Mia's heart lurched. Everything about Nick was a lot sexy and a little bit dangerous.

"I wanted to see you." His smile was forced, like the admission cost him more than he wanted her to know.

Mia curved her cold hand into his warm one. "I want to be with you. Even though we're not teenagers anymore and I don't have that green bikini."

Nick's gaze skimmed her body from head to toe and lingered at her breasts. Then he gave her a grin that was pure bad boy. "I was always a lot more interested in what was underneath that bikini anyway."

She looked at him from under her lashes and flirted like she'd wanted to do all those years ago but had been too shy. "You were, were you?"

"Oh yeah." In the sudden silence, panic rolled over her again. Except, there was excitement too...

Acclaim for Jen Gilroy
The Cottage at Firefly Lake

"Gilroy's debut contemporary is packed with potent emotions...[Her] protagonists tug at the heartstrings from the beginning of the story and don't let go. The strong group of supporting characters includes Charlie's sister, Mia, and her daughter, Naomi, whose stories are to be later told. Long on charm, this story invites readers to come in and stay a while." —*Publishers Weekly*

"4 stars! Memories, regrets, and second chances are front and center in Gilroy's fantastic debut. The first book in the Firefly Lake series is complex and mired in secrets. The Vermont setting adds a genuine feel to the story, and the co-stars are highly entertaining." —*RT Book Reviews*

"Such a sweet love story. 4.0 stars for this second-chance romance!" —TextTeaserBookBlog.com

"The first in a promising new series...I most certainly will be on the look for more books from Ms. Gilroy."
    —Reviews by Crystal (reviewsbycacb.blogspot.com)

"There's a lot to love at Firefly Lake. I'm looking forward to a return visit." —ReadingReality.net

"A touching story that will resonate with those who enjoy women's fiction and contemporary romance."
    —NightOwlReviews.com

*Summer on
Firefly Lake*

Firefly Lake

JEN GILROY

FOREVER

NEW YORK BOSTON

Copyright © 2017 by Jen Gilroy
Preview of *Back Home at Firefly Lake* copyright © 2017 by Jen Gilroy
Cover design by Elizabeth Turner.
Cover copyright © 2017 by Hachette Book Group, Inc.

Forever
Hachette Book Group
1290 Avenue of the Americas
New York, NY 10104
forever-romance.com
twitter.com/foreverromance

First Edition: July 2017

Forever is an imprint of Grand Central Publishing. The Forever name and logo are trademarks of Hachette Book Group, Inc.

The publisher is not responsible for websites (or their content) that are not owned by the publisher.

The Hachette Speakers Bureau provides a wide range of authors for speaking events. To find out more, go to www.hachettespeakersbureau.com or call (866) 376-6591.

ISBNs: 978-1-4555-6960-1 (mass market), 978-1-4555-4035-8 (ebook)

Printed in the United States of America

OPM

10 9 8 7 6 5 4 3 2 1

*For my daughter, with all my love. I'm
so lucky to be your mum.*

Acknowledgments

As always, I'm indebted to Dawn Dowdle, who is not only my literary agent but also my friend. Both personally and professionally, Dawn's support is invaluable, and I'm grateful she's a partner in my writing career.

I also extend appreciation to my fabulous editor, Michele Bidelspach; Elizabeth Turner, art director; and the entire Grand Central Forever team who work so hard to help make my books shine.

Thanks to the anonymous reviewer who critiqued an early version of this story via the Romantic Novelists' Association (RNA) New Writers' Scheme (NWS). That feedback helped me dig deeper into character and taught me much about writing craft.

My RWA Golden Heart class of 2015, the Dragonflies, are a steadfast source of friendship and encouragement. Once again, the dragonfly reference is for you.

Jennifer Brodie, Tracy Brody, and Arlene McFarlane

have lifted me up through some very tough times. Thank you, my friends.

Special thanks are also due to Jennifer Brodie, who provided insightful comments on the first chapter of *Summer on Firefly Lake* when I needed a wise and detached sounding board.

My dear friend Susanna Bavin is the best supporter any author could hope for. Generous, loyal, and kind, she's a blessing in my writing life and beyond.

To the women who have shared their experience of divorce and single parenting with me, thank you. Your devotion to your children is exemplary, and your strength and courage in building a better life inspire me.

I have also walked alongside loved ones on their cancer journeys. Those experiences shaped this story as well.

To my husband, Tech Guy; our daughter, English Rose; and Heidi, the sister of my heart. Thank you for your love and support and always being in my corner.

Not least, I'm grateful to my parents, who gave me both roots and wings. Their abiding love reaches beyond death to nurture and sustain me.

*Summer on
Firefly Lake*

Chapter One

"Y ou want to hire me?" Mia Connell laced her fingers together, and the pad of her thumb lingered on the bare space where her wedding and engagement rings had once nestled.

"Why not? Friends help each other out." Nick McGuire's smile had a sexy edge, and Mia's breathing quickened. "In this part of Vermont we all depend on one another."

That sense of community was one of the reasons she'd moved to Firefly Lake last month. "I appreciate the offer, but I've already got a job. Two jobs. When school starts, I'll have private music students and substitute teaching. Besides, you've helped me out so much already."

And Mia had a plan. To be independent and stand on her own two feet. To take control of the life that had gotten stuck on hold when she'd married young and given everything to her family.

Nick's smile broadened. "Why can't my hiring you to

help my mother be part of your new start? It'd only be for a few weeks."

The new start was part of the new life she was determined to build out of the rubble of the old one. Mia glanced around the gracious hall that led to a country-style kitchen, where July sunlight flooded through the French doors at the back of the house. "I'm surprised your mom wants to sell Harbor House."

"This place is way too big for her." Nick scrubbed a hand across his face. "We've made an offer on a new bungalow in the development by the lake. She's thrilled. She won't have to go up and down flights of stairs every day, and the house has a small yard, so it'll be easy to maintain."

"She's lived here so long." Mia looped his mom's dry cleaning over one arm and backed toward the kitchen.

"Too long." Nick took the dry-cleaning bag, hung it on a hook behind the kitchen door, and followed Mia.

He nudged six-four, and with his wind-ruffled dark hair, white shirt open at the neck, and loose tie, Nick was a lifetime away from the badass kid Mia remembered, the one who'd hung around the edges of her life for those endless vacations she'd spent at her family's summer cottage on Firefly Lake outside town. He was the kid who'd become a man who never lost control and who, in the last year, had also become her friend, cheerleader, and steady compass in a world that had spun off its axis.

"I'm not a professional organizer." She tried to ignore the flutter in her chest that was new. It had nothing to do with friendship and everything to do with the way Nick's shoulders filled out his shirt.

"Mom doesn't want a stranger in her house. She wants

someone she already knows and trusts. With all the moves you've had, you'd be a natural."

"Surely your sisters want to be involved. They're her family."

"They'd help if I asked them to, but..." A pulse ticked in Nick's jaw. "Cat's teaching summer school in Boston. As for Georgia, she couldn't organize herself or anyone else. Besides, she's at that retreat center in India until Christmas."

"My daughters..." Mia's chest tightened and her throat got raw.

"Are with their dad in Dallas for the next month." Nick closed the distance between them.

As if she needed a reminder of the custody and visitation agreement with her ex-husband. Sending her two girls thousands of miles away to stay with him and another woman had torn Mia apart. "My sister needs me to help get ready for the baby. It's Charlie's first, and I'm the only family she has."

"Her husband and his whole family hover over Charlie twenty-four/seven."

Mia sucked in air as Nick moved even closer.

"Besides, if Charlie needs you so much, why did I find her barricaded behind her laptop yesterday in the back booth of the diner? And why did she make me promise not to tell anybody, you included, where she was?"

"She's almost eight months pregnant. Pregnant women are hormonal."

A shadow flitted across Nick's face and was gone almost before Mia registered it. "Charlie didn't look hormonal. If you ask me, she looked pissed off."

"See, she's hormonal."

Mia looked out the French doors at the terraced gardens surrounding the stately Victorian perched high above Firefly Lake. The small town was spread out below, and the spire of the Episcopal church rose out of the trees near the town green. A patchwork of rooftops sloped toward the gentle scoop in the lake from which Harbor House took its name. The whole scene was encircled by the rolling Vermont hills, which made her feel safe and protected in this little corner of the Northeast Kingdom.

"Please?" Nick's breath warmed her cheek, and the scent of his aftershave enveloped her, cedarwood and amber topped with something crisp, confident, and suave. "While your girls are in Dallas, you could stay here. Mom could sure use the company."

His mellow baritone tugged at an almost forgotten place inside her, and Mia smoothed a wayward strand of brown hair. She was being ridiculous. Why shouldn't she help Gabrielle? The money Nick offered was more than generous, and it was money she needed as more security for the girls. Besides, staying in Harbor House would be perfect. She wouldn't have to live in a construction zone while the new kitchen was installed at her place.

It was time to stop the excuses. It was also time to stop the self-doubt, which had made her defer to others and ignore what she wanted and needed.

"I'd have to have a contract." She tried to sound competent and professional. "To get this house ready for sale is a bigger job than you might think."

"Of course." Nick gave her an easy smile, all business. His eyes were dark blue with a hint of steel. "We can work on one together."

"I couldn't work set hours." She smiled in return. The

kind of smile she'd perfected as the doctor's daughter, the executive's wife, and the queen of more beauty pageants than she could count.

"Completely flexible. You'd be doing me a big favor." Nick pulled at his tie, took it off, and stuffed it in the pocket of his suit jacket.

"I can start today if you want." Mia's stomach churned.

"Mom will be thrilled. I knew we could count on you."

Everyone had always counted on her. First her parents, then her husband and daughters and all the organizations where she'd volunteered in each new city her husband's job had taken them to. She was helpful and dependable Mia. But she was also a thirty-nine-year-old woman, and it was more than time she learned to count on herself. Depend on herself.

"There's one more thing." She plumped a stray cushion and slid it back onto a chair in the breakfast nook, a sunny alcove that overlooked a pond thick with water lilies.

"Anything." Nick gave her the smile again that almost made her forget he was her friend—the only male friend she'd ever had who didn't want something she couldn't give.

She nudged a dog basket aside with one shoe, and the red kitten heels gave her a confidence she didn't feel. "I agree your mom needs help. She hasn't gotten her strength back after being sick. You work all the time and your sisters aren't around much, so she's here alone."

"I gave her Pixie."

At the sound of her name a tiny whirlwind barreled past them with its tail up. It had fluffy white fur and short legs. It also had a bark at odds with the dog's small size.

A laugh bubbled inside Mia and rippled out before she could stop it. "Your mom needs more in her life than a dog."

The Maltese gave her a bright-eyed stare.

"But—"

Mia lifted a hand as she glimpsed a flash of orange under the weeping willow by the pond. Nick's mom in her garden smock. "You think your mom needs to move, but I'm not so sure. This house has been in her family for generations. She's rooted here."

With the kind of roots Mia longed for.

"It's not like she has to leave Firefly Lake. She'll still have friends nearby and all her clubs." Nick avoided Mia's gaze.

"Harbor House is her home. To leave it, even if she's as excited about the new bungalow as you say, is bound to be a wrench." Mia stepped around Pixie and gestured toward the window. "Look at those beautiful gardens. Those plants mean the world to her."

It wasn't only the plants. It was the memories of children who'd toddled on chubby legs around the garden paths, and the pencil scratches on the kitchen door to mark how they'd grown. The memories of Christmases and Thanksgivings and birthdays that, when put together, made the fabric of a life and a house a home.

Mia swallowed. This wasn't her house or her garden. She had to focus on her daughters. To provide for them and be a mother they could be proud of.

"I'm looking out for Mom." Nick's expression hardened. "That's my job."

"Of course it is." One of Mia's heels snagged Pixie's basket, and she grabbed a kitchen chair to keep her balance. "But if I help your mom like you want, looking out for her becomes my job too. It means more than dropping off her dry cleaning and popping in every few days with cookies or a casserole." She took a deep breath and straightened to her full height, which even in the shoes only brought her to Nick's collar, stiff, white, and unyielding.

"That's what I'd pay you for."

Mia channeled the woman she wanted to be instead of the one everyone expected. "If your mom changes her mind about selling Harbor House, will you accept her decision and not stand in her way?"

"Why would she change her mind?" Nick picked up the dog, who eyed Mia, unblinking. "I want you to help Mom, but I don't want—"

"You can't have it both ways. I'll help your mom and live here with her for the next few weeks, but I won't let you push her into anything."

Or let him push her into anything, either.

"I'm only doing what's best for Mom." Nick's features were a careful blank.

"Best for her or best for you?"

Nick opened his mouth, closed it, and fiddled with his watch strap.

Before she lost her nerve, Mia turned and walked out of the kitchen, her heels a comforting staccato on the tiled floor.

Nick set a wiggling Pixie in her basket and pressed his fingers to his temples in a vain effort to erase the image of the little sway to Mia's hips as she walked away from him in those sexy red shoes. How her hair, fastened away from her face with a clip, was like a sleek, dark pelt, except for one rogue curl that had escaped to brush the perfect curve of her cheek.

He balled his hands into fists and looked out the window. On the upper terrace, a breeze off Firefly Lake stirred the patio umbrella, and his mom walked up the gravel path to the old summer kitchen. His breath caught as she wrestled the light screen door open. She didn't want his help, but illness had made her *need* his help, made her vulnerable.

Mia was vulnerable, too. It was in the tight set of her jaw and the stiff way she held herself. It was in the tension that radiated off her and the pain that lurked in the depths of her beautiful brown eyes.

That pain caught him unaware and sparked feelings as unwelcome as they were unexpected. Mia was his friend and a single mother. Two good reasons, if he'd needed any, why he couldn't let those feelings go anywhere.

He shrugged out of his suit jacket and draped it over a kitchen chair. His mother had to move. That was the plan. Then he could go back to New York City, leave the apartment over the law office on Main Street behind, start his life over, and claw back the self-respect his ex-wife had yanked away.

Nick moved into the hall. The formal dining room was to his right. The massive oak table where he'd eaten Christmas dinner for thirty of his thirty-nine years was piled high with art supplies, and an easel stood in front of the bay window. Sunbeams bounced off the crystal in the glass-fronted cabinets and gleamed on his great-grandmother's silver tea service.

"Mia?"

Pixie bumped his leg and yipped, her steps muffled by the thick carpet.

He shook his head at the dog and crossed the hall again toward the living room at the front of the house. Pale sunlight filtered between heavy patterned drapes. Decorated in faded gold and cream, it was an obstacle course of side tables, spindly chairs, two Victorian horsehair sofas, and a baby grand piano nobody ever played.

"You don't know what your help will mean to me, honey." His mom's voice came from the alcove off the living room. Connected to the summer kitchen by a short passage, the small room had once been his dad's office.

"I can stay here while my daughters are with their father."

Mia's gentle voice comforted him like the liquid amber of single malt Scotch whiskey. Except those days were long gone. He'd turned his life around. In all the ways that counted, he wasn't the guy he'd once been.

"Nick's right. This house is too big for an old woman to rattle around in alone." His mom's trademark silver bracelets jingled.

"You're only sixty-two," Mia said. "That's not old."

"The cancer was a wake-up call." His mom's voice was low. "I thought I had all the time in the world, but it turns out I'm as mortal as anybody else. Besides, this house needs a family."

Nick's body was heavy. It should have been his family here. Before he'd found out he couldn't give his wife the children they both wanted and he'd never be a family man.

"I'm happy to help you, Gabrielle." Mia said his mom's name with the musical French intonation that was a legacy of her Montreal childhood. "Whatever you need, all you have to do is ask."

"Oh, honey." His mom's voice had a wobble Nick hated because it reminded him how close he'd come to losing her.

He cleared his throat and stuck his head into the room. "Hey, Mom. Mia."

Perched on a low blue love seat, his mom wore an orange smock that lit the room like a beacon and was in stark contrast with her cropped silver hair. She gave an elegant shrug and glanced at Mia beside her. Cool, confident, and still as out of reach as the glamorous girl who'd spent her summers in Firefly Lake and all the boys had wanted to date.

Nick moved into the alcove. His dad's law books were long gone, as was the big desk and the black chair Nick and his younger sisters used to spin around in until they got dizzy. They'd been loaded into the moving van with the clothes, football trophies, golf clubs, and mug emblazoned NUMBER 1 DAD Nick had given him for Father's Day. It was as if his dad had never existed.

"I told your mom I can help with whatever she needs to get ready for the move." Mia's voice was brisk and efficient, and that loose curl of hair still mocked Nick and made him want to yank the clip out and run his hands through the thick, dark strands.

"I'll miss my flowers." His mom's tone was wistful as she glanced out the half-open window, where white roses tumbled over a wooden trellis.

"Think how much fun you'll have this winter planning the garden at your new place," Nick said. "Besides, you can take cuttings from here."

"I suppose so." His mom sighed and set her sketchbook and watercolor pencils on a side table. "Some of those plants are irreplaceable, though. Like the trees I planted when you and your sisters were born, and when my parents died. To leave those behind, well..."

Mia covered one of his mom's hands with hers. Her chest rose and fell under her clingy top. From the top of her glossy dark head to the tips of her designer shoes, Mia was a walking, talking reminder of the world he'd left behind. The woman who'd left him behind.

"Do you ever think this house and everything in it holds you back?" Didn't his mom realize he wanted to protect her? That it had been his job since he was eleven?

Mia looked up and something sizzled between them. Then she flashed him a smile that made her look younger and a lot more available. "Leave the psychology to the professionals. You need to relax."

"I am relaxed," he lied. Lately, just when he'd gotten his life stable again, being around her had him wound up tight and wanting something, someone, he couldn't let himself have.

"No, you're not. You should try yoga. I got Charlie into yoga, and she's a new person."

Nick's laugh spilled out, rusty. "Your sister's a new person because she's blissed out with Sean." And his friend was blissed out, too, and settled into married life like he'd never known anything else, a cozy domesticity as strange as it was unsettling. "Next thing you'll tell me I need a cat."

Mia shrugged, and a dimple dented her right cheek. "Even though I've never had one, I like cats. They're low maintenance and independent."

Cool and aloof, too, a lot like her. Yet another reason the two of them weren't suited. If he had time, he'd have a dog. Open and uncomplicated, dogs wagged their tails because they were happy to see you, unlike cats, who strolled along with their noses in the air and a twitch in their tails.

"Like I told you, I want what's best for my mom."

"I do too." Mia's smile didn't reach her eyes.

"I'm glad we agree." Nick jammed his hands into his pants pockets.

Pixie clambered onto the love seat and gave him a fixed stare.

"See, Nick, you got what you wanted. You go back to work, and Mia and I'll get started." His mom waved a hand to dismiss him. "I'm sure you have lots more important things to do."

He did, but as he looked at Mia and his mom, with Pixie sandwiched between them, maybe what was most important of all, what he really wanted, was right here.

Chapter Two

Four days later, Gabrielle shut her sketchbook and abandoned the half-finished outline of a rose, budded tight. She tugged at her wide-brimmed straw hat and stared at the lake.

She'd told Nick and Mia she'd miss her flowers, these terraced gardens her French-Canadian mother had carved out of the rocky northern soil when she'd come here as a bride, but she'd miss this view of Firefly Lake even more.

The lake, her lake, was still and ice-locked in winter, snug in a blanket of silver-blue snow. It came alive in spring as the sun-warmed ice cracked, and the boom echoed off the cliffs below Harbor House, where dark water foamed onto the beach. In summer, it was a gentle blue, dotted with green islands and white sails. And come fall, it was framed by a panorama of red and yellow leaves with splashes of orange, a paint box of colors she looked forward to all year.

Yet as the seasons rushed past, day by day and year by year, so did her life. And it had slipped through her fingers.

"I'm a foolish, sentimental woman, Pixie."

At the foot of the sun lounger, Pixie opened one sleepy eye, her expression quizzical.

"And you're a very wise dog." Gabrielle drained her glass of ice water. "Nick's right. I can't stay in this house. Neither he nor the girls want it. But that bungalow? Promise me you won't tell him how much I hate the idea."

Pixie whimpered and moved to lick Gabrielle's face.

"I know you promise." Gabrielle sighed, long and heavy. "Maybe you can tell me where I went so wrong with my children. Cat and Georgia only come home when they have to. As for Nick, even though he'd never say so, he can't wait to leave."

"You ever think your kids might share some of the blame?"

Gabrielle jumped and her sketchbook hit the terrace with a *thud*. She swung her legs off the chair, grabbed Pixie's collar with one hand, and smoothed her light sweater with the other. "Who's there?" she called as Pixie barked.

"I'm sorry." A man near to her age stood at the top of the stone steps from the lake. "I didn't mean to frighten you." He wore jeans and a blue shirt with the sleeves rolled to his elbows. A backpack was slung over one shoulder, and a camera dangled from a strap around his neck.

Pixie barked louder. Gabrielle scooped the dog into her arms and got to her feet. Although Firefly Lake wasn't a hotbed of crime and the man didn't look threatening, a woman on her own couldn't be too careful. "This is private property."

"I realized that as soon as I spotted you." When he smiled, deep grooves between his nose and mouth creased his face. A shock of gray hair stuck out beneath a battered red ball cap. "By then, though, it was too late to go back the way I came." His warm blue eyes searched hers. "Your dog had already seen me."

"What are you doing here?" Gabrielle stroked Pixie's ears. "Hush."

He whistled, soft and musical. Pixie stopped barking and cocked one ear.

"I was taking pictures by the lake. When I saw steps through the trees, I had to see where they went." He stuck out a hand. "Ward Aldrich."

"Gabrielle Brassard." She slipped her hand into his, the handshake cool, firm, and decisive. Pulling her hand away, she patted Pixie, her fingers still tingling from Ward's brief touch.

"You've got a beautiful place here." His eyes were deep blue, almost violet, the color of the irises she'd planted in the border by the house the year Nick was born.

"Thank you."

Pixie squirmed and she set her on the flagstones. The dog scampered over to Ward and sniffed his shoes.

"Pixie, no." Gabrielle stepped forward, but Ward laughed.

"She's okay."

More than okay. What was he? Some kind of dog whisperer? Pixie was wary of strangers and, apart from

Nick, she usually didn't like men. "Are you here on vacation?"

"A working one." Ward touched the camera. "I'm a filmmaker, nature documentaries for the most part, but also the people who live in those places." He grinned, all of a sudden boyish. "When I was a kid, I wanted to be an explorer. It's pretty much what I grew up to be."

Gabrielle's breath hitched. He was an attractive man, but she was a woman with a whole lot of life behind her, not the impressionable teenager who'd papered her bedroom walls with peace signs and David Cassidy posters. Not the girl who'd fallen into lust and mistaken it for love. "I should let you get back to work."

"No rush." He gestured to her sketchbook. "Are you an artist?"

"An amateur one. I taught art at the high school here." Before she got sick and her body betrayed her. When life was still rich with possibilities.

"May I take a look?"

She picked up the book and handed it to him. Gabrielle's little hobby, Brian called it, her ex-husband's smile patronizing like she was one of the children. "They're nothing special."

"I disagree. The detail and the way you've captured the light are extraordinary." He squinted as he flipped through pages. "You have a keen eye."

Warmth stole through her at his words of praise. "I always liked drawing but—"

Pixie barked and shot back to Gabrielle's side.

"I didn't realize you had company." Mia moved onto the terrace, her ballet flats soundless on the flagstones. She held out a tray. "I brought you a snack, but there's more than enough for two. I'll get an extra cup and—"

"No, wait." Gabrielle inhaled the heavy scent of the roses. The buzz of a bee half drunk on nectar punctuated the sudden stillness. "Ward, this is my friend Mia."

Ward exchanged a greeting with Mia, then took the tray from her and set it on a low table with the sketchbook before he looked back at Gabrielle. "I don't mean to intrude, but if it's not an inconvenience, would you show me your garden sometime?"

Her gaze locked with his and shut out Mia, shut out everything. "Of course." She gave garden tours all the time. Or at least she had. There was no reason for the little quiver in her chest.

"What about tomorrow morning? Around ten?"

"Fine." His eyes were so blue she could swim in them. Gabrielle tried to work moisture into her dry mouth.

"Nice to meet you, Mia. You too, Gabrielle." He paused, his gaze still intent, like he could see into her soul. Then, with another smile, he moved to the steps and disappeared into the trees, like a mirage she'd imagined.

Mia knelt by the table and poured a cup of tea from Gabrielle's favorite chintz-patterned pot. "That's what my daughter Naomi would call one hot guy."

"He's a filmmaker. He's interested in plants." Gabrielle's face heated as she sat back on the sun lounger.

"He's interested in more than plants." Mia gave her a pointed look before she straightened and her expression sobered, the lovely face hiding a hurt Gabrielle could imagine too well. "About Nick, I don't want you to think I'm—"

"Forcing me to move?" Gabrielle reached for the teacup Mia held out.

"He cares about you, but if leaving Harbor House isn't what you want, you have to tell him." Mia shook a linen napkin over Gabrielle's lap.

Gabrielle sipped some tea, and the hot liquid eased the tightness in her throat. "Nick's my son, but he can be..." Judgmental and controlling but passionate, too. And so wounded Gabrielle's heart ached. "He thinks I need looking after. He has ever since his dad left us. But maybe he's right about this house. For once in my life, I have to be practical." Gabrielle set her cup aside and covered Mia's hand.

The younger woman gave her a too-bright smile. "I don't want to come between you and Nick, but I'm on your side, whatever you want."

Gabrielle bit back a sigh. Mia was another wounded soul. "Thank you, honey. This past little while, you've been more of a daughter to me than my girls." Although Cat and Georgia cared about her as much as Nick did, they darted in and out of her life like dragonflies, never still, always looking ahead and never back.

Mia squeezed Gabrielle's hand before she untangled her fingers. "Your daughters are busy, and Firefly Lake's a small town. You know the sign out on Lake Road that says population twenty-five hundred? Nick jokes that since the girls and I moved here, the town should change it to twenty-five oh three because of how slow the population grows." She gave Gabrielle a wry smile. "See, I made you melon balls with the fresh berries I got at the farm stand."

Gabrielle took the bowl of fruit Mia had prepared and picked up the silver fork. Its monogram was worn with age but shone with fresh polish. Maybe Ward was right and what had gone wrong between her and her kids wasn't all her fault. Maybe she had a chance to fix it, starting with Nick.

And even to help Mia.

Gabrielle eyed Mia from beneath the brim of her hat. Mia needed a good man in her life, one who'd treat her and those beautiful daughters with the care and respect they deserved. Her son was a good man who needed a good woman. And Harbor House needed a family. Her family.

It was so simple. Gabrielle bounced and the sun lounger wobbled. And so perfect she should have thought of it before.

"Can I get you anything else?" Mia bent beside Gabrielle's chair.

"Not a thing. Just keep me company for a bit. You're already doing a lot more than Nick hired you to."

"It's a pleasure." Mia patted Gabrielle's knee. "I don't want you to overdo things."

Gabrielle popped a raspberry into her mouth and savored the sweetness of the fruit, like sunshine. She gave Mia her most innocent expression. "I won't."

At least not overdo in the way Mia meant. But was it wrong for her to look out for two people she loved? She glanced at Pixie, who spun in circles after a butterfly. No, it wasn't. Her dear mother always said the Lord helped those who helped themselves.

Gabrielle spooned a perfect melon ball as Mia sat on the chair across from her. All she'd do was give Mia and Nick a nudge in the right direction, so subtle they'd never even notice.

And she'd help Pixie, too. The little dog nosed Mia's

slender ankles. Pixie would hate being cooped up in a bungalow even more than Gabrielle.

"No." The following evening, Mia eyed her sister across the patio table on Sean and Charlie's deck. The sun hung low and dipped behind the hills, while its rays tinged the water of the lake pink.

Sean's gray clapboard house hugged the edge of Firefly Lake five miles outside town near the cottage that had belonged to Charlie and Mia's mom, and where they'd spent childhood summers. After their wedding last Christmas, Sean's house became Charlie's, too, and Mia and her girls had stayed here when they first moved to town.

"Why not? The fashion show is for Mom's foundation. I thought you'd be happy to help." Charlie rested one hand on her rounded belly covered by a green maternity top. Her dark hair was glossy and her brown eyes sparkled. "Even if I weren't the size of a whale, parading on a runway was never my thing."

"You don't look anything like a whale. You're cuddly and cute like a koala bear." Sean dropped a kiss on his wife's hair. The two of them exchanged a loving smile before Sean went into the house with empty plates and leftover food from the barbecue.

Her younger sister glowed, and although Mia didn't begrudge Charlie the happiness she'd found with Sean, her childhood sweetheart with whom she'd reunited almost a year ago, it sometimes made Mia feel even more left out and alone. "Parading on a runway isn't my thing either these days."

Maybe it had never been her thing, but by entering all

those beauty pageants she'd coaxed a rare smile onto her mom's face and basked in her dad's approval, the family peacemaker who calmed troubled waters. She'd been a different and more confident Mia than the insecure and frightened girl she often was inside.

"Okay, you've made your point." Charlie got to her feet and rested a hand on her lower back. "I need to help Sean clean up and fix dessert." She flashed Mia a cheeky grin. "Which I got from the bakery in town since I was never a Betty Crocker wannabe like my big sister."

"Charlie..." Mia began, but her sister had already left, a surprisingly quick exit for a woman due to give birth in six weeks. "I agreed to organize the fashion show. I don't want to be in it."

"Then don't." Nick shut the barbecue lid and sat in Charlie's abandoned chair. "Nobody has a gun to your head."

"Even though she backed off, I know Charlie wants me to. The foundation board wants me to. I don't want to disappoint people, and it's for Mom, sort of."

Nick's blue eyes were serious. "Your mom's gone, so how can you disappoint her?" Even summer casual in navy shorts and a white polo shirt open at the neck, he still had a corporate look. Like he'd been on a golf course doing deals with guys who'd gone to Yale and Princeton and Harvard. "As for everybody else, why do you care?"

"That's not the point." Mia looked out at the lake, where wisps of pink clouds drifted across the western horizon like cotton candy. "I want to honor Mom's memory. You still have your mom but I don't and..." She stopped. The ache of that loss was still raw and maybe always would be.

"I understand. You need to do what's right for you." Nick's expression softened. "About my mom, I talked to her again like you asked me to. She's fine with moving, really."

"She's lived in Harbor House her whole life. It's her home. She's spent her life tending those gardens like her mother did before her. Uprooting Gabrielle is like uprooting one of those old plants."

"I know you care about Mom, but you worry too much." He rubbed his jaw, shadowed in dark stubble. "She's anxious about change, that's all."

Mia didn't want to talk herself out of a job, but she didn't want Nick to put Gabrielle out of her home either. She'd seen the sadness in Gabrielle's eyes and how she looked at the lake and the gardens when she didn't think Mia noticed. She'd also seen how Gabrielle's touch lingered on the burnished wood of the stair railings, and the tenderness in the way she traced the floral pattern in the small stained-glass window in the hall. "You could hire more people to help her."

Nick's dark brows shot up. "Mom's always looked after herself. She's fine. She doesn't want me to hire anyone but you." He laughed without humor.

"Did she say so?" Mia had managed to avoid Nick when he'd come by to see Gabrielle, but tonight, when he'd dropped by Charlie and Sean's place to talk to Sean about a Rotary Club golf tournament and stayed for dinner, she couldn't avoid him any longer.

"Of course not." He gave her a tired look. "But I know my mother. She'll be fine once she's settled into the bungalow. Everything new and convenient, no stairs and an attached garage so she doesn't have to go outside to get to her car in the winter. It's perfect."

Mia got to her feet to put distance between them. Since she'd moved to Firefly Lake, Nick unsettled her in a way she didn't want to be unsettled. A way that was more than friendly. "I understand, but maybe your mom doesn't want new and convenient. Or perfect."

The unhappiness and loss in Gabrielle's eyes when she talked about leaving Harbor House were stamped on Mia's heart.

"She has to want it. I can't have Mom living in that big house alone. She's fragile and..." Nick's voice cracked, and he coughed before he joined Mia at the railing that encircled the wooden deck.

Below, a sandy path curved toward the lake and Carmichael's marina and boat yard, the family business Sean ran. Crickets chirped, and the wind whispered in the pine trees.

Mia looked at Nick in the half darkness. "What is it?"

"You lost your mom, so you know what it's like. I'm not ready to lose mine. I can't." He clenched the railing. "After her surgery and chemo and..."

"You're never ready to lose your mom. You can't control whether it's her time, either." Mia covered his hands with one of hers, and her fingers tingled with the warmth of his skin. "But Gabrielle's doing great. I only want to help her get better and better."

"I know." He took his hands away and turned toward the lake. "What I need you to understand is Mom's been through a lot, and Harbor House is way too much for her to handle. My sisters agree."

Mia linked her hands behind her back. The way he'd pulled away from her said it all. Nick wasn't interested in her as a woman, but why didn't she feel more relieved?

"Hi, Mrs. Connell, Nick." The voice came from the path below, and the name Mia had answered to for almost seventeen years was all of a sudden wrong. Like the pair of pointy black shoes that pinched, but she'd kept anyway and squeezed her feet into for all those black-tie dinners her ex had insisted they attend.

"Ty." She fixed her face into a smile. "Call me Mia."

"Okay." Sean's sixteen-year-old son, Charlie's stepson, smiled back and his sun-bronzed face reddened.

"Hey, Ty." Nick's voice rumbled beside Mia.

"Are Dad and Charlie in the house?" The setting sun glinted off Ty's blond hair, and his blue eyes were honest and open.

"In the kitchen," Mia said. "Charlie saved dinner for you, unless you want dessert first."

"Cool." Ty's smile widened. "You hear from Naomi today?" He dug the toe of his sneaker into the sandy path.

"She called me this morning. I talked to her and Emma both." And there'd been a note in her daughters' voices that had worried Mia, even though she couldn't pinpoint what it was or why it made her uneasy. "She said her dad was taking them to a waterpark today."

"Yeah, she told me. We FaceTimed last night." Ty hesitated. "You think she's okay? She sounded, I don't know, sad, I guess. She looked sad. Not like her. She's not real excited about her birthday, either." The flush on his face deepened as he came up the steps and joined Nick and Mia on the deck.

Shadow, Sean and Charlie's black lab, followed at his heels.

"I'm sure Naomi's fine." Mia tried to make herself believe it.

Naomi's sixteenth birthday was in three days, and Mia would experience it via FaceTime. She wouldn't be there to bake Naomi a cake or do anything else to make it a special day for her daughter to cherish. A lump lodged in her throat.

Jay had laughed off her worries and said Naomi was a teenage girl, and all teenage girls were moody. Except, her ex had never spent enough time with Naomi to know what she thought or felt, moody or not.

"Of course the girls are fine," Nick said. "Why wouldn't they be?"

Mia guessed he meant to reassure her, but how could he know? He'd never had kids, whereas her daughters were her whole life and Emma was only eight, too little to be away from her mom. "Naomi sent me some pictures." She dug in the pocket of her sundress for her phone. "See?"

Ty took the phone and stared at the screen. The longing in his eyes tugged at Mia's heart. Naomi was almost grown up, and Mia wasn't ready for it. She wasn't ready for her daughter to get more serious about Ty than she already was, either.

"Naomi's still going to the high school here, isn't she?" Ty handed Mia the phone.

Shadow nosed at her shoes and Mia scooted backward. "That's the plan."

After a lifetime of living by plans and schedules, that was Mia's only fixed plan. There was no way she'd break up her family and send Naomi to that Connecticut boarding school Jay insisted would do her good and prepare her for college.

Ty's ready smile spread across his face. "She'll make friends in no time."

Mia's stomach knotted. Ty and her daughter were already friends, more than friends, despite what they both wanted her to think.

"Hey, Shadow." Nick whistled and the dog ambled away from Mia's feet. "You know she likes shoes."

"Not my Jimmy Choos." She gave him a half smile. "Another reason I prefer cats."

"Cats claw furniture." Nick tossed a battered slipper to the dog.

"No cat of mine would." Mia moved back to the chair, sat, and tucked her feet under it.

Nick's deep laugh rang out. "Haven't you learned you can't control everything?"

Yeah, she had, over and over again. Instead, she gave him her perkiest smile. "Wise words you might want to think about."

"Okay, I've got chocolate and vanilla cupcakes and ice cream." Charlie came through the patio door from the house, followed by Sean with a tray. "And watermelon for Mia." She put a bowl of fruit by Mia's place. "I even used that scoop you gave me because you like fruit cut like Mom did."

"Thanks." Mia's vision blurred.

She picked up her fork and moved the pieces of fruit around in the bowl. Across the table, Charlie and Sean talked to Ty about his day at work, their plans for Charlie's birthday, the same day as Naomi's, and when his mom, stepdad, and two stepsisters would be back from vacation. The three of them were a family her sister had blended with patience, kindness, and a whole lot of love.

Mia chewed and swallowed a watermelon ball, the fruit tasteless in her mouth. She stole a glance at Nick and shoved the bowl away. "What kind of ice cream do you have, Charlie? If there's enough to go around, I'd like a cupcake too."

"You what?" Her sister stopped midsentence, her mouth half open in surprise. "Except at birthdays and Christmas, you never eat ice cream or cake."

"Maybe it's time for me to make some changes." In the flickering light cast by the candle lantern on the middle of the table, Nick's gaze caught Mia's and held. Her heart pounded and she looked away.

"There's strawberry, vanilla, chocolate, maple walnut, and tiger tail." Charlie counted the ice cream flavors on her fingers. "There are plenty of cupcakes. I feed a growing boy, remember?" She grinned at Ty.

"Tiger tail ice cream from Simard's Creamery?"

"The same and your favorite." Charlie took the ice cream scoop and another bowl from Sean. "I got tiger tail for Emma, but all she wanted was chocolate."

"I'll have two scoops." Back when Mia was Emma's age, the orange ice cream with the black licorice ripple was one of the few good things about coming to Firefly Lake every summer. She'd looked forward to it all winter in Montreal, and then in Boston after they'd moved there when her dad got a job at Massachusetts General.

Her mouth watered as she picked up her spoon again. She didn't have to answer to Jay anymore. She didn't have to starve herself to stay the size her ex-husband wanted her to be. The size she'd been before she'd had two children. When she'd walked those endless runways to claim the crown for the prettiest girl and the one with the best smile. The one who'd hidden what she thought and felt. The girl all the other girls wanted to be.

She looked back at Nick, and the edges of his smile warmed her. He raised his spoon in mock salute and her face got hot.

She dug into the ice cream Charlie set in front of her and savored the sweetness as the coldness trickled down the back of her throat.

"Tiger tail ice cream, huh?" Nick's blue eyes had a teasing glint that catapulted her back to adolescence. "You always say you don't remember much about Firefly Lake, but I guess there's at least one thing you didn't forget."

Shadowy memories of the girl and boy she and Nick had once been tugged at the edge of Mia's consciousness. She dipped her head, thankful for the darkness to hide her face. She remembered all right. Remembered more than the ice cream, and enough to wonder if she'd played it safe too long. And what her life might be like if she loosened a few of those controls.

Chapter Three

Nick stole a glance at Mia in the passenger seat of his Lexus. Even before she'd dug into the ice cream with a passion that surprised him, he'd kidded himself. He wanted her. Once she'd have been the kind of woman he could get serious about. Except, after his ex-wife he didn't do serious.

"You didn't have to drive me back to town. Sean would have taken me home." Etched by moonlight, her profile was sculpted like a marble angel he'd seen at a church in Rome.

"Sure he would, but he picked you up because he was already in town. He doesn't want to leave Charlie unless he has to, even for half an hour." He put the car in gear and they bumped along Sean's rutted driveway. "Mom's place is on my way."

"Thank you." Her voice was cool. Like he'd imagined the heart-stopping look they'd shared on the deck. "Your mom said I could borrow her car while mine's in the shop, but she had plans tonight."

Nick braked at the junction with the main road. "What kind of plans?" It wasn't her garden club night, and her book club and sketch group didn't meet in the summer. When he'd seen her earlier, she hadn't mentioned anything about going out.

"Maybe you should ask her." Mia looked away, but not before Nick glimpsed a wariness in her expression that put his internal radar on alert.

"Is there something you haven't told me?" He signaled left and pulled onto the two-lane highway. A single yellow line divided it in the middle, and tall pines marched along both sides like sentinels.

"Gabrielle met a friend for dinner." Mia's tone chilled several degrees further. "I didn't think she had to ask your permission to go out."

"Of course she doesn't." Nick exhaled. He'd over-reacted. His mom had lots of friends. It was good she was getting out of the house and having fun. He wanted her to get back the life the cancer had almost taken away. "I worry about her, but maybe I'm being a controlling jerk."

"You said it, not me." Mia's tone turned warm and amused. "I agree with you as a friend, of course."

But thinking of her as a friend was going nowhere fast. He slowed the car and searched for a gap between the dark trees. Maybe he was going about this situation all wrong. He needed to think about Mia like she was one of his sisters, or the women he worked with. Except, every time he looked at her, his feelings were far from brotherly. Or collegial.

She inclined her head toward him. "Where are we going?"

"Where does it look like?" Even though he'd promised

himself he'd take her straight back to town, he turned left again into another rutted driveway where white lights twined around the fence posts illuminated a small wooden sign.

"Nick." Her breath hitched. "I spent too many summers here. Unhappy summers. Charlie loved this cottage. I didn't."

"It isn't the Gibbs cottage anymore. It's Camp Rainbow. You did all the work to organize a summer camp so kids who need some good times have a place to make happy memories. Apart from the ribbon cutting, though, you've never been out here. Don't you think your mom would be proud of what you accomplished?"

She bit her bottom lip. "You and Charlie helped me."

"A camp for underprivileged kids was Charlie's idea, but you're the one who made it happen. Charlie was busy with her wedding and her new job at the Associated Press in Boston. Then she got pregnant, and you'd think nobody ever had a baby before the way Sean carries on."

"He loves her. Charlie is Sean's whole world. The baby is too. At any age, a pregnancy is a blessing, but at hers it's extra special. Sean worries because things can go wrong."

"Charlie will be fine. Didn't she tell us tonight the doctor said her pregnancy was textbook normal? You should give yourself credit. You did the work to make the cottage property into Camp Rainbow. Charlie and I only pushed papers around."

"Important papers." But there was a smile and sense of purpose in Mia's voice.

At the end of the driveway, Nick pulled into a parking space beside the white, two-story clapboard cottage and cut the engine. Faint piano music and a chorus of crickets and frogs broke the quiet of the night.

This spur-of-the-moment detour was for her. Not because he wanted an excuse to spend more time with her. "Ten minutes. You can do ten minutes. Go inside, say hi, and I'll have you back at Mom's place in half an hour."

Her smile hit him full force. "Did anybody ever tell you you're pushy?" She unclipped her seat belt and slid the car door open while he was still blindsided by that smile, the way it changed her face and wiped away the sadness he'd grown used to seeing there. How it wiped away the mask she usually wore to keep the world at a distance.

"All the time." He got out of the car to join her and tried to smile back, even though the ground had dropped from under his feet. "It's one of the reasons I'm a good attorney."

His work meant everything to him. It defined who and what he was. No longer the out-of-control kid, Brian McGuire's son following in his old man's footsteps. He might be a lawyer like his dad, but he'd forged his own path, an honest one.

Mia stumbled on the rough ground, and he reached out to steady her. She let go of him like she'd been burned and turned toward the original summer cottage, which had been converted into the camp's offices and recreational hall. "It sounds like a singsong in there." Her voice was brittle and the mask was back on her face.

Guilt sliced through him, hot and sharp. "You don't have to do this. Not if it reminds you of your mom and when you were a kid."

This wasn't work. This was Mia. And as a guy who

had a black belt in avoidance, he got where she might be coming from. "Say the word and I'll take you back to town."

"I'm here, aren't I?" She moved around the building, and her white dress with red flowers gleamed in the darkness. "Besides, like you said, it's not the Gibbs place anymore. It's Camp Rainbow. Mom and Dad are gone. Charlie and I are adults with families of our own."

He stopped at the foot of the steps. An out-of-tune rendition of "On Top of Old Smokey" came from inside. A lot of things had changed since he was a kid, but camp songs weren't one of them.

"That music sucks."

The voice came from Nick's right. A girl of around eleven sat on the porch swing. Her feet hit the porch floor with a rhythmic thump.

"You think so?"

"It's so sucky it couldn't be suckier." The girl hunched into a purple hoodie. Her light hair was half hidden by a ball cap worn backward.

Nick glanced at a red-haired woman who poked her head through the half-open window behind the kid. One of the camp leaders he'd interviewed smiled at him before she disappeared back into the cottage.

"What would you like to sing?" Mia leaned against the porch rail and looked at the girl like she cared about the answer.

"Whatever." The kid gave an elaborate shrug and made a face. The kind of "fuck you" face Nick remembered on young offenders back when he was in law school and did legal aid work one summer. The face he'd worn pretty much permanently between the ages of twelve and seventeen.

"I'm Mia and this is Nick." Mia gave the girl a warm smile. "We helped set up this camp. When I was your age, I used to spend summers here with my mom and dad and my sister. Back then it wasn't a camp. This recreation hall was our cottage."

"Lucky you." The girl's sarcasm was worthy of a Hollywood diva. She tugged on her hat, and a clump of blond hair tumbled over one eye. Painted purple, her nails matched her hoodie, and her nose sported a small silver stud.

"Not so lucky me. I hated it here." Mia tapped one high-heeled sandal on the porch floor. Her legs were long and toned. Legs Nick had found himself thinking about in lots of inappropriate ways. Like wrapped around his waist in the middle of his king-size bed.

"You did?" The kid looked up and shoved her hair away. Her green eyes, like a cat's, glinted in the moonlight.

"My sister loved it here, but I didn't. I couldn't wait to get back to the city." She smiled at the girl again, who gave her a tentative smile back. "I was stuck here for almost three months, every year from when I was a baby until my late teens. You're here for three weeks, right?"

"Eighteen more days." The girl unfolded her legs, thin like a spider's below a pair of black shorts, and leaned toward Mia. "Unless you can get me out of here sooner?"

Nick choked back a laugh at the girl's hopeful expression. She'd asked the wrong woman to spring her out of jail.

"No." Mia shook her head like she was sad about not being able to help. "You need to talk to the camp counselors. If you're not happy, it's their job to make things better for you." She hesitated. "You are?"

"Kylie," the girl muttered. The swing squeaked and her bare feet landed on the floorboards again.

"The counselors can help you, Kylie, if you'll let them. I don't want any more kids to hate being here," Mia said.

"I never said I hated it. Not exactly, but I don't know…those songs are dumb and the games are dumb. The other girls laugh at me, and there could be bears out there, and I don't know how to swim, and it's so dark at night except for these little flashes of light like lightning." She stopped like a wind-up toy that had run down.

"I understand." Mia lowered her voice. "When she was little, my sister used to tag after me everywhere. Until I convinced her a bear with sharp yellow teeth lived in our boathouse and it would gobble her right up if she put one foot off this porch. But there's never been a bear around here since my grandfather built this cottage."

"Mia's right," Nick said. "I've never heard of a bear around this side of the lake, but I'll check if you want."

"You will? Like really?" Kylie's lower lip wobbled, and she rubbed a hand across her face. Her purple polish was chipped, and her fingernails were bitten to the quick.

"Sure. As for those little flashes like lightning, I bet they're fireflies. Do they look like that?" He gestured toward the darker shadows beyond the cottage where sparks of light darted and dipped.

"Yeah. You mean bugs?" Kylie's eyes narrowed.

"Insects, beetles actually, although some people call them lightning bugs or moon bugs." Nick smiled at Kylie. "They put on a magical light show for us every night. That's what my mom says, anyway. Since this is Firefly Lake, they're an extra special part of summer around here."

"They sure are, and fireflies aren't anything to be afraid of," Mia said. "As for the bears, if there are any, which I doubt, Nick will scare them so far away they'll never come back. Won't you?"

"Absolutely."

The frightened expression on Kylie's face got to him in a way those scared kids had gotten to him long ago. Back when he'd wanted to be a lawyer to do some good in the world and help people who needed a break. To be a different kind of man than his dad.

Mia smiled like he'd given her an all-expenses paid trip to Paris. "While Nick checks for bears, you come inside with me and we'll find a flashlight to help with the dark. I'm sure the counselors can do something about the music and those other girls. As for the swimming, I bet all you need is extra help to catch up. We can fix this, Kylie. Will you give the camp staff a chance?"

Heat spread through Nick's chest. His ex-wife would have walked past Kylie. He hadn't recognized it at first, but Isobel was shallow, selfish, and self-centered. Mia was different. Even though most of the time she kept it hidden, there was a real person behind her perfect face and designer wardrobe. A loving and caring person.

"Nick?" Mia half-turned, her expression quizzical. "The bears?"

"I'm on it."

Kylie looked at him, her eyes less like a feral cat's and more like a scared girl's. "Can you check out near the cabins and the dining hall? I never saw anything, but last night I heard this scratching noise and well, you know?"

"Yeah, I do." Although he'd never admitted it to any-one, back when he'd been at summer camp in Quebec, away from home for the first time, he'd convinced himself a wolf pack lived in the woods behind the dining hall. "I'll check everywhere you want me to."

"Before she went to the state prison, my mom said you can never trust guys. Especially guys who wear fancy clothes and drive fancy cars." She flicked a glance at his silver Lexus.

"If Nick says he'll check, he means it, Kylie."

Kylie shrugged. "Whatever." She got off the swing and it hit the wall behind her with a thud. Her eyes were bleak, like she'd seen too much of life too soon. The kind of eyes no kid should have.

"It's true, Kylie. Nick's a good man." Mia's look was so warm and loving, Nick ached. It made him wonder how it would feel if she ever looked at him that way. "He wouldn't be my friend if he wasn't."

And didn't that sum things up? Nick went down the steps into the darker shadows cast by the cottage, where the fireflies glowed bright. He'd turned his back on the path he'd been headed down at seventeen, and by keen intelligence and force of will, he'd turned himself into a good man, an honorable man. But it hadn't stopped Isobel from cheating on him. It hadn't stopped him from feeling like an impostor either, like if he'd been good enough and the son his dad wanted, the guy might have stuck around longer.

Nick moved to the edge of the lake, where the sand was soft under his shoes. Water slapped against the wooden dock, in time with the beat of the music from the cottage. Music that had nothing to do with the camp songs he remembered and everything to do with a green-eyed sprite called Kylie. The kid who had him out here in the dark when he should be in his office at work on a pile of legal briefs.

The kid who'd helped him see Mia in a whole new light and who'd made him face a truth about himself. Although he still didn't do serious, he couldn't maintain this friendship farce much longer, either.

He tossed a piece of driftwood into the fire pit encircled by a blackened ring of stones and stared at the dark water of the lake. It was slick, impenetrable, and deceptive, waiting until he let down his guard to suck him in.

What was he thinking? As soon as he got his mom settled, he was out of here and back on the fast track. He wouldn't let anything or anyone, especially not a woman, distract him ever again.

No more excuses and no more self-doubt. Mia repeated the words like a mantra as she slipped out of Harbor House early the next morning. The air was cool and the sun stained the eastern sky red. For the first time in a long time, she was building an independent life.

Her house. Her lips curved into a smile as she pictured the cozy rooms in the little clapboard cottage Sean and his brother were renovating for her. They planned to put in a new kitchen with cabinets salvaged from a friend of a friend. Sean wouldn't let her pay anything because she and the girls were family.

Her job. Her smile broadened. For the first time since college, she had money she'd earned through work she'd done. Although she only had one music student so far, she'd had lots of inquiries for September.

And friends who'd never been part of her life with her ex-husband. Gabrielle. Nick.

Mia's pulse sped up and her insides quivered. Like she was sixteen again, when she'd lingered outside the North Woods Diner in the hope she'd catch a glimpse of Nick as he cruised by on that motorcycle of his, with some girl with big hair and tight clothes riding pillion. Back then, he'd gone out with girls who had what Mia's mom and the other women at the golf club called a bad reputation.

A sharp, high-pitched bark yanked her back to the present. "Pixie?" She eyed the dog through the screen door. "Okay, but only because I don't want you to wake Gabrielle." She opened the door again and grabbed the dog's leash to clip it to her pink, rhinestone-studded collar.

The dog whined and Mia put a finger to her lips as she closed the door behind them. She slid a baseball cap onto her head, tucked headphones into her ears, and gave a little skip in time to Abba's "Dancing Queen." Her mom's happy song.

Last night she'd even faced the cottage, no longer the Gibbs place, where she'd spent all those summers with an unhappy mom and a dad who'd cheated, but Camp Rainbow, where kids like Kylie could make new memories.

Mia picked up speed, and Pixie kept pace beside her as they passed the grand old houses once owned by the mill bosses, where big maple trees shaded wide porches. At the foot of the hill, they crossed the intersection to her house. It was tucked into a marshy curve of the lake, where Nick had told her loons nested in the spring. The little house that already felt like home.

This early the town was quiet and the lake was still. A train rumbled through the level crossing at the end of Main Street and its faint whistle echoed. At the foot of the hill, she turned right onto Main, where the lone traffic light was stuck on green. The sidewalks were empty and the storefronts dark. Outside McGuire and Pelletier's law office, Pixie tugged on the leash and Mia faltered. The gold letters across the window glinted in the morning sun, and two tubs of red petunias on either side of the door were wet with dew.

Her phone vibrated. She glanced at the screen and yanked the headphones out of her ears as she fumbled to answer. "Naomi?"

"Mom?" Her elder daughter's voice was muffled. "I didn't wake you, did I?"

"Of course not. What's wrong?" Mia's maternal radar went on high alert. "Are you hurt? Is Emma hurt?"

"No, we're okay." Naomi sniffed and there was a rustle like she'd dropped the phone in bedding.

"Naomi? Sweetheart?" Her legs shook, and Mia sat on the bench in front of Tremblay & Sons Plumbing and Heating, two doors from McGuire and Pelletier. Pixie squeezed beside her. "What's wrong? You never call this early."

"Dad got a job offer in San Francisco." Naomi made a choked sound. "He wants Emma and me to move there with him because he said us living in Firefly Lake was only ever temporary." The choked sound turned into a sob. "Why didn't you tell me?"

Because a job in San Francisco was news to her. "Sweetheart, listen." Mia clenched her fist around the phone and sucked in a breath, rich with the smell of yeast from the Daily Bread Bakery. "Your dad hasn't said anything to me about a new job or you girls moving. He agreed the two of you would live with me in Firefly Lake."

Naomi hiccupped. "Dad promised he'd look for a job in Boston or New York to be closer to Emma and me."

"When did he promise that?" Mia's stomach heaved, and she gripped the phone tighter.

"Before we left Dallas. He said it was our special secret." Naomi's voice was thick with tears. "Then last night he told me he got this great opportunity. He's already taken it, and Tiffany's all for it. Dad wants his new family more than us."

Tiffany, the beautiful blond marketing intern Jay had cheated on her with. The one who'd gotten pregnant and given Jay the son he'd always wanted. "That's not true." Mia forced the words out and hoped she was right. She also hoped Jay wouldn't betray his daughters like he'd betrayed her.

"Apart from work, all he cares about is Tiffany and the baby."

"Your dad, he..." Mia stopped. Her days of making excuses for Jay were over.

"Why did Daddy break his promise?"

Mia's heart turned over. Naomi hadn't called Jay *Daddy* since she was six. "I don't know, honey."

Except, she did. Her ex-husband was a liar and a cheat, more concerned for himself than anyone else, even his daughters. And she'd fallen for it, over and over again. Mia shifted on the wooden bench. She ached to take her daughter in her arms to soothe her and tell her everything would be okay.

"He promised me. I trusted him. I don't want to move to San Francisco."

"Of course you aren't moving to San Francisco."

Pixie squirmed onto Mia's lap and licked her face.

"We chose to move to Firefly Lake together, remember? So we could be close to Charlie and Sean and the baby. Your dad was fine with that."

Maybe *fine* was an exaggeration, but Jay had agreed, which was all that counted, and Mia had a legal agreement to prove it. She took another breath of warm, yeast-scented air.

"In Firefly Lake I can be close to Ty," Naomi added.

Mia's throat constricted as yet another worry crowded in. Naomi's friendship with Sean's son was the one reason she'd first hesitated about the move to Vermont. "We have friends in Firefly Lake, sure, but your dad loves you and Emma and—"

"He loves us as long as we do what he wants."

"What do you mean?" Mia's mouth went dry. She eased Pixie away and stared at Firefly Lake's Main Street without seeing it.

"Nothing, forget it." Naomi's voice was guarded.

Jay couldn't take the girls from her. Not without going to court. Besides, he'd always said his work schedule was too unpredictable for him to have Naomi and Emma for anything more than vacation visits planned at least three months in advance.

"Mom? Dad wants to talk to you. He says he—"

"Amelia?" Mia flinched as Jay's voice boomed across the miles. He'd never called her Mia because he thought the name wasn't sophisticated enough.

"Jay." Mia tucked Pixie into the crook of her arm and stood, then ducked under the awning of the plumbing and heating store. "What's this about you moving to California? You didn't say anything to me, and Naomi's upset. She thinks you want her and Emma to move, too."

"I planned to tell you when I brought the girls back. I didn't expect Naomi to get all emotional. I thought she'd be thrilled and want to surprise you." Mia caught the impatience in her ex-husband's voice. "She had some idea I'd move to New York or Boston."

"She said you promised her."

Once, Mia had loved this man with her whole heart. When she met him in college, she'd imagined them building a life and making the family she'd wanted and that they'd grow old together. A dream that had started to die a long time ago, the first time he'd hooked up with a girl like Tiffany and Mia had pretended to not notice.

Like her mom had pretended to not notice her dad's women.

"I may have said I'd look for a job in Boston or New York, but I didn't expect Naomi to take me seriously."

"You're her father. Even though she'll be sixteen in two days, Naomi still believes what you tell her." Mia held on to her temper by a thread. "And why did you upset her so close to her birthday?"

"It was a misunderstanding. Naomi's a big girl and she can handle it." Mia pictured Jay running a hand through his sandy hair as his pale blue eyes narrowed. "I've got a great job offer, and Tiffany has friends in the Bay Area who can help out with the baby."

"You decided this when? Without a word to me? We agreed the girls would live with me in Firefly Lake. I gave you all the vacation visits you wanted, but Naomi and Emma need me. They need stability, roots, and—"

"Hang on. You're making a problem out of nothing. Didn't Naomi tell you?" His tone turned persuasive and became what Mia had always thought of as his salesman voice. "The whole point is you'll move, too. I'll still pay child support. I'll even add extra so you can get a place in San Francisco. It's not like you have anything to keep you in Firefly Lake."

Mia tensed, and sweat trickled between her breasts. "My sister's here. I've got a job. I bought a house and—"

"Sell the house. As for your job, it's not like substitute teaching or a few music students is a big commitment." His laugh was the one Mia hated. The one that diminished her and made her doubt herself. "Naomi said you're working for some old woman, clearing out her house."

"Gabrielle isn't old, and she needs my help." Mia curled her toes inside her sneakers. "As for the teaching, I've always wanted to use my degree and—"

"You can teach in California if you want. What you do about teaching is your decision, but I won't let you put my daughters at risk." He clicked his tongue against his teeth. "Emma told me all about your house and that boy Naomi messages all the time. She's not interested in the sons of my friends, boys who are going somewhere in life. Instead, she gets mixed up with the guy who cuts your grass. He's as good as related."

"They're our daughters and my house is my business." Mia set Pixie on the sidewalk and made her voice decisive. "As for Ty Carmichael, he's a good kid, and he and Naomi are friends."

"As soon as she's in California, Naomi will forget all about him." Jay's tone sharpened. "You've always been too lenient with the girls. Naomi especially needs a firm hand. She's strong-minded and willful like your sister."

Maybe if Mia had been more strong-minded she wouldn't have stayed with Jay as long as she had.

"You've already wrecked our family because you wanted somebody new. I won't let you uproot the girls again."

Jay gave the kind of sigh Mia was too familiar with. "You and I hadn't been right for each other for a long time. And Firefly Lake—"

"Is my home." Mia steadied herself against the wall of the plumbing and heating store, the brick cool against her back.

Pixie looked at her with anxious brown eyes.

"Besides, my sister needs me."

And she needed Charlie too. Apart from the girls, Charlie was the only close family she had.

"Visit your sister a few times a year. When we lived in San Francisco before, you loved it, remember? You even talked about applying to the music conservatory."

She had loved it, but San Francisco was right after they got married and she'd been starry-eyed in love with her husband. As for studying at the conservatory, she'd let go of that dream when Jay got his first promotion and she got pregnant with Naomi. The first of a whole lot of sacrifices she hadn't realized she'd made until it was too late.

"San Francisco was a long time ago." Dizziness and nausea rolled over her in a wave. "I have a teaching certificate I never used because we moved around so much for your job. But Jay, we have a custody and visitation agreement, and there's nothing in it to say the girls and I have to follow you around anymore."

"You'll do what's best for the girls." Jay narrowed in on her weak spot like a heat-seeking missile. "Once she calms down, Naomi won't miss an opportunity to live on the West Coast. As for Emma, she's excited already. I can commute to the city and get a place in the country to keep that pony she wants."

Mia swallowed the angry retort she could have made. Emma wasn't old enough to understand what moving to California meant. Or what having a pony meant she'd give up.

"You can't drop this on me. The girls have been through a lot and—"

"Think it over." His voice became soft and cajoling. "Like I said, you can teach in California if you want, but what about the girls? In San Francisco they'll have access to good schools and lots of cultural experiences. Naomi will apply to colleges soon. Apart from granola-crunching, tree-hugging hippies, who lives in Vermont unless they have to? The Northeast Kingdom is great for a vacation, but you have to be realistic. A choice between a cosmopolitan city and a little backwoods town is no choice at all."

Except, maybe it was the most important choice of all because it was her choice and her life. As for the girls, she wanted what was best for them. Security, family, and an independent mother they could be proud of.

"I live in Vermont because I want to, and I can't make any other decisions yet." She picked a hangnail on her thumb.

"Okay, I hear you. Maybe I got ahead of myself, but this is such a good opportunity. It's the big time." His laugh was intimate. "I know what I want and I go for it. You think about it, babe, and we'll talk when I bring the girls back."

Mia winced at the meaningless endearment. She'd always gone along with what Jay wanted because he and the girls were her family. But because of that, she'd lost sight of what she wanted. She mumbled a good-bye and disconnected then grabbed a corner of the building until the brick cut into her palm.

"He won't get away with it, Pixie. He won't, I tell you."

Pixie barked once and cocked an ear.

"Listen to me. I talk to you like you understand." Mia texted Naomi, then forced herself to put one foot ahead of the other to go back the way she'd come.

Back to Harbor House, where Gabrielle needed her and her work made a real difference in her friend's life.

Back past her little house, where she was happier than in any of the big houses she'd lived in with Jay.

As she passed Daily Bread the door swung open, and the scent of cinnamon and coffee wafted out to the street. Her stomach rumbled and she paused, drawn by the row of cinnamon buns displayed on a shelf in the bakery window.

"There's nothing in there for you, Pixie." She'd done it again, talked to a dog. It was all Jay's fault. He'd stirred her up.

"Mia?" The bakery door swung open again, and Nick came out. He had an insulated Boston Bruins mug in one hand and a paper bag in the other. "You're out early. Did Pixie pester you for a walk?"

Mia opened her mouth but the words wouldn't come. Instead, she shook her head.

Nick's white shirt was open at the neck, and he didn't have a jacket above his navy pinstripe suit pants. He came closer, and his eyes changed from clear blue to stormy gray. "What's wrong?"

"Nothing." She jerked her chin like a puppet on a string.

Pixie strained against the leash to climb Nick's legs, and Mia fixed her gaze on the cinnamon buns.

"Come on." Nick took her arm and awareness shot along her nerve ends. "I know when something's wrong. Remember?"

She remembered all right. Remembered what she'd trained herself for years to forget.

Chapter Four

Mia's lips were tinged with blue, and she fiddled with her phone before she slid it into the pocket of her black athletic pants. "Nothing's wrong." She wound Pixie's leash tighter around her fingers.

"If you say so." Nick dug in the bakery bag and handed her a cinnamon bun. "Eat. It'll boost your blood sugar."

"You're Dr. McGuire?" She licked her lips, and his heartbeat sped up. "You save lives as well as estates?"

"I wish, princess." He gave her a teasing grin. "Cat's the only doctor in the family, and she's an historian, remember?"

The ravaged look on Mia's face made him think about taking her in his arms right in the middle of Main Street and promising her he'd protect her and fix whatever was wrong. Apart from his mom and sisters, though, he was done protecting women and fixing their problems.

"Princess?" She gave him what he guessed was meant

to be a smile, but it didn't reach her eyes. Then she bit into the sweet pastry, chewed, and swallowed.

"It's what the guys around here used to call you. I thought you knew." He fell into step beside her and Pixie.

She shook her head. "No." A bit of icing clung to one corner of her mouth and shone against her still-pale lips.

Nick focused on the basket of flowers suspended from one of the Victorian-style lampposts along Main Street. It was a look the summer tourists loved because it mirrored the nineteenth-century buildings and the time when one of his mom's ancestors, a mill owner from Boston, had built the big house on the hill. If he focused on that long-ago ancestor with his mutton-chop whiskers, captured in a stern portrait in the dining room at Harbor House, he wouldn't reach out to run his fingers along Mia's jaw to her mouth and brush the icing away.

"Is princess what you called me?"

He shrugged and sipped coffee. "If the name fits." Back then, she'd been as beautiful as the princesses in the bedtime stories his younger sisters had demanded he read to them when his mom had to work late. And, because of that beauty, she'd been as unobtainable.

"I'm not a princess." She ate more of the cinnamon bun, and the expression in her eyes was bleak.

No, but a part of him would always think of her that way. "I get things aren't great for you but—"

"I'm fine." Her tone was as regal as the princess she claimed not to be, and a hint of red colored her cheeks. "Naomi and Emma love these cinnamon buns. Once a month, they're our Saturday morning treat."

He flinched at the change of subject with its reminder of who she was now. A single mom who struggled to make ends meet. "Mom says you're making great progress on her house." At the law office, he found his keys, unlocked the door, and punched in the code for the security alarm.

"We sure are and...Pixie, no, you can't, oh..." Mia let out a breathy whoosh and lurched forward as Pixie wiggled out of her collar and scampered into the office. "Come back here. How did you do that? You mustn't...Nick, you have to do something."

"Mom didn't tell you her sweet little Pixie is an escape artist?" Nick shut the door behind them and tried not to laugh.

"No, she didn't." Mia twirled Pixie's pink leash, and the dog's collar and tags rattled. "I'm not a dog person. Pixie knows it, the little monkey." She took off the baseball cap and her hair slipped free of its ponytail. "Come back here, you..."

"You have to show Pixie who's in charge." Nick followed Mia into the office and set his coffee and the bakery bag on the reception desk under a picture of his great-grandfather, one of the founders of McGuire and Pelletier.

"Pixie?" Mia put her fingers in her mouth and let out a whistle. "Nick, you gave that animal to Gabrielle. You have to fix this."

"Way to go, princess," he murmured.

"What?" She turned to face him, stuck her fingers back in her mouth, and whistled again, louder this time.

"Where did you learn that?" A whistle so unexpected and hot he wondered what other surprises were hidden beneath her cool, elegant exterior.

"Charlie's my little sister." Her eyes narrowed and

amusement mixed with frustration glimmered in their chocolate depths. "As a toddler, she was the original escape artist."

He grinned. "Not something Sean ever mentioned." He put a finger to his lips. "Follow me," he whispered.

"What?" Mia asked in her normal voice. "Pixie's got to be in here somewhere. All we have to do is capture her and then I can leave."

Nick shook his head. "It's part of the game."

Mia's expression said he was deranged. "She's a dog."

"Come on, play along." He moved into the short hallway. "Not in here." He poked his head into the first half-open office door, still empty because, like all the other staff, his cousin, the other partner in the firm, didn't start until nine.

"She's not in here, either." Mia ducked into the smaller office that belonged to their part-time paralegal and ducked out again. "What?"

"Nothing." Nick dragged his gaze away from her sexy butt outlined in the stretchy pants. She should wear pants more often. But he liked her in dresses and skirts, too. In fact, he liked her in pretty much anything. And he bet he'd like her even more in nothing.

"Nick?" Mia popped out from the cubicle occupied by the summer student who helped with office work. "Pixie's not here either, and I have to get back to Harbor House. I'm planning to start on your mom's bedroom closets today, and they're a big job."

His laughter died. Although Mia hadn't said so, it was a dumb game. The kind he'd have played when he was thirteen to spend more time with a pretty girl. "Pixie's in my office. I keep dog cookies in my desk drawer."

"Dog cookies?" Mia raised a groomed eyebrow.

"Mom brings Pixie along when she comes here because everyone loves that little dog. It makes Mom happy. When she was so sick, Pixie was the only one who could make her laugh, and I came up with this game to help Mom, okay?" His throat got tight, and he made fists with his hands.

"More than okay." Mia's eyes softened. "It's sweet."

Nick suppressed a groan. *Sweet* was right up there with *nice*. The kind of word no man wanted to hear from a woman, especially a woman like Mia. A gorgeous, sophisticated woman who could pick and choose men like chocolates in a box and discard the ones she didn't want. Like his ex-wife had done.

"Pixie's in here." He pushed his office door all the way open.

There was the big mahogany desk with the black swivel chair behind it, his suit jacket draped across the back. Glass-fronted bookcases that had been part of McGuire and Pelletier since his great-grandfather's day. A round table with four chairs and filing cabinets topped with pictures of Rotary club dinners and the annual Firefly Lake Fishing Derby. Modern computer equipment and a cactus the firm's receptionist kept alive. A typical small-town attorney's office, but, except for the jacket, nothing to mark it as his.

"Pixie, I know you're in here." Mia strode by him, and a light floral scent lingered in her wake. She headed behind Nick's desk and pulled out the chair. "Here you are." She scooped up the dog and slid the collar over her head then snapped the leash back into place. "Don't think you'll get a treat out of this trick, either."

Pixie barked and licked Mia's face.

Nick leaned against the door frame. "She likes you. She wouldn't kiss you if she didn't."

Mia frowned and avoided Pixie's pink tongue. "Neither you nor Pixie will turn me into a dog person. I took her for a walk because if I hadn't, she'd have barked the house down and disturbed your mom."

He crossed the office and kept the desk between them. The floral scent was stronger here—freesias maybe? His ex-wife had favored spicy fragrances with incense and amber that were mysterious, exotic, and sensual. Isobel had been mysterious, all right, and he'd been the sucker who'd fallen for it.

"Pixie will miss you when you go back to your house." This closeness between him and Mia was temporary, but he'd miss her too, more than he wanted to admit. In only a few days, he'd gotten used to her being at his mom's place when he dropped by, and he looked forward to chatting with her.

"About my house." She fingered the thin gold chain around her neck. "I might have to sell it."

"You only bought it a few months ago. Sean's doing all that work on it." Nick didn't rush to fill the silence.

Her chin jerked. "Jay…he's got a new job in San Francisco. He's moving and he wants the girls nearby. So he wants me to get a place there, too."

"Do you want that?" Nick shifted from one foot to the other.

Mia's head shook like it was disconnected from the rest of her body. "Of course not."

Pixie nuzzled Mia's throat, and something broke inside Nick. Something frozen for a long time came free in a sudden rush of emotion.

"I'm scared if I don't move, though, he'll take the girls from me." Mia's shoulders heaved as she buried her face in the dog's silky fur.

"You have a custody agreement." Nick moved around the desk toward her. A friend would comfort her without a second thought, and he was her friend.

"Naomi called me this morning. Then Jay got on the phone and..." Mia's voice faltered and broke.

"Hey." Nick slid his hands around her shoulders to pull her close. The floral scent was mixed with cinnamon, sunshine, and something honest and real. The scent of the woman she was. Sweet, sexy, and vulnerable. "What did Jay say?" Warm and soft in his arms, Mia's curves fit against him like the other half of a whole.

"He said I was putting the girls at risk. If I wanted to teach, I could do it in California." She stiffened. "I won't let him do this. If I have to take him to court and sell the house to raise enough money to pay the legal fees, I will."

"Don't even think about selling your house." Nick tried to ignore the need that slammed through him, half frustrated and half relieved Pixie formed a barrier between them to keep Mia's breasts from pressing into his chest. "That house is security for your future."

"My girls are more important than any house." She eyed him over Pixie's head, her expression stern. "For almost seventeen years, I did what Jay wanted. I moved from city to city each time he was promoted or headhunted. I made a home for my family, but I never put down roots, not real ones anyway, because as soon as I did, he changed jobs and we were uprooted all over again."

"That's the past." Nick trailed a hand across her back

to relax the tension in her tight muscles. Which did nothing to relax him and the pressure behind the zip of his pants.

"It is." A half smile played around her mouth. "For the first time in my life, I'm standing up for myself. I choose what's right for me and the girls." Her smile broadened. "It feels good."

Nick tried to smile back. After Isobel, he'd told himself he didn't need a woman in his life. At least not a permanent one. He'd filled his days and weeks with work, but maybe he'd made a mistake. Maybe the gaping hole in his heart wasn't about Isobel any longer.

"You know something else?"

Nick shook his head.

"I'd never thought about Firefly Lake or Vermont as home. Not until Jay went on about how I could pack up and leave. But I've got family here, the girls love it, and you and your mom are my friends. Even though I never expected it to be, this is my home. I've got roots here, my roots." She leaned forward and gave him a quick hug. "Thank you."

"For what?" Awareness churned through Nick of what he'd missed and how he'd fooled himself.

"For being a good listener and not judging me. I should have left Jay long ago. I should never have married him in the first place. It's as if my life stopped the day we got engaged, but you've never made me feel stupid for any of the choices I made." She lowered Pixie to the floor and looped the dog's leash around one wrist. "Thank you for being my friend and, like today, comforting me even when I didn't think I needed it."

Except friendship and comfort hadn't been at the top

of Nick's mind. He'd wanted to take her here in his office, on the desk or the table. Or pull her onto his lap in his desk chair and wrap those endless legs of hers around his waist. He bit back a groan as he pictured her head thrown back as he ran his hands through her cloud of dark hair. Her eyes and hands on him, too.

"It's not a big deal. What else are friends for? You should talk to Allison."

"Allison?" Her expression was puzzled.

"Allison Pelletier. My law partner and cousin on mom's side of the family. If Jay's up to anything, you need a good attorney." It wasn't like he could help her. It would be a conflict of interest, and he always kept his private and professional lives separate. At least he did when he'd had a private life. "When it comes to family law and wronged women, Allison's a pit bull in stilettos with the soul of a pussycat."

"A pussycat, huh?" Laughter lurked in the depths of Mia's eyes and warmed him. It also made him want her so much he ached.

"Absolutely." He fixed his face into an expression he hoped was friendly and reassuring. "At McGuire and Pelletier, we give a discount to family and friends." They didn't, but he'd talk to Allison and pay the difference.

"Really?"

"All part of small-town service." He picked up Allison's business card from the holder on his desk. "Jay's probably bluffing, but if it turns out he's not, Allison's your woman."

"Thank you." This time Mia didn't hug him, didn't even let her fingers brush his when she took the card. "I'm going out to Camp Rainbow later. One of the counselors called and asked if I could help Kylie with swimming, one-on-one. Charlie told them I taught swimming at a summer camp when I was in college. Do you want to join us?"

Nick's tongue got stuck to the roof of his mouth. He didn't swim. Not anymore. His vision blurred as memories pressed in on him. Back when he was seventeen and pissed off at the world. He and two of his buddies, drunk on a cocktail of Jack Daniel's and beer. Suspended for endless seconds in midair as the truck hurtled off the cliff on the highway outside town. Then the dark water as it pulled him toward the lake bed and he'd fought for breath.

"Earth to Nick? Swimming with Kylie and me?"

He forced the past back where it belonged. "I . . . uh . . . I have a lot of work today. In fact, I'll have to work late." To fix broken families and broken lives and find a neat legal solution to messy human traumas.

Another memory blindsided him. This one of Mia's killer body in the bikini she'd worn as a teenager when she'd hung out on the town beach.

"If you change your mind, drop by. Kylie would love to see you." Mia snapped her fingers at Pixie. "The way you took care of the bears, you're that girl's hero."

With another smile that made Nick's stomach knot and his breath get even tighter, Mia slipped out of his office, with Pixie walking beside her in an obedient, un-Pixie-like way.

Mia had him wound up in a way he never got wound up. She made him think about things he'd avoided for years. Like a home, a family, and a dog. Things that were permanent and not broken. She made him feel alive for the first time in a long time, too, and made him want her, even as she made him want to run as far away from her as possible.

And she made him wonder what it would be like to be her hero.

Mia put another armful of clothing on Gabrielle's bed. The vintage four-poster was flanked by a matching walnut dressing table and chest of drawers. A floral-patterned easy chair was tucked into an alcove by the window that overlooked the gardens and lake, and a bank of closets ran along one wall, stuffed with clothes, shoes, and accessories that were a treasure trove of styles through the years.

Apart from a one-line text, Mia hadn't heard anything more from Naomi. She sat on the edge of the bed and checked her phone yet again. Since her daughter texted as much as she talked, often at the same time she talked, the silence pressed in on Mia. Like the worries pressed in, too.

Damn Jay. And damn her for pretty much falling into Nick's arms in his office earlier.

She fingered a beaded white cocktail dress. Its simple, elegant lines contrasted with the rest of Gabrielle's clothes, which tended toward the artsy. It was the kind of dress Mia's mom would have worn. As a child, she'd spent hours dressing up in her mom's old clothes and bribed a reluctant Charlie to join in. She'd tottered in her mom's heels and pretended she lived someplace far away, like London, Paris, or even Australia. So far away she could start over and be someone else. Mia slid the dress off its padded hanger and took it to the window to examine the beading in the light.

"I'd forgotten all about that dress. Where did you find it?" Gabrielle came into the bedroom. A paint-spattered smock billowed around her slender figure to expose a pair of white capris and a turquoise top.

"In a garment bag at the back of one of your closets. It's beautiful."

"My ex-husband didn't like it on me. He said it was too fancy for small-town Vermont, as well as too short, but I wore it anyway. You should try it on."

"I couldn't."

Gabrielle took the dress from Mia and lowered the side zipper. "Sure you can. We're about the same size, so I bet it would be a perfect fit."

Five minutes later, Mia looked at herself in the dressing table mirror. Gabrielle was right. The dress was a perfect fit, although it was shorter than anything Mia had worn in years, ending well above her knees. She tugged at the hem. "I don't think a dress like this is right for me either."

"You're a beautiful woman, and Jay is a fool."

Mia's reflection in the mirror blurred, and she blinked away the sudden moisture at the back of her eyes. "I trusted him."

"Of course you did, but he broke your trust, so you're getting on with your life, aren't you?"

"For the girls."

"No." Gabrielle smoothed a strand of Mia's hair away from her face. "I don't deny you have a big responsibility to Naomi and Emma, but I mean for you."

"Me?"

"Yes, you." Gabrielle eyed Mia from head to toe. "If you went out in this dress, every single man in Firefly

Lake under the age of sixty would be knocking at your door within a day. Even the older ones, at least those who can still breathe on their own, would think about it."

"I don't want another man." Nick didn't count. He was her friend.

"Don't make the same mistake I did." Gabrielle wrapped her arms around herself and looked at the rug. "When Nick's dad left, he took a shedload of my family's money and his clients' money with him, and he embarrassed me in front of the whole town and half the state. He almost destroyed the law firm our families had built, and his behavior put his parents into an early grave. I had three young kids, and I was hurt, angry, and so ashamed. If it hadn't been for the children, I'd have wanted to curl up and die."

She rested a hand on Mia's shoulder. "I hurt so bad I closed myself off. I took back my maiden name as soon as I could, and I told myself I was over Brian and what he did, but I wasn't, not really. Then I woke up one day. Nick and his sisters had left home, and I was almost sixty and all alone in this big house."

"You had a job, your garden, hobbies, and lots of friends." Mia unzipped the dress and let it pool around her feet while she slipped her T-shirt and skirt back on. "From what I remember, nobody blamed you. Besides, after what happened, why would you want a man in your life?"

Firefly Lake had talked of nothing else for months. The money Brian McGuire had embezzled from McGuire and Pelletier. The big deal he'd orchestrated that had bankrupted a slew of investors. How he'd somehow escaped the jail term everybody expected he'd get and disappeared to Las Vegas, leaving his family to face the resultant scandal.

"After a few years, Nick and his sisters were older and my bed was pretty big and empty. Now I've got two daughters who rarely come home, a granddaughter I don't really know, and a son determined to pack me off to a retirement bungalow and make me old before my time." Gabrielle stared at the lake, her expression sad. "Don't wait for something like cancer to make you see everything you did wrong."

Despite the warmth of the room, Mia shivered. "Nick loves you, and he wants what he thinks is best for you."

"If he keeps on the way he's headed, he'll make some of the same mistakes I did."

"What do you mean?" Mia picked up the dress and hung it on a hanger on the hook behind Gabrielle's bedroom door. For an instant, she imagined wearing it for Nick and the expression on his face, the spark of desire in his deep-set eyes.

"I'm not surprised he didn't tell you. My boy was always close-mouthed, and he's turned into a close-mouthed man. His wife cheated on him with someone at work. He came back here, supposedly to look out for me when I was sick and turn around McGuire and Pelletier, but I think he's hiding out."

"She cheated?"

"Yes, but they're divorced and have been for more than a year."

Mia moved toward the bed and the scattered piles of clothing. Everyone in town knew Nick had been married, but surprisingly for Firefly Lake, folks were vague about the details.

Gabrielle sat on the edge of the bed. "Nick still does some ad hoc criminal law work for another firm in New York, on top of McGuire and Pelletier. I tell him he'll kill himself working such crazy hours, but will he listen?"

Jay worked all the time too. Like her dad. Mia was an expert when it came to workaholic men, and there was no way she'd let another one into her life, at least not permanently. "Nick, his wife, she..." Nick's marriage was none of her business. Not even if he'd been betrayed like her.

"Isobel's married to someone else now and has a little boy." Gabrielle answered the question Mia hadn't asked. "She was beautiful, smart, and a rising star in the legal world. I tried to like her for Nick's sake, but I never saw much of a person behind her pretty face and designer clothes. I don't know the whole story, but Nick was hurt bad, even though he'll never admit it."

Mia's breath hitched. "So he's—"

"Very much single." Gabrielle's tone was amused. "Despite the best efforts of every eligible woman hereabouts to catch him like one of those largemouth bass Firefly Lake is famous for."

"I wasn't..." Mia's face heated.

"Fishing?" Gabrielle's eyes twinkled. "Underneath his conservative, buttoned-up exterior, there's still a good bit of the teenage hell-raiser left in my son. Except Nick turned his life around, and these days he wants to save the world, not fight against it."

And Mia had always played it safe and never dated a hell-raiser. She'd always gone for the kind of boy her dad would approve of, and she'd chosen the perfect husband and the perfect life. Which had turned out to be a mirage of cheating and lies that had broken her heart and betrayed two innocent girls.

"What do you want to do with all these clothes?" She didn't want to talk about Nick with his mother. Or about the unknown Isobel who'd put the look in his eyes Mia had wondered about. A guarded look that kept her and the rest of the world at a distance.

"I'll never wear them again." Gabrielle rose from the bed, and her smock floated around her like a sail. "Give them to charity, I guess."

"You've got some good labels, so those could go to a costume museum, or a vintage clothing store might take pieces to sell on consignment. Before that, though, what would you think of letting me use them in the fashion show for my mom's foundation? I still need a final number, and you've got enough clothes here for a through-the-years showcase."

An almost forgotten excitement coursed through Mia. It would be the perfect tribute to her mom. Thanks to her mom, clothes were something Mia knew about. How to wear them to project an image and how to hide behind them.

"What a great idea." Gabrielle cocked her head to one side, her cropped silver hair an ever-present reminder of what the older woman had been through. "I kept some of Cat and Georgia's old things in those trunks up in the attic. Do you think the girls from Camp Rainbow would like to wear those clothes in the show?"

"I'm going out to the camp this afternoon, so I'll ask. Most girls like to dress up."

"There are even some of my mother's clothes in the attic. I'll call Cat and see if she and Amy can come here that weekend. Amy's such a tomboy we'd never get her into a fashion show, but Cat loved my mom's wedding dress and maybe she could wear it. It was made in Montreal by a Paris-trained dressmaker. I was too big to wear it, but Cat's petite like my mom was and I always hoped..." Gabrielle swallowed hard, and her shoulders drooped. "Never mind. If I ask her, Cat might wear the dress in memory of my mom, and you can wear my white dress."

"I couldn't." Mia's breath caught. "Besides, I won't be in the show."

"Honey, you'd be the star."

Which was what Mia was afraid of. "I'm happier these days behind the scenes."

"Your husband sure did a number on you, didn't he?"

"This has nothing to do with Jay." Mia turned her back on Gabrielle and put several silk blouses into a garment bag.

"I'm sure Nick would like to see you in my dress." Gabrielle's tone was light.

Mia's heartbeat sped up. "He...I..."

"You don't need it, but you have my blessing."

Mia swung around, but Gabrielle had gone and the house was silent. The white dress still hung on the bedroom door and swayed in the breeze through the open window.

Jay was the only man she'd ever been with. For all its virginal color, that dress might as well have had a neon sign to tell the world the woman who wore it was ready for sex. Which she wasn't. Mia closed the zip on the garment bag with a sharp tug. Even if she couldn't remember the last time she'd had sex.

That dress was temptation on a hanger. Like Nick was temptation in a suit.

Outside the house, Gabrielle greeted someone, her voice high and musical, and a deep laugh rang out in response. Mia moved to the window and stayed hidden behind one of the floral drapes.

On the patio below, Ward looped an arm around Gabrielle's shoulders and pointed to a boat on the lake. Their heads were close together and Pixie pranced between them, dainty on her tiny paws.

Mia backed away. She wasn't Gabrielle. She wasn't ready to let a man into her life, let alone one like Nick. Besides, if what Gabrielle said was true, Nick wasn't ready for her either.

Chapter Five

Ten days later, Mia sat on the edge of a table in Firefly Lake's town hall and swung her feet in time to Jace Everett's "Little Black Dress," which blared out of the speaker system.

It was only a song. It had nothing to do with the little white dress hanging in its garment bag backstage. Mia hugged herself as the girls from Camp Rainbow clustered with two of the camp counselors at the top of the makeshift runway. She'd done it. Close to the wire but, thanks to Gabrielle's clothes, the fashion show would end on a high.

Even Kylie had joined in. From her neck to her knees, the girl looked sweet in a pink ruffled party dress that had once belonged to Nick's sister, Georgia. However, Kylie had customized the outfit with a pair of black and white high-top sneakers, white lace gloves, several pink streaks in her blond hair, and black nail polish.

"There's something hot about guys doing physical

work, isn't there?" From beside Mia, Charlie's voice carried above the music. "It makes you want to haul them away somewhere and do them."

She whistled at Sean, who cleaned away the last of the construction debris with an industrial-sized vacuum cleaner. Then she poked Mia in the ribs and waved at Nick, who wielded a hammer to tack a curtain to the side of the stage. They were part of a crew of volunteers from across the county who'd pitched in to transform the hall, more suited to town meetings and the annual Christmas pageant, into a venue for the fashion show Mia had first imagined last winter.

"You're pregnant," Mia said.

"You're also a professional woman. We don't like it when men ogle us, so we shouldn't ogle them." From Charlie's other side, Cat's disapproving tone was at odds with the teasing glint in her eyes. "Besides, one of those guys is my brother, which is downright icky."

Charlie gave them a cheeky grin. "How do you think I got pregnant, sister dear? As for you, Dr. McGuire, I wasn't ogling, I was appreciating like I would sculptures in an art gallery. Aren't I lucky one of those yummy pieces of art is all mine?" Charlie whistled at Sean again.

Cat's laugh bubbled out, engaging and infectious. "True, but don't tell some of my more serious women's history students I said so. Or that an avowed spinster like me will be up on that stage tonight in a white wedding dress to rival the meringues served at Firefly Lake's annual strawberry supper."

"Spinster? That word went out of use a hundred years ago." Charlie gave Cat a warm smile. "You're a closet romantic who hasn't met the right man yet. And speaking of men, the always-thoughtful Mia has paired you with a super sexy groom who is Firefly Lake's very own Olympic and all-American hockey hero. Luc Simard is so hot he might as well have steam coming out of his ears."

"He's also widowed and a retired hockey player who has come back to Firefly Lake because it's his home." Mia covered Charlie's hand with hers. "Luc only agreed to take part because he remembers Mom and the show's to benefit the health center. Sure, he's a media draw, but he wants to keep his participation low-key. The way he talked about his late wife...Cat, what is it?"

"Nothing." Cat slid off the table and knocked a spray of artificial flowers to the floor. "That's why you paired us up for the show. Nobody could be more low-key for Luc than me. He's a jock, and the kindest thing anyone could say of me is I'm athletically challenged and have my head in a book most of the time. Nor am I a knockout like Mia, who the press would fall over themselves to get a picture of him with. And don't get me started on all those jokes about tall men and short women." She cleared her throat, bent to retrieve the flowers, then stuck them back on the table behind Charlie. "Sorry. I have to check on my daughter. I'll catch you later."

"No, I'm sorry. I didn't mean..." Mia stared at Cat's retreating back. "Cat never gave any indication she was uncomfortable being part of the show with Luc. As for him, he said it was great to see her again and laughed about how he sat on her Care Bear at some play group they both went to."

"Don't worry about it. As far as I know, there's no history between Luc and Cat beyond going through school together." Charlie gave Mia's arm a comforting pat. "I guess it's one of those nuances of small-town life you have to be born here to understand. Cat's super smart. She skipped a grade and, even then, at least from what I've heard, she was still way ahead of everyone else in most subjects. It must be hard to grow up different like that. You can talk to her later, but for now let's ogle as much as we want."

Mia zeroed in on Nick and the way the old jeans he wore cupped his ass. A great ass. How his white T-shirt hugged his chest. A great chest. The guy was eminently ogle-worthy and built in a way those suits he wore from Monday to Friday kept hidden.

"Mia?" Charlie's voice faltered, teasing gone. "I'm glad you're here. I need you. Sean's done this baby thing before with Ty, but I'm scared I won't know what to do."

"Sean's never done it with you or this baby." Mia squeezed Charlie's shoulder. "You'll be fine. Babies have pretty simple needs. Food, sleep, clean diapers, and cuddles. It's when they get older things get trickier."

Like with Naomi and Ty. Mia glanced at the stage, where Ty was perched on a ladder. Sean's son was also built, which wouldn't have escaped her pretty daughter's notice.

"Have you heard anything more from Jay?" Charlie's brown eyes, like their mom's, softened in sympathy.

"No." And when Jay brought the girls back to Firefly Lake, he'd barrel into her life like a Texas tornado in spring, destroying everything in his wake. "Naomi texts me a couple of times a day and we FaceTime every night. On her birthday, it was like a chunk of my heart was missing, but although I was afraid this trip might mean she'd want to move back to Dallas, she says there's no way she'll leave Firefly Lake. Jay will have to drag her across the Vermont state line kicking and screaming."

"Atta girl." Charlie gave Mia a thumbs-up.

"I also talked to Allison, Nick's colleague. She was reassuring, but she said we can't make a move unless Jay does something concrete."

"Allison Pelletier's great." Charlie levered herself off the table to loop an arm through Sean's. "Behind that angelic face she's a real kick-ass woman. After I deliver this baby, I'd be happy to kick that bullying rat of an ex-husband of yours right where it would hurt most. Sean and I are here if you need us."

"I know."

"I mean it." Charlie cradled her enormous belly covered in a white-embroidered maternity top, a vintage gem also from Gabrielle's closet. "A loan, a safe place to stay. Whatever you need, it's yours."

"Thank you." Mia met her brother-in-law's steady gaze.

Sean was a good man who looked out for his family, and that family had expanded to include her. He'd become the brother she'd never had, the brother of her heart. Like Nick, he was in her corner, no question.

"Hey, gorgeous pregnant lady." Nick appeared at Charlie's side and gave her a quick hug. "Are you one of the models tonight?"

"Get your hands off my wife." Sean gave Nick a mock glare.

Charlie chuckled. "I'm only the MC, but my stylish sister said I needed to look the part."

"Hey, princess." Nick's voice was low and, as he turned to Mia, his gaze changed from teasing to something hot and dark that made her breath short and remember the bad boy he'd once been.

"Nicolas McGuire." She moved away from Charlie and Sean toward the little vestibule at the entrance to the hall.

He raised an eyebrow as he followed her. "Mia Connell."

"It's Gibbs again." At least it would be once the official paperwork was done. Even though the girls would keep Connell, losing Jay's name gave her back part of herself. One more step to being her own woman.

His expression changed. "Mia Gibbs." In his mellow baritone, the name she hadn't used in so many years sounded like it belonged to someone else. "Amelia Gibbs."

"No." Her stomach muscles clenched.

"Okay." Nick's voice was steady. "You've always been Mia to me." His gaze caught hers and held.

Or princess. The word he didn't say hung between them. Except, she didn't want to be a princess either, locked in a castle and shut away from the world. She dredged a smile. "Jay calls me Amelia, and I don't like it."

"Mia Gibbs it is." He dug in the back pocket of his jeans and pulled out an envelope. "I have something for you."

"What?" She eyed the envelope he held out.

"A check for the work you've done for my mom so far."

She fumbled with the flap and took out the thin slip of paper. "It's too much, more than we agreed. I can't take it."

"You've already done much more for Mom than we

agreed. She told me you mended the slipcovers on the living room chairs and steam-cleaned the rug. You polished all that old silver. You make snacks for her all day long. You even arranged for the piano to be tuned and paid for it."

"That piano's a beautiful instrument. I don't think it's been tuned in fifteen years." She folded the check in half and her hands shook. "It's a privilege for me to be able to play such an instrument, and it's a crime not to maintain it. As for everything else, if I see something that needs doing to help your mom, of course, I'll do it. She doesn't like big meals, but snacks will help her get her strength back just the same. It's what I did for my mother."

"It isn't fair for you to not be paid for the work you do. Sure, it's for my mom, but it's also business." Nick's expression softened. "You have a good heart, but if you're not careful, people will take advantage of you."

They already had and she'd let them. But this was different, and not only because it was for Gabrielle. Mia fingered the check. She needed the money. Naomi and Emma needed things this money would buy. The extras Jay's child support didn't stretch to cover.

"You wouldn't take advantage of me," Mia said.

Like Sean, Nick was a good man and an honest one.

"No, which is why I insist you take this check and cash it." He covered her hand with his and gave it a brief squeeze. "Like you'll cash the check I'll give you next week and the week after that until your work at Harbor House is done."

Mia's heart pinched. He was right. Despite what she felt for Gabrielle, it was a job. Somehow, though, she'd lost sight of the job and the business arrangement, swamped by the new feelings she had for Nick. "Okay." She tried to smile. "Thank you."

"No problem." He gave her hand another squeeze.

Footsteps pounded on the linoleum, and Kylie bounced to a stop in front of them. "Nick. Did you see me?"

"Sure did." Nick pointed to her hair. "How could I miss you?"

"Great, isn't it? Too bad the dye washes out." Her green eyes sparkled. "Mia told me fashion is all about creating your style and being you."

"Nobody could ever say you weren't you," Nick said.

"Mia helped me. Do you know she used to model, like for real?" She bounced like her feet were on springs.

"Yes." Nick's smile was tight.

Kylie looked at Mia, and her green eyes were softer in the muted light of the vestibule. "She even won beauty pageants."

"Back then, Mia was the prettiest girl anybody around here had ever seen. The prettiest girl in the whole state, some said, when she was crowned Queen of the Fishing Derby." Nick looked at the worn floor.

Mia gritted her teeth as the past crashed in on her. "None of that was real. It was fun, sure." A lie, but she couldn't destroy the excitement in Kylie's face. "Girls to-day have lots more choices."

"Really?" Kylie stuck her thumb in her mouth, the childish gesture at odds with her tough-girl demeanor.

"Absolutely. You don't have to choose what someone else wants for you. Or the first thing you think you want, either. You need to take the time to figure out what's right for you." Which Mia hadn't done, and she'd paid for it in heartbreak.

"Maybe I could be a hairdresser." Kylie gave a little twirl. "Or I could work in a restaurant. I like to cook." Her grin popped out.

"Mia likes to cook too," Nick said.

Mia stiffened. A faded beauty queen and a domestic goddess. Was that how he saw her?

"I used to cook for my mom and brother." Kylie's smile slipped away. "Before my brother went away."

"Went away how?" Nick's voice sharpened.

"He got himself killed. In a car accident. Last summer." Kylie fingered the ruffles on her dress. "He was racing with some friends, and they crashed into a guardrail on the freeway."

"Sweetie, I'm so sorry." Mia moved closer to Kylie.

"Dylan did some bad stuff, but he was still my brother." Kylie pressed a fist to her chest.

"Of course he was." Nick moved to Kylie's other side. "Maybe if Dylan had had someone to help him make better choices, he wouldn't have done the bad stuff. I did some bad stuff when I was a teenager, but I was lucky because my mom never turned her back on me."

So he'd never turn his back on Gabrielle. She reached behind the girl for Nick's hand. He was motionless for a second before his fingers curled around hers.

"There are people who care about you, Kylie," she said.

Nick's touch sent heat ricocheting through Mia's body, and the hair on her arms stood up.

"Your social worker for a start. And the staff at Camp Rainbow. They'll help you make good choices. Trust them."

"People pretend they care but then they let you down.

I've had five social workers in three years. One retired, one got pregnant, one moved out of state, and the other two got transferred." Kylie shoved Nick and Mia aside, and the sullen expression was back on her face. "The camp counselors are okay, but it's not like they'll stick around for me either."

"Hold on a second." Nick's hip bumped against Mia's thigh. His big body was solid, and her face heated. "You still need to give people a chance. Sometimes they can surprise you."

"Yeah, right." Kylie's expression said she was mad at the world, had been let down too often in her twelve years, and was scared of being hurt again.

Mia tightened her grip on Nick's hand, and he pulled her into the shelter of his muscular side. "While you're here, the staff at Camp Rainbow can help. They're good people. You can talk to them whenever you need to and about whatever you want."

"They're paid to talk to me. It's their job. Not like you. I bet you tuck your girls into bed at night, even Naomi." Kylie crossed her arms.

"I'm their mother." Except, in the curve of Nick's shoulder, with the clean cotton smell of his T-shirt, his crisp aftershave and a musky scent that was all male, she didn't feel like a mom. She felt like a woman. A desirable, sexy woman.

"See? That's what I mean. You cook nice things for them to eat and make sure they have the right stuff to wear so other girls won't laugh at them." Strands of pink hair fell onto Kylie's forehead and hid her eyes. "You love Naomi and Emma because you're their mom. They're the most important people in the whole world to you, and you'd never go away and leave them. Ever, no matter what, even if they fucked up or you did."

Nick sucked in a breath, imperceptible, but enough to make Mia's body cool. Kylie was right. Once you got the mom role, it was who you were forever. And she was a single mom, which was an even bigger job.

"Kylie, I—"

"Whatever." Kylie shoved the hair out of her eyes. "I gotta go change. The Camp Rainbow staff is taking us to the diner for burgers before the show. Just like one big, happy family." She raised her hand in a mocking salute then turned on her heel and was gone in a froth of pink ruffles and a whole lot of attitude.

"You need to get ready for the show." Nick uncurled his hand from Mia's and stepped away.

"I do, but what you said to Kylie was great." Mia twisted her hands together. She missed Nick's touch, wanted and needed it like she'd never, not even at first, needed Jay's.

A pulse worked in Nick's jaw beneath the dark stubble. "As someone who also, to quote Kylie, 'fucked up,' who am I to dish out advice?"

"Maybe that makes you the best person of all."

"I'm not a family guy. Never have been and never will be."

"From what your mom told me, you helped raise your sisters."

Nick gave a harsh laugh. "Because my dad skipped out and never looked back except to throw money at us. Money he probably got illegally from his so-called business investments, the con man." He turned, and the sunlight from the pocket window in the vestibule slashed across his face like bars. "Don't make me out to be some-one I'm not." He reached out and touched the curve of Mia's face, the faint caress both a promise and a threat.

Mia flinched. Unlike Jay, who'd been smooth and charming but, in the end, full of lies, Nick was honest and real, heartbreakingly so. "I know who you are."

"Then why do you keep pretending you don't?" Nick's expression changed, and the shaft of sunlight changed too and softened the hard angles of his face. He touched her face again like he couldn't help it.

Mia's stomach knotted. Despite her brave resolutions, she wanted him. Wanted him in a way far beyond her teenage crush that had been stunted before it had a chance to grow. "Nick, I know you think—"

"Forget it." His blue eyes darkened. "I have."

Except, Mia hadn't and someday soon she'd have to face the truth and stop pretending. Stop lying to him and to herself.

Part of standing up for herself and being independent was standing up to her past.

All of it.

Nick stretched in a vain effort to get comfortable on the folding metal chair. He was squeezed between Sean and Josh Tremblay, from Tremblay & Sons Plumbing and Heating and, despite the air conditioners wedged into the windows, the town hall was stuffy.

He wanted to get on his bike. Tear up the highway around the lake or head over to Burlington. He'd ride the big Harley until the buzzing in his head stopped and he'd tamed the restlessness that made him chafe at the confines of his life. Confines he'd put there.

Except, he'd sold the bike years ago, part of his campaign to turn himself into the man a woman like Isobel wanted. To get as far away as possible from Brian McGuire's son, the wild kid who'd given his mom too many sleepless nights and who the cops came after first and asked questions of later.

On the temporary runway in front of him, Cat walked with Luc Simard, who'd been four years behind him in school. Their grandmother's wedding dress trailed behind her as Cat swayed in time to an old song about a bicycle built for two.

Nick whistled, which earned him a glare from his mom two rows over. "Sorry," he mouthed as Cat laughed.

Her blue eyes shone like they used to when she was little, and her smooth, blond hair gleamed in the overhead light. The serious expression she usually wore was absent as she looked up at Luc.

"This place is packed. There are folks here from all across the state as well as lots of tourists. Who'd have thought there'd be such a heatwave the one night we're all crammed in here like sardines in a can?" Sean wiped a hand across his brow and leaned forward to smile at Charlie, who stood silhouetted in a spotlight, a microphone in one hand and a framed photo of Beatrice McKellar Gibbs propped on an easel beside her.

Mia and Charlie's mom had been a beautiful woman, but Mia was more beautiful still.

Nick searched the stage to find her, the need as surprising as it was sharp. Except she'd stayed backstage to orchestrate the show out of sight, not front and center like Isobel would have been. "We'll sure raise a lot of money for the health center."

"They're wrapping up," Sean said, as the Partridge Family's first hit, "I Think I Love You," echoed from the speakers. "The girls from Camp Rainbow are the last. It was a genius idea getting those kids involved and—"

"Whoa." From Nick's other side, Josh broke in, and there was a collective intake of breath.

Nick's chin jerked up. Mia stood five feet in front of him, one hand on her hip and the other holding Kylie's arm. The girl stared into the audience and trembled like a frightened rabbit in the bright lights.

A white beaded minidress sculpted Mia's small breasts and almost pushed them out of the halter neckline. Outlined in smoky black, her dark eyes smoldered. Beneath the short skirt, her legs finished at a pair of high-heeled white sandals with jeweled straps that flashed silver in the light. Her tongue darted out to moisten her full lips, and Nick bit back a groan.

"You think she'd go out with me?" Josh asked. "I could get her a real good deal on a new furnace. I'd even throw in free parts and labor and a five-year, free maintenance plan."

Nick swung around and fought an unexpected urge to take a fist to Josh's blameless face. "You're too young for her."

"Only a few years, and some women like younger men." Josh raised a hand. "Relax. I got you two are friends. I didn't know she was your woman."

"She's not..." Nick stopped.

"Okay." Josh searched Nick's face. "But she's a nice woman and you better do right by her."

Nick bit back another groan. Josh was right. Mia was nice—too nice—and she'd already been hurt. She deserved a guy like Josh, a divorced dad with a son going into sixth grade, who could be a real father to her girls.

A guy like Josh could even give her another kid. Josh wasn't flawed. He hadn't sat in a doctor's office and been told he'd been shooting blanks since forever. Nick balled his hands into fists as Mia walked the runway, Kylie still glued to her like one of the leeches that plagued the bays along the eastern side of Firefly Lake.

Except, he only had eyes for Mia. How the dress outlined each curve of her body with every sway of her sexy hips and how the skin of her bare shoulders was luminous in the light. How a curl of hair had escaped from its complicated twist to brush her jaw.

He didn't love Mia. He didn't even think he loved her. It was one of those songs his mom and her friends had listened to when they were young. But as David Cassidy and the Partridge Family started again and the audience clapped along as the Camp Rainbow girls took a bow, Nick got to his feet and shoved the chair away with a clang of metal.

"What's up?" Sean raised an eyebrow.

Nick sat and tried to steady his breath. "Nothing." He focused on Mia, who looked at him with a heartbreaking expression in her eyes that made him want to run through the crowd of people and hold her. A look that told him she was playing a role and that she'd put herself on a stage she didn't want to be on because she didn't want to let Kylie down. And a look that told him once again she was so much more than a beautiful face and a killer body.

A guy behind him whistled, and then a few of his buddies joined in with catcalls and foot stomping. Mia untangled herself from Kylie's grasp and disappeared backstage. Nick turned and gave the guys the badass look he'd perfected as a kid. The look that said back off or he'd take it outside.

He pushed by Sean, his mom, and the friends and neighbors who'd given him a second chance. Adrenaline pumped through him as he ducked backstage and elbowed his way around tables stacked with clothes, garment bags, and shoes. He pressed his fingertips to his temples. The heat of the hall, the beat of music, and the scent of perfume and hairspray pressed in on him.

Mia had to be here somewhere. She wouldn't have left the building. Not in that outfit. Besides, the sole exit back here was through the fire door, which was alarmed.

He scanned the room again before heading toward a rough pine door with GALS painted on it in crooked black letters. The hinge squeaked as he pushed the door open.

"Mia?" He edged into the small room. Three industrial-green metal stalls were fronted by a line of sinks and a speckled mirror that made his reflection wavy.

"Nick?" From inside one of the stalls, Mia's voice rose an octave. "What are you doing in here? This is the women's restroom." Clothing rustled and then a zipper lowered.

"I wanted to make sure you're okay." He closed his eyes. The image of her slipping out of that dress less than a foot away made his heart beat faster and his body throb.

"I'm fine."

He leaned against the sink vanity, the tiles cool against his back. "You didn't look so fine out there."

The stall door swung open, and Mia emerged in a denim skirt and pink tank top with the white dress folded over one arm. Her face was flushed, and a big purse was slung over the arm that didn't hold the dress. "See? Fine." She patted her hair and looked in the mirror instead of at him.

"I don't believe you."

Her face crumpled. "Okay. You want the truth?" She tugged at the pins in her hair, and the dark mass fell loose around her shoulders.

"I do, actually." Except, he also wanted to run his hands through her hair. Bury his face in it and then spread it out on a pillow next to his face.

She faced him, and her eyes shimmered with unshed tears. "Tonight, I did what I always do. Like I told you, I didn't want to model. I said no to the foundation board, to Charlie and everyone else. Then in the blink of an eye, there I was in this dress in the spotlight. I did what somebody else wanted. I caved."

"You did it for Kylie."

"Exactly. Don't you see? It wasn't my dream. It was somebody else's, and I went along with it." Her voice cracked.

"Kylie was scared. You put yourself out there for her so she'd fit in with the other girls."

"I still did something I didn't want to do." She gathered the hairpins and dumped them into her purse.

"It wasn't about pleasing your mom, or your dad either."

Despite the makeup, Mia's face blanched. "Remember all those beauty pageants I was in? Mom was so happy when I won. Dad was proud of me, like all that mattered was how I looked. Even though I hated the whole contest circuit, I could never tell anybody. I did it for Mom, and she thought I loved the pageant experience as much as she did."

Nick inhaled the scent of the floral perfume Mia always wore, sweet with a subtle sexy edge. "Tonight you helped a young girl who needed you. It was your choice, not anybody else's. You might not have seen Kylie's face, but I did. You gave her confidence in herself, and you helped her feel like she belonged in a group, maybe for the first time in her life. But now you can do what you want, and I guess you want out of here."

"I can't just walk away." In flip-flops and without her usual skyscraper heels, Mia's head only grazed the middle of his chest. "I have to pack up after the show. I'm the organizer. I told Sean to make sure Charlie gets home early because she's tired."

"You're tired, too. Everything and everyone else can wait until tomorrow. You've been here all day and you need a break." She was the kind of woman who didn't take breaks and who never disappointed people.

"I can handle it."

"Sure, but you don't have to." Nick held out a hand and, after a long moment, Mia slid her smaller one into it. He pushed open the restroom door, and the red light over the fire exit winked in the shadows.

"What are you doing?"

"You want to leave, don't you?" He tracked the play of expressions on her face as resolve replaced uncertainty.

"Yes, but the door's alarmed. See?" She pointed to the sign.

"That would be a problem, how?" He reached up to temporarily disable the alarm then eased the fire door open to tug her out into the cooler night air. "Where's your car?"

"Back in the shop again. Charlie gave me a ride."

He scanned the rows of vehicles. His Lexus was boxed

in by Josh's plumbing van and a florist truck. "Charlie still has her car, right?"

"It's over by the road. She parked there so she could leave as soon as the show ended."

He headed for Sean's pickup with the Carmichael's logo on the side and pulled open the passenger door. "Hop in."

He reached under the floor mat and pulled out the spare key Sean kept there for emergencies. Mia stared at him wide-eyed as he slid into the driver's seat and the engine roared to life. "You can't take Sean's truck."

"Why not? He can go home with Charlie. I'll text him." He grinned. "Buckle up."

She grinned back and clicked the seat belt into place, a reckless gleam in her beautiful eyes. "Where are we going?"

He pulled out of the parking lot with a squeal of tires and accelerated onto Lake Road, the highway out of town.

"Wait and see, angel."

Chapter Six

Angel?" Mia glanced at Nick's profile.

His jaw was straight and the wind through the cab's open windows ruffled his dark hair.

"You don't like it when I call you princess." His voice was rough.

"I..." She shut her mouth fast. This was the Nick she remembered, sexy as sin and with the wild streak that had excited more than scared her. "I don't want to go back to Gabrielle's."

"You're not up for bedtime milk and cookies with my mom and Cat?" He shot her another spine-tingling grin.

Mia shook her head. She didn't want to go back to the town hall either, even though it would be the sensible option. Except, she was tired of being sensible.

She rested a hand on the dress on the seat between them. Even if only for a moment, she wanted to be the kind of woman Nick had seen in that dress. She gave him a slow sideways smile.

His breath hissed as she fiddled with the radio dial until the notes of a mellow country song filled the cab.

The LEAVING FIREFLY LAKE, COME BACK SOON sign flashed past, and then Nick turned off Lake Road and headed away from the lake along a country lane. Moonlight reflected off the thick curtain of old-growth forest and etched it with silver.

"If you don't text Sean right now, he'll think somebody stole his truck. He'll call the state troopers." Mia raised her voice above the guitar riff.

Nick took one hand off the wheel and rested it along the back of the bench seat. "The show just ended. He'll still be inside the town hall talking to folks, but since you're so worried, why don't you text him?"

Mia found her phone in her purse and swiped at the screen. "Nick borrowed your truck to take me home. Let Charlie know."

Within seconds the screen lit up with a reply. "Way to go, big sis. Have fun." Mia's face heated as she hit DELETE.

She hadn't meant what Charlie assumed. That she and Nick were going home together to his place. An apartment above the law office on Main Street she'd never seen but wondered about. Was it a home or only a place to live?

"Well?" Nick's voice, sexy and comforting, wrapped around her in the velvety darkness of the cab.

"You're right. Taking Sean's truck isn't a big deal." She curled her fingers around the phone. She might never have another chance to tell Nick the truth. He deserved the truth. Maybe she did, too. "I'm sorry."

"No worries." He turned up the radio on a Sam Hunt song, "Breaking Up in a Small Town."

"I didn't mean about the truck. I meant for pretending I didn't remember about us." She hated the catch in her voice almost as much as she hated peeling back the layers of herself to feel things she hadn't felt in a long time.

Nick switched the radio off. "There was never an 'us.'"

The breeze caught Mia's hair and whipped it around her head. Like it had all those years ago the only time she'd ridden behind him on his motorcycle. When they'd cruised along Lake Road and Firefly Lake's Main Street past the movie theater, the creamery, and the bowling alley, and she'd tucked her face into the back of his jacket in the hope nobody would recognize her.

The truck slowed as Nick hung a left along a dirt road, where tree branches dipped and tangled overhead. She held on to the side of the cab as they bounced down a hill then up the other side. He took another left farther into the trees and braked in a small clearing. The truck shuddered into silence.

Her heart pounded as her stomach knotted. "The summer before senior year I liked you. I couldn't believe it when you asked me out."

"Why not?" Nick unclipped his seat belt and turned to face her.

"I wasn't like the girls you usually went out with, and you dated a lot."

And she hadn't because she'd never been sure if boys liked her for her, or wanted to be seen with the beauty queen, as if her pageant ribbons were all that mattered.

"You were different, special." He looked at the pattern of stars against the inky sky. "Every guy in Firefly Lake wanted to have a date with you."

"All the girls wanted to have a date with you, not only the locals but the summer ones too."

"Except you." His voice hardened. "You couldn't wait to get rid of me. Why did you say you'd go out with me if you planned to ditch me in front of half the town?"

"I didn't plan it. Back then, I wanted to go out with you more than anything." She focused on the half moon that cast a white light on the dark trees and encircling hills. "I couldn't believe it was me at the diner with you on a Saturday night."

"So why did you make some excuse and leave? You could at least have waited to finish your meal."

"I was scared."

"Of me? What did I do?"

"You didn't do anything. You were the perfect date. I was never scared of you." Despite his reputation, she'd known there was a goodness in Nick and that he'd never hurt her.

"Then why did you leave?"

"I didn't tell my mom I had a date with you. I told her I was going to a movie with a friend so I needed to borrow her car. That's why I said I had to meet you in town. My dad was in Boston on call at the hospital that weekend."

"And Daddy wouldn't have wanted his little girl to go out with me." Nick's voice was as brittle as ice pellets against her skin.

"No." Mia dug her nails into her palms. She'd spent her life trying to be who her dad wanted, date who he wanted, and even marry who he wanted. All that effort to make him and her mom happy, when she hadn't understood until years later she couldn't fix what was wrong between her parents. And she shouldn't have had to try.

"So you came to your senses and bailed. You couldn't take the risk somebody would tell your dad you were out with Brian McGuire's son."

"Not exactly." Mia flinched and nausea threatened. "It turned out Dad wasn't in Boston after all. I saw him through the diner window."

As if in slow motion, she'd watched him park the new, dark blue Cadillac. A blond woman, the afternoon tea hostess in the dining room at the Inn on the Lake, sat in her mom's place. A woman with bright red lipstick and artificial eyelashes who'd leaned over and kissed her dad on the mouth, long and intimate. Her hand lingered on his jaw and then on the collar of the shirt Mia and Charlie had given him for Father's Day.

"I didn't want..." Her voice trailed away.

"You didn't want him to see you with me. End of story."

"No, wait." She had to make him understand and tell him a truth she'd never told anyone, not even Charlie. "He had a woman with him. It wasn't Mom, and he'd lied. Again."

Nick pushed the white dress aside and slid toward her along the seat until his breath feathered the hair at her temple. "I'm sorry, I—"

"He cheated." Mia's heart raced, and if she didn't get the words out now, she never would. "Even though Dad promised Mom, and then me, that there wouldn't be any more women. That's why I didn't want him to see me, not because I was with you."

"So you left through the back door."

"If he'd seen me, he'd have come in and told some story, like the woman was a friend." Mia gulped as the years of buried hurt and anger tumbled out. "Like he always did, like it meant nothing and I was some gullible little kid. Then he'd have taken me home, and he'd have yelled at me for being with you, but that wasn't why I left, I—"

"Mia—"

"No, I have to finish. I was so ashamed. Afterward, I pretended everything about that night hadn't happened. I didn't want it to be real because if it was real, my family and my whole life were based on a lie. When I got up the next morning, Dad was at the cottage and he and Mom were drinking coffee on the porch. He said he'd gotten someone to cover for him at the hospital so he could surprise us."

Nick reached for her hand and squeezed it. The warmth of his touch gave her courage.

"Dad took us out for brunch, and then we spent the afternoon on the lake in his boat. Mom was so happy. I couldn't tell her what I'd seen. When you helped me establish Mom's foundation and we became friends, I was scared you'd talk about that night. I was sure you must have seen him with that woman, so whenever you mentioned anything about back when we were kids, I pretended I didn't remember. I've pretended for so long, but I can't keep pretending with you anymore."

How could she expect Nick to understand? Even she didn't understand why she'd done what she had. She choked on a sob as Nick looped one arm around her shoulders and held her tight.

"I brought you out here because I want to show you something." He unbuckled her seat belt and maneuvered them out of the truck. Then he took her hand and guided her through the trees into an even smaller clearing, where a miniature waterfall cascaded over rocks and tumbled into a pocket-sized pool.

Mia drew closer to him. The carpet of pine needles on the forest floor was soft under her flip-flops, and the trees were dark, silent and listening. "What is this place?"

"It's supposed to be a healing place." In the moonlight, his teeth gleamed white in the shadows of his face. "It's sacred land for the Abenaki, the Native American tribe who live in this area. Mom used to bring me here." He knelt at the edge of the pool, and Mia crouched beside him.

"Back when you were..." Mia stopped as Nick eased their joined hands into the stream of icy water.

"Back when I was a mixed-up, out-of-control kid. I drank. I picked fights. You name it, I did it." The water trickled over their hands, and its coldness numbed Mia's fingers.

"Did this place help you?"

"Mom swears it did. To hear her talk, this waterfall turned my life around. It washed away all the bad stuff and gave the good a place to grow." He clasped her hand tighter. "I still come out here when life gets complicated."

"Complicated how?" The water against the rocks blurred the night sounds, and the carpet of stars far above gleamed mysterious and timeless.

"Mia." His face was inches from hers as Nick ground out her name.

"What?" The familiar knot in her chest loosened, and the heaviness she'd carried there for years lifted.

"I wanted to do this when we were kids." The Vermont lilt he'd lost during his years in New York was back. His lips brushed her jaw in a faint caress before his mouth covered hers, warm and insistent.

She kissed him back, and a needy little moan slipped out as he drew them onto the grassy bank and fit her body against his. She ran her hand along his arm, where the muscles were corded tight, and a faint sheen of sweat dampened his skin. He deepened the kiss and, despite herself, Mia moaned again and arched into him. She ran one hand across his jawline, the beard stubble rough beneath her touch.

He tore his mouth away, breathing hard. "Mia."

She lurched upright. "It's fine." Her hand shook as she tugged on the hem of her top.

"No, it's not. I'm sorry, I..." Nick raked a hand through his hair.

"No need to apologize." She scrambled to her feet and brushed pine needles, twigs, and soil off her clothes in sharp, jerky motions. "We got carried away. Forget it. I will."

Nick got to his feet, too, and his expression was dark with the same edge to it she remembered from all those years ago. "Forgetting and pretending. Despite what you said, you're still good at those things, aren't you?"

Mia sucked in a harsh breath. He was right. She'd pretended for so long she'd forgotten what was real and what was pretend. What she was supposed to feel masked what she really felt. The good girl who'd always followed the safe path. Except, the safe path hadn't been the right path and that supposed safety was a lie.

Nick dug in his pocket for the truck key. "I'll take you back to Mom's." He walked away from her and slipped out of the circle of moonlight that had bewitched her, bewitched them both.

The healing place that had made everything a whole lot more complicated.

Something had changed for Mia and Nick tonight. Gabrielle glanced between the two of them as they hovered outside her living room doorway. "You're welcome to join us. Amy's asleep upstairs, and Cat's grading papers in the kitchen."

"Us?" Nick lounged against the door frame as far away from Mia as possible, and so like Brian that Gabrielle's scalp prickled. In all the ways that mattered, Nick wasn't anything like his father.

"I don't think you've met Ward." Gabrielle inclined her head in the older man's direction.

"You know I haven't." Nick's casual demeanor was at odds with the sharp, assessing look in his eyes that hid a pain only a mother could see. He turned to Mia. "Have you met him?"

"Yes." Mia flicked a glance at Ward. "He's interested in plants. He helps your mom in the garden."

A muscle worked in Nick's jaw. "Why didn't you—"

"Your mom's business is her business." Mia's smile disappeared, and she turned back to Gabrielle. "Although I'd love to join you, I'm tired after the fashion show. I want to call the girls and have a shower." She put a hand to her mouth, dropped it again, and shifted from one foot to the other.

"Oh, honey, I didn't think. The show was fabulous but you must be exhausted. You go on and give your sweet girls my love." Gabrielle lifted her mother's Wedgwood teapot and refilled Ward's cup.

His smile started deep in the blue of his eyes and

pulled her in. It warmed almost forgotten places inside her, like she was a young woman again and life was rich with possibilities.

Without another glance at Nick, Mia escaped up the stairs, her footsteps light on the wooden treads.

Nick moved farther into the room and crossed his arms over his chest. "Ward, is it?"

"Ward Aldrich." Gabrielle made the introductions.

Mia was right. It was none of Nick's business who she made friends with.

"Good to meet you." Ward stood and shook Nick's hand. "Your mom's told me a lot about you."

"Funny, she never mentioned you." Nick returned Ward's handshake then sat in a blue velvet armchair and crossed one jean-clad leg over the other. "Mia didn't either." He flicked a glance toward the empty staircase, and his expression changed to one of such longing Gabrielle's breath caught. Her boy felt something for Mia, she was sure of it. She only had to keep nudging the two of them in the right direction.

"I stumbled across your mom's garden and we got talking." Ward dug in his pocket for his wallet and pulled out a business card. "I'm on a working vacation and based at the Inn on the Lake for a few weeks."

Nick took the card and studied it. "It must be interesting to travel all around the world and make nature films."

"It sure is. I'll be in northern China in October for a documentary project." Ward's eyes lit up as he launched into a description of his work and travels.

Gabrielle tightened her grip on the handle of her teacup. Of course Ward would leave. Whatever was between them was temporary. It had to be. She hadn't told him she'd been sick, and she wouldn't. Even a shopping trip to Burlington or a visit to her sister and cousins in Montreal was still too much. China might as well be the moon.

"You and my mother are…?" The warning in Nick's voice was unmistakable.

"Nick." Gabrielle set down her cup with a thud. Amber liquid sloshed over the fluted edge and splattered across the Victorian tea cart to stain the embroidered tray cloth.

"The boy's looking out for you, is all." Ward got to his feet. "I'd like to think your mother and I are friends."

"Boy?" The corners of Nick's mouth twitched as he rose to his feet, too. "You know I'll check you out, don't you?"

"Of course you will. I'd do the same in your shoes." Ward moved to stand next to Nick, the two men almost equal in height. "An attorney like you must have contacts in the right places."

"A few." Nick's smile came out and then he laughed, awkward, but still a laugh.

Ward's expression sobered and the sadness in his eyes was in stark contrast to the warmth and good humor Gabrielle was used to seeing there. "My wife, Carol, died almost twenty years ago. I've been alone since my daughter went off to college and then married. Now she has a little girl of her own."

"I'm sorry about your wife and…everything." Nick cleared his throat. "I can be a bit—"

"Overprotective." Gabrielle joined the two men and linked an arm through her son's. The sweet little boy who'd grown into the angry teen and then the disillusioned man. Damn Brian and damn Isobel, too.

Ward's expression changed again, and he shot Gabrielle a teasing glance. The kind of look that made her heart beat faster and made her forget about those traitorous cells that might still lurk inside her body to pounce when she least expected. "What checking me out won't tell you is I've still got all my teeth and most of my hair. I broke my right leg climbing in the Himalayas three years ago, but I got a clean bill of health at my last physical in March. I also play a decent game of pool."

Nick laughed again, less awkward. "Pool, huh?"

"You play?" Ward looped his arm through Gabrielle's free one, the gesture as familiar and comfortable as if they'd known each other for years, and she shivered. A shiver that reminded her she'd once been a woman, not a cancer patient. Not a fighter and not a survivor but a woman who was healthy and whole.

"When I have time, yeah, I play with a group of guys at the Moose and Squirrel, the bar down by the lake." Nick opened his wallet and slid out his card. "Wednesday's our pool night. Give me a call if you're interested."

"Sure." Ward took his arm away from Gabrielle's to take Nick's card. "Thanks."

They assessed each other the way men did, and Gabrielle watched them, her heart full. She loved Nick, more than she could ever tell him. For her sake, he'd try to get to know Ward and accept him, so he'd opened himself up in a way he rarely did.

Like she'd opened herself to Ward. Even though, if she let herself, she could fall for him. And fall hard. But she couldn't let herself.

She bent to pick up Pixie, who snoozed on a needlepoint-covered footstool. The dog nestled into the curve of her chest, and her small body was warm and soothing. The old house creaked in the wind, and an upstairs window banged. Nick's head jerked toward Gabrielle.

"I've given Mia Georgia's old room. The window's sticking again, but neither of us is strong enough to fix it." A little white lie, which was justified if it got Mia and Nick to talk to each other. Gabrielle gave him as helpless a look as she could muster.

"I'll come by at lunch tomorrow and take a look," Nick said. "Mia's going to Camp Rainbow, so I won't disturb her. The sooner you get this place sold and you move into that bungalow, the better. It has new windows and frames and everything is energy-efficient and maintenance-free. You'll be warm, no matter what the Vermont winter throws at you, and cool if it's a hot summer."

"What bungalow?" Ward's expression was puzzled.

Gabrielle looked at Nick and summoned the courage to tell him the truth she'd avoided for weeks. The truth he'd never wanted to hear. "I've changed my mind. I'm not selling Harbor House."

"But I hired Mia to help you and—"

"She has helped me," Gabrielle broke in. "Mia's helped me see how much I love my home and how it would about kill me to leave it and see strangers living here."

"Mom, be reasonable, you can't—"

"Don't use that 'I know best' tone with me." Gabrielle straightened, strong and sure. "If you want that new bungalow so much, buy it for yourself. Pixie and I are staying right here where we belong."

Chapter Seven

His mom was stubborn and contrary, but whenever Nick thought about losing her, he got so damn scared he couldn't think straight. He drained his soda and rested his elbows on his office desk, where the endless stack of paperwork mocked him.

The time on his laptop was twelve thirty a.m., and he'd sat here for almost two hours, trying to lose himself in work and deal with other people's problems in a futile attempt to stop thinking about his own. Like what he'd do about his plan to go back to New York if his mom insisted on staying in Harbor House. And why he'd kissed Mia.

That mind-blowing kiss he couldn't stop thinking about. The taste of her mouth, sweet and rich, and the softness of her lips under his. How, if he hadn't come to his senses, he'd have taken things further and ruined a friendship he counted on.

Since work was going nowhere fast, he should at

least try to get some sleep. Outside the office window, Main Street was quiet. Dark clouds scudded across the moon and cast long shadows over the silent buildings. He flipped off the desk lamp and headed upstairs to the apartment, which, like the office, was supposed to be temporary, so there were no personal touches to make it a home.

As he unlocked the door, his cell phone buzzed. He tensed and grabbed it from his pocket to answer on the second ring.

"Thank God you're still up." Sean's voice echoed like he was at the bottom of a well.

"What's wrong?" Nick stood inside the compact apartment foyer with its plain white walls and table with a stack of junk mail.

"It's Charlie." His friend's voice broke. "There's something wrong with the baby. Charlie's bleeding. I called the paramedics and they're taking her to the hospital in Kincaid."

"No." Nick's palms were damp and his heart pounded.

"I need you to pick Mia up from your mom's place. That old clunker of hers is in the shop again and Charlie needs her." Sean's voice was muffled and there were noises in the background. Noises Nick didn't want to hear. Moans and a high-pitched cry. Official voices too, brisk and meant to reassure.

"Of course. Whatever you need." He cared about Charlie and Sean like family. Nick's hand slid on the phone and his body was ice cold.

A car door slammed, and Sean took a rasping breath. "Thanks, buddy. I already called Mia. She'll wait for you outside Harbor House."

Nick grabbed a sweatshirt from a chair, checked to make sure he had his wallet and car keys, and fought the panic in his throat.

"I have to go." Sean's voice yanked him back to reality. "I knew we could count on you."

"I'm on my way." He hit the stairs at a run, even though his legs were numb.

The accident was a lifetime ago. He'd driven that road to Kincaid hundreds of times when his mom was in the hospital. Tonight was no different and, unlike his friends, Charlie and the baby would make it. They had to.

Five minutes later, he pulled his Lexus into the circular drive in front of Harbor House, where Mia stood on the bottom porch step. In dark sweats and a hoodie, her hair in a messy ponytail and square-framed glasses perched on the bridge of her nose, she looked like she'd rolled out of bed minutes earlier. Before the car came to a complete stop, she had the passenger door open and was belted into the seat beside him. Her face was ashen and, behind the glasses he'd never seen her wear, her eyes were stark with fear.

"Hurry. Please hurry."

His mom and Cat stood on the porch in fuzzy bathrobes and slippers. His gaze locked with theirs, and then he eased the car out of the drive between the line of trees older than he was.

"It sounds like Charlie's hemorrhaging. I couldn't talk to her but Sean..." Mia stopped and dropped her head into her hands. "It's not good. I can't lose her."

"You won't lose her. She's a fighter. When she was a foreign correspondent, she survived a roadside bomb, didn't she? Her colleague died, but she didn't. It wasn't her time. This isn't either."

"She was younger and she wasn't pregnant then. She and Sean only found each other again last summer. After she miscarried their first baby all those years ago, this pregnancy is a second chance." Mia's voice wobbled.

"Charlie and the baby will be fine." Nick sent a silent prayer to a God he'd almost stopped believing in. "She needs you to be strong for her." At the foot of the hill, he hung a left toward the lake and headed for the highway and the county hospital in Kincaid, twenty miles away across the twisting mountain road.

"Of course I'll be strong. She's my sister and the baby is my niece or nephew. My only niece or nephew."

And family meant everything to Mia. She was still rigid beside him, but there was a new determination on her face and in her voice.

"Can't you go any faster?"

"Not without the cops coming after us." He'd been there and done that on this road on a night a lot like this one. "I'll get you there as fast as I can. I promise."

Nick gripped the wheel and stared into the night, where the car headlights sliced a yellow path through the darkness. A guardrail loomed silver along the side of the road to separate the narrow highway from the jagged rocks that dropped to the water below.

Mia clenched her hands together in her lap in silence.

"I didn't know you wore glasses." Anything to make conversation, because if Nick kept talking, maybe the memories would stop circling in his head.

"I usually wear contacts, but tonight when Sean called, I didn't have time to put them in."

"They suit you." The glasses made her more real and gave her a sexy librarian look that was a surprising turn-on.

"Jay never liked them." Her laugh was forced. "That's one bonus. I don't have to care what he thinks anymore."

"Why did you marry him in the first place?" Nick took his foot off the accelerator in anticipation of the place where the road narrowed more into a hairpin turn. The dark forest was on one side and vertical granite cliffs on the other.

"I loved him and I thought he loved me. I believed him when he said he wanted us to make a family together."

Nick gave her a sideways look.

Her face was sad and pale in the moonlight. "The family I grew up in wasn't the greatest, so I wanted a new family, a happy one."

"You still have a family. You, Naomi, and Emma. You're a good mom, and sometimes one good parent compensates for everything the other one can't give."

"Like your mom did for you and your sisters?"

"Yeah." He stared out the window, where the double yellow line bisected the twisty road, and the lake loomed dark and cold out of sight below. "Why did you stay with Jay?"

"The same reasons any woman stays with a man long after the time she should." Mia hugged herself. "I was afraid if I left, I'd mess up my girls' lives. I'd worked so hard to create the perfect family, I didn't want to admit I'd made a mistake. I convinced myself Jay would change. I believed his lies and excuses, like my mom did with my dad."

"It's not only women who do that." Despite Nick's

doubts, he'd stayed with Isobel. He'd believed her stories because he hadn't wanted to look like a fool in front of his family, friends, and colleagues. Instead, she'd run off with the senior partner, which had made him look like an even bigger fool.

"Like you and your ex-wife?" Mia fiddled with the seat belt, and her nails clicked against the buckle in the darkness.

"My mom told you about Isobel?" Nick navigated into the turn.

"Only because she's worried about you. She didn't tell me any details, so you don't need to think...what is it?"

"Nothing." He kept his eyes on the road. He wouldn't let Mia down. Or Charlie, Sean, and their baby. Or, most of all, himself.

"I should have remembered. The accident happened near here, didn't it?"

He nodded as cold sweat trickled down his back.

"You were lucky to get out alive." Mia's voice was clear and nonjudgmental.

"Lucky?"

"Compared to your friends."

As if he needed the reminder.

"It wasn't your fault. You went along for the ride. You were seventeen and made a bad choice."

Except, it wasn't okay because he'd been as drunk as the others. He hadn't spoken up, he hadn't taken the keys, and so two of his buddies had died.

They'd screamed as the truck skidded off the road and through the guardrail. Then silence and blackness before he'd clawed his way out through the icy water and the twisted metal that had shredded his flesh.

"The accident was a long time ago." And he was a man, not a boy. "Tonight's about Charlie and the baby." He hadn't been able to save his friends, but now he had a chance to help make something right for someone else.

All these years he'd avoided feeling much of anything, apart from the guilt he alone had survived, but with Mia, he felt everything. Desire but also affection and a huge, aching sense of loss. Which went to show it was a lot safer to stay numb.

He stole a glance at her. She was the kind of woman a guy could count on. But she'd been hurt once and, despite that kiss earlier, he wouldn't be the one to hurt her again.

Or make her promises he couldn't keep.

Mia couldn't think about Nick. How she felt about him, or the way he'd come through for her tonight.

He pulled the car into a parking space outside the white and red sign marked EMERGENCY. The hospital was on the outskirts of Kincaid, encircled by rolling hills, the 1950s brick building fronted by a new wing where glass and concrete soared skyward. Colorful flower beds sat in front of a bank of double glass doors, and fluorescent light spilled out into the night.

He turned off the car, and Mia grabbed her purse.

"Do you want to wait here?" She opened the car door.

After that moment near the accident site, he hadn't said a word the rest of the way here.

"Like I'd let you handle this by yourself." Nick unfolded his big frame from the driver's side and came around the car to take her arm. He propelled her along the concrete walkway to the hospital entrance, where the automatic doors opened to let out an antiseptic smell.

Behind the information desk, a middle-aged woman looked up. Her brown hair glinted in the overhead light, and "Donna" was written on the name tag pinned to her white sweater.

"We're here to see Charlotte Carmichael. I'm her sister and she came in by ambulance." Charlie had to be okay. Maybe this was all a mistake. A bad dream she'd wake up from.

Donna tapped on the computer keyboard below the desk. When she looked up again, her expression was guarded. "Her husband is in the small waiting room at the end of the hall. Follow the signs to Emergency, and the room's the next one along."

"The waiting room?" Mia clutched Nick's arm. "Why isn't he with her? She's having a baby." Sean had been at Charlie's side for every step of the pregnancy. He'd never have left her alone now.

"I'm sorry. I can't give out confidential patient information." Donna looked back at the computer screen and avoided Mia's gaze.

"Come on." Nick tugged Mia's arm and led her along the hall, where watercolors of Vermont covered bridges hung at regular intervals on the pale blue walls.

"I have to find Charlie. She needs me." Mia broke into a jog and pulled Nick along with her.

Nick matched her steps as he kept hold of her arm. "Here." He steered her into the waiting room. It had more blue walls, more pictures of bridges, and a row of upholstered chairs, empty except for one.

"Sean?" Mia broke free of Nick's hold and skidded to a stop in front of her brother-in-law.

He was hunched over in the chair, and his head was buried in his hands.

"Where's Charlie?" Her heart raced. She was too late. She'd lost her sister, the same as she'd lost her mom.

Sean lifted his head. His blue eyes were rimmed with red, and his face was haggard like he'd aged ten years since the fashion show. "She's in surgery."

Mia's legs went weak and she sank into the chair beside him. "The baby?"

"They're taking it out by caesarian section. Everything happened so fast they had to put Charlie under. The doctor said she started to bleed because the placenta came away." Sean dropped his head into his hands again, and Mia wrapped her arms around him. "They wouldn't let me stay with her."

"Charlie will be fine." Mia held back a cry. "The baby, too. Everyone says this is a great hospital."

Over Sean's bent head, her gaze locked with Nick's. Although his face was ashen, his expression was steady and full of reassurance. Mia seized on it, amidst the horror that engulfed her.

"My mom had terrific treatment here." Nick sat on Sean's other side. "Charlie and your baby couldn't be in better hands."

"Charlie needed me and I failed her."

"Of course you didn't." Mia took a deep breath and gripped Sean's shoulders. "They didn't let you stay because it was an emergency. Charlie would have understood."

"Apart from my son, she's the best thing that ever

happened to me. Every day, I tell her I love her first thing in the morning and last thing at night." Sean blinked and buried his face in Mia's hoodie. His shoulders shook beneath his polo shirt. "Except tonight, I didn't get a chance to say it. Before I knew it, they'd wheeled her away."

"Charlie knows you love her. You and Ty are the best things that have ever happened to her, too."

With Sean, her sister had found the kind of love Mia had never known. An accepting, all-encompassing love she'd pretended she'd had with Jay, but it had been a lie.

Sean raised his head. "You think so?" His eyes were haunted and desperate, and his forehead was beaded with sweat.

"I'm sure of it." Mia's throat clogged. Even if the worst happened, Charlie had been loved. She held Sean tighter.

"Charlie loves you more than anything." Nick's voice was low. "In my job, I see all the couples that don't work and the families that fall apart, but the two of you have something special."

His gaze locked with Mia's again, and heat rose in her face. Even though she didn't want to admit it, there was something special between her and Nick. The kiss they'd shared hadn't been casual or meaningless.

"Mr. Carmichael?" A door to Nick's left swung open, and a petite woman in green surgical scrubs came through it. Her dark hair was streaked with gray and pulled away from her face in a neat twist. "I'm Dr. Anne Sullivan."

Sean stumbled to his feet, and Mia and Nick followed. "My wife, how is she?"

"Mrs. Carmichael came through the surgery well, but she's lost a lot of blood." Dr. Sullivan's expression softened, and the lines around her nose and mouth eased. "You have a little girl."

"A girl. She's okay?" Sean's voice was hoarse.

"Yes. She's about four weeks premature and there may be some issues there, but so far so good." Dr. Sullivan pulled several sheets of paper from a clipboard tucked under her arm. "We have to airlift the baby to the Dartmouth-Hitchcock Medical Center because she requires special care. I need you to read and sign some forms. We don't have a neonatal intensive care unit here, so we refer cases like your daughter's to Dartmouth-Hitchcock."

"In New Hampshire? But Charlie, my sister, she's here." Mia's hands were clammy.

"Your sister can't be moved at the moment, so I suggest Mr. Carmichael goes with the baby." Dr. Sullivan held out the papers and a pen to him. "It will be a while before your wife comes out of the anesthetic."

"I can't leave Charlie or the baby, either." Sean took a step forward.

Mia gripped the back of a chair. "I'll stay with Charlie. I won't leave her alone for a second."

"Can I see my wife?"

"Of course. Give me a moment." Dr. Sullivan patted Sean's arm, and her dark eyes, framed by bluish-purple shadows, glistened with sympathy. "Try not to worry. Things went as well as they could, all things considered."

After the doctor had disappeared back through the door, Sean sat on the chair again. "A daughter. I've got a daughter."

"And Naomi and Emma have a cousin," Mia said. "They'll be so excited."

"Ty's still the only boy in the family." Nick half-hugged Sean and slapped his back. "Congratulations. What will you call her?"

Sean turned to Mia. "Charlie would have wanted us to tell you together, but in case…" He gulped. "If the baby was a girl, we planned to call her Alexandra Beatrice Mimi. Lexie for short."

Tears pricked at the back of Mia's eyes. "Beatrice for our mom and Mimi…" The tears spilled out.

"Mimi for you," Sean finished, "like Charlie's pet name for you when she was little. We want you and Nick to be godparents."

"I'm honored." Mia bent to kiss Sean's cheek. "While you're in New Hampshire, we'll look after everything here. Don't worry about anything except Lexie and Charlie."

"A godparent?" Nick looked back at Mia, his expression tinged with panic. "I don't know anything about kids. There must be someone in Sean's family who'd be a better choice and—"

"You have a niece, don't you? I'm sure Charlie and Sean won't ask you to change Lexie's diapers." Mia grinned.

Except, instead of teasing back, Nick's expression became so sad Mia caught her breath.

"Of course, I'd be happy to be a godparent to Lexie." The sadness disappeared so fast Mia wondered if she'd imagined it. "Like Mia said, it's an honor. You send us a picture of Lexie as soon as you can, you hear?"

A slow smile broke across Sean's face. "You bet."

Mia dug in her purse and pulled out a small penguin toy, soft and cuddly. "Take this with you. I got it for the baby a few weeks ago. Charlie loved penguins when she was little."

"I never knew that." He got back up and wrapped Mia in a bear hug. "Look after Charlie for me?" His voice was husky.

"Of course I will." Mia blinked back more tears.

From the doorway, Dr. Sullivan gestured to Sean. "We've got the flight arranged and the children's hospital at Dartmouth-Hitchcock is on standby." She turned to Mia. "A nurse will come and get you as soon as we move your sister to the ward."

Mia hugged Sean back before she pushed him toward Dr. Sullivan. Her heart clenched as his blond head disappeared through the door. This was all wrong. Charlie and Sean should welcome their baby together. Instead, by the time Charlie woke up, Lexie would be gone without even a cuddle from her mommy. A whimper escaped, then a sob.

"Hey." Nick moved closer to her. "Charlie and little Lexie will be fine."

"You don't know for sure." Mia dug in her purse for tissues and yanked a handful out of the package.

"No, but I can't let myself think they won't be, either."

"Charlie should have the baby with her." After Naomi was born, the nurse had tucked the baby against Mia's chest, skin to skin and heart to heart, a miracle that had changed Mia's life forever. "Lexie will be miles away and Charlie can't even go to her."

"Lexie will get the care she needs to come home healthy and grow up healthy." Nick took off Mia's glasses and patted her eyes with a tissue.

"My mom...she should be here. Charlie needs her."

And Mia needed her mom. The ever-present grief she

carried deep in her heart overflowed, and she buried her face in Nick's worn Yale sweatshirt. It was soft and she inhaled his scent, lemon laundry soap and fresh air.

"Your mom was taken way too soon." He held her close, and the steady thump of his heart slowed Mia's jerky breathing. "But your mom's a part of you and Charlie, Naomi, and Emma, and little Lexie, too."

"Right before she passed, Mom said..." Mia shredded a tissue between her fingers. "She said she'd always watch over us."

"There you go." Nick still held her tight. "Your mom was a special lady, and you're a lot like her."

Mia tilted her head to look at him. Without her glasses, he was blurry and unfocused. "You mean I made the same mistake she did? I married someone who cheated on me and lied about it."

"No, you're like her in other ways, more important ways." Nick stroked her hair, his touch gentle. "You care about people and you help them, like I remember she did. I've seen you with my mom and Kylie."

"Anybody would have—"

"No, anybody wouldn't." Nick traced the outline of her lips. "What about all those cookies and casseroles you made for Mom long before I hired you to help her? What about how you helped Kylie at the fashion show and how you're as good as coaching her so she'll learn to swim? And it was you who planted those flowers on the bare patch outside the seniors' home, wasn't it?"

"Older folks like flowers. If I lived there, I'd want to look at something pretty." Mia's face heated. "As for your mom, she's a sweetheart. With your sisters so far away, of course I'd help her."

"Kylie's not a sweetheart." Nick's voice held a hint of laughter.

"She would be if she had the mothering she deserves, and if she'd had a chance to be a normal child in a real family instead of shunted between foster homes for most of her life."

"See, that's what I mean. People around here still talk about your mom and how if anybody needed help, Beatrice Gibbs was the first one to step up. Unlike the other summer people, she was a real part of Firefly Lake."

"Her mom's family came from here, don't forget."

"She could still have turned her back on this place, but she never did." Nick's voice was a comforting rumble. "She donated money to local charities anonymously until the day she died. I know because McGuire and Pelletier handles the legal side for most of them, and we see the books from the accountant."

His finger lingered at the corner of her mouth before he traced the outline of her jaw, under her ear, and along her neck. "Your smile is her smile. Who you are and the way you treat people, always know your mom is still a part of you."

Mia shuddered when his finger connected with the sensitive spot on her neck she'd forgotten existed. "Nick?" she whispered. "What—"

He dipped his head to kiss the spot and brought her even closer against his hard body.

She closed her eyes and leaned into him.

It wouldn't hurt to lean on him for a few minutes. Having glimpsed death tonight, she needed to seize the warmth and life Nick offered. His mouth grazed her neck again, and then he captured her lips in a gentle kiss.

A kiss that pushed her right over the edge she'd teetered on for weeks. It wasn't a kiss fueled by lust, but rather a caress so intimate, tender, and sweet that it undid her. It whittled away her defenses and made her think about what it would be like to trust a man again. And to hope and believe in a future.

Chapter Eight

Nick shifted the bag with a carrot muffin from the Daily Bread into the hand that also held his laptop case and ducked under the awning in front of McGuire and Pelletier. As he reached the door, a woman who'd been friends with Georgia pushed it open from the inside.

She gave him a big smile as he held the door open for her to maneuver a stroller and its blue-clad occupant through the narrow entryway. "You're sure a dark horse."

"Me? Why?"

"You and Mia, of course. I've already emailed Georgia to make sure she checks Facebook." Her voice was amused.

"Why should my sister check Facebook? And what about me and Mia?"

"You were never one to kiss and tell, were you?" She giggled, gave him a little wave and continued along Main Street.

Nick's heart thudded. How could that kiss he shared

with Mia at the hospital have ended up on Facebook? He'd stopped, but only because anybody could have walked in. Mia had given a nervous laugh, then taken her glasses from him and mumbled something about fixing her hair before the nurse came to take her to Charlie.

He'd sat in the waiting room long after she left, aching with wanting her, his heart hurting most of all.

"You head right on over." The voice came from behind the reception desk. It was Lori's voice, but he couldn't spot McGuire and Pelletier's fifty-something receptionist.

A dog barked, and Sean and Charlie's black lab darted out from behind the desk with a pink ribbon tied to her collar.

"How did you get here, Shadow?" He bent to pat her. "I left you in my apartment. You had the radio, snacks, water, and toys. What else did you need?"

"I brought her downstairs." Lori disconnected her call and stuck her caramel-blond head out from behind an arrangement of pink and white flowers stuffed into a basket with a pink teddy bear wrapped in cellophane. "I didn't want Shadow to miss any of the fun."

"Fun?" Nick handed Lori the muffin bag and scanned the reception area. A gaggle of gray-haired women sat knitting in the chairs where clients usually waited. Coffee mugs and several open cookie tins were on the low table where business and golf magazines were ordinarily stacked.

His second grade teacher, Miss Crandall, waved a knitting needle at him and beamed.

He'd been at the courthouse in Kincaid for a couple of hours on a Monday morning, but his ordered world had flipped upside down. Again.

"What's up?" He turned back to Lori.

Lori pointed to the picture of Lexie propped against the basket of flowers. The photo Sean had emailed where all you could see of the poor kid was a tuft of dark hair and wires and tubes stuck out everywhere. "You know Ty set up that Facebook group for Lexie?"

"Yes?" Even though he hadn't seen Lexie yet, Ty was already head-over-heels in love with his baby sister.

"Since a lot of the older ladies aren't on Facebook, they need somewhere to get up-to-the-minute news about that precious baby." Lori pushed a box of disposable diapers aside. "Everyone also wants to bring presents, and you can't do that on Facebook. Since you're Lexie's godfather, it makes sense to have everyone come here like a central mission control. I put a notice in the post office earlier."

"You what?" Surprise made the words sharper than he'd intended.

"Right on the door as you go in. I did the same at the bank, the North Woods Diner, and most of the stores." Lori gave his hand a soothing pat. "Even the New Vermonters and the summer people are involved. Everyone loves Charlie and Sean, so they love Lexie. You did a good thing to get Mia to the hospital so fast in the middle of the night. It must have been real scary, like one of those TV dramas, and you were part of it. A real hero."

No, he wasn't a hero. He'd done what he had to for his friends. The knitters advanced on him like a gray-haired battalion led by Miss Crandall.

"Ladies."

Miss Crandall enveloped him in a perfumed hug. "Thank you for letting us gather here. At a time like this, the community has to rally together. Do Sean and Charlie need help with the medical expenses?"

"Sean said they're lucky. Their insurance should cover almost everything, even the air ambulance because the doctor certified Lexie had to go to Dartmouth-Hitchcock. But thanks. I'll let you know if anything changes." And if there were any issues with the insurance coverage, Nick would chip in and be the first to organize a fund-raiser.

"We're filling the big freezer at the town hall with as many meals and desserts as we can so they don't have to cook when they bring their beautiful little girl home." Miss Crandall patted Nick's arm. "We also popped a few things into the fridge here for you and your dear mother. You always look like you need a home-cooked meal, and Gabrielle's not strong yet."

"Thank you." Nick's throat got tight. He'd missed this sense of community in New York. The caring and connections that went back years, if not generations.

"It was wonderful to see Cat in the fashion show. She looked like a fairy princess in your grandma's wedding dress," Miss Crandall added. "We don't see enough of Cat or that daughter of hers, either. How old is Amy? Ten?"

"Eleven. She'll be twelve in December." Nick didn't see enough of Cat and Amy either. Like he had, his smarty-pants younger sister, Dr. Catherine McGuire, had cut her ties with Firefly Lake and made a life somewhere else as soon as she could.

"Cat called me and she'll be here again next weekend. She wants to surprise your mom." A smile tugged at one corner of Lori's mouth. "She saw that picture of you and Mia on Facebook. She didn't realize you'd been in the middle of all the action."

Nick fingered his phone. He needed to escape from these kind, well-meaning women and get to the privacy of his office to check Facebook. "Look, I—"

"Cat didn't know you still had the hots for Mia." Lori stacked files in color-coded piles.

Nick gritted his teeth. "Can I have my messages, please?"

"Here you go." Lori handed over a stack of green slips. In any other office, messages were emailed, but Lori had used the same system for twenty-five years and wasn't about to change. "Georgia called, too. She got the news about Lexie all the way over in India at her retreat place."

"Georgia says phones are bad karma." Once, he and his baby sister had been close, but when she turned eighteen she'd left town to travel the world and, apart from Christmas and birthdays, they were rarely in touch.

"Don't be silly. She was teasing." Lori gave him the patient smile she'd used when she babysat Nick and his sisters when his mom had parent meetings or other evening events at the high school. "Georgia wanted to talk to you, but since you were in court, I filled her in on the latest. She sent me some yoga exercises for you and told me to tell you to pay more attention to your posture and breathing."

"My posture and my breathing are fine." At least they would be if he could check Facebook. Nick gripped the edge of the reception counter, where a woolly sheep on wheels and several packages wrapped in pink foil paper had replaced his great-grandfather's picture.

"Cat and Georgia were sure mad at me for not telling them about you and Mia." Lori handed him the Johnson-Peters file before he asked for it. "I told them you hadn't said anything to me, either."

"There's nothing to tell."

He glanced at the women, who'd abandoned any pretense of knitting.

"It didn't look that way," Miss Crandall said. "Lori showed us Facebook, and the two of you are real sweet. Like you'd see on a cover of a romance novel. The tasteful ones, where they leave something to the imagination. The way you had a hold of Mia's glasses was so tender it made me tear right up."

"You have to be careful of people with phones these days." Lori shook her head. "Before you know it, you're the local celebrity. Even though whoever took the picture didn't name names, it's you all right. As for Mia, well with her looks, she'll never be invisible."

He'd sue. He was an attorney and a good one. This was a total invasion of privacy. Mia's, as well as his.

Mia. Nick dragged air into his constricted lungs. He doubted she'd seen the picture or anyone had told her about it since she was at Charlie's bedside. Maybe it would be better if he told her first and prepared her.

"You need to think about having a baby. You're not getting any younger." Lori winked.

Nick's stomach rolled. Lori couldn't know how her words were like a knife to his heart. Not only did she run the office like clockwork, but she'd always been like a big sister, and she'd never do or say anything to hurt him.

"Hold my calls for the next hour, please." He bit back angry words and gestured to the file. "I have a lot of work to get through here." Starting with Facebook.

Lori's gaze shifted to a point somewhere to the left of Nick's ear. "There's a client in your office." She inclined her head to the ladies still clustered around him. "I couldn't have her wait out here."

The bell above the door jangled and more women came in, younger ones with strollers and baby slings. And babies, lots of babies. His office had become the venue for an impromptu mom and baby group. The headache Nick had battled all morning slammed into him full force.

"Who's the client?" He didn't have a meeting in his calendar. Someone must have called while he was out. Since Allison was on vacation for a few days, he had to hold the fort.

Lori checked a note on her desk, and he'd have sworn she tried to hide a smile. "A Miss Kalinowski."

"Kalinowski?" Nick leaned over the desk to check the name. It wasn't local.

"She's a new..." Lori hesitated, "client." She grabbed the phone as it rang.

Clients were good. Clients meant money to keep the firm on its feet so he could hire someone else and go back to New York after Labor Day. While he'd miss Firefly Lake's caring, he also craved big-city anonymity. He'd be done with this Miss Kalinowski in an hour, tops. Then he'd check Facebook and head to the hospital to talk to Mia.

Nick pushed open his office door. This Lexie mission control center was temporary. His life would soon be back to the way it was. He and Mia would laugh about that Facebook picture because they were friends. At least he hoped they were still friends.

He scanned the room. No baby stuff in here. Only a stack of files in the in-tray and the whir of the air-conditioning. Afternoon sunlight filtered through the slatted wooden blinds.

Except, his chair had gotten turned the wrong way round so it faced the window.

As Nick moved toward the desk, the chair spun around.

"Hey." Kylie grinned at him from the depths of the black leather seat. Her hair was still pink streaked, and she wore a red Camp Rainbow T-shirt above a pair of dirty white shorts.

"Miss Kalinowski, huh?" Nick set his laptop bag on the floor and sat in the client chair across the desk from her. "How did you get here?"

"Easy." Kylie blew a pink bubble with the wad of gum in her mouth then popped it. "Half the Camp Rainbow kids went to some dumb museum to look at fossils and Vermont life crap, and the other half went bowling. Which is also dumb. Both groups think I'm with the other one. I told that woman out there in reception I wanted to surprise you."

Nick hit the intercom on his desk, spoke to Lori, and then turned back to Kylie. "You're busted, kiddo, so, in the twenty minutes or so until someone from Camp Rainbow gets here, what can I do for you?"

Kylie blew another bubble before she took the gum out of her mouth and rolled it between her fingers.

Nick grabbed a tissue from the box on his desk, and Kylie stuck the gum in it, her green eyes wary.

"You're smart, right? You went to lawyer school?"

"Yale Law School."

"Whatever." Kylie spun around in the chair again.

Nick shrugged out of his suit jacket and waited.

"See, I gave the Camp Rainbow staff the slip because I thought you were the only one who could help me."

"Help you how?"

Kylie Kalinowski was a tough girl with a smart mouth and a super-size chip on her shoulder. But something about her tugged at Nick and reminded him of when he'd been a tough kid with a smart mouth and a chip on *his* shoulder. Behind the attitude, he'd been a scared kid who was lonely and angry at the world, and wanted something he'd lost forever.

"It's my mom." Kylie took a pen out of the holder on his desk and clicked the top. "She's in jail, right? But I still see her almost every Saturday afternoon." She dug in the pocket of her shorts and pulled out a mini photo album, her expression at once fierce and so vulnerable Nick's heart skipped a beat.

The album fell open at a picture of a blond woman, hardly more than a child herself, with a toddler on her lap. An older dark-haired boy stood beside them. "You and your mom?"

"And Dylan, my brother, remember?" Kylie flipped the pen across the desk, and Nick caught it. "Mom was sixteen when she had Dylan. She's pretty, isn't she?"

"Yes, she is." Nick studied the picture.

Although the woman was pretty, her smile was tight and there was a desperate look in the same green eyes that looked out of Kylie's face and spoke of a life lived close to the edge. "You can see how much your mom loves you." The girl had one arm wrapped about Kylie and the other around Dylan, like a mother bear defending her cubs.

"She didn't love us enough." Kylie picked at a mosquito bite, a red and swollen blotch on her forearm. "Not like Mia loves Naomi and Emma."

Nick tented his hands on the desk. Do not get involved. Except, like it or not, Kylie was here, so he was already involved and, as much as he wanted to, he couldn't distance himself. "What do you want from me?"

"My foster family's moving to Chicago. They can't look after me anymore. It's no big deal. Families move all the time or they have another kid." She shrugged, but Nick caught the hurt in her eyes. "I'm the disposable kid."

"You're not disposable." Nick swallowed the unexpected lump in his throat. How could a girl of twelve see herself as disposable?

"Whatever." Kylie shredded a tissue between her thumb and forefinger. "I heard my social worker on the phone when she didn't know I was listening. She said Mom might be moved somewhere else. A new 'facility,' she called it, which is a fancy word for jail. She said it'd be too far away for a new family to take me to see Mom."

"Kylie." Nick took a deep breath. Why were kids like Lexie wanted and, before they were even a week old, cherished by the whole town as one of their own? While kids like Kylie lived on the margins, invisible. "I can see it's a problem, but how do you think I can help?"

"I don't know." Dwarfed by the chair, Kylie looked even smaller than usual. "I didn't know who else to ask." She stood. "I'll go. I'm sorry I bothered you."

"No, wait." Nick caught her arm as she came around the desk. Like the rest of her, the arm was small and skinny. "I could call your social worker and your mom's attorney to find out more. She has an attorney, doesn't she?"

"Yeah." Kylie dug in her pocket again and pulled out a tattered slip of paper torn from a notebook. "Here, I wrote down their names and telephone numbers for you. Mom's attorney is the first one, and my social worker's Kim." She eyed him. "You're not bullshitting me, are you? To get rid of me?"

"Of course not." Guilt pricked Nick. Although the last thing he needed was to get involved in somebody's family, a troubled family moreover, it was only a few phone calls. "I can't make any promises, but I'll try to find out more for you."

"I've got thirty dollars saved from doing extra chores so I can pay you." She pulled a red plastic purse from her shorts. "It's real money, not fake."

"You keep your money." Nick pressed the purse back into Kylie's hand. Her fingers were long and slender like Mia's, but unlike Mia's, her nails were bitten to the quick. "I'll do any work *pro bono*."

"Pro what?" She put the purse and photo album back in her pocket.

"It means for free, like a volunteer or a public service."

"I won't take no handouts." Kylie didn't smile back. "Mia says girls have to pay their way and not depend on men to look after them."

"Mia's right. Usually you would pay your way." He stood and tried to choose the words to make her understand. "But in this case, I want to help you."

"Why?" Kylie's sharp gaze drilled into him. "My mom says guys always want something. Like when you kissed Mia. You wanted sex from her."

Nick bit back a groan. "When I...Mia...no..."

Kylie was a street-smart kid, and whatever he said was bound to make things worse.

"I saw you two on Facebook." Her grin popped out.

"All the girls at Camp Rainbow think you must be an ace kisser, the way Mia was into you."

"Kylie..." For the first time, Nick wondered if maybe it was good he couldn't have children. He had no idea how to handle them, almost-teenage girls especially. Without a dad to show him the way, he wasn't cut out to be a father. "I want to help you because back when I became a lawyer, I did so because I wanted to help people."

Until recently he'd forgotten about that. He'd been focused on making money to reestablish McGuire and Pelletier so he could get out of Firefly Lake.

"Oh." Kylie studied him for a few minutes. "Thank you." Her grin widened. "Some of the girls printed out that Facebook picture and stuck it in the dining hall on the 'specials of the day' board. You're old, but they think you're hot."

Nick shoved the chair back. Maybe it was time to check off that trip to Argentina from his bucket list. Or he could go to New York for the weekend. Far away from people who'd seen a picture of him on Facebook and had nothing else to talk about.

"I don't think you're hot." Kylie's grin faltered. "Well, you are, I guess, but I think you're nice. That's better than being hot. If I'd ever had a dad, I'd have wanted him to be like you." She reached up and gave him a bony hug. "You got anything to eat in here? I'm starving 'cause I missed lunch."

"There are Snickers bars in my desk." Still reeling from Kylie's hug and the feel of her scrawny arms wrapped around him, the simple trust and affection in the innocent gesture, Nick forced himself to move forward and open the bottom drawer. "You want one?"

"Like yeah." Kylie caught the bar when he tossed it to her. "Snickers are my favorite."

"Mine too." Nick sat in his chair and locked his knees together to stop them from shaking.

"See you." Kylie spoke around a mouthful of chocolate. "I'll wait with those old ladies out there so you can get started on my mom's case right away. I can play with Shadow. Lexie's sure getting a lot of shit, isn't she?"

"Gifts." Nick choked back a laugh.

"Sorry." Kylie stuffed the last of the Snickers bar into her mouth. "I never swear around Mia because she's like so proper and perfect, but I forget with you because you're a guy." She chewed and swallowed. "Maybe she's not so perfect if she's having sex with you."

Why was a twelve-year-old girl talking to him about sex? "She's not, we're not—"

"Check Facebook. You've got it bad, Nick. Real bad." With another grin, Kylie closed the office door behind her.

Nick swiped the Facebook icon on his phone. Ever since Isobel, he'd kept his life uncomplicated. No ties and no commitments. No diamond rings and no kids, his or some other guy's. The couple of women he'd dated understood it was casual and wanted a good time, and kids weren't yet on their agenda.

Except Mia was a woman he couldn't stop thinking about. She wasn't casual, her kids were central to who she was, and her kisses had spun his world off its accustomed axis.

And somehow the two of them had ended up on Facebook and become the talk of Firefly Lake. He navigated to the picture. It was him all right. There was no mistaking Mia either, or the way they were wrapped around each other.

Her lips had opened under his. They'd been soft, warm, and sweet. Her body had curved into his like the missing piece of a puzzle, and he hadn't wanted to let her go.

Except, now their private moment was out there for everyone else to see. That was something he could fix. He scrolled to his contact list.

Laughter erupted outside his office, followed by Shadow's deep bark and Pixie's higher-pitched yelp. Which meant his mom was there to coo over Lexie and talk about the evils of retirement bungalows to anybody who'd listen.

Nick shoved his phone in his pocket and grabbed the last Snickers bar from the drawer.

Pixie yelped again before being drowned out by the insistent beat of a Katy Perry song. Sure, the first week in August was always slow. They didn't have any client appointments this afternoon, either. But McGuire and Pelletier was a law office. His law office.

Maybe Kylie was right. He might have it bad. So he had to get this situation under control fast.

Mia wouldn't think about Nick. The next time she saw him she'd be friendly like always. Maybe they'd even laugh about the kiss. Or not. She blinked as the television screen on the wall at the end of Charlie's hospital bed went blank.

"When did the news get so depressing?" Charlie dropped the remote and pulled at the sheet. "Wars, pollution, death, and destruction. What kind of world have I brought Lexie into?"

Although Charlie was still pale, she'd lost the waxy gray color that had scared Mia so much when she'd first seen her after Lexie's birth.

"The news has always been depressing. You're a journalist, so you cover it, don't you? But when you become a mom, it changes you. All of a sudden, there's danger everywhere."

Charlie plucked at the sheet again. "I don't feel much like a mom. I haven't even seen Lexie yet."

Mia poured a glass of water from the pitcher on the bedside table and held it out. "The doctor said if you keep on progressing the way you are, you should be able to go to New Hampshire by the weekend."

Charlie waved the water away. "If that's the case, why won't people give me facts? My boobs hurt. I'm supposed to be pumping milk for a baby who can't nurse. Not that that matters because I'm not even there to nurse her. And my stomach hurts so much that getting out of bed takes at least five minutes." Her voice wavered and a tear spilled down her cheek. "And although I can't imagine I'll ever want to have sex again, I miss Sean. Texts and phone calls aren't the same as having him here. I need him to hold me."

"Of course you miss him." Mia reached over to give her sister a gentle hug. "As for sex, give it time. Sean will wait and when you're ready, I'll go with you to buy sexy lingerie and watch Lexie to give you some couple time."

Charlie gave Mia a half smile through her tears. "Like I'll ever look sexy again. My hair's a mess, my stomach's as flabby as a deflated balloon, my body's leaking all sorts of weird fluid, and I haven't had the courage to look at my C-section scar yet."

"You just gave birth, honey, and sexy comes in all shapes and sizes. You look beautiful."

"Says the woman who was back to her immaculate stick-figure self within minutes of popping out her babies." Charlie's smile broadened. "I'm sorry. You're so sweet. You've hardly slept in two days and all I can do is complain."

Mia laughed. "It's the hormones."

"I am *not* hormonal." Charlie stuck her tongue out like she'd done as a kid.

Mia shifted in the straight-back chair, and the vinyl seat stuck to the backs of her legs beneath the skirt Gabrielle had brought her to change into. "Let's look at the pictures of Lexie again. I asked the nurse if she could print them out so we can pin copies to your bulletin board. I think Lexie looks like Mom." Mia tapped at her phone.

"You'd think any baby of mine or yours looked like Mom." Charlie's expression softened and she gave an engaging little chuckle. "Whoever she looks like, Lexie's a miracle. You said that about Naomi and Emma, but I'm only their aunt. I didn't know."

"How could you?" Mia patted Charlie's hand. "You want me to help you take a walk?"

"The nurse already did while you went to find a vase for my flowers." Charlie gestured to the bouquet of pink roses her colleagues at the AP in Boston had sent. "What I want is for you to tell me what's going on between you and Nick."

"Nothing." Mia folded Charlie's discarded newspaper into neat creases.

"I guess you didn't check Lexie's Facebook group.

There's a picture of you and Nick kissing." Charlie poked Mia's arm then winced.

"What? I've been here with you, so I haven't checked Facebook in a while. When did you see it?"

"When you went to the bathroom. Oh, no you don't." Charlie knocked the phone out of Mia's hand. "Not until you tell me why you kissed Nick if there's nothing going on."

"Okay, I kissed him. Or he kissed me, I can't remember." Mia's face heated. "We were upset. Lexie was being flown to Dartmouth-Hitchcock and you were still unconscious. It was a reaction to stress." At least that was how she'd tried to rationalize what had happened.

Mia retrieved her phone, swiped to Facebook, and groaned. Why would somebody take a picture of them? And how had Ty Carmichael gotten hold of it and posted it for everyone to see? Even her daughters. Mia's hand shook. She had to call Naomi right away and explain it was a big mistake.

Liz Carmichael, Sean's aunt by marriage, a widow in her mid-sixties who worked part-time at the North Woods Diner and mothered half the town the other part, came through the doorway. She had bleached blond hair piled on top of her head, and a gold charm bracelet jingled on her wrist.

Nick followed her, dressed like he'd come straight from court and carrying a bag from the Firefly Lake Deli.

"Charlie, you poor thing." Liz kissed Charlie before turning to Mia. "Look who I bumped into in the parking lot? I told Nicky I'd stay with Charlie so you could take a breather. Hospitals are full of germs, so Gabrielle shouldn't be here. With Sean's mom in New Hampshire with Sean and that precious baby, and everybody else in the family working flat-out to fill a big Carmichael's order, you girls need help."

"I'm fine. I want to stay with Charlie." Mia looked at her feet as Charlie shook with suppressed laughter.

"You're a devoted sister, but you need a break." Liz tapped Mia's knees with red-lacquered fingernails. "I brought popcorn, my portable DVD player, and movies. Matt Damon and Colin Firth will distract us in no time. Charlie and I will be as happy as clams at high water."

Charlie made a choked sound, and Mia shot her a silencing look.

"We can watch movies together." Then she could slip out and call Ty to get that Facebook picture removed.

And avoid being alone with Nick.

"Hey, Charlie." Nick approached the bed and leaned over to give Charlie a careful hug. "You and Lexie gave everyone a big scare. How are things?"

"I've been better, but the doctor says it's still early days." Charlie hugged him back. "Lexie's great. Sean says she's a real fighter."

"Who does she get that from, I wonder? You fought pretty hard, too." Nick handed Charlie an envelope with the logo of the spa at the Inn on the Lake embossed on one corner. "This is from my mom, my sisters, and me. We figured you'd have enough flowers and maybe you could use a gift certificate once you're home from the hospital. It's for one of those pamper days."

"That's so thoughtful." Charlie grinned at Mia. "Can I count on you to babysit?"

"Of course." Mia's throat clogged. Nick cared about other people in a way Jay never had. It was in the way he'd hugged Charlie and his genuine concern for her and Lexie.

"If there's anything else I can do, I told Sean to say the word. I offered to help out at Carmichael's, but he said he's got it covered. I don't think he trusts me with that fancy equipment."

Charlie's smile was warm. "My husband loves his power tools, but thank you. Everybody has pitched in to help. Even though I've lived here for almost a year, I was surprised. Sean says it's the Northeast Kingdom way, though."

"Of course it is. Real Vermonters stick together in good times and bad." Liz rubbed Mia's back. "You go on with Nicky. You look like a wrung-out dishrag, you do. You'll be the next one to fade away."

"I haven't faded away." Charlie's brown eyes twinkled. "Mia won't either."

"Mia looks pale." Liz dug in her tote bag and popped open a DVD case. "Your blessed mother was always pale, like a puff of wind would have blown her away. Then the cancer carried her off too young, God rest her soul. You're not anemic, are you?"

"No." Mia stood and forced a smile.

Liz meant well and she and her mom had been acquaintances, even friends of a sort. The kind of friendship fostered by a small, isolated town.

"Still, there's no harm in Nicky taking you out to fill your lungs with some good, clean air. An ounce of prevention's worth a pound of cure." Liz plumped Charlie's pillows with brisk efficiency. "Charlie can show me pictures of sweet little Lexie."

"Great idea." Laughter lurked in the depths of Nick's blue eyes.

"Nicky always had a good heart. Even through all those wild times, I told Gabrielle he'd turn out right in the end and he sure has. You two kids run along. We'll be fine." Liz sat on the end of Charlie's bed.

Giving Charlie the "I'm your big sister and I'll get you for this later" look she hadn't used in years, Mia grabbed her purse and went to the door. "I'll be back in half an hour."

"You aren't running off without me, are you?" Nick caught her halfway down the hall.

"Nicky?"

A hint of red colored his cheeks. "Liz served me my first ice cream cone over at the diner when I was about a year old. She started calling me Nicky and the name stuck, but Liz is the only one who gets away with using it nowadays."

Whereas Jay would have made an issue of the nickname, Nick had been considerate of the older woman, respectful even.

Mia dodged an empty wheelchair and headed to the elevator at the end of the hall. "I need to make a phone call."

"Wait." Nick put out his hand to stop her from hitting the elevator button. "I didn't expect to meet Liz out front, but I came here to talk to you."

"Sure. As soon as I make this call."

"Is something wrong with the girls?" Concern shadowed his face. "Or Charlie?"

"Naomi and Emma are fine." At least they would be if they didn't see Facebook. She pushed his hand away and tapped the elevator call button. "The doctor says Charlie's doing really well."

"Would that phone call be to Ty?" The elevator doors slid open, and Nick came in with her. He filled the small space. "If so, I beat you to it."

"You did?" The elevator swooped downward, and Mia's stomach swooped along with it.

"I told Ty if he didn't delete that Facebook picture of us, I'd slap him with an invasion of privacy lawsuit he'd still be paying for when he's thirty."

The doors slid open again and Mia followed Nick into the hospital lobby.

"He's sixteen. You can't sue a sixteen-year-old."

"Ty doesn't know that. I also told him you wouldn't let Naomi so much as walk to the high school cafeteria with him if he didn't remove the picture within forty minutes of my call. I'd have made it five, but he was over on the other side of the lake with a canoe rental and Internet's spotty there."

"Thank you." Her heart felt full. "But what if Naomi and Emma have already seen the picture? I have to call them and try to explain."

Nick guided Mia along a short hallway past a flower shop, where the scent of roses masked the sterile hospital smell. "Ty said Jay took Naomi's tablet and phone away last night. No Facebook, Twitter, or Instagram, no games or YouTube, no e-mail, nothing for twenty-four hours. She can only use the phone when she wants to call or text you, or if you call or text. Jay's got her phone with him."

Which explained why he'd answered when Mia had called the girls earlier. But when she'd probed for the reason why, Naomi had made a joke.

"How does Ty know all that?" Something was wrong, big time. She and Jay only took away Naomi's phone and computer privileges for something serious. Yet, mixed with the worry was relief. Mia might not have to explain to her daughters why she'd kissed Nick, when she couldn't even explain it to herself.

"When everyone else was out by the pool, Naomi snuck the cordless phone into the bathroom to call a friend from her old school. She told the friend Jay cracked down because he doesn't want her in contact with Ty so much. Then the friend called Ty." Nick gave her a lopsided smile. "You might not approve of Naomi's methods, but you have to give her credit for ingenuity and determination."

Mia stepped through the door Nick held open for her. "Naomi shouldn't have gone behind Jay's back, but the more he tries to push Ty and Naomi apart, the more determined she'll be to see him. There's a reason people still relate to *Romeo and Juliet* and...oh."

A patio shadowed by maple trees was tucked into a corner of the old wing of the hospital. A large-flowered, purple clematis climbed a trellis on a red brick wall, and a garden swing sat between two tubs of flowering lavender. In the center, water trickled over a pair of chubby cupids in a stone fountain.

"I had no idea this place was here." Mia sat on the swing and slipped off her sandals.

"I brought food." Nick sat beside her. "If I had to tell you about that Facebook photo, I wanted to make sure you were fed first."

"You didn't take the picture. You didn't post it on Facebook."

"No, but I knew it would upset you and maybe even hurt you." His voice got low and intimate. "I don't want that. I'd never want it. You don't look like a 'wrung-out dishrag.' Liz is wrong about that. But you do look like you could use a breather." Nick handed her the deli bag. "I know what it's like to spend too much time by a hospital bed and eat hospital food."

Mia closed her hands around the top of the bag so they wouldn't shake. Sitting with Charlie had brought back those awful weeks she'd sat with her mom. When she'd known she'd lose her but pretended she wouldn't. How she'd been afraid to leave her side for more than a few minutes. And how she'd wanted her mom to be free of pain but didn't want to let her go.

Then those memories had gotten tangled with the worry over Charlie and Lexie because she couldn't lose them as well. With too much time to think, she'd also worried about Naomi and Emma. She missed them, of course, and, from the moment she'd kissed them goodbye, had counted the days until Jay would bring them back, but now she had a whole new worry beyond if they ate and slept right and brushed and flossed. She worried what her ex-husband might be plotting.

Somehow Nick had sensed how troubled she was, and he'd brought her here, to a place that was part of the hospital but as far removed from it as possible.

It was sweet, wonderful, and caring.

But it also meant she couldn't pretend whatever was between them was superficial and casual or joke about their kiss like she'd planned. For a woman who'd lived her life by plans and schedules, the feelings that churned through her were unplanned, unscheduled, and terrifying.

Chapter Nine

Nick was supposed to get things under control, not shoot the breeze with a beautiful woman on a sunny weekday afternoon. Except, this was Mia, a woman he was at ease with in a way he hadn't been at ease with anyone in a long time, maybe ever.

She dabbed at her mouth with a paper napkin. That luscious mouth with a little dimple at one corner. "Avocado and tomato is my all-time favorite sandwich."

"On seven-grain bread with no mayonnaise and Greek olives on the side." Nick rocked the swing with one foot, and Mia's breasts moved under her yellow T-shirt.

"Whereas you like mayonnaise, the more the better, wouldn't eat an avocado if your life depended on it, and snuck half the olives when you didn't think I was looking." Mia grinned, and he glimpsed the teenage girl he remembered.

The one who was sweet and a bit shy and had a sexy smile and an even sexier walk. The girl whose picture he'd cut out of the *Kincaid Examiner* when she was Queen of the Firefly Lake Fishing Derby then hid in the back of a math book so his nosy little sisters wouldn't find it.

The only girl he'd wanted, but the one who'd always remained elusive and out of reach.

"Your point is?" Nick handed her the plastic olive tub, where a lone olive rolled around the bottom.

Mia popped the olive into her mouth, her eyes fluttered closed, and Nick caught his breath at the pleasure on her face. Her eyes popped open again. "That wasn't the last olive. You hid a few somewhere."

"Busted." He dug in the deli bag and handed her another container. "I got a double order."

She batted his hand away and, at the brief touch, sensual fire ricocheted through him. "Paws off."

"Has Pixie finally turned you into a dog lover?"

"No." Mia gave him an impish grin. "But your mom loves that little dog, and I love your mom. Besides, Pixie keeps me on my toes."

Nick looked at Mia's bare feet. Her toenails were painted a soft coral color, and all he could think about was sweeping her off those toes and into his bed.

"You can get cute clothes for dogs like Pixie." Mia wiggled her toes, and one of her slender feet brushed Nick's ankle.

"You're dressing Mom's dog?" He breathed in the lavender of the flowers mixed with the soft floral scent that was Mia. A scent he could pick out anywhere.

"It was your mom's idea. When I took her shopping last week, we bought Pixie a pink coat for winter, a scarf, a new carrier, and a few T-shirts. She'd like to get

Pixie a dress for Christmas from this store we found online."

"A Christmas dress for a dog?" His mom had lost it and taken Mia along with her.

"You should be happy your mom wants to make plans for Christmas. She hasn't given up." Mia's voice got a catch in it that made his heart turn over. "If dressing Pixie makes her happy, who are we to judge?"

"I..." Nick stopped at the dejected expression on her face. Unlike Mia, he still had his mom. "Do you think Mom would like a gift certificate to get something for Pixie?"

"I think she'd like it more if you spent time with her." Mia dug in the bag and handed him a Snickers bar.

"I do spend time with her. I fix stuff around the house, manage her investment portfolio, and do anything else she wants. I want to help her buy that new bungalow, don't I? It's the top-of-the-line one with European finishes and an attached garage so she wouldn't have to go outside to get her car in the winter."

"You do lots of things *for* her, sure. Maybe even things she doesn't care much about or could do herself, but how much do you do *with* her?" Mia eyed him over a fruit tart, and her brown eyes, edged with those thick dark lashes, were serious.

Nick opened his mouth and closed it again. The woman would have made a good lawyer the way she cut right to the chase to ambush him. "Well...I...not much, I guess."

"In that case, what will you do about it?"

Mia nibbled the fluted edge of the tart, and Nick forced himself to look away. This was about his mother. He had to stop his wayward thoughts about Mia's mouth. How soft it felt on his. How sweet it tasted. How he wanted her to use it to explore every inch of his body.

"Mom has refused to sell Harbor House. If she doesn't sell, I don't know what else to do. That's all we talk about these days."

"Talk?" Mia brushed pastry crumbs off her skirt, and a pair of sparrows hopped over to investigate.

"Okay, argue." Like he was a teenager again, and the two of them were pitted against each other with neither one prepared to compromise.

"Your mom's made a choice. Her choice. You might not like it, but you need to respect it."

Like hell he didn't like it. Before he went back to New York in a few weeks, he had to make sure his mom was safe. Apart from the cancer, which Nick couldn't control, the biggest threat to her safety was that ramshackle old house.

"Maybe you could..." He shut his mouth fast.

"What?"

"Help me out. I hired you to organize Harbor House, but maybe that's not what Mom needs. Except, I don't know what she needs." He dropped his head into his hands, and the sparrows took off in a flurry of wings.

"Gabrielle needs help to clear out more than a hundred years of stuff from that house. She's bogged down by memories and expectations of family members who died long ago, and she's lost sight of which things truly mean something important to her. The problem isn't clearing out the house. It's selling it that has her in pieces. Harbor House means more to her than any of the things in it."

"I—"

Mia raised a hand to silence him. "Your mom doesn't think she can talk to you because when she tries, you don't listen. Your sisters don't, either. The three of you are so afraid of losing her you're treating her like a child. I understand you're doing it out of love, but it's not working for any of you."

"Mom can't manage in Harbor House all winter alone." At least not with Nick back in New York, which had always been the plan. Once his mom was healthy again and settled in a new place, he'd go back to his real life. "What if there's an ice storm and the power goes out? What if she slips and falls on one of those staircases and nobody finds her for days?"

"Firefly Lake is a tight-knit community. Gabrielle's friends call her every day. She could have an accident alone in that bungalow, and an ice storm could cut off her heat and light there the same way as in Harbor House. Maybe Harbor House is too much for her, but your mom doesn't see it that way, so you'll have to figure something out." Mia's gentle smile warmed places in Nick's heart he'd locked away long ago.

"You won't help me out?"

"You're such a guy. I already did." Her smile broadened. "You're part of the problem, so you have to be part of the solution. Start by listening to her, really listening. Pretend she's a client. You listen to your clients, don't you?"

"Of course I do."

The swing creaked, and water gurgled in the fountain as Mia's words seeped in and made Nick think about things he didn't want to think about. Like when his dad had left, and how overnight Nick had become the man of the family. Except, somewhere along the line love had been eclipsed by duty, and his mom had become yet another item on his to-do list.

The truth hit him like the truck had hit the lake all those years ago. Sudden, shocking and life changing.

"Your mom loves you." Mia's soft voice was like a cool glass of water on a hot day. "And you love her, so you'll figure it out."

"You think so?" Although he prided himself on always being in control, around Mia that control slipped to expose the essence of who he was and the man he kept hidden.

"Sure you will." Her smile told him she believed he'd do the right thing.

"When I was in rehab after the accident, I spent a lot of time out here trying to figure out my life." He'd asked questions nobody could answer, wanted reassurances nobody could give, and prayed for another chance to make things right.

"You turned your life around." Mia squeezed his hand like she understood what it had taken for him to change. "Although it can't have been easy driving that road by the lake in an emergency situation, you came through for all of us."

"It wasn't a big deal."

"Yes, it was. You're human, not a robot. Maybe you remembered the accident, but you didn't let me down, or Charlie and Sean, either."

"I almost didn't make my eighteenth birthday. I wouldn't have, except for luck and the skill of the doctor on call that night. I also don't underestimate my mom's stubborn refusal to believe anybody who dared suggest I might not pull through."

Above all, it was his mom's force of will that had

helped Nick see he had to make something of his life because his buddies couldn't.

"Your mom is one determined lady, and that's why she's so set on staying in Harbor House." Mia gave his hand one last squeeze then moved away. "I should get back to Charlie. She needs me and—"

Nick caught her wrist. This was it. He might not get another chance. He had to tell her the truth. His mom's illness had shown him you got one chance at life and couldn't hit rewind.

"Charlie will be fine with Liz for a little while longer. They'll call you if there's a problem. For weeks we've pretended there isn't anything more than friendship between us, but those kisses say something else."

"We're attracted to each other, sure." Mia wriggled out of his grasp and got to her feet. "But it can't go anywhere." She shoved her left foot into the right sandal, realized her mistake, and took the shoe off again.

"Why not?" He'd been blind. It was the same as with his mom. He was part of the problem, so he had to be part of the solution. And the solution was obvious and perfect in its simplicity.

"We're friends, good friends, and that's enough. My entire life I haven't stood on my own two feet. First, my dad told me what to do, and then Jay did. This last year is the first time I've been an independent woman. I like it. I don't want a relationship." Mia's chest with those little breasts he ached to touch rose and fell.

"See, that's what great." Nick forced himself to look in her eyes and not at her chest. "I don't want a relationship either. Wife, kids, and cut the grass on Saturday morning? That whole white picket fence scene isn't for me."

Everything that went with a family. The family he couldn't have with Isobel or anyone else.

"I don't want you to cut my grass. Ty does it because we're family." Mia's mouth quirked into the half smile Nick liked, cute laced with sexy. "My house doesn't have a white picket fence, either."

"It was a figure of speech."

Her smile broadened. "As for the wife thing, I've been there, done that, and got the T-shirt. Ditto the kids." Her smile slipped. "Do you mean we can be friends but with...." Her ears turned red, and she glanced around the empty patio.

"Why not? Thanks to that Facebook picture, the whole town already thinks we're sleeping together, so it's not like we'd give people anything more to talk about." Nick stood and his heart got stuck in his throat. "I'm attracted to you, and you're attracted to me. We like each other, and neither of us would go into anything with false expectations."

"True." She half-turned into him, and her breasts brushed his chest.

His body hardened as he pulled her close. "Feel what you do to me?" He rocked into her then moved away when she gave a breathy little moan.

"I should go." She ran her hand across his chest like she couldn't help herself.

"If you can leave Charlie, will you have dinner with me on Saturday night? We could drive around the lake to Fairlight Cove and see a play at the summer theater there." They'd had dinner together lots of times, but this invitation was different.

Mia nibbled her lower lip, and the ache in Nick's

body ratcheted up another notch. "If the doctor says she can travel, Sean will take Charlie to New Hampshire on Saturday morning to see Lexie." She touched his chest again before she stepped away. "If that happens, dinner and a play sound good."

She picked up the almost-full olive container and, with a little wave, walked back into the hospital building, her hips swaying in the way that had always made him crazy.

Nick sat on the swing again and stared at the fountain. He'd gotten what he wanted. With Mia's help, he'd get things under control with his mom, and he'd proven the memories of the accident no longer held the power over him they once had.

Most of all, he'd get his feelings for Mia out of his system once and for all. Even though she hadn't said so, he'd read the truth in her eyes. She was ready to take things further between them.

So why did he suspect if they started something, no strings attached, it might make him want her even more? And maybe not give him that control he craved after all.

Gabrielle had forgotten what it was like to spend time with a man. To enjoy a man's company and wake in the morning and look forward to seeing him. Even though she had plenty of reasons to not get used to having Ward in her life, she couldn't stop the sense of expectation as if she was a young woman again.

"Take a look." Ward crouched at the edge of her rose garden and handed her his camera.

She focused on the image on the screen. A bumblebee was perched on a pink rose petal to drink the nectar. "It's beautiful. I could paint that." Her fingers twitched, and she could almost feel the watercolor pencil and the sure and steady strokes she'd make across the creamy page.

"I hope you do." Ward got to his feet and grimaced. "Inside, I still feel twenty-five, but then my knees creak and I realize I'm not."

Gabrielle laughed. She'd laughed a lot since Ward had come into her life, honest laughter that came out when she least expected it. "Me too." She let him take her arm to help her to her feet. "I may not be twenty-five, but I'm not eighty-five either, which my son doesn't seem to understand."

"Is Nick still pushing you to sell this house?" Ward led her to the terrace overlooking the lake, and the breeze ruffled the tendrils of gray hair at his temples.

"Not directly. Nick doesn't push the way most people push." Gabrielle leaned against the stone wall. "He still wants me to come around to his way of thinking, though."

"You're not?" Ward shoved up his shirt sleeves to expose tanned forearms.

"No." Gabrielle tried to smile. "Nick thinks he's doing what's best for me. He's right that Harbor House is too big for one person. I don't want to spend another winter by myself in it, but I always thought he or the girls would have a family and want to live here."

She'd been a fool and wished and hoped for something that hadn't happened. Despite her bold assertion she wouldn't sell, unless she found another plan fast, the house that had been in her family for generations would have to pass to strangers. The house she'd clung to when Brian took off and mired her in scandal and debt. The only thing that had been hers, owned jointly with her parents, and that neither Brian nor his creditors could touch.

Ward lifted his camera and snapped a picture of a crow perched on the branch of a pine tree. "What about Cat and her daughter?"

"I don't see Cat ever coming back here. She's smart, and I'm proud of her for what she's achieved, but she's outgrown Firefly Lake. She's looking for a permanent job, but for now she and Amy rent an apartment in Boston near the university where she does contract teaching. As for Georgia, she's a rolling stone and nothing will anchor her. As long as she has a backpack and a yoga mat, she's happy."

Ward's blue eyes twinkled. "Never say never."

"You haven't met Georgia, and you've only met Cat briefly. Both of them come to see me, sure, but they're in and out of here so fast the dust doesn't have time to settle. Even Vermont mud season doesn't make them stick. I long to see more of Amy, too. Cat's always been a single mom, but she's so set on doing everything herself. I've never been able to help her much with Amy, although I'd love to."

Gabrielle bit back a sigh. What kind of mother got most of her information about her daughters from Facebook? Along with being more a part of Amy's life, she yearned for more grandbabies.

"I love my granddaughter." Ward's face softened into the look he always wore when he spoke of his daughter and her little girl. "When my wife passed, it was only Erica and me for a lot of years. Now she's a mother and so happy and settled, I can rest easy. Her husband's in the Navy, and it's been a gift these past two years he's been based near Seattle so I see them all the time." He pulled Gabrielle into the crook of his shoulder. "Are you sure about Nick? He and Mia look close."

"Not that kind of close. Neither of them can see what's

right in front of them. I've come to love Mia like another daughter and she'd be perfect for Nick, but will he see it? No."

Despite her subtle attempts to ease them together, they were friends, nothing more. Maybe not even friends anymore after whatever had happened between them after the fashion show. She'd been so hopeful, especially after Nick charged after Mia that night and set the whole town talking.

"You might be surprised." Ward rested his head on top of hers, as comfortable as if they'd known each other for years. "At the Moose and Squirrel last night, he almost decked one of the guys he plays pool with. The fellow said something about Mia that Nick didn't like and, unless I miss my guess, Nick would have taken it outside if the bartender hadn't stepped in. What about that Facebook photo of the two of them?"

Hope flared in Gabrielle's heart then dimmed. "He wants her, that's what the Facebook picture says. But love her and make a future with her? I doubt it." First Brian and then Isobel had destroyed her son's trust and faith in love.

"You can't live Nick's life for him, Gabby." Ward brushed a strand of cropped hair away from her ear. "You've got your own life." His voice deepened, and Gabrielle's heart skipped a beat.

"Gabby?"

His fingers were still in her hair, the spiky strands she hated but which were better than no hair at all.

"You don't want me to call you Gabby?"

"It's fine." Except, the pet name was one more thing to make her fall for him. Like she'd fallen for Brian when she was young and foolish and he'd been the high school football hero. The boy who'd convinced her he wanted to stay in this little town and grow old with her. Who'd assured her he'd be happy to work in the law office like his father and grandfather before him, alongside her uncle and cousin.

"You've been sick, haven't you?" Ward rested his hand on her shoulder, and his gentle touch was warm through the gauzy fabric of her top.

She twisted away because his touch, like his words, was too intimate. "How did you find out?" She hadn't planned to tell him, but she couldn't deny it either. He'd be gone from her life in a few weeks, and if she didn't have to tell him, she could pretend she was still the woman she'd been before her diagnosis.

"One of the waitresses at the Moose and Squirrel asked Nick how you were doing, and I put two and two together." He pulled her close again and massaged her shoulders. Like magic, his fingers found and eased the knots in her tense muscles. "Besides, you'd be at the hospital with Mia and Charlie day and night if you could."

Gabrielle blinked away the sudden moisture behind her eyes. "I'm fine."

If she told herself often enough, it would be true. The cancer had been caught early. She was done with chemo and radiation, and her last checkup had been clear, nothing to worry about, the doctor said. At least for another three months when she had to go back, be tested again, and worry all over again.

"Of course you're fine." Ward's voice was warm. "None of us knows how much time we've got, so you won't waste it, will you?" He dipped his head toward her ear and she breathed in the scent of sunshine, earth from the garden and good health.

"I can't." She avoided his mouth.

"Why not?" He touched a finger to her lips.

"You live in Seattle for a start." She waved a hand toward the lake. "It's thousands of miles from here."

"I live there because I don't have a reason to live anywhere else. It's close to Erica right now, but her husband could be posted anywhere on his next assignment. Since I travel to Asia for work, Seattle's convenient for flights, but I'm not rooted there, not like you are here."

Rooted. More tears pricked and threatened to spill over. Nick and the girls had broken free of those roots without a backward glance, but this little slice of Vermont with its lake, green hills, moose crossings, and salt-of-the earth folks wasn't just a place, it was *her* place. Where she'd been born, where she'd spent her life, and where she wanted to die, preferably with several generations of her family around her.

"Gabby?" Ward cupped her chin. "What is it? What's wrong?"

She sniffed and rubbed a hand across her eyes. "I'm a foolish old woman like Nick wants to turn me into." She sniffed again, and Ward pulled her into the curve of his chest.

"You're not foolish, and if you're an old woman, then I'm an old man." His laugh rumbled and, beneath the blue cotton of his shirt, his heart thumped in a steady rhythm. "Life isn't over until it's over. Meeting you has been a gift."

Gabrielle tilted her head to his. "For me too," she murmured, "but I can't…"

His mouth caught hers in a gentle kiss. "Then I'll wait until you can," he said against her lips.

He kissed her again, not so gentle, and Gabrielle's knees buckled as her toes curled. No expectations, she reminded herself, even as she kissed him back. No promises, either.

"Okay?" Ward's blue eyes searched hers.

Before he dipped his head for another earth-shattering kiss, she whispered, so soft she wasn't sure he'd hear. "Okay."

Chapter Ten

When Mia was in high school and college, Saturday night was date night, but she hadn't been on a real date with someone new in almost eighteen years. She was so out of practice she wasn't sure if this was a date, either.

Fairlight Cove's summer playhouse had once been a barn, and the conversion was so new the place still had a scent of sawdust and fresh paint. It also had a whiff of Firefly Lake from the reedy cove at the bottom of the sloping field out back.

She shifted on the wooden bench and stole a glance at Nick to her right. His dark hair blended into the darkness of the theater, and his muscled forearms rested on his lap. He wore faded jeans and a white shirt, and his long legs were stretched out in front of him. She was a single woman, and single, independent women went on dates all the time. Those women also had sex with men they liked. Men they wanted, and who wanted them.

The audience laughed, and Mia tried to focus on the

stage to still her panic. She hadn't had sex with anyone except her ex-husband. Scene after scene went past her in a blur, and when everyone around her clapped, Mia made herself clap, too. The sound echoed in the high rafters and in her head.

"Did you enjoy the play?" Nick leaned over to speak into her ear.

She jumped and then blinked as the overhead lights went on. "It was nice."

"Nice?" He raised one dark eyebrow and grinned. "It was a murder mystery where the villain killed his so-called friends with poisoned martini olives. *Nice* isn't the first word that comes to my mind."

"I meant it had a good plot. I didn't guess who did it until the end." Probably because she hadn't paid attention.

"I knew it was the town clerk all along."

"The town clerk? I thought it was the caterer."

"When he isn't on the boards, the actor who played the caterer is the town clerk over in Kincaid." Nick chuckled. "He's always cast as the villain in local theater productions. Cat says it's because he has evil eyes. He grew up in Firefly Lake, and every Halloween when we were kids, he dressed as a monster and scared her half to death."

"I'm a city girl, remember?" Easy banter, keep it light and pretend everything was like it had always been between them. "I'm still not used to the kind of community here and how everyone seems to be connected to everyone else."

"There's a lot that goes along with that community." Nick got to his feet and shepherded Mia through the crowd to the exit. His big frame sheltered her and made her feel safe and protected. "People know your business and think they have a right to talk about you because their grandmother's second cousin was related to your great-aunt by marriage three times removed. They post pictures of you on Facebook."

Mia's face heated. A copy of that Facebook picture had appeared on Gabrielle's kitchen table. She should have gotten rid of it but instead, Mia had taken it upstairs and tucked it into the bottom of her suitcase. Then ignored Gabrielle's pointed looks.

"Do you want to get ice cream? Simard's Creamery has a stand across the street from where we had dinner." The intimate bistro with tables for two, where the muted candlelight had softened the planes of Nick's face, and they'd bumped knees under the small table to send jolts of awareness through her.

"You like your tiger tail ice cream, don't you?" Although Nick's voice held a teasing note, something hot and elemental sparked in his eyes. Then his expression changed again, and he was the Nick who'd helped her with her mom's foundation on all those late-night phone calls last winter. The friend she called when she wanted to talk about anything and everything.

Mia stopped in the middle of the rutted track in the field where they'd left the car. The long grass tickled her bare legs below her sundress, and she shivered in the cool night air. They'd go for ice cream and then Nick would take her home. They'd drive the familiar highway back to Firefly Lake and talk about the play and how well Charlie and Lexie were doing. Safe, easy topics.

He'd drop her off at Harbor House, and she'd go upstairs and get into Georgia's single bed beneath the tattered travel posters. Alone. Like all those other nights she'd spent alone, denying what she wanted and making excuses.

"I changed my mind. I don't want ice cream." Her voice shook.

"Mia, I—" He made a choked sound.

"I thought about what you said." If she didn't go for this, she'd always regret it and wonder about what might have been. And maybe a fling with Nick was exactly what she needed to put the last ghosts of her marriage behind her. "You're right. We're both single and neither of us wants something the other one can't give."

"Are you sure?"

She tried to laugh. "We'd have to be discreet."

"Of course." The raw desire on his face was replaced by a glimpse of what might have been vulnerability.

"I like you, and I know you won't hurt me." Because she'd locked the part of her that could be hurt deep inside. "We both have needs." She kicked the grass with her sandals and rubbed her bottom lip.

"I like you, too. What Jay did was wrong, and I want to make sure you understand I'd never do anything like that." A pulse fluttered in Nick's throat. "We might not have a relationship, but I wouldn't sleep with anybody else if I slept with you."

Mia looked at the night sky, where stars twinkled above the forested hills. When she was little, she'd wished on stars and believed in a happy-ever-after. But she was an adult, and life had made her wiser and destroyed her childish belief in magic and wishes. "Where do we go from here?"

"I'll take you back to Mom's if you want me to."

Nick's arm brushed the curve of her shoulder through her light sweater, and the tremble inside her kicked up. "If you're not ready."

She was ready all right and had been even before he kissed her the first time. "I want this." She lifted her face to his as a cloud scudded across the moon. "I want you."

Even if it could only be for tonight, she was Mia, not a mom, not a sister, and not a wife who'd been tossed aside for someone younger and curvier. For this one moment, she didn't have any responsibilities except what she wanted and needed.

"I want you, too." He took her hand and led her toward the car. "A part of me has wanted you since I was fifteen and you hung out at the town beach in that green bikini with the white flowers."

Her heart lurched. He'd noticed her enough to remember the bikini she'd hidden from her mom. The one she'd bought because she'd heard Nick say he liked green. "You were always with the guys by the lifeguard station."

His fit body was encased in a pair of board shorts, and his eyes were hidden behind mirrored sunglasses. Everything about him was a lot sexy and a little bit dangerous.

"I wanted to see you." His smile was forced, like the admission cost him more than he wanted her to know.

Mia curved her cold hand into his warm one. She'd guessed she'd hurt him the one time they'd gone out, but until tonight she hadn't understood how much. She couldn't regret the past, and she couldn't predict the future, but she could do something about the present. "I want to be with you. Even though we're not teenagers anymore and I don't have that green bikini."

Nick's gaze skimmed her body from head to toe and lingered at her breasts. Then he gave her a grin that was pure bad boy. "I was always a lot more interested in what was underneath that bikini anyway."

He opened the passenger door for her to slide in.

She looked at him from under her lashes and flirted like she'd wanted to do all those years ago but had been too shy. "You were, were you?"

"Oh yeah." He shut the car door and, in the sudden silence, panic rolled over her again. Except, there was excitement too. She was going do what she'd hardly let herself think about, but she wouldn't let herself fall for him or care about him as anything other than a friend.

Want wasn't love. Love needed commitment. And without love and commitment, there couldn't be a forever.

Nick stood on the log cabin's front porch with Mia's hand tucked in his. The leaves in the big trees near the house rustled in the wind, and night birds called to each other. Out back, beyond the old maple sugar shack, a creek gurgled, and the bass note of a bullfrog reverberated like a bow across the strings of a fiddle.

"Who owns this place?" The innocence in Mia's face tore at his heart. No relationship and no ties. Both of them were okay with that. It wasn't like he'd take advantage of her or promise something he couldn't give.

"I do." He unlocked and opened the door then flipped on a light switch.

Soft light gleamed off the honey-colored oak boards dotted with colorful rag rugs. A sectional sofa sat in one corner near the bedroom door.

Mia's gaze darted around the room, and tension

radiated off her. "You never mentioned you had a place at Fairlight Cove."

"It never seemed important." He'd always kept people at arms' length, and he didn't share much of himself, even with the ones he cared about. He closed the door behind them to shut out the night.

Mia slipped off her sandals and followed him into the living area, her bare feet a soft patter on the floor. "It's gorgeous. If this cabin were mine, I'd be here every weekend."

"Mémère Brassard, Mom's mother, left it to me in her will." More than Harbor House, more than his apartment in New York, and way more than the place above the law office in town, it was the closest Nick came to having a home. "My grandfather built it for her when he came back from the Navy after the Second World War. It was their special place."

A smile curved Mia's mouth as she perched on the edge of the sofa. The white sundress with the red flowers he liked so much billowed around her. "That's sweet."

He sat beside her as unsure as he'd ever been. He liked sex, and he liked to think he was good at it, but with Mia, he didn't know where to start. Or what to do so he wouldn't scare her any more than she already was. "You're so beautiful and—"

She put her index finger on his lips to stop him. "My whole life, people have told me I'm beautiful. Maybe I am, but that's not all I am. With you, I don't need pretty words." Her brown eyes were sad. "I want you to look at me and see who I am. All of me, not the girl I was, but who I am now."

"I don't see that girl. I see the woman who's my friend,

who I respect and admire for the way she's put her life back together."

"Good." She let out a shuddery breath. "I don't see Brian McGuire's son or the kid you were. I see you." She touched his jaw, and her fingers lingered on the faint triangular scar from the accident.

For the first time, the weight of his dad's legacy lessened. The expectations, the mistakes, and the regrets didn't matter, at least for tonight. The fear of loving and losing didn't matter either. He cupped her face in his hand and looked into her eyes. "Angel, you're sure about this, you and me, here?"

She got to her feet and tugged him with her. "I already texted your mom and told her not to wait up for me."

"Did you tell her where you were?"

"No and she didn't ask. She's so happy to have Cat and Amy staying, she can't think of much else." Mia gave him an impish grin. "Besides, I didn't know where you planned to take me."

Nick chuckled as he eased Mia's sweater off her shoulders. One of the straps of her sundress came along with it. "Mom's smart. She knows we went to Fairlight Cove tonight. She'll guess I brought you here."

She'd also guess why, and Nick's throat thickened. All those hints about Mia his mom had dropped made it clear she wanted to see the two of them together. She'd never understand tonight was casual with no strings for either of them.

Mia trembled as he eased the sweater and dress down her arm. "Did you . . ." She gasped as he licked the curve of her neck and his hand grazed the underside of her breast.

"Did I what?" He breathed in the intoxicating scent of

her floral perfume and eased her back toward the half-open bedroom door.

"You and your ex-wife..." She stopped with her dress hanging off one shoulder.

"I never brought Isobel here. Or any other woman, either." He wrapped a strand of her hair around one finger. "Sean and I came here a few times last winter to go cross-country skiing, but those are guy weekends. Charlie stays home."

"This place isn't anything like Harbor House." Mia gestured to the room with its modern furniture accented by a few vintage pieces, like the oak Vermont blanket box he'd gotten at an auction and his grandfather's snowshoes, which hung on the wall next to the woodburning stove. "You've even got accent pillows, and all the colors complement each other. Greens with touches of red and brown to pick up the tones of the wood."

"What?" Nick dragged his attention away from her mouth.

Mia grabbed a sofa cushion. "You're a guy. Don't tell me you picked this out by yourself." Although her eyes teased him, wariness lurked in their depths.

"Okay, I lied." He chuckled. "There's been one woman here. The decorator I hired to update the place. I loved Mémère, but I didn't love all the pink roses she had everywhere." He moved toward Mia, and she backed even closer to the bedroom door.

"You have a kitchen?" She hitched at her dress and exposed more creamy skin.

"Top of the line." He caught the neckline of her dress with one finger. Her skin was hot, and she hissed when he dipped his finger lower into her cleavage.

"I can cook us breakfast tomorrow morning." Her eyes widened as his finger snagged the lace of her bra. "I mean if…"

"I don't plan to drive back to Firefly Lake in the middle of the night." Nick slid her sweater all the way off. As it dropped to the floor, the buttons bounced with staccato pings. "We'll be discreet, but I don't want to sneak around. I wouldn't have brought you here if I didn't want you to stay the night." He pushed the bedroom door open and backed Mia through it toward the bed.

"I don't have any other clothes or—"

"I have a spare toothbrush, and you can use one of my shirts if you get cold." He slid her dress all the way down her arms and unbuttoned the tiny buttons at the front until the top half came away, and she stood naked from the waist up, apart from an ivory strapless bra. "I want to keep you real hot, though." He found the switch for the bedside light and flipped it on.

Mia's face reddened as she covered her chest with her hands. "I'm small. I always was, but after having the girls, I got smaller. Charlie got the good breasts in the family." Her laugh was high and tinny.

"Your breasts are perfect." Nick yanked his shirt off and pulled her against his chest. He dipped his head and kissed her neck, then her mouth as she trembled against him. "Your legs are perfect, too." He scooped her up and sat her on the bed, then ran a hand under the hem of her dress.

As Mia wiggled across the bed, her dress came off, and Nick sucked in a breath.

"What?" She jackknifed upright and tried to cover her breasts and the panties that matched her bra.

"You're even better than you looked in that bikini." He clasped her hands in his and held her gaze. "You have nothing to be embarrassed about. Not with me and not ever." He moved beside her and shoved her dress onto the floor on top of his shirt.

She took one of her hands out of his and traced the contours of his chest, then his back and the indentations of his spine, her touch light. He shivered.

"I'm sorry." Her hand stilled like she'd done something wrong.

"Don't stop." He bent, kissed her mouth, and waited until she opened for him to deepen the kiss and taste the dark chocolate they'd shared at the play. Rolling onto his side, he pulled her toward him so they were face to face and heart to heart.

Mia let out a soft sound and pulled him closer. She touched his back again, then her fingers dipped lower beneath the waistband of his jeans and boxers.

He eased away and unbuckled his belt one-handed. "Help me, angel?"

She fumbled with the button on his jeans, then the zipper, and brushed his erection before she pulled her hand away.

Nick got rid of his pants and reached for her again. He lowered his head to kiss the curve of her jaw, her neck, and then her breasts. He found the clasp on her bra and opened it, those little breasts he'd wondered about within reach, and the nipples already hard for him to touch and taste.

"Nick." Mia breathed his name as he squeezed then sucked one of her nipples into his mouth.

His free hand skimmed over the curve of her hip and

under her panties. She arched her hips and he continued his intimate exploration, tugged her underwear down, and wrapped one leg around both of hers.

She stiffened and twisted away. "I thought I could do this, but I . . ."

Nick lifted his head. Her breath burst in and out, and her body shook.

"What's wrong? What did I do?"

"Nothing. You didn't do anything wrong." Her eyes were too bright. "It's me."

"Hey." He grabbed the fleece blanket from the end of the bed and wrapped her in it. "It's okay."

"I haven't done this in a long time, and I'm scared." She buried her face in the curve of his shoulder and curled into a fetal position.

Nick rubbed her back through the soft blanket. "You were married. I don't understand."

She tilted her head to look at him, and her eyes were enormous in her white face. "Yes, I was married, but Jay and I hadn't had sex, not really, since before Emma was born."

Her younger daughter was eight. Nick's heart ached. "Why not?"

She shrugged like she didn't care, but her eyes told another story, bleak and so sad that tenderness, as sharp as it was unexpected, welled inside him.

"Emma's birth was hard. Jay didn't make it back in time because he was closing on a big sale in Germany. He couldn't understand what it meant for me to go through that all alone, or how I felt, physically and emotionally. When I was ready to make love again, I tried." Her voice cracked. "I bought lingerie, cooked romantic dinners, booked weekends away, and arranged for the girls to stay with a friend. Except, by then he always had an excuse, like work or he was tired."

"He was with other women?" Nick clenched a fist around the blanket and wished it were Jay's face.

"He didn't want me anymore, and it turned out he hadn't for a long time, even before I got pregnant with Emma." She swallowed a sob. "He's the only man I was ever with, so I panicked because, even though you said you wanted me, maybe you don't. I'm like one of those born-again virgins you read about in the magazines at the supermarket checkout."

"I never read those magazines." Nick cupped Mia's chin to make her look at him and make sure she understood. "I want you, and if you give me a chance, I'll show you how much. I'll do everything I can to make this good for you."

"You promise?" Her lashes were wet with unshed tears.

"I promise." He didn't do promises, but this was different. This was Mia.

He tapped down the spurt of anger at Jay and how he'd treated her and how she'd lived for years. Most of all, anger at how the girl he remembered had become a woman so unsure of her sexuality she could doubt what he wanted. And what she wanted, too.

He kissed the tip of her nose. "Isn't it about time you had some good sex?"

"I don't know if I can make it good for you." Her eyes were wary.

"Doesn't this tell you anything?" Nick took her hand and wrapped it around his erection.

She gave him a small smile, and he eased the blanket

down her body. Her breathing sped up as he stroked her breasts. He found her nipple again and tweaked it between his thumb and forefinger. "Tell me what you want."

She leaned closer and whispered in his ear.

"Oh yeah." He flipped her onto her back in one quick move. "Don't worry about getting it right the first time or making it good for me." Nick trailed a hand across her midriff and she gasped as her body relaxed and melted into his. "You can bet I'll want to try this again."

What Mia wanted was for Nick to keep touching her. She pulled his head lower and guided his mouth to her breast.

He gave a soft chuckle then gave her what she wanted until she squirmed against him. "Take off my boxers."

Mia fingered the elastic waistband. Beneath it, black cotton covered an erection that left her in no doubt he wanted her. She slid her hand under the fabric and touched his skin. It was hot and a bit damp. "Nice." She tugged the underwear down his muscular legs.

"First the play and now me?"

"Is *impressive* better?" He was big, hard, and all male, and her insides clenched with anticipation. She touched his knee then ran a hand across his thigh. His skin was smooth and unmarked, apart from the ridged scar tissue along his right side from the top of his ribcage to his hip.

"Way better." His voice was hoarse and strained.

She traced the outline of the scar. "Is this from the accident?"

"When I crawled out of the truck, the metal—"

She silenced him with a kiss. "It's over." Then she wrapped her hand around his erection and stroked to learn his shape and feel.

"I wanted to take this slow, but if you keep doing that..." Nick closed his eyes and the pleasure on his face, pleasure she'd given him, gave Mia confidence and an unexpected sense of power.

"Maybe we should get the first time out of the way. Since I haven't had sex in so long, I have a lot of catching up to do."

His eyes flipped open. "Are you sure?" His mouth was inches from her nipples.

"Yes." If she didn't have time to think about what she was doing, what it meant or didn't mean, maybe she wouldn't lose her nerve again.

He reached for his jeans, found his wallet, and took out a foil packet. The condom she'd forgotten. The package crinkled as he tore it open, then he rolled the condom on and covered her body with his.

"No." She wanted this to be different and wanted to take charge in a way she'd never done before.

"No?" Nick stilled almost before the word was out of her mouth.

"Yes, but not this way."

"You want to be on top?" In the soft light of the bedside lamp, his eyes gleamed blue-gray like the color of the lake early in the morning.

She dipped her head as her face got hot, but he grinned and lifted her over him.

Mia held her breath and eased down on him, slow and steady. It hurt and she tensed but relaxed again when he stroked her. Her body opened and adjusted to his as he held himself in check. "Yes."

He thrust upward, so gentle, and held on to her hips while his gaze never left her face. "Yes?"

"Oh yes."

His smile had the sexy edge that always gave her a shivery feeling. She gasped as he thrust again, harder.

"I don't want to hurt you."

"You won't." She looked at where they were joined then back at his face and her breath caught.

Nick wasn't thinking about anybody or anything else. Not work, not himself, and definitely not another woman. He was only focused on her and giving her pleasure.

He increased the pace as she did, and they fell into an instinctive rhythm until his breathing got hoarse. "Angel, I can't wait, not..."

"You don't have to." She braced herself as he came hard, hot even through the condom.

Tremors still rocked through him as he reached for her and touched her where she needed it most. His thumb circled and sent her spiraling as the orgasm slammed into her.

"Nick." From a distance she registered her voice calling his name. Her body quaked as he still pulsed deep inside her like he belonged there. She collapsed on top of him, and tears pricked behind her eyes.

"I'm right here, angel." He kissed the top of her head and his gentle fingers caressed her cheeks. "Hey, you're crying. Was I too rough?"

"No." She swallowed hard. The tears she couldn't hold back weren't because of any physical hurt. Instead, it was the emotions sex with him had stirred up. Emotions she'd hidden so deep she'd never expected them to bubble out. "It got me, you know? I'd forgotten."

Forgotten what sex felt like when it touched her heart and soul and reached to the core of who she was. If she'd ever known.

"Got me too." Nick smoothed back the hair stuck to the side of her face, and his touch was tender as he brushed the teardrops away. "For a woman who says she's out of practice, you're amazing."

Swallowing more tears, Mia breathed in the notes of his aftershave, her lighter perfume and sex. A musky scent of the two of them together. "I . . . I could make us a snack."

She couldn't let herself think about what he meant by *amazing*, what they'd done and how sex had changed things between them. Somehow she had to make this situation normal and get back some semblance of what was real and familiar.

Nick let out a sexy chuckle. "I thought what we just did was the snack." He eased away from her. "Give me a minute and then we can figure out what we want to do for the main course."

"You mean you . . . ?" He couldn't want her again, could he?

"We only got started, angel." He rolled out of bed toward what must be a bathroom behind a door on the far side of the bedroom.

Mia slumped on the pillows and wrapped herself in the blanket. He did want her again, as much as she wanted him. That was the easy part.

What they'd started, though, was something else that, at least for her, might not be so easy to stop.

Chapter Eleven

Mia stretched and stuck her toes out from under the quilt. Sunlight poked through a gap in the curtains and illuminated the room with its mellow log walls. She was in Nick's sleigh bed in the bedroom of his cabin, a place and a part of himself he'd kept hidden until last night.

She turned her head on the pillow. Nick was sprawled on his back beside her. His hair stood on end, and beard stubble darkened his jaw. His chest was bare above the sheet and, when she snuck a peek, he was bare beneath the sheet too. Even without her glasses, his magnificent body reminded her of what she'd missed throughout all those years of enforced celibacy.

Her body ached in unfamiliar places, and she stretched again as she eased a foot out of bed. She was also naked, the first time she'd ever slept without a nightgown or pajamas. She reached for her bra on the floor by the bed, and stopped as her arm was caught in a firm grip.

"Where are you going?" Nick's voice was gravelly.

"I need to get my glasses and put on some clothes." Mia blinked to try to bring him into focus. After what he'd persisted in calling the snack, she'd taken her contacts out while he'd watched, touched, and distracted her.

"Get your glasses, but I like you naked." Nick rolled over and kicked the sheet away. He was hard.

Mia flushed and put her hands to her face. "I have to find my purse." She gestured with one hand and then caught his stare at how the movement made her breasts rise and fall.

"Sure." Nick laughed. "I'll watch. I like to watch you."

Clearly, he liked to have sex with her too, four times, finishing in the whirlpool tub in the adjoining bathroom, his body slick against hers.

Mia wrapped herself in the quilt, got out of bed, and grabbed the purse she'd dropped by the door the night before. She dug in it for her glasses case when her phone vibrated.

As she slid her glasses on, her breath caught at the name on the screen. Naomi. She hit ANSWER and moved to a rocking chair near the window. "Hi, honey? What's up?" It was almost eleven, later than she'd slept in years, except last night she and Nick hadn't done a lot of sleeping.

Still naked, Nick moved behind her and massaged her shoulders.

"Naomi? I can't hear you."

Nick eased the quilt away, and Mia shivered as his hands moved south.

"Where are you?" Naomi's voice broke through loud and clear. "You didn't answer your phone earlier, and I've sent you like a gazillion texts. Don't freak out. Emma and

I are at Ms. Brassard's." She hesitated for a heartbeat only a mother would clock. "With Dad."

"You and your father are in Firefly Lake?" Mia lurched away from Nick's touch. "You aren't supposed to be back for another week."

She'd counted the days last night like beads on a string, to plan how many times she could see Nick before the girls came home and she had to be a mom first.

"Dad wanted us to surprise you. We flew into Boston last night and drove here this morning. He had this great idea we should all be together."

"We?" Mia reached for her panties on the floor and tried to wiggle into them. "Your father and I are divorced."

And she'd spent the night having great single sex with a hot guy. Sex that had gone a long way to restoring her confidence and reminding her of the woman she wanted to be.

"Dad says the divorce is only a piece of paper." Naomi sounded younger than sixteen. "He thought you two could talk. Besides, Dad and Tiffany had this big fight, and Tiffany took the baby and went to her mom's two days ago."

So Jay had gotten himself and the girls on a flight to Boston as soon as he could. Mia's lips tightened. She'd talk to him all right. They had a custody agreement that included all the scheduled vacation time with the girls he wanted. He couldn't drop in and out of her life when he felt like it.

Mia stood and bumped into Nick, who eyed her with a mixture of lust and concern. "I'll see you in an hour, Naomi." She tried to smooth her hair. "An hour and a half tops." It would take at least half an hour to get back to

Firefly Lake, and Mia couldn't turn up looking like she'd done what she had.

"Where are you, anyway?" Naomi's voice sharpened with curiosity. "I took Dad to our house first and you weren't there. Ty was cutting the grass and he said he hadn't seen you, so I was sure you'd be at Ms. Brassard's."

"What did Gabrielle say?" Mia leaned into Nick, the one solid point in a world that tilted like a ride at an amusement park.

"She told us you left really early to meet a friend. Some place the other side of the lake."

Mia pressed a finger to her temples, and the dizziness subsided. Bless Gabrielle. She hadn't lied exactly, but she'd covered for her. "That's why it will take me a while to get back. The cell reception isn't great here. That's why I didn't get your calls or texts."

Mia tamped down the guilt that needled her. Every parent had to stretch the truth to their children on occasion, didn't they? Besides, she couldn't be entirely honest with her daughter. She couldn't tell her she'd been so into Nick and how he'd made her feel, she'd forgotten to check her phone for messages. She'd even forgotten to turn the phone's sound on again after the play.

"Emma and I are hungry. Dad said you'd make us lunch." Naomi's tone was accusing.

The old Mia would have, but not the new and improved version. "What are Emma and your father doing?" She retrieved her cuff bracelet from under the bed and shook out her dress as Nick shrugged into his boxers.

"Dad's working on his laptop on the patio, and Emma's playing a computer game with Ms. Brassard's granddaughter." Naomi let out an aggrieved breath. "We wanted to surprise you so we left the airport hotel really early. Ms. Brassard already has plans for lunch."

Mia clenched her clammy hand around the phone. "Tell your dad to take you to the diner. I'll meet you there." That would give her more time to think and plan.

"Okay." Naomi's voice became a whisper. "Dad really wants to talk to you. He told me a lot of things were a mistake, but he'd work it all out. Tiffany was so mad and Dad was, too. He said she could never compare to you. Tiffany made Emma eat processed cheese, and then Emma threw up. Twice."

Do not react. "Naomi, honey—"

"Emma's fine," Naomi interrupted. "She might even have faked it so Tiffany would freak. I have to go." Naomi made a kissing noise. "I can't wait to see you."

The phone went dead, and Mia dropped it onto the bedside table beside the pile of condom wrappers.

"Trouble?" Nick pulled her into a hug.

She bobbed her head, not trusting herself to speak. The panic and self-doubts were back and licked at her. To remind her sex with Nick had been an interlude and escape from reality.

Except, it had been more than sex. It had been making love. And there was a world of difference between the two.

Mia had been silent on the drive back to Firefly Lake. And, as she hesitated outside the North Woods Diner, she looked defenseless and dwarfed by the square, red-brick building where a neon sign in one of the windows overlooking Main Street advertised ALL-DAY BREAKFASTS.

Nick's stomach rumbled to remind him he hadn't eaten

since the night before. But with Mia in his arms and in his bed, he'd forgotten about food. All he could think of, even with her ex-husband and daughters here, was when he could have her again.

He pulled the heavy door open, held it for Mia, and then followed her into the diner. The black and white checked tile floor and high red booths were the same as when he was a kid. Probably the same as when his mom was a kid.

"You don't have to come in with me." Mia stepped behind one of the big Boston ferns, which were Liz Carmichael's pride and joy. "I'm sure you have stuff to do." Behind her glasses, her eyes were blank and washed clean of emotion.

"Nothing pressing." Nick scanned the diner packed with the Sunday after-church crowd. He zeroed in on Naomi and Emma at a table near the back. And the man with them. Jay, the guy who'd walked away from his family without a backward glance, destroyed Mia's life, and made her doubt everything about herself.

Like his dad had done to his mom.

Mia tensed, and her face went white. Then she gave a little cry, and her heels clicked across the floor as she ran to her daughters with her arms outstretched.

When Naomi and Emma spotted her, they jumped up and ran too. The three of them met in the middle of the diner in a group hug.

Nick put one foot in front of the other, the movement mechanical. He'd seen Mia with her daughters before. He'd even grabbed a pizza with them once when he'd bumped into all of them in town.

But that was when Mia was his friend and not his

lover. The step from friend to lover had changed how he saw her and how he saw himself.

"Hey, Nick." Naomi gave him a high five.

Although the teen had Mia's brown hair and eyes, she looked more like Charlie, with her aunt's curvy but athletic build. Returning the gesture, he turned to Emma. The younger girl didn't resemble either Mia or Charlie, and he'd always assumed her blond hair and blue eyes came from Jay's side of the family.

"Hi." Emma tilted her head to look at him. "Do you know I've got a cousin?"

"I do. She's a real cutie." Nick wasn't any judge of babies, but that's what his mom and everybody else said about Lexie.

"My dad says, except for my hair, I looked exactly like Lexie when I was born." Emma stared at him and she angled her head to one side. "Why are you here with my mom?"

Because he'd made love to her all night, and because he cared about her and wanted to make sure nothing bad ever happened to her again. The realization hit him out of nowhere like he'd been punched. "Your mom and I are friends."

Emma's eyes narrowed, and for the first time Nick noted a similarity to Mia: the look she got when something made her suspicious. "Well, since we're here now, you can leave."

"Emma Rose Connell, you will apologize to Nick at once," Mia said. "You know better than to be rude."

"Sorry," Emma muttered and held her arms tight to her body.

"I'm sure Emma wasn't rude." Jay joined the group and looped an arm around Mia's waist. "She's tired. We had an early start this morning, and since you weren't here to make lunch, we ate later than she's used to."

Mia slid out of Jay's grasp and retied the bow on Emma's sundress. "I don't think you've met Nick."

"You're the guy who helped Amelia with her mom's foundation, aren't you?" Recognition dawned in Jay's sharp blue eyes. "My wife never had a head for business." His laugh boomed.

"I have to disagree." Nick forced himself to sound calm and polite. "Mia did a great job with the foundation. I only handled the legal side." He stuck out his hand. "Nick McGuire."

Jay gripped Nick's hand in a firm shake. An executive handshake. He wore executive-on-vacation clothes, too. A white designer polo shirt, pressed jeans, and shiny black loafers.

"I'll call you later, Nick." Mia pulled at her sweater.

"Why would you call him later?" Jay slung an arm around Mia a second time, and again she shook off his touch. "And why are you wearing those awful glasses?"

"If she says she needs to call me, she needs to call me." Nick stuffed his hands into the pockets of his jeans as he pictured his fist connecting with Jay's long nose.

"I'm helping Nick's mom." Mia's voice was strong and even. "Besides, we're divorced, so it isn't any of your business who I call or why. Or if I choose to wear my glasses."

Jay shrugged and gave a polished smile. "I'm looking out for my family, that's all."

He'd had work done, Nick was sure of it. The guy was forty, but his face had only a few strategically placed lines.

"Table for one?" Liz stopped at Nick's elbow and rested a hand on the small of his back.

He read the warning in Liz's eyes and the concern. "Sure." He made himself smile back at Jay and the girls, but when his gaze landed on Mia, the smile slipped away. "Okay?" he mouthed for her alone.

"Later." She linked arms with Naomi and Emma and moved toward the table they shared with Jay.

After Liz had led Nick to a table on the other side of the diner, hidden behind another one of those damned ferns, she filled his coffee mug and slid into the booth across from him. "Want me to drop a jug of ice water on his lap? I'd make real sure it looked accidental."

The teenage Nick would have gone over and punched Jay out, but he hadn't been that guy for a long time. "I'd say yes, except he'd probably sue and put you out of business."

Liz's chuckle was warm and comforting. "You're worth ten of him. He criticized my biscuits. Said they had too much butter in them, which was bad for his heart."

As if Jay had a heart. Nick clocked the hurt in Liz's brown eyes behind the banter. "Your buttermilk biscuits that have taken first prize at the fair every year since forever?"

"The same." Liz straightened the already straight silverware and paper placemat.

"The man has no taste." Except, he'd chosen Mia, so he must have had some taste once. From the way he'd touched her and called her his wife, maybe he was set to make a play for her again.

"Mia can see right through him, Nicky." Liz patted his hand like she'd done when he was five and he'd accidentally dropped his ice cream cone on the floor in front of the diner counter, the chocolate waffle cone his mom had promised him as a special treat.

"I don't want her hurt again. She's my friend." Maybe if Nick said it often enough, he'd believe that was all Mia was, all she could be and all he wanted her to be.

"You took her to your gran's cabin at Fairlight Cove last night, didn't you?" Liz gave an order for the farmhouse breakfast with eggs over easy to a waitress before Nick asked.

"How did you..." Nick stopped. He'd as much as told Liz the truth.

"Your great-aunt Bernice was at the play at that summer theater, and she saw you and Mia there. She left her umbrella under her seat. When she drove back to get it, she passed you turning into Lost Loon Road. There's nothing along that road but your gran's cabin and the hunting camp that got burnt out two winters ago."

"It hasn't rained in weeks. What did great-aunt Bernice need an umbrella for?" Nick took a mouthful of coffee, and the hot liquid burned his throat.

"Don't change the subject. First thing this morning, Bernice called me. You remember she's a distant cousin on my mother's side?"

Nick pressed his thumbs against his temples. He had to get out of Firefly Lake soon before he got trapped here like the proverbial fly in the spider's web, stuck so tight he'd never escape. "Who else did she call?" He couldn't punch old ladies, and he couldn't sue them either.

"Nobody." Liz's eyes took on a steely glint. "Facebook was one thing. Ty's young, and to him the picture of you and Mia was a joke. With Sean away, I soon set Ty straight, but Bernice is a different kettle of fish. As I reminded her, when I mentioned I knew all the beds her shoes have been under."

"Great-aunt Bernice?" Nick's mouth fell open. Bernice was over eighty, favored fussy floral prints and sensible shoes, and had been widowed as long as he could remember.

"You think she's too old?" Liz poked Nick's chin with a forefinger and closed his mouth. "We women have needs, and there are lots of lonely and able widowers in this town."

"All I meant was..." Nick tried to unstick his tongue from the roof of his mouth.

"I know exactly what you meant. Mia has needs, you do too, and I'm glad the pair of you finally did something about it. She's a nice woman, and you could do a lot worse." Liz got to her feet as a teenage waitress slid Nick's breakfast in front of him with a shy smile. "You already did a lot worse with that Isobel minx. Behind Mia's pretty face, there's a woman who's the kind to settle down, and her apple pie is outstanding."

"How..."

"She made an apple pie for your mother to take to her garden club meeting. Gabrielle saved a piece for me so I could check out the competition." With a wink, Liz disappeared behind the fern and left Nick to stare at the plate of eggs and bacon with three silver dollar pancakes and a pot of maple syrup on the side.

He wasn't the kind to settle down, but he was alone at a table for one when he should have been with Mia, talking about important stuff and not so important stuff, the way good friends did.

He picked up his fork and stabbed at a pancake. From the jukebox at the front of the diner the Elvis classic "Can't Help Falling in Love" rang out.

Nick chewed a pancake, and the taste was like sawdust in his mouth. He pushed several fern fronds aside and stared across the diner at the couples, the families, and one family in particular. Mia was squeezed into the booth with her daughters on either side. Jay sat across from them, his sandy blond head bent over his phone. Then he raised his head, said something to Mia, and reached across the table to touch her wrist, the gesture intimate and possessive.

Nick dropped the fern back into place. Sex, even though it had been great sex, didn't mean he was involved. He had his plan. Get his mom healthy and moved and go back to New York after Labor Day.

His phone lit up with Cat's number and he hit ANSWER. "Hey, Muppet."

"Hey yourself, Big Bear. What kept you so busy you couldn't see me this weekend?"

His younger sister's voice held a teasing note that didn't quite mask the tremor of insecurity. The vulnerability she'd had since their dad left, and which no amount of academic success had ever erased. Back then, he'd called her Muppet and he'd been her Big Bear, the brother who'd helped her tie her shoes and throw a ball, and protected her from schoolyard bullies.

"Give me a break. You've been in town less than twenty-four hours."

"Sorry." Her voice softened. "Amy and I are already on our way back to Boston. Amy needed the bathroom so we're at a rest stop. It was only a short trip because I'm up to my ears in work, but I wanted to see Mom again. Make sure it wasn't only excitement about the fashion show that made her look so great last weekend."

"And?"

"Mom looks fabulous. I admit I questioned it at the time, but you were right to hire Mia. She's amazing. So kind and yet firm. I could never have convinced Mom to get rid of so much stuff. Mia's worked miracles in that house."

Nick's throat tightened. "She's a miracle worker all right."

"Even Amy liked her right away. I expected the teen years to be hard, but nobody warned me a tween would be such an emotional volcano." Cat's tone was wry. "Mia knew just what to say to Amy. It was like magic."

Mia had worked that magic on him, like she'd done on his mom and, from the sounds of it, his sister and niece.

"Ward's great, too. He's so good for Mom. Really kind and caring. She's been alone far too long. Do you think the two of them are serious?"

"I don't know." Except, he'd seen how the older man looked at Gabrielle. The care and tenderness paired with respect and admiration.

"I wouldn't worry about Mom as much if she had a man like Ward in her life for the long haul." Music blared in the background then faded. "Enough about Mom. When did you plan to tell me what's going on between you and Mia?"

"Nothing's going on." At least nothing he was ready to share with his sister, who, like her childhood heroine, Nancy Drew, had never encountered a mystery she didn't want to solve.

"Sure it isn't. Like you were at work last night, and Mia was tucked up in bed at Mom's with a mug of chamomile tea and a book. Please." Cat's laugh rippled out, as unfettered and joyful as it had been when she was a kid.

"So? We had dinner and went to the summer theater at Fairlight Cove. It wasn't a big deal." That part of the evening hadn't been. It was what had happened later that was the mega deal.

"Liar, liar, pants on fire." Cat laughed harder.

"Little ears?"

"Amy's still in line for the bathroom. There's a bus tour group in front of her."

"It's none of your business." Nick's voice got tight.

"I saw the picture of the two of you on Facebook. I know you and Mia went out last night. I also know she hadn't come home when I went to bed. When I got up this morning, Mom said Mia had gone out early, but I don't think so. Her towel wasn't even damp, and her toothbrush hadn't been used." Cat's tone was smug.

Nancy Drew had nothing on his sister. "So?"

"I hope there is something between you and Mia. The way you looked at her the night of the fashion show was special." Cat's voice warmed. "You're my brother and I might not say it often enough, but I love you. I don't need anyone in my life right now, but you're different. Mia's good for you, and I think you'd be good for her."

Except Nick hadn't counted on what making love with Mia would mean. Or how he couldn't think of her in the same way, no matter how much he wanted to.

"Like I said, there's nothing to tell." Nick shoved the fern aside again, but Mia's table was empty. "I love you, too, Muppet. Don't be a stranger. Stay longer next time."

"I'll try, but I'm working toward a permanent job at a university. Amy has back-to-school stuff, and between all the practices and games, her hockey schedule gets crazy in the fall."

Cat had been as eager to leave Firefly Lake as he had, as keen to bury the ghosts of the past in a shiny bright future.

If only those ghosts didn't come back to haunt you when you least expected.

Gabrielle let go of Ward's hand to shade her eyes against the sun, which reflected off the diner window. Nick sat at a table alone, and the lost expression on his face tore at her heart. Her son needed her in a way he hadn't for years.

"You go on." Ward patted her shoulder. His touch was warm through her blouse, and his blue eyes were kind. "Once you're a parent, you're always a parent, no matter how old your kid is." He pointed across Main Street where a striped awning shaded the entrance to the Firefly Lake Craft Gallery, and a wooden bench carved in the shape of an easel invited passersby to stop and sit a while. "I'll grab a coffee from the bakery and wait for you over there. Take as long as you need."

"I'm sorry. I know we'd planned to rent a boat and go out on the lake after Cat and Amy left, but Nick's in there and I have to talk to him." Gabrielle had already spent far too long avoiding her son and filling the silence between them with meaningless arguments about that bungalow.

Creases indented Ward's cheeks as he smiled. "The boat will keep for another day. I'm not going anywhere." He brushed his lips against her cheek, and her pulse raced.

"Thank you." Her eyes misted. Maybe this was her chance to start over with both her life and her son.

With a little wave to Ward, she went into the diner to Nick's table. His shoulders were hunched as he twirled a spoon in an empty coffee cup next to a plate where the remains of bacon and eggs congealed. The lunch rush was over, and most of the tables were empty. A few waitresses cleared up behind the front counter.

"Nick?" She hovered by the table and twisted her hands around her straw tote bag.

"Mom?" His expression changed to a careful blank. "What are you doing here?"

She slid into the booth across from him. "I want to talk to you."

As always, she was struck by his resemblance to Brian. Nick had the same square jaw, dark hair, and deep-set blue eyes as his dad. But there was a new vulnerability in those eyes, which gave her the courage to press on.

"I was about to leave." Nick pulled a wallet from his back pocket and took out several bills and some change.

"Then I'll come with you."

Nick's mouth thinned. Also like Brian. "This isn't a good time."

"There never seems to be a good time." Gabrielle rested her elbows on the table and stared at him. "Where's Mia?"

Nick clanged his spoon against the cup. "She left with Jay and the girls."

"You let her walk away?"

"She was with her family." He looked at his plate.

Gabrielle studied his bent head and the telltale red mark on his neck. "You're a grown man and she's a grown woman, so whatever's between you two is your business, not mine."

Even though Mia's text the night before had given her hope one of her dearest wishes was about to come true, she wouldn't interfere. Like her mother always said, you could lead a horse to water but you couldn't make it drink.

"I really have to go." Nick half rose, and Gabrielle reached across the table and pushed him back into his seat.

"What's between you and me, though, is my business. I want to fix it if you'll help me." She took his hand in a firm grasp.

"You do?"

"After you went to college, you became someone I didn't recognize. I'm proud of what you've achieved in your work, but although you're my son, I don't know who you are anymore. Sometimes I miss the boy you used to be."

Gabrielle looked out the diner window. As if he sensed her gaze, Ward looked up from his phone and smiled; a smile to warm her heart and soul.

"You miss the hell-raiser?" Nick's voice was dry but tinged with amusement. "You hated me riding that motorcycle. You also hated it when I punched people out, and when I drank too much."

"True, but now I don't like how you work all the time and deny who you are, all of you." She paused to let her words sink in. "The Nick I knew would never have packed me off to some retirement bungalow."

"I don't want to lose you. I thought a nice new house would make your life easier and more comfortable." He rubbed a hand across his face. "I'm going back to New

York, and if you're in a new place, I won't worry about you as much. Harbor House—"

"Is my home. I'll die sometime anyway, so until I do, why can't I live in the place where I'm happy?"

"You've already made your point." Nick's shoulders sagged. "I'll pay off Mia and leave things as they are, if that's what you want."

"No." Gabrielle tried to hide a smile. "Having Mia clear out all those old things has been a blessing. Already I feel lighter, as if I've reclaimed my life, and she hasn't even started on the attic yet."

"The attic?" A glimmer of the boy she'd raised sparked in Nick's eyes. "A lot of my stuff is still up there. My tabletop hockey game, my collection of baseball pennants, and my glove signed by—"

"There wouldn't be space for those things in a bungalow, would there?" Gabrielle sat back in the booth. "You can help Mia sort through your boxes and take everything you want to keep back to New York with you."

"Smooth, Mom." Nick laughed and it was a real laugh, not the bitter, cynical one she'd gotten used to.

"There's no way I'll let you pay Mia off, so we'll have to make another plan."

"We?" Nick's eyes narrowed, and his expression changed into his lawyer face, the smooth mask that shut out the rest of the world. "You and Mia have talked, haven't you?"

"This isn't about Mia. It's about you and me. We need to get past me being sick and the bungalow business and start over. Your dad hurt all of us, but sometimes I think he hurt you the most. In all these years, you've never tried to see him, never even tried to talk to him."

"He left." Nick's mouth flattened into a stubborn line. "He chose to leave us, remember? Why would I want to talk to him again?"

"To put what happened behind you. I admit I'm not one to talk. I held on to my anger for years, and I only spoke to Brian when I had to about you kids, but you're his son—"

"Drop it." Nick's voice was clipped. "We'll figure something out about the house, and we can do more stuff together." He passed the money to a waitress and gestured to her to keep the change. "But as for Dad, I won't go there."

"I want to spend time with you. I want to get to know who you are, but you can't run away from the past forever." Gabrielle grabbed his wrist. "It catches up with you. Getting sick like I did was a big shock. I want us to be a real family again."

"We are a real family." Nick patted her hand like she was Pixie. "I never needed Dad to be a family. Ward seems like a good guy. If you want to be friends with him, I'm okay with it."

Which wasn't what she'd meant. "I love you, and I want you to be happy." The start of a headache, sharp and insistent, throbbed behind Gabrielle's temples.

"I am happy." Nick's laugh was bitter again. "I've got a good job and lots of friends." He pulled away from her. "I've got you, and Cat and Georgia, even though they aren't around much. I've arranged to meet Cat and Amy in Boston for a Bruins game in December. Since Amy loves hockey, the tickets are my treat for her birthday."

"You're her favorite uncle." Gabrielle tried to smile.

"I'm her only uncle."

Which was why Gabrielle wanted Nick and the girls settled with their own families. For each of her children to know the love of a good partner, and for Amy to have cousins, along with a father. "We're okay?"

"Never better." Nick leaned across the table to give her a quick kiss on the cheek. "I've had some ideas about the house so you can stay there but be safe and comfortable. Why don't we spend an evening together this week? We could have dinner at that new vegetarian place in Kincaid you said you wanted to try."

He sat back with a look of satisfaction like he'd already solved the problem and had moved on. Whereas Gabrielle was stuck with unfinished business and loose ends that, no matter what happened with Harbor House, would lurk beneath the surface like one of those submarines her dad had served on during the war.

"About Mia, did you ever think Jay's a lot like your dad?"

"If you mean Jay's a liar and a cheat, then yes." Nick got to his feet, the little boy who'd been her shadow all those years ago unrecognizable in the tall, handsome man. "Don't go there, either." He held out a hand. "I'm heading over to the office. Do you want to get ice cream and walk with me?"

"Sure." Gabrielle stood too. This was progress. "Why do you have to work on Sunday afternoon?"

"I'm trying to help one of the girls at Camp Rainbow." Nick's face got a tender, maybe even paternal expression Gabrielle had never seen there before. "Kylie's had a rough life. She never knew her dad, and her mom's been in and out of correctional facilities for armed robbery, drug offenses, and fraud. This kid has spent most of her life in foster care. I want to make things better for her."

This was the Nick who'd almost disappeared thanks to Brian and Isobel.

"You're a good man, and I'm proud to call you my son."

For an instant his gaze connected with hers and something changed. Something important. "I'm proud you're my mom, too." He gave an awkward laugh. "You want to get chocolate waffle cones?"

"Are there any other kind?" Gabrielle tucked her arm through his. "Maybe...I mean if you don't mind, I could ask Ward to join us?" She tried to keep the hope and anticipation out of her voice. "He's waiting for me across the street by the gallery."

"Fine by me." Nick guided her through the diner to the front counter. "You go get him and I'll order. Does he like chocolate waffle cones as much as we do?"

"He sure does." He'd bought one for both of them last week. Gabrielle might not know much about Ward, but she knew that. Like she knew his favorite color was blue, he had a deep love for his daughter and granddaughter, and he was the kindest man she'd ever met.

There was still a lot she wanted to know about him but, for now, she knew what she needed and both of them were taking baby steps.

Her gaze met Nick's again and held. Like she was taking baby steps with her son.

Chapter Twelve

Despite being in Nick's old room, Mia wouldn't let herself think about last night and how he'd rocked her world. She secured one end of the fitted sheet over the single mattress as Naomi grabbed the other. The small bedroom under the eaves overlooked the circular driveway in front of Harbor House. However, if Gabrielle hadn't told her, Mia would never have known it had been Nick's.

The narrow bed, chest of drawers, and battered student desk didn't hold any reminders of the boy who'd once lived here, and the pale green walls hadn't held any pictures. But then Mia had discovered the posters on a shelf in the closet beneath a pile of winter blankets. Posters of the Harley Davidson motorcycles that had once been Nick's passion. She'd rolled them into a cardboard mailing tube and waited for the right time to give it to him. So far, she hadn't found it.

She shook out the top sheet and Naomi tucked it in.

There was a new maturity about her daughter, as if she'd grown up in the weeks they'd been apart. As if her sixteenth birthday, which Mia would always regret missing, marked a milestone between the girl Naomi had been and the young woman she would become.

Mia sat on the end of the bed and squeezed the pillow into a white case edged with knitted lace. "You're sure you're okay here? Your dad wanted you to stay at the Inn on the Lake with him to finish your vacation there."

"Dad forgot all about Emma and me as soon as he saw that business center. We hadn't even left before he was on the phone to somebody in Tokyo." Naomi's long brown hair gleamed in the light from the desk lamp.

"I'm sorry, sweetie." Never again would Mia excuse Jay's behavior, but she'd always share her daughter's hurt.

"That's how Dad is. He cares about us, I guess, but most of the time he's so busy he forgets to show it." Naomi set a battered teddy bear on the pillow. "Besides, how could you think I'd want to stay with him when I could be with you? I missed you so much. My birthday wasn't the same without you there. Before this one, I've never had a birthday without a cake you made for me."

Mia's heart warmed. This was who she was. A mom who was always there for her girls. She'd had fun with Nick, and she'd always be grateful, but she wouldn't be greedy and want more than she could have. "I missed you so much, too. We'll have a belated birthday celebration for you here, and when school starts, you can have a party with your new friends."

"I know." Naomi sat beside Mia on the bed. "But I'd always thought my sixteenth birthday would be this amazing day, and it wasn't. Dad took us out for dinner, but he didn't make it special, not like you would have. Tiffany was busy with the baby, and Emma…she…well…she's gotten really weird."

Mia reached for Naomi and pulled her close. In only a few weeks, Emma had also grown up and grown closer to Jay. This was what divorce was like, a constant tug of divided loyalties with children in the middle who had to choose. Birthdays, Christmas, and Thanksgiving. The annual calendar of celebrations now divided into his and hers, no longer theirs.

"Emma's confused. I wish—"

"It's not your fault." Naomi nestled closer to Mia. "Emma thought, we both thought from what Dad said, that maybe you could work things out. He made it sound…I don't know…like everything was a big misunderstanding."

Because Jay was a consummate sales guy, a smooth talker who could sell anything to anyone. "It's not a misunderstanding. Your father and I aren't getting back together."

Almost twenty-four hours later, Mia could still feel the imprint of Nick's body on hers and in hers. She could smell the lingering fragrance of his aftershave on the sweater she'd worn to the play. The sweater she'd slung around her shoulders before having dinner with Jay and the girls as a reminder of who she was, and not who she'd been.

"Dad and Tiffany argued all the time, even before the last big fight when she left. Tiffany's only seven years older than me, and she wanted to hang out with her friends sometimes. Dad didn't get it."

Mia drew in a breath. "Your dad—"

"Can be an idiot sometimes." Naomi's legs stretched out on the bed were long and tanned below her pink sleep shorts, and her breasts beneath the matching vest top were more defined than they'd been a few weeks ago. "Tiffany's okay. Not as a stepmom, of course, but if she wasn't Dad's girlfriend I could like her. She just wants to have some fun. Dad still works all the time, and he's not really a fun guy."

Mia got up and went to the window. According to Jay, she hadn't been fun either. She looked out into the night. The wind ruffled the leaves on the century-old maple trees near the house, and stars dotted the blue-black sky. Through the half-open window, a train whistled at the level crossing at the far end of Main Street.

"Your dad has to figure out what he wants." Mia turned and tried to smile at her daughter. "You need to get some sleep. It's been a long day."

Naomi crawled under the covers then reached over and flipped off the light to plunge the room into darkness. "Today, you and Nick seemed different."

"Different how?" Mia forced herself to sound casual, like what Naomi had said wasn't a big deal.

"How he looked at you."

"I didn't notice." Mia tried to make herself believe the lie. She'd felt Nick's eyes on her from across the diner, and she'd been hyper aware of the invisible thread that linked the two of them together.

"Come on, it was obvious." Naomi thumped the pillows and yawned. "Even Emma noticed."

"You both have overactive imaginations." Mia kissed Naomi good night.

"I know what I saw." Naomi rolled onto her side and tucked one hand against her cheek like she'd done as a baby.

Mia got a lump in her throat. Her baby was almost a woman, and the years had flown by in the blink of an eye. Years she'd wasted waiting for Jay to change and trying to change enough for both of them. Always feeling she wasn't good enough and couldn't meet his standards.

She closed Naomi's bedroom door, then peeked in on Emma in Cat's old room. Her younger daughter was curled in a ball, and her silky blond hair was tousled above pink pajamas patterned with hearts. Unlike Naomi, Emma had clung to Jay and wanted to stay at the inn with him. And she'd spent the short drive back to Firefly Lake staring out the car window and giving one-word answers to Mia's questions.

"Did the girls settle in all right?" At the end of the hall, Gabrielle's bedroom door swung open, and she came out tying the belt on a purple bathrobe. Pixie followed at her heels.

"Fine. Kids can sleep anywhere." A knack Mia envied, although last night with Nick she'd slept better than she had in months. Once they'd finally slept.

"If you want to go out for a while, I'll listen for the girls if they wake." Gabrielle's eyes were warm in the muted light cast by the lamp on top of a bookcase.

"Out where?"

"For some fresh air." Gabrielle scooped up Pixie and thrust the squirming dog into Mia's arms. "You'd help me if you could take Pixie for a walk. I was too tired to take her earlier. You'd love a walk, wouldn't you, baby dog?"

Mia's heart thumped. Maybe Nick wouldn't be home.

Maybe he'd be busy. And maybe those were more excuses to deny what she wanted.

"Well..." Mia struggled to keep hold of a protesting Pixie. She might not know much about dogs, but if ever a dog looked less like wanting a walk, it was this one.

"Go on." Gabrielle made a shooing motion. "It's a mild night and we won't get many more of those this year. A nice stroll into town will do you good."

Being with Nick would do her good. Mia had said she'd call him, except she hadn't. Every time she picked up her phone she'd told herself she didn't know what to say. Even though she'd never dropped by his place before, maybe she needed to take that next step.

Twenty minutes later she stood in front of McGuire and Pelletier. Nick's office was dark, but there was a light on in the upstairs apartment. "What do think, Pixie? Do you want to say hi to Nick?"

The dog yelped and strained at the end of her leash.

Mia wound the leash tighter around her fingers with one hand and hit the doorbell with the other. The sound echoed and made her jump. Above her, a window opened with a squeak.

"Mia?"

She tilted her head to meet Nick's gaze and clocked the surprise in his expression. "Hey."

Pixie whined and scratched the door.

"Hang on. I'll be right down." He disappeared from view.

Mia smoothed her hair, which had curled into spiky tendrils in the mist off the lake. She couldn't run even if she wanted to, but she didn't want to. The lock clicked and the door swung open. On the other side, Nick wore a pair of low-slung jeans and a white T-shirt, and his feet were bare.

Mia swallowed as she tried to look anywhere but at him, and how the T-shirt molded to his broad shoulders. Now she knew what was beneath that shirt and those jeans, too. "The girls are asleep at your mom's. I took Pixie out for her, but I've caught you at a bad time. I'll go, I—"

"It's not a bad time." Nick pulled her inside and shut and locked the door behind her. "You didn't call." He led her past the law office and up the carpeted stairs.

"I wanted to. I planned to." She stopped outside his open apartment door. The Bruce Springsteen classic "Born to Run" spilled out into the stairwell. "After last night..." She let go of Pixie's leash, and the dog scampered into the apartment.

"And this morning." Nick led her into the foyer. "Don't forget the tub. I haven't." His blue eyes teased her before he dropped a kiss on the top of her head.

"I don't do one-night stands. Or mornings." Mia moved through the foyer into a sparsely furnished living and dining area. The music was louder here, and there was a smell of roasted vegetables and yeast. "With Jay and the girls here, it's complicated."

"Last night wasn't a one-night stand. At least it wasn't to me." Nick turned the music off, and in the sudden silence, the tick of the clock on the wall above the table was unnaturally loud. "Are you hungry?"

Mia started to shake her head and then stopped. She'd only picked at the two meals she'd eaten with Jay and the girls, so she was hungry. "Yes." She pushed away the memory of Jay's comment about her having gained a few pounds.

The oven timer dinged from the galley kitchen tucked off the living room. Nick grabbed a pair of black oven mitts from the counter and slid a pizza pan out of the oven. He gestured to the cupboard above the sink. "Dishes and glasses are up there, and there's silverware in the drawer." He sliced the pizza into triangles.

"How have we been friends this long and I didn't know you could make pizza?" There was no cardboard takeout box, only a dusting of flour across the white countertop and rich, good smells. Mia grabbed two plates from the cupboard, knives and forks from the drawer, and paper napkins from a metal holder shaped like a sailboat.

"When my dad left, and Mom went back to teaching, I had to cook for my sisters. Liz helped me." Nick balanced the pizza tray in one hand and two cans of soda in the other as he led Mia to the round table with four chairs at the end of the living room.

Mia pulled out a chair and sat across from him. "Nobody makes pizza dough unless they want to."

A faint flush crept up Nick's cheeks. "I like to cook. Is that a problem?"

"No, it's great." She set the table and then took a piece of pizza. The tomato sauce and melted cheese base was topped with a colorful medley of grilled vegetables, and her mouth watered in anticipation. After years of making meals for Jay and the girls, a man who liked to cook was a major turn-on. Along with all the other things about Nick that were a major turn-on.

"I already know you like to cook. What else do you like?" His eyes had a mischievous glint.

"Simple things, like spending time with my girls. I also like the roses in your mom's garden when they're wet with dew, and the smell of fresh-baked bread. How the sun rises over Firefly Lake in the morning and makes the sky all pink, and the first hint of red on the maple leaves here."

"I like the fall colors too." Nick's voice deepened. The man could arouse her with his voice alone. "I also like the dress you wore last night and the way your hair is all curly right now." He reached across the table and tugged on a strand near her jaw.

"It's a mess. The humidity on a night like this gives my hair a mind of its own." Mia's skin burned as he traced a path along her jaw and down her neck.

"I like a woman who knows her mind."

Which Jay hadn't. Mia chewed a piece of pizza. It was crisp, flavorful, and everything homemade pizza should be.

"I like you, and I also like what happened between us last night." Nick hitched his chair around the table next to hers. "I'd like to talk about what happens now."

Mia had two daughters asleep at his mom's place and an ex-husband settled into a suite at the Inn on the Lake, going on about the family he'd destroyed like he was still part of it. Her sister and brother-in-law were camped out at a New Hampshire hospital with their premature baby, and her house was still under construction since the baby and keeping Carmichael's boat yard going were way more important than Mia's new kitchen cupboards.

And she had a friend who'd turned into a lover and feelings she didn't know what they meant or how to handle them. Talking wasn't high on her list of priorities, but if Nick was so set on conversation, she had a question. "What happened between you and your ex-wife?"

"Isobel?" Nick's hand slid away from the curve of her thigh. "Why do you want to know?"

"We slept together." She wanted to sleep with him again, but she also wanted to know the truth Gabrielle had skirted around.

"Yeah, we did." Nick's voice got flat. "And Isobel slept with the senior partner at the law firm where we both worked. She had sex with him in the thirty-second-floor boardroom on the big conference table. I came back one night to get a file I needed for court in the morning and caught them."

"Nick—" This was so much worse than Mia imagined.

"I never thought people really had sex on those tables. I'd read about it in books and seen it in movies, but when it's your wife and a guy you work for..." He stopped and rubbed a hand across his face. "Isobel told me she'd be at a baby shower for a friend at her gym. I believed her. She even had a gift in one of those fancy bags."

"I'm sorry." Mia put an arm around his shoulders. "Jay played a lot of golf, but I never caught him doing it in a golf cart."

Nick's laugh sounded more like a sob. "Count yourself lucky."

Except Jay had still made her look like a fool in front of everyone. The women who'd pretended to be her friends whispered behind their hands at the country club, at the girls' schools, and even the grocery store. She'd taken to doing the weekly shopping at a store two suburbs over to avoid meeting anyone she knew. If your spouse cheated, everyone thought there must be something wrong with you.

"You came back to Firefly Lake after..." Mia twined her fingers with his to give and seek comfort.

"Not right away, but when Mom was diagnosed, she needed me. The other lawyer at McGuire and Pelletier had just retired. Allison needed help, so I said I'd cover for a while. My dad was the last McGuire to head the firm, so maybe I had something to prove."

"What did you need?"

He stiffened. "I needed a place to get away, where I didn't have to see Isobel in the office and in court. A place where people gave me a second chance."

Apart from the office and the courtroom, those were pretty much the things she'd needed. She dipped her head, found the sensitive spot on his neck, and nipped at it.

He twisted into her touch and groaned. "Angel, you're killing me." He pulled her onto his lap and his hands sought her breasts, the nipples already tight. "I want—"

"I want, too." She straddled him and rocked over his thighs. Talking was overrated, especially about things she didn't want to talk about.

Pixie gave a sharp bark and scooted under Nick's chair.

"Hang on, there's someone at the door."

The door? So the ringing noise wasn't in her head. Mia lurched to her feet, bumped into the table, and grabbed Nick's soda before it spilled. "You go and I'll..." She sat in her chair and found her abandoned cutlery.

"Hold that thought." Nick's kiss was hot and intense. "I'll get rid of whoever it is and be right back."

Nick took the stairs two at a time as the doorbell rang again, like the person outside was leaning on it. His mom would have called his cell if something was wrong. Sean and Charlie were still in New Hampshire, and everything had been fine when he'd spoken to Sean earlier. Most of the guys he played pool with had families and weren't the kind of friends to drop by without a phone call first. And McGuire and Pelletier didn't have the kind of clients who needed an attorney on a Sunday night.

He unlocked the door and opened it. "What do you think you're...Kylie?" He took a step forward.

"I didn't know where else to come or who else to ask." The streetlight turned her blond hair silver. She wore her purple hoodie and cradled a knapsack with a faded New York Mets logo. Beneath her denim shorts, blood oozed from a cut on one bare knee.

"Kylie?" Nick said again, the sight of her like a cold shower that banished thoughts of Mia upstairs.

"No, the tooth fairy." Kylie made a face that was rude, defensive, and a whole lot scared before she pushed past him through the doorway.

"Okay." Nick stopped himself from saying "Kylie" one more time as the door hit his elbow before it slammed shut. "What are you doing here? What's in that knapsack? How did you get here?"

"I already told you. I'm here because I didn't know where else to go." Kylie looked him up and down. "All my stuff's in the knapsack. As for how I got here, I snuck a ride in the back of a plumbing van. A pipe burst in the camp kitchen so a guy got called out from town. Josh with a weird last name."

"Tremblay. It's a French name from Quebec."

"Where?"

"It doesn't matter." At least Kylie hadn't hitchhiked. Nick's heart, which had almost stopped, started to beat normally again. Even if he'd found her, Josh was a good guy, a father, who'd have taken his little stowaway straight to the police station.

"You better come upstairs." Even though he should take Kylie to the police station, he didn't want to scare the poor kid any further. He'd call the cops instead.

"Do I smell pizza?" Halfway up the stairs, Kylie's face brightened. "I hid in that van for hours, so I'm starving."

Nick bit back a sigh. His night had gone to hell fast, and how he'd explain all this to Mia he had no idea. "Yeah, it's pizza."

"Pepperoni?"

"Vegetarian."

She wrinkled her nose. "I hate vegetables."

"Tough." Nick ushered her through the apartment door. "Kids need to eat vegetables." He shut the door behind them as Pixie darted out from the living room with a series of short, sharp barks.

"You sound like a dad." Kylie patted Pixie, and the little dog bounced around her ankles.

No, he didn't sound like a dad. He sounded like an adult. A sensible adult. The police station was a few blocks south on Main. Forget about not scaring the kid, he should take Kylie there, hand her over to whoever was on duty, and rescue his evening. And keep free of any messy entanglements to boot.

"Nick?" Mia stood by the sofa. Her sweater was buttoned to her neck, and her face was flushed. "What's going on?"

"I...uh..." He shrugged and gestured at Kylie, who hovered inside the door.

"I ran away." Kylie dropped the knapsack and folded

her arms across her chest. "Camp ended today. I don't have anywhere else to go."

"Oh, honey." Mia opened her arms, and Kylie ran into them.

"Nick helped me with my mom. I thought he could help me with this, too." Kylie snuffled.

"This? Nick?" Mia raised an eyebrow at him over Kylie's head.

"I made some phone calls. I talked to her mom's attorney and found out why she was being moved to another facility." He couldn't hug Kylie. He was a guy, and guys didn't hug young girls who weren't family. "Like I told you, Kylie, I talked to your social worker, and she's got a nice foster family organized for you from next week. Until then, you have another nice temporary family. Sure you've got somewhere to go."

Kylie raised a white, tear-stained face. "How do you know they're nice? You've never met them. But even if they're the nicest foster family that ever was, they live miles away from where Mom's gone and I'll never see her again, ever." Her voice rose. "That attorney can say what he wants. Mom needs help, but a jail's still jail, isn't it? She won't be out for years this time and I'll be grown up and—"

"Sweetie." Mia made soft and soothing noises. Mom noises. "We'll figure something out, but the staff at Camp Rainbow must be frantic looking for you."

Of course they'd be frantic. What had he been thinking? He hadn't been thinking. Nick grabbed his phone, glad to have something practical to do to escape the emotion that engulfed the small apartment like a tidal wave. "I'll call the camp and—"

"No." Kylie reached for the phone and knocked it out of his hands. "Nobody at Camp Rainbow knows I've gone."

"What?" Mia's eyebrows furrowed into a worried crease. "When I came to say good-bye this afternoon, you were in the line for the bus with everyone else. All the staff was there to check."

"I got on the bus all right. They ticked me off the list. But when nobody was looking, I went out the back door open for the luggage." Kylie gave Mia an earnest smile. "I'm small and I'm quick. Besides, nobody ever notices me anyway."

Mia made more soothing noises and patted Kylie's hair. "You must be hungry and cold, and look at your knee." She knelt at Kylie's feet. "What happened here?"

"I fell and scraped it on something in the van."

"What van?" The crease between Mia's eyebrows deepened, and Nick shook his head.

"Never mind," Mia said, "one problem at a time. I'll get you cleaned up and fix you something to eat. Nick will call Camp Rainbow—"

"No," Kylie said again.

"Yes," Nick said.

"I can stay here." The silver stud in Kylie's nose gleamed, and Nick flinched. Young girls shouldn't have their noses pierced, and even though this was rural Vermont where moose were more of a threat than people, young girls shouldn't wander the streets alone at night or hide in a stranger's van.

"No, you can't stay with me." Because young girls definitely shouldn't spend the night at a single man's place who wasn't family.

"Then I'll run away again so far nobody will ever find me. Never, ever." Kylie backed away from Mia like a cornered animal and grabbed for her knapsack.

Nick crossed his arms and stood in front of the door. Kylie had come to him because she believed he could help her, and he didn't want to let her down. "Here's the deal, kiddo. I'll still call Camp Rainbow and your social worker. However, if they give the okay, you can stay at my mom's place tonight."

"With Mia?" The hope in Kylie's voice almost broke his heart.

"Only for tonight." His mom wouldn't turn Kylie away if he asked her to help.

"Nick, you want to do what you think's best, but there are rules about child protection and I—"

He waved away what Mia had been about to stay. "I practice family law. I know the rules. You've been checked to be around kids, and Mom was a teacher so she has, too. Kylie can't stay at Camp Rainbow tonight, not in a cabin without the other kids, and most of the staff will have already left. Besides, it's late. How will anyone from the family services office in Burlington get here before morning?"

Nick's throat got tight at the look on Kylie's face. The trust and the faith in him.

"I knew you'd help me." Kylie flung her arms around him. "You're the best."

"We have to see what your social worker says." Nick stood stiff. He couldn't let himself get close. He just didn't think he could give Kylie the love and the home she needed.

"What about some pizza and a glass of milk?" His

voice came from far away. Milk was good for kids and, from the look of her, Kylie needed to grow.

"You got any Snickers bars?" Kylie stepped back, and her face was transformed by a grin.

"I always have Snickers bars." He grinned back, the tension broken. "But you have to eat some vegetables first."

Mia laughed. "Gabrielle raised you right. While Kylie eats, I'll do first aid on her knee, and you call Camp Rainbow and her social worker." She looked at Kylie and her mouth trembled. "Before you know it, honey, you'll be tucked up safe in bed."

Nick needed Mia in his bed tonight, but Kylie needed her more. And Kylie needed him, too. Apart from his niece, he'd kept kids out of his life, but one had turned up and, against all the odds, he didn't want to let her go.

Nick's breath caught as Mia unbuttoned her sweater and slid it off her shoulders. Her skin above her tank top was dewy in the light, and her expression as she looked at Kylie was warm and loving.

He didn't want to let Mia go, either, but her family was back in town. He'd delude himself if he thought he could have anything more than he already had.

Chapter Thirteen

Mia slid the last batch of cowboy cookies onto a wire rack to cool on Gabrielle's kitchen table. The oatmeal, raisin, and chocolate chip treat had been Emma's favorite since she was a tiny girl. "Do you want to put some of the cooled cookies on a plate?" She glanced at Emma hunched over the tablet Jay had given her. "Nick and Kylie will be back with her social worker soon, and I bet they'd like a snack."

"Kylie can get her own snack." A curtain of golden-blond hair half covered Emma's sulky face. "It's bad enough she had to share my room last night. And Dad says Nick spends way too much time with you."

"Nick grew up in this house. His mom still lives here, so he has every right to drop by." Mia steadied her breathing. "Your dad and I are divorced. It isn't any of his business who I spend time with."

"You're my mom, so he says that makes it his

business." Emma took a cookie and ate it, scattering crumbs on the floor.

Jay had cheated on her, walked out on her, and, although they might have looked like a family when they'd gone to the hospital to see Lexie, it was a myth. Mia didn't love Jay anymore, and maybe she never had.

At least not in the way Charlie loved Sean. Mia's ribs squeezed as she remembered the expression in Charlie's eyes when she looked at her husband and baby daughter. Even though Lexie was still in the hospital, the three of them were already a family in the best sense of the word.

"Nick and his mom are our friends. They helped us get settled in Firefly Lake, remember?" Mia couldn't risk her daughters guessing there was more than a casual friendship between her and Nick. Besides, it was an interlude. No relationship and no commitment, like they'd both agreed.

"Kylie isn't my friend."

"No, but Kylie needed our help last night, and if it's okay with her social worker, she'll stay here for a few days. Like I already explained to you." Mia walked around the table to sit beside Emma. "Your bedroom's the only one with bunk beds. It's good to share with others in need."

Emma's lower lip trembled. "Dad's got baby Riley, so I'm not the youngest anymore." A fat tear rolled down her face. "All Naomi talks about is Ty Carmichael, and now there's Kylie. Do you like her more than me?"

"Of course not." Mia wrapped her arms around her daughter. "No matter how big you get, you'll always be my youngest and Naomi's only sister. I want to help Kylie, sure, but I love you. When you were with your dad, I missed you every moment of every day."

Emma sniffed and wiped a hand across her face. "Really?"

"Of course I did. I know everything's topsy-turvy right now, but things will be better when we're back in our house and can be a real family again. Since Uncle Sean has to be at the hospital with Aunt Charlie and Lexie, Nick asked some of the guys he plays pool with to help him finish the renovations. He texted me earlier to make sure he got the right paint color for your bedroom."

"Dad doesn't like our house." Emma's chin jutted. "He said so when we went there to look for you yesterday. Besides, we're not a family without Dad, not a real one anyway."

"Your dad doesn't have to like it, does he?" It was Mia's house, bought with her divorce settlement. "And of course we're a family. Like your dad and Tiffany and Riley are a family. You've got two families." Mia manufactured what she hoped was a neutral smile. She could be civil for Emma's sake.

"I don't want two families. Besides, Tiffany and Riley left to go to her mom's house, so they aren't my family anymore. You and Dad can get back together."

"Honey…" Mia hesitated. She hated to destroy the longing on Emma's face, but she needed to make sure she understood the truth. "Your dad and I won't get back together. As for Tiffany, that's for her and your dad to work out."

"You might get back together because Dad said it wasn't appropriate for me and Naomi to live in our house here." Emma cocked her head to one side. "What does that mean?"

Pixie barked and darted to the kitchen door, saving

Mia from answering. Nick came into the house, a blue shirt open at his neck above dark suit pants. Behind him, Kylie carried two bulging plastic shopping bags. "Hey, ladies." Nick picked up Pixie and tucked her into the crook of his elbow.

"Nick." Mia busied herself with the cookies.

"You made these cookies?" Kylie set the bags on the floor and eyed the plate.

"Sure she did." Nick's smile was warm, with a sensual edge for Mia alone. "She's a woman of many talents." His smile turned wicked, and Pixie slithered out of his grasp.

"May I have one, please?" Kylie's gaze was still fixed on the cookies.

Emma scraped her chair across the kitchen floor to the other side of the table, as far away from Nick and Kylie as possible.

"Of course, as long as you wash your hands first."

Kylie's face brightened at Mia's words, like the sun coming out from behind a cloud.

"Emma, do you want another cookie, too?"

"No." Emma slid the tablet across the table. "Cowboy cookies are for babies."

Ignoring Emma, Kylie moved toward the sink. "I had the best day ever." Her smile softened the sharp edges of her face and made her look younger and more innocent. "Nick got me some clothes. New ones nobody wore before." She gave a little twirl to show off her denim skirt and purple T-shirt.

"Very pretty." Mia kept one eye on her daughter.

"If you like purple." Emma rolled her eyes.

Mia shot the girl a warning glance. "Emma."

"I also helped Nick in his office." Kylie's usual

defensive expression was replaced with one of shy pride. "I made coffee for everyone and filed things and scanned documents."

"So?" Emma closed the tablet. "I go to my dad's office all the time. At least I used to before Mom made us move." She stood with her hands on her hips, and her chest heaved beneath a shirt with a rainbow on it. "My dad has a very important job. He's a senior vice president, which is like almost a president, and thousands of people work for him." She pushed the chair back so hard it hit the edge of the kitchen counter.

"Emma." Mia reached for her daughter, but the girl twisted away.

"My dad doesn't work in some hick town in the middle of nowhere. He has his very own secretary, maybe even five secretaries, so he doesn't need me to file things." Her voice rose and she turned and stumbled over the chair leg.

"Emma, you're out of line." Mia reached for her again. "Where are you going?"

"The front porch to wait for Naomi to come home. Leave me alone."

"Emma, I—" The kitchen door banged, and Mia put a finger to her temples. In the past few weeks, she'd lost the closeness she'd once shared with her younger daughter. And she had no idea how to get it back.

"Kids say stuff. I said stuff when I was her age. It's okay." Nick's blue eyes were calm.

"No, it's not okay. Emma needs space right now, but I'll talk to her later." She turned to Kylie, who'd finished washing her hands. "Take your new clothes to the bedroom and put them in one of the empty dresser drawers."

"She doesn't want me here, does she?" The sharp look was back on Kylie's face and her eyes were bleak.

"Emma doesn't know what she wants." Mia bit back a sigh. A lot like her.

She wanted Nick, but she wanted her daughters, too. And she wanted her new life, but parts of her old life had come back and threatened to suck her in, as unexpected and treacherous as quicksand.

Kylie gathered the bags with the clothes and took the plate of cookies Mia held out to her. "I'm used to people who don't want me. My mom didn't, not really. Dylan was always her favorite. Mom's boyfriends said I was a nuisance. Most of the foster families are okay, but I don't belong with them either."

"Ah, Kylie." Nick's voice cracked.

"As soon as my social worker gives the word, I'll be out of here. A guy like Emma's dad wouldn't want someone like me around her anyway. If he has a problem with Ty Carmichael, he'd sure have a problem with me."

"Emma's dad has a problem with a lot of people," Mia said, "but Emma misses him and she wants..." Wanted what Mia couldn't give her. She'd expected the divorce would be harder on Naomi, but she'd been wrong. It was Emma who'd suffered the most, and Emma who still yearned for the family she'd lost.

"Whatever." Kylie herded Pixie out of the kitchen.

After the kitchen door shut behind her, Nick wrapped his arms around Mia. "I didn't think about how having Kylie here would make things awkward for you and the girls."

"Naomi's fine with it. She's always off with Ty anyway." Another worry that kept Mia awake at night.

"Wasn't Kylie's social worker supposed to come back with you?"

"She had to make a few calls, so she's outside in her car. She thinks Kylie's a sure risk to go missing if she takes her back to Burlington today."

"Missing?"

"Kylie's already run away from three temporary foster homes. The last time, she made it across the New York state line before she was picked up by the police at two in the morning outside a convenience store. Kim, the social worker, has to fix an emergency home study and meet you and Mom, but if it goes okay, she'll recommend Kylie stays here until her permanent foster family can take her."

"I see." Mia rolled her tight shoulders. "Your mom and Ward went to a photography exhibition at the gallery, but she should be back soon. At least your mom likes Kylie."

Gabrielle had welcomed the girl with a hug and a glass of warm milk and said Harbor House was her home as long as she needed it.

"Since Mom isn't here, I can do this." Nick bent his head and kissed her. The heat from his body generated an answering heat in Mia's.

"Stop." She pulled away.

"You don't like me kissing you?"

"I do, but Emma could come back. Or Kylie."

"I'm sure Kylie's seen lots of people kissing and more." Nick snagged a cookie from the cooling rack. "She talked about us having sex."

"What? To who?"

"Me." Nick grinned. "Even before you and I had sex. Kylie's smarter than her years."

"Too smart. I'm worried Emma will get a whole new vocabulary before Kylie goes back to Burlington."

"I already talked to Kylie." Nick's expression turned serious. "I told her she had to behave around you and the girls. No bad language and no talking to Emma about stuff she shouldn't. She gets she has to watch her mouth."

"I hope so."

"She'll be fine. At work with me today she was great. She sat at the conference table and worked at some puzzle books I got her. While I met with Kim, she helped Lori with scanning and filing. Lori said she was polite and helpful."

"I'm sure she was."

Nick was Kylie's hero, and the girl was desperate for his approval.

"Do you think Kylie would like a tablet?"

"I'm sure she'd love one, but you can't..." Mia bit her lip.

"I know." Nick blew out a breath. "Even if Kim approves foster care here, it's only temporary. We can't get attached to Kylie."

"Did Kim say so?"

"No, it's what I think. Kylie's had a lot of losses in her life. If she gets attached to us, it'll be another loss. If she stays here, though, I'll take some time off work to help you. It's the least I can do." He gave her a slow smile. "There are lots of other things I'd like to do, too." His fingers slid down her arms and brushed the side of her breasts.

"We can't."

"You won't sneak me in after lights out?" Nick's chuckle was low and sexy. "I can be very quiet."

He might be, but Mia wasn't sure she would. Not if Saturday night and Sunday morning were anything to go by. "In case you've forgotten, this is your mother's house. She'll be home any minute, and Kim will knock on the front door to assess our suitability as foster parents."

"Yeah." Nick gave her a wry smile and took his hands away from her breasts. "Mom might have told you I've had a few ideas about this house. If we convert the old pantry to a full bathroom and make a bedroom out of the small parlor beside it, she could live on the main floor this winter. Mom seemed to like that plan."

"Sure she did." At last Nick had tried to understand Gabrielle and had listened to her. And when she'd come home from having dinner with him, Gabrielle had been happier about the prospect of a new relationship with her son than the changes he'd suggested to Harbor House.

"I already called some contractors for quotes. Once your place is finished, I can help with the work here. Best of all, after you move out and I go back to New York, Mom can rent out a room to have some company. There must be people who've just moved here who need a place to stay. Mom said it would be perfect."

"Perfect," Mia echoed, although all she could think about was what her life would be like when Nick had gone back to the city. The friend she counted on. The lover she wanted.

"You look tired. After we meet with Kim, why don't you have a nap and I'll take the girls to the beach?" He patted her shoulder. "Afterward, I'll cook. Or order in, whatever you want."

"Great." Mia had gone into this situation with her eyes wide open. She didn't want a relationship, but she hadn't expected Nick to get tangled in her life, either.

"Tomorrow I'll swing by and help you clear out the

attic. Most of the stuff up there hasn't been touched in years. Some of it's my stuff, as Mom reminded me."

"You don't have to—"

He gave her a quick kiss, sweet, tender, and a little sexy. "What else are friends for?"

Friends weren't to have sex with. Despite what her body told her.

And friends weren't to fall in love with. Despite what her heart said.

Although Nick hadn't come here in years, the triangle of sand at the base of the granite cliffs below Harbor House had once been his favorite place.

He dropped the beach towels near a rocky outcrop and scanned the horizon. The red sun hung low in the sky and dipped behind the hills. Watching Emma and Kylie was a small thing he could do for Mia, especially since Kylie's social worker had approved the girl staying at Harbor House for at least the next forty-eight hours.

His chest ached as he pictured the purple shadows beneath Mia's beautiful eyes and the lines of strain around her mouth. The look on her face when Emma had slammed out of the kitchen. A look he couldn't fix.

And the other look he'd put on her face when he'd talked about renovating Harbor House and going back to New York.

"Stay close to shore, girls. It gets deep fast." Even though he hadn't swum in Firefly Lake in over twenty years, Nick remembered the rogue currents and sharp rocks that lurked beneath its tranquil blue surface and how the sandbar fifteen feet from shore here dropped off into the dark, cold depths of the glacial lake.

Scrawny in the purple bathing suit he'd bought her earlier, Kylie waded into the water to her ankles. "This is awesome. Your mom has a private beach."

"My dad's house in Dallas has a swimming pool." Emma slipped out of her flip-flops without looking at him.

"That's lucky, isn't it?" Maybe this was a mistake. Without Mia to run interference, Nick was way out of his depth. He didn't know much about kids, but at least if Emma had been a boy, or a tomboy like his niece, he could have talked about guy stuff. Sports or action movies. But not only was Emma a girlie girl, she was one who didn't like him much.

Emma rolled her blue eyes. "Yeah, I'm so lucky. I don't live in that house. I have to live here."

"Did you hear me about not going in too deep?"

"I'm not deaf." Her small shoulders were stiff in her pink two-piece as she marched toward the water's edge.

Nick took a deep breath and sat on the sand. Far above him, a broad-winged hawk circled before it disappeared into the trees. As a kid, he'd loved this time of day, when the lake was quieter and most of the tourists had gone home.

He squinted against the setting sun. The wooden swim raft he and his dad had built the summer he was ten still bobbed out on the lake. The raft must be rotten, even though his mom took it in every winter. He toed off his sneakers and walked to the water's edge for a closer look.

"Nick?" Kylie waved at him from the water near where the sandbar started. "Watch me swim. Mia helped me, so I'm a lot better."

"Sure, but don't go out any farther."

Kylie floated on her back and kicked her legs.

"Anybody can do that. Watch this." Emma did a somersault and disappeared below the surface before she popped up five feet beyond Kylie.

"Emma, come back here." Nick waded into the icy water, glad he'd changed into the board shorts he kept at his mom's.

"Emma?" Kylie's voice rose. "Nick? What's she doing?"

"Emma." Nick called again, but the girl ignored him and broke into a choppy front crawl.

She scrambled onto the swim raft. "Bet you can't do this either, Kylie." She jumped high in the air then launched herself off the raft, cannonball style, and a wall of water sprayed high.

Nick's heart pounded. She'd surface any minute. He'd jumped off rafts in this lake when he was younger than Emma. Cat and Georgia had too, but they'd all been strong swimmers.

"Nick?" Kylie's gaze met his. Her lashes were spiky from the water, and her face was white.

"Wait on the beach. Don't move unless I tell you."

Her pointed chin jerked in agreement. He had to go after Emma. Mia's daughter needed him.

He stripped off his shirt and tossed it onto the sand, together with his phone, wallet, and keys. Surfacing from a shallow dive, he slipped into a fast crawl, the rhythm instinctive, and he reached the raft seconds later.

Still no Emma. Nick scanned the lake then dove under the water. It was cloudy from mud on the bottom, and he rubbed a hand across his eyes. His lungs burned and he surfaced again to gulp in air before he went back under.

One of his knees knocked the chain that anchored the raft to the lake bed.

Emma's swimsuit was caught on the rusty chain, and blood trickled down the side of her face.

He tugged on her swimsuit strap before he tore the top off. Swinging her over his shoulder, he battled to the surface and maneuvered Emma into a rescue hold before he struck out for shore.

"My cell, call nine-one-one," he yelled at Kylie, but she already had the phone at her ear.

Emma was a dead weight, and she wasn't breathing. He took one stroke after another until his feet caught the lake bottom and he stood, staggered to the beach, and put Emma on her back.

He had to do CPR. Which he knew, thanks to the lifeguard qualification he'd earned as a teenager.

"Breathe, sweetheart." Nick pressed Emma's tiny chest and counted.

"I said it was an emergency." Kylie's voice was high and reedy. "The ambulance is on the way."

Nick nodded, still counting, before he put his mouth to Emma's and willed her to breathe.

Kylie crouched beside him. "She'll be okay, won't she?"

Nick couldn't answer. The world telescoped to counting, watching Emma's chest and then counting some more.

Emma coughed and struggled to sit, then flopped back on the sand, her eyes unfocused.

"Emma." Nick pushed hair away from her face where a jagged cut oozed blood across her forehead. "It's me, Nick. You're okay." At least he prayed she was. He couldn't face Mia if anything happened to her baby girl.

He was the one who'd offered to take the girls to the beach. Why hadn't he chosen the diner or the bowling alley? Anywhere but here.

Emma blinked. "Nick?"

"Yeah." He grabbed a towel and covered her then pressed his shirt to her forehead in an effort to stop the bleeding.

"I want my mommy." Emma coughed again then threw up lake water.

"She'll be here any minute." He inclined his head to Kylie. "Run and get Mia and then wait for the ambulance out front so they know where we are."

"Mommy," Emma said again. "I'm cold."

"Here, sweetheart." Nick grabbed another towel and piled it on top of the first one.

"What's wrong? What happened?"

Nick looked at Mia partway down the steps to the lake.

"My baby." She made a high, keening noise and ran the short distance to the beach.

"I did CPR. Emma's breathing. She jumped off the swim raft and—"

"Baby girl..." Mia's voice cracked, and she knelt on the sand beside Nick to gather Emma into her arms.

"Don't move her. The ambulance is on its way."

"It's my fault. I wanted to show Kylie and—" Emma coughed again, a raspy sound that twisted Nick's insides, and more water came up.

"Hush. It's okay. You don't need explain." Mia pressed the shirt harder to her daughter's forehead. "You'll be fine, Emma bear." Her worried gaze met Nick's in a silent plea. "I couldn't sleep so I came outside and saw you here. And Emma..."

"I'll uh..." Kylie twisted her hands.

Nick glanced at her. Kylie's lips were blue, and shivers wracked her small body. "You were great." He took the last towel and wrapped it around her. "You didn't panic, and you did what I told you to. Good job."

Her eyes widened.

"Kylie?" Emma looked up. "I'm sorry. I said mean things to you and I shouldn't have."

"It's okay." Kylie dug a bare toe in the sand. "I better go meet the paramedics. I can get Emma some clothes."

"Thank you." Mia raised her head. "Thank you both." Her gaze lingered on Nick. "If you hadn't known what to do, it could have...she could have..."

"She didn't." He touched Emma's hair. The strands were heavy with water, and near her temples blood matted with mud. "You get some clothes for yourself too, Kylie. We don't want you to catch cold."

"Sure." Kylie turned toward the steps, her shoulders hunched. "Emma, she has to go to the hospital." She turned back to Nick, and he read the fear in her face.

"She'll come home again, Kylie. I promise." Her brother had gone to a hospital and hadn't come back. From what Kylie's social worker had said, maybe her mom hadn't either. She'd been strung out on heroin, bleeding from a knife wound, and her daughter, who'd witnessed everything, had been taken into care again, permanently this time.

Kylie held his gaze for a long moment before she turned, skipped up the steps, and disappeared into the trees.

Across Emma's body, Nick took Mia's free hand. "I'm sorry. It's all my fault. I brought the girls here. I didn't think."

"I didn't either. Emma's always been sensible around water. But she...you went in the lake after her, and since the accident you—"

He squeezed her hand tight. "Your little girl was in there, hurt. I'd have searched the whole lake to find her if I had to.

"Nick?" Emma blinked at him. "It isn't your fault. It's mine. I didn't listen, and I was mean to you, too." Her voice came out in a croak. "Even meaner than I was to Kylie."

"You didn't say anything worse than I said to people when I was older than you, and old enough to know better." His throat tightened.

"I'm really sorry. Sorry about everything." Emma's hand cupped his on top of Mia's. "It's okay if you and my mom are friends."

"Thanks." The one word was all Nick could manage. His gaze met Mia's, and the man he was shifted and changed.

Except, Mia was beautiful and sweet, and she'd rebuilt her life. She deserved a better man than him. A man who wasn't afraid to love.

Emma's grip on his hand tightened. Mia also deserved a man who could be a father to her girls, and who'd stick around Firefly Lake longer than he ever planned to.

Chapter Fourteen

Two days later, Mia pushed an empty trunk aside and sat on the shallow seat beneath one of the attic windows in Harbor House. Rain tapped against the glass, and she traced the pattern of drops with her index finger.

The lake was choppy today, a pewter gray dotted with whitecaps. She shivered as she remembered what might have been. But Emma was safe and, for the first time in a long time, life was good. Not perfect. In this new life she'd given up on perfect, but good was more than enough.

Turning away from the window, she stretched, and her T-shirt rode up over the top of her cotton skirt. Thanks to Nick's help, she only had a few more boxes to go through and the attic would be cleared out. She'd be one step closer to finishing her work in Gabrielle's house. And one step closer to when Nick would leave Firefly Lake. Although he hadn't mentioned a date, Labor Day was coming up, and he'd always said he planned to leave after the long weekend.

She had to stop fantasizing about him and wondering what if.

The attic door creaked open, followed by footsteps on the plank stairs. "Mia?" Nick appeared at the top of the stairs and ducked his head until he reached the middle of the big room away from the eaves. "Mom said you were still here."

Her heart somersaulted. All this time she'd tried to pretend she only cared for Nick as a friend, but when he saved Emma's life, feelings she'd tried to deny had surfaced. New and scary feelings she'd never, in all their years together, had for Jay.

"Hi." She tugged one of the remaining boxes toward her, and a cloud of dust floated in the air between them.

"Let me give you a hand." Nick lifted the box onto the trunk and leaned in close to give her a quick kiss. He lifted the flaps on the box to reveal Christmas decorations. "Mom never threw anything away, did she?" He fingered a cardboard angel. "I made this for her one year in elementary school."

"When kids make you things, it's special. You keep them forever."

"I wouldn't know." His voice was flat. "My niece has never been a crafty kid."

Mia propped the angel on the window seat and straightened her tinsel halo. "Your mom's doing crafts with the girls, and Kylie's really into it. When I stuck my head into the dining room earlier, she was decked out in sequins, purple felt, and feathers. She told me she's making a surprise for you, so you better act surprised."

Nick picked up the angel then put it down again. "I missed all that. I came in through the kitchen with the contractor. He can start on the main floor bathroom tomorrow. Mom's already picked out paint colors and tile, as well as a tub and shower stall. He's also updating the existing powder room so it will be more convenient for Mom."

"What you're doing so she can stay in the home she loves is good."

Gabrielle had gotten what she wanted, so why didn't Mia feel better about it?

"You were right. I hadn't listened to Mom, but compromising isn't as hard as I thought it would be." Nick gave her a dry smile.

"So why won't you open your heart to Kylie? Her heart's wide open to you."

Nick's smile disappeared. "She'll have a new family soon. Kim approved Kylie to stay with you and Mom for what, five days tops? I don't want to unsettle her."

"Don't you think never seeing you again, never even hearing from you again, will unsettle Kylie even more?" Mia took three more angels out of the box, porcelain ones this time.

"Kylie's a kid. She'll forget all about me." There was a catch in Nick's voice as he turned away.

"She's twelve. That's old enough to remember summer camp and the first father figure who made her feel special. A man who showed her all men aren't like her mother's deadbeat boyfriends." Mia remembered exactly what it was like to be twelve, and how she'd vowed to never marry a man like her dad.

"What if Kylie does remember? I can't be part of her life." Nick bent his head over one of the angels and tightened his jaw.

"Why not?"

"That's not the kind of guy I am. I can't change because Kylie's got some crazy idea in her head."

"You mean because she thinks you're a hero?"

"Exactly." Nick raised his head and his expression was blank. "I'd forgotten about these angels. Mémère Brassard gave them to my sisters and me one Christmas. They came from her family in Quebec."

Typical Nick. Whenever Mia or anyone else got too close to something he didn't want to talk about, he shut down, changed the subject, or both.

"This one's yours." Mia turned the angel over and pointed to his name on the base in a spidery script. "You should take it back to New York with you."

Nick's expression softened. "I want you to have it. Someday you can give it to Emma."

"It's a family heirloom. You should keep it. Maybe you'll have children to share it with."

"No, take it. I like you and I...care about you, so when you look at it, remember..." He stopped and dug in the box for tissue.

"I care about you, too." After years of trying to live up to Jay's expectations and never meeting them, Nick had accepted her for who and what she was and helped restore her faith in herself.

"Hey." Nick set the tissue paper aside. "What is it?"

"I was thinking about Emma," she lied.

"She'll be fine. Remember what the doctor said? In a few days she'll be back to normal. If she has a scar, it'll fade and be covered by her hair anyway."

"I could have lost her, and you..."

"I'm the reason she was at the beach in the first place."

His voice was gruff. "I'm surprised you aren't mad at me. I'm mad at myself. I can't forgive myself for what happened."

"You have to. If it's anybody's fault, it was Emma's." Mia worried her lip. Jay had berated her for letting Emma go to the beach with Nick. He refused to admit Emma had made a mistake and laid the blame for the accident solely on Nick's shoulders.

"Emma must have had a guardian angel watching over her. Which is all the more reason you should keep Mémère's angel for her."

"Thank you."

Nick smiled at her, and Mia's heart caught at the sweetness of it and the way it warmed his eyes.

"Mémère would have liked Emma. She was a spunky old lady, and she admired that quality in others."

"Emma's spunky all right." Mia wrapped the angel and set it aside. "I think she finally understands Jay and I won't get back together. She's talking to me again more like she used to, but it's still hard for her." And it was hard for Mia not to give her daughter what Emma wanted most.

"It'll be hard for a long time, but you're a good mom and you'll help Emma through." Nick traced the curve of Mia's cheek.

"Jay's still moving to California, but with the mess he's gotten himself into with Tiffany, he seems to have dropped the idea of wanting the girls there." And Mia hadn't mentioned it, grateful for the sudden business trip to Atlanta that had taken him away from Firefly Lake the day after Emma's accident.

"What if he changes his mind again?"

"The girls and I will still stay here. Emma and I talked about how when you make a commitment, you stick to it." Except when that commitment was to someone who broke it as often as Jay had.

"She's okay with that?"

"Not entirely." Mia's breath hitched as Nick's finger touched the sensitive spot on her neck. "All Emma sees is a California move would mean she'd get the pony Jay promised her, but I think she understands some of how I feel. At least as much as a girl her age can. Even in California, Emma wouldn't see much of Jay because he travels all the time, and she'd have to compete with Riley for his attention."

"Mmm." Nick's hand reached the neckline of her T-shirt.

Mia wiggled away from his sinful touch. "We can't, not here, your mother—"

"Never comes up to the attic." His hand slipped lower to graze her breast. "Besides, I locked the door behind me." He fingered the hem of her skirt and, in one quick motion, slid his hand under it. His touch was warm on her bare thigh.

"Stop." But even as she protested, Mia's breathing sped up, and she reached for the button on his polo shirt.

"Say it like you mean it." With his other hand, Nick eased her toward the wall as he rained kisses along her jaw.

"I do mean it." Mia's back hit the wall with a gentle thud.

Nick's laugh was low and sexy. "No, you don't. You want this as much as I do. All I can think about is being inside you again. Not being able to touch you is driving me crazy."

Like it was driving her crazy. "Nick, I..." He tugged on her panties, and she arched against his hand.

He captured her mouth in a blistering kiss, sensuality mixed with the subtle sweetness of the maple sugar cookies she'd baked earlier.

Although she wasn't about to admit it, she'd never had sex anywhere but in a bed and never been anything but conventional. "I...uh..."

The faint echo of the bells from the church at the bottom of the hill blended with the rasp of the zipper on his jeans. He pulled off her panties, and she gasped as cooler hair hit her skin.

"Nick." His name came out in a moan. "We have to be quick. And quiet."

"I can be quick." He undid his belt one-handed and continued his sensuous exploration. He slipped one finger inside her, then another to stretch, twist, and intensify the sensation. "And I can be very, very quiet."

Mia's head lolled against the wall. "Don't stop," she whispered as she gave in to his touch and the sensations he aroused.

"I won't. I've only gotten started." He dropped to his knees. And gave her a whole lot more to fantasize about.

From the home team's bench beside Firefly Lake's ball diamond, Nick scanned the crowd and zeroed in again on the little group in the front row of the stands. Naomi and Emma flanked Mia, who was in jeans, a white T-shirt, and red flats. Kylie sat between his mom and Ward, and Pixie was perched on Kylie's lap. When she spotted him, Kylie waved and then stuck two fingers in her mouth and whistled.

Mia glanced at Kylie before she waved at Nick, too. The setting sun turned her hair russet brown, and although he'd seen a lot of women in his life, women dressed for work in sharp suits and killer heels, and women dressed to impress in thigh-high dresses with plunging necklines, in her simple outfit, Mia was the most beautiful woman he'd ever seen.

The crowd erupted into cheers, and Nick tore his gaze away from the stands to look back at the field in time to see Ty slide home.

"Good one." Nick tossed Ty a towel.

"Thanks." Ty's face was red and his chest heaved beneath a Firefly Lake Eagles baseball shirt as he dropped to the bench beside Nick and mopped his forehead. "Even without Dad, we still won."

Nick slapped Ty's back. "Your dad's not the only good ball player. You earned your place on the men's team tonight."

Ty grinned and grabbed a bottle of water before scanning the stands in his turn. "That Kylie's sure something else. Mia took all of us out for creemees to celebrate Naomi's belated birthday, and from how Kylie went on, you'd think soft ice cream drizzled with maple syrup was better than Disney World." He waved at Naomi.

Nick lifted his sports bag onto his shoulder and his good mood slipped. He'd talked to Kylie's social worker earlier, and her new family could take her in forty-eight hours. A wake-up call to stop pretending his life over the past week was something it wasn't. With Kylie, as well as with Mia and her girls.

"The doctor says Dad and Charlie can bring Lexie

home in a few days." Ty fell into step beside Nick and headed toward Naomi, like a homing pigeon. "My mom traded weeks with Dad so I can stay here and help Lexie get settled. I bought her this elephant toy like I had when I was little. What did you get her?"

"A bond. It's never too soon to start to save for college." He was a practical guy, but he hadn't wanted to go into a store and be surrounded by baby things, had he?

"For real? Money's fine and all, but you have to get her something else. Naomi helped me pick out my gift and wrap it. Girls are good at stuff like that. Maybe Mia can help you. Since you two are friends...and everything." The tips of Ty's ears reddened.

The kid might play ball with the men, but it didn't mean he was one of them. The friends with benefits thing, or whatever was between him and Mia, was none of Ty's business. "I can pick out something else for Lexie, no problem." That's what online shopping was for.

Nick's heartbeat sped up as Mia came across the field. She smiled when he met her halfway, like he was her man, and her T-shirt hugged those little breasts he loved to touch. While he'd never been a big fan of flat shoes, the red ones with bows on the toes were as sexy as any of the heels she usually wore.

"Great game." Her smile included Ty. "Your mom and Ward have invited all of us for milkshakes at Simard's Creamery store."

He should say no. He should put up some of those barriers he planned to, but it was only milkshakes. "Sounds good."

The full force of Mia's smile turned on him, and Nick slipped a little more into something with her. Something he didn't want to put a label on but he'd felt for a while, which had intensified after they'd been together in his mom's attic. When he'd been as close to her as a man could get to a woman, and he'd looked into her eyes and the raw emotion there had winded him and ripped a protective strip off his heart.

"Mom?" Emma's pink sneakers pounded into the dry grass of the ball diamond as she darted toward them. "Did you tell Nick?" Her blue eyes sparkled, open and friendly again.

"I haven't had a chance." A flush crept over Mia's cheeks.

Emma let out a breath and turned to Nick. "You know the article about us in the *Kincaid Examiner*?"

"Yeah." Nick tensed. The front page article had made him out to be some kind of hero. Which he wasn't.

Emma skipped, and the ruffles on her pink top caught the breeze. "The principal at Firefly Lake Elementary read it and remembered Mom was on the sub list. One of the music teachers is really sick and just got signed off, and since school starts soon, the principal hired Mom to fill in until next spring."

"Congratulations." Nick stretched his mouth into a smile. The job was perfect for Mia. Of course he was happy for her. Except, it was another reminder she had a life and roots here, while he didn't.

Mia patted his arm. Her touch was gentle and right, like coming home after a long day, but not to any home he'd ever had. "The principal only interviewed me this afternoon. It was last minute, and there's a lot of paperwork before the offer's official. I'll still start off as a substitute teacher. Emma got a bit ahead of herself."

"It's good news." He studied Mia's face as Emma ran back to his mom.

"The best." Mia's smile was so sweet and full of affection his heart ached. "Although I'm sorry the regular teacher is sick, this job is more security for the girls and me, and to be in the same school every day until next year is a dream come true."

Nick looked at his baseball shoes. "I'm happy for you."

"I lost sight of what I wanted for a while, but I've found it again." She stood on tiptoe and kissed his cheek. "Thank you."

"For what?"

"For being my friend and helping me remember what I wanted."

As Mia talked, unfamiliar emotions churned through Nick, and his heart pounded more than it had when he'd rounded third base and headed for home as the crowd cheered. "Sorry, what did you say?"

"Are you okay to walk to the creamery store from here? It looked like you twisted your knee when you slid into third base on that home run."

She'd noticed and was concerned for him. "It was nothing."

"You limped when you walked across the field. Do you need an ice pack?"

"I already iced my knee. I'm good." His breath caught at the tenderness in her face.

"I know you're good," she murmured, even though Ty had gone ahead with Naomi, and his mom and Ward were with Emma and Kylie. "But I still think we should take my car and meet the others there." Mia licked her bottom lip, slow and teasing, and Nick went from soft to hard in a second.

He glanced at the bulge in his tight baseball uniform and shifted his sports bag, but not before her mouth quirked in amusement. "You see what you do to me, angel?"

"Me?" She gave him a naughty grin before she called to Emma that she'd see her at the creamery in ten minutes and then dug in her bag for her car keys.

"Yes, you." He pulled her close and caught his mom's smile of approval. He liked how Mia's head fit into the curve of his shoulder. He liked lots of things about her, especially sex with her, but most of all he liked the way she got him, at least the parts he'd chosen to share.

"Nick?" She stopped by her blue Honda. "What is it? Should I take you to the hospital to get your knee checked out?"

He let out a breath as sexual desire faded. "It's not my knee." For the first time in a long time he needed to talk to someone, and maybe Mia would understand. "My dad got in touch. He wants to catch up."

"Will you?" Mia slid into the driver's seat, and Nick got in on the passenger side and tossed his bag onto the seat behind.

"No." Nick's body tensed. "He walked out on Mom and us kids. He sent money, sure, but he never wanted anything to do with us." Apart from once. He'd come to the hospital after the accident and stayed until Nick told the doctor to make him leave. "He's more than twenty-five years too late."

"If you talked, maybe you could make peace. I never had a chance with my dad. He had a massive heart attack and died before he even got to the hospital. Although I don't think I could ever have forgiven him for how he treated my mom and Charlie and me, it would have been easier to let it go if we'd talked."

"My sisters can talk to him if they want, but I won't. After what he did, even his parents never spoke to him again, so why should I?"

"It's your choice." Mia's brown eyes were tender and wise. "But you don't want to regret anything." She started the car, and her hair fell forward to hide her face.

"No regrets." Except in name, he wasn't Brian McGuire's son. He'd left that guy behind long ago.

Nick leaned back in the seat and angled his knee in front of him as the car bumped along the rough track to the road. Mia hadn't given him the answer he wanted. She hadn't assured him it was the right thing to not contact his dad.

Instead, she made him want to be the kind of man who didn't fail at relationships and who wasn't so afraid of loss he could take a risk and let himself love again.

The kind of man who could head back to New York without regrets.

Chapter Fifteen

Mia paced the flagstone path around Gabrielle's rose garden for the fourth time, all thirty steps of it, as Pixie ambled beside her. Where was Jay? He'd promised to have Naomi and Emma back straight after lunch, a brief visit on his way from New York to Dallas.

Pixie flopped in the shade under a tree, and Mia breathed in the scent of the roses, heavy in the warmth of the August afternoon. Harbor House drowsed in the sunshine, solid and safe. Gabrielle stuck her head out of an upstairs window and waved. Mia shook her head in answer to the older woman's unspoken question.

She checked her cell for the tenth time in five minutes. No message.

A car door slammed, and Mia turned toward the house as Jay and the girls came through the side gate. After he hugged them and they disappeared into the house, he came across the patio and down the steps to the garden to meet Mia by a white rose of Sharon bush.

"Don't you need to catch a flight?" Her palms got clammy.

"Yes, but I need to talk to you first without the girls around."

Her heartbeat sped up. "What about?"

"I want us to get back together." His voice was firm, decisive.

"What?" The words reverberated in her head and sunlight gilded his features. A golden god who'd turned out to have feet of clay. How had she ever loved this man and given him almost twenty years of her life?

"I want to marry you again and be a real father to the girls." Jay took a step forward, and Pixie got up from under the tree to sit at Mia's feet.

"You're the one who left and who wanted the divorce. You're the one who said you didn't love me anymore." Mia's throat burned as bile rose. "What about Tiffany? And the baby?"

"Tiffany and I...it's over." Jay's hair had thinned on top. He shifted from one foot to the other. "I'll support baby Riley, of course, but Tiffany's young, too young."

Mia crossed her arms over her chest. "You dumped me and destroyed our family and all of a sudden you come here and say you think we should get back together? No."

Jay gave her the easy smile she'd fallen for back in college. As if all he had to do was snap his fingers and she'd run to him. "I didn't handle things right before. Of course you wouldn't move to California by yourself, but if we're a family again, where better to have a fresh start? I've already sounded out Naomi and Emma, and they're all for it."

"Even Naomi?" Mia forced the words out as heat flashed through her body.

Jay hesitated for a fraction of a second. "Sure. I told her Ty can come visit." He gave her that smile again, urging her to believe him, trust him. "Of course, once she's in a new school with new friends, she'll forget all about him."

"If you think Naomi would forget Ty so fast you should talk to your daughter and listen to her. As for you and me, we're over. There's no way I'll move to California."

"I made a big mistake and I'm sorry. Maybe it was one of those midlife crisis things or stress. You know how stressful my job is." Jay reached for her and his tone was coaxing. "Come on, babe, you have to believe me. You and the girls are the best things in my life. Tiffany's a great girl, but she's not you."

"No." Mia picked up Pixie to evade his touch. "I've got a new life here, my life, and you can't walk in and take it away."

Not even if he was sorry. The word he'd never said before. The word that might once have made a difference.

"You don't want to let people down. I finally get it, okay?" Jay took another step forward, and Mia took one back. "We'll commute for a while. You can finish the work for Gabrielle and teach here until Christmas and move to California then. Emma's still young so changing schools midyear won't hurt her. As for Naomi, I talked to that boarding school and they can take her last minute. There's a uniform so you'd have to—"

"No boarding school for Naomi, ever. You didn't listen to anything I said. If you had, you—"

"Okay, forget the boarding school for now." Jay gave her the look of love she'd once been powerless to resist. "You're the most important person in my life. Without you, everything's meaningless. I need you."

"You think you need me. But you don't, not really. I don't need you either. Not anymore."

To her surprise, it was true. She couldn't go back to the woman she once was, even if she'd wanted to. Although it hadn't seemed that way at the time, Jay had done her a favor. She was stronger now, more powerful, and it felt good.

"It's Nick McGuire, isn't it?" Jay's blue gaze narrowed, and his smile slipped. "You're sleeping with him."

"That's none of your business."

Pixie quivered in Mia's arms, and she stroked the dog's head.

"If he's around my daughters, it sure is my business." Jay's voice held a sneer. "He was with Emma when she had her accident."

"We've already been through this." Mia made her voice calm. "Emma had the accident because she went too far out in the lake, even though Nick told her not to. He apologized for taking her to the beach, but I said he could so it's as much my fault as his. If Nick hadn't been there and known CPR, Emma would've died."

"Still, he—"

"It was a mistake, but it's not as if you haven't made mistakes with the girls. Remember when you took Naomi to the park and she jumped off the top of the slide and broke her arm? You didn't expect a four-year-old to jump from such a height. Like I never expected Emma to ignore an adult who told her to stay close to shore."

"Point taken." Jay's smile was sulky. "But what about that Kylie the girls told me about? Nick's mixed up with her, and what kind of influence is she?"

"Kylie's a girl in foster care. She needed help for a few

days, and Nick and I, as well as his mom, met with her so-cial worker as part of a risk assessment. If we hadn't said we'd look after Kylie, the social worker was convinced she'd run away, and who knows what would have hap-pened to her." Mia tightened her grip on Pixie's collar. "I want to make a positive difference in a child's life, and it's good for the girls to see not everyone's as fortunate as they are."

"They can help out at a food bank or a senior center. A girl like Kylie shouldn't live in the same house as my daughters or share Emma's room."

"Naomi and Emma are my daughters, too, and I'd never put them at risk. Besides, Harbor House is Gabrielle's home. Kylie's only here temporarily, as Gabrielle's guest, because her social worker requested it."

"You always were too soft-hearted." Jay's mouth flat-tened into a hard line. "You're naïve too, because all a man like Nick's after is sex."

"Which you'd know all about, wouldn't you? You never wanted to have sex with me after Emma was born." Mia spoke through stiff lips. "You'd never go for couples' counseling either, even though I begged you."

"I wasn't the one with the problem." Jay kicked a low-hanging rose of Sharon branch.

"You never understood. You weren't there for Emma's birth, so you didn't see how hard it was. I needed time but—"

"The doctor said you were fine."

"Physically maybe, but…" Mia stopped. She'd needed tenderness and gentleness, patience and under-standing. Everything that wasn't in Jay to give.

"You were frigid." He tossed the word at her. The

one he'd always used to describe what he called her "problem."

Except, it didn't wound her like it had before.

"This conversation is over."

Pixie growled and showed sharp little teeth.

"I have to get to the airport, but this conversation isn't over." Jay turned and crushed several blossoms under one polished shoe. "I've apologized and admitted I was wrong. What more can I do? I want you back, Amelia. I want our family back. If you won't agree to come back to me, I'll fight you for full custody of the girls."

"You . . . you wouldn't." Mia's voice caught.

Pixie growled again, louder this time.

"Try me." Jay raised his hand, and Mia flinched and backed away. He held his hand poised for several seconds before he dropped it back at his side.

"You travel so much for work, and you always said you didn't want Naomi and Emma full time. Although we make decisions about the girls' upbringing together, you agreed they would live with me here. Vacation visits were all you ever wanted."

"I want the four of us to be a family again." Jay's smile didn't reach his eyes. "I'll do whatever it takes to make that happen."

"What if I don't want that family?" Mia set Pixie on a flagstone, but the dog stayed close beside her and yipped.

"You always wanted a family. You never wanted anything but a family." He dug in a pocket of his navy chinos and fished out the keys to his rental car. "From what people say about Nick McGuire, he's not a family man."

Jay walked away across the grass with the swagger Mia hated, and flower blossoms fluttered in his wake.

Jay was right about one thing. She'd always wanted a family, but she and the girls were that family, and she'd fight with all she had to keep the three of them together and safe. She wouldn't let him control her again, either.

From the driveway, Jay's car started. Pixie growled then barked.

Mia stared at the dog for a long beat. "You looked out for me, didn't you? You wanted to protect me." Four pounds of fur might not be fierce, but Pixie was on her side.

Like Nick. He'd be on her side, too. But did she have the courage to trust him? Maybe the real question was if she had the courage to trust herself and trust what she wanted along with her family.

"Mom?" Nick came through the side door of Harbor House with a can of paint in one hand and a dropcloth in the other. He scanned the empty kitchen before he moved into the hall.

"In here." His mom's voice was muffled.

Nick went into the dining room. "What's wrong?" She sat at one end of the long table and rested her chin in her hands.

"Nothing." She tried to smile as she ran a finger over the cover of one of her sketchbooks. "I'm fine."

"You don't look fine." Nick set the painting supplies on the floor and sat on the chair beside hers.

Her face was pale and drawn.

"Should I call your doctor?"

"No." She flipped the sketchbook open and rifled through pages.

"These are good." Nick took the book from her. Her

usual delicate watercolors of flowers and the Vermont landscape were juxtaposed with abstract sketches and bold arcs of color across the page.

His mom took the book back. "I tried something different but..." Her throat worked, and she touched the soft wisps of hair against her jaw.

"Is it Ward?" If the guy had hurt her, Nick would make him pay.

Her blue eyes filled with tears. "He flies back to Seattle tonight. He had to leave all of a sudden because something came up with work." She dabbed at her eyes with a tissue. "He said he'd come back as soon as he could so we could talk, but I told him he shouldn't and I don't think..."

"Ah, Mom." Nick wrapped his arms around his mother's shoulders where the bones protruded.

"After your father, I can't..." Her chest heaved. "Besides, I can't ask a man like Ward to tie himself to a sick woman."

"You're not sick." Nick held her close. "You were sick, but you're fine."

"For how long?"

"Don't even think that. All through your treatment you were so positive. You fought so hard."

"I didn't want to worry you and your sisters any more than you already were." His mom sniffed and pulled another tissue out of the box on the table. "I'm still fighting and I'm still positive, but sometimes the disease gets you anyway. It's not fair to ask Ward to deal with all that, a man I only met a few weeks ago who doesn't even live here."

"Shouldn't that be his choice? When I was growing up,

you always said go after what you want, no matter what. Don't let anyone stop you. Do you want me to go after him?"

"No, you won't go after Ward." She gave him the ghost of a smile and tapped his hand with the sketchbook. "I never expected to have any of you kids give my advice back to me."

"It was good advice."

"Maybe he doesn't want me. Maybe work was an excuse and he was glad to leave." Her shoulders drooped.

"Ward's crazy about you."

"Nicolas." She said the name in the French way, and her cheeks went pink.

"Well, he is. Mia said so, too. I bet she'd tell you to at least email him and explain."

"Has Mia called you?" His mom's eyes got a worried expression.

Nick tensed. "No. She had to do some things to get ready for school while Jay took the girls out for lunch. Why?"

"Jay dropped the girls off a while ago, and then he talked to Mia in the garden." His mom twisted her hands together. "I didn't mean to spy on them, but I happened to look out my bedroom window and see his face. He scared me. I think he scared Mia. The way he raised his hand..."

Nick shoved the chair back and got to his feet. "Where did she go?"

"Upstairs to talk to the girls, and then they all left in her car." His mom's hand shook as she gathered watercolor pencils into a holder. "Kylie's watching a movie in the living room, but Mia didn't stop to talk to either of us."

"I'm sure everything's fine." Nick wasn't sure at all,

but he didn't want his mom to worry. "You and Kylie stay here, and I'll go look for them."

"Where would they go? Sean and Ty are finishing the new kitchen at Mia's house today."

"I have an idea."

"I called Mia and it went straight to voice mail." She stood and squeezed his arm. "You try, too."

"I will." But if he knew Mia like he thought he did, she'd gone underground. No calls or text messages. He squeezed his mom's arm back before he released her and fumbled in his pocket for his phone. "I'll call you as soon as I find out anything."

"You'll go after what you want?" His mom eyed him, as sharp and knowing as ever. "Promise me?"

"I'll make sure Mia and the girls are okay."

He couldn't go after what he wanted. Because what he wanted, he couldn't let himself have.

Nick left Harbor House at a jog and scrolled to Allison's number on his phone. If Jay had threatened Mia, he needed to get Allison onto the situation fast. After he left her a message to call him ASAP, he jumped in the truck he'd borrowed from Sean to haul painting supplies around and headed for Lake Road, out of town.

Fifteen minutes later, he pulled into the driveway at Camp Rainbow and cut the engine. There was no sign of Mia's car in the empty parking lot, and the buildings were shuttered because the staff and all the campers had gone home. He got out of the truck and circled around the cottage on foot to the lake.

Mia sat on the end of the dock, with her back to him, her head resting on her knees.

Nick pulled out his phone but, as if she sensed his

presence, Mia turned. He caught his breath at the expression on her face. A mix of loss, despair, and fierce determination.

He moved across the strip of beach to the dock. "I thought I'd find you out here."

"Did Charlie tell you where I was?" Mia hugged her bare knees below a pair of black shorts that showed off those endless legs Nick couldn't stop thinking about.

"No, I haven't talked to Charlie. Are Naomi and Emma with her?" He toed off his shoes and socks, rolled up his pant legs, and sat beside Mia to dangle his feet in the cold water.

"With her and Lexie. I told Charlie I needed some time by myself. She understood."

"Mom said Jay came by the house." Nick battled to keep the anger out of his voice.

"He said if I didn't come back to him and give our marriage another chance, he'd fight me for full custody of Naomi and Emma."

Nick made a fist. "That's a threat."

"It sure sounds like it." Her voice was devoid of emotion.

"Did he hit you?" Nick held his breath.

"No, but I thought... he looked like he wanted to. If we hadn't been in your mom's garden... maybe... I've never seen him so angry." She stared at the water as if she didn't see it.

"What will you do?" Nick relaxed his fist.

"I've already called Allison."

"Good for you." His heart resumed its normal beat.

"I don't know if Jay's serious, but I can't take any chances." Mia's dark eyes were bleak.

"You won't go back to him?" Nick fought the urge to wrap his arms around her, hold on tight, and never let go.

"Even if getting back together with Jay was right for Naomi and Emma, it's not right for me." A sad smile curved Mia's mouth. "It's not right for the girls, either."

The pressure in Nick's chest loosened. He had no long-term claim on Mia, but, for reasons he didn't want to examine, he didn't want Jay to have any such claim either. "He doesn't deserve you."

"No, he doesn't. He lied to me, cheated on me, and betrayed his daughters and what our family stood for. I tried to convince myself he'd change, although he never did. But I changed, and I can't go back to the woman I was when I was with him."

Nick squeezed her hand. "You stood up to him. I'm proud of you."

"I'm proud of me, too, but I'm also scared. I came out here to think because it's a link with my mom. This cottage is the place she loved most in the world. She came here from Montreal with her parents when she was a child, but Dad... she was so unhappy with him he spoiled this place for her. Even though I didn't plan on it, I married a man just like my dad."

"That's the past."

"Yes, but until Jay left me, I never believed I had choices. He said all I ever wanted was a family." Her gaze locked with Nick's, her expression firm. "Jay's right. I did want a family. I still do, but I only had one idea of what a family was, what a family could be, or what I could be."

"And now?" Nick held his breath. Even Jay's name made him angry.

"I've got my family. My girls, and Charlie, Lexie, and Sean are my family. I moved to Firefly Lake because I thought Charlie needed me, but I need her even more. And although I didn't realize it until today, I need this place. It's a special part of my mom and her family, and it'll always be a part of me and my girls."

Nick hadn't needed Firefly Lake or Vermont. He'd broken away from his home, family, and friends when he went to college, and until last year, he'd never looked back. But he needed Mia, more than he'd ever needed any other woman. And maybe, like her, he needed this place with its memories and roots both good and bad.

He looped one arm around Mia's shoulders and pulled her close. "Allison will handle Jay. It's the kind of challenge she thrives on. After she crushes him under those spiky heels of hers, you won't ever have to worry again. I bet she even skewers him for more child support while she's at it."

Mia's eyes widened. "She seems so nice."

"You haven't seen Allison in court. When she's on a mission for justice, grown men cower like little boys." Nick laughed then sobered. "I...I..."

"What?" Mia nestled closer to envelop him in the scent of the north woods and floral shampoo. She was tender, trusting, sexy, and so sweet his heart twisted, and his desire for her became mixed with something that felt an awful lot like love.

"If Jay ever threatens you again, or if he even raises a little finger to you, call Allison or me anytime, day or night. We can slap him with a temporary relief from abuse order so fast he won't know what hit him."

Which wasn't what Nick wanted to say, but he needed

to put the brakes on until he figured out how to handle these new feelings for her.

"Thank you." A faint flush stained Mia's cheeks.

He dropped a gentle kiss into her hair. He wanted her in all the ways it was possible for a man to want a woman. Body and mind, heart and soul. But friends with benefits was what he'd said he wanted, and what she'd agreed to.

Except, it wasn't what he wanted after all. Mia wasn't the only one who'd changed. If she wasn't the woman she'd been before, he wasn't the guy he'd once been either.

Chapter Sixteen

Nick respected her. Mia read the truth in his eyes. More important, though, she respected herself in a way she hadn't back when she'd been the girl who sat by this lake for hours and whiled away the endless summer days with fashion magazines and books she'd borrowed from the library in town.

He kicked up a spray of water and splashed her shorts.

"Hey." Mia scrambled to her feet. "Charlie will think I fell in."

"A wet T-shirt look would be real sexy on you."

"In your dreams. If I go into this lake, I'm taking you with me." She stood with her hands on her hips and gave him a mock glare. "And those pants of yours look like dry-clean only."

"I went straight from the office to Mom's. Since I was worried about you, I didn't stop to change." He pulled her into his big body, and his smile warmed her inside and out. "The past few weeks have been good."

"Yeah, they have." She ran a hand along the dark stubble on his jaw.

"I'm still going back to New York after Labor Day, but there's no reason we can't keep on seeing each other. I'll visit my mom, and you can come to the city. Mom would love to have the girls stay."

Mia curled her toes into the edge of the dock, where the wood was wet and slippery. She didn't want to lose Nick's friendship, but she wanted more. "You mean we could see each other on weekends?"

"Sure." He gave an awkward laugh. "I'll miss you. You're one of the best friends I've ever had."

He was one of the best friends she'd ever had, too, but friendship was only one part of everything else she felt for him. "Nick, I…"

"Don't answer right away." His breath was warm at her temple. "Think about it."

"Okay."

She wanted to say yes, but she had to be true to herself. Despite Nick's reassurance, what if Jay took the girls from her? What if he twisted her relationship with Nick to depict her as a bad mother? Naomi and Emma were already churned up about what they wanted and clutching at straws that, like Humpty Dumpty, their fractured family would somehow fit together again.

Nick cleared his throat, and when he spoke again, there was a catch in his voice. "I guess you need to think about the girls. They're your family."

"Yes." Mia slipped her sandals on and rubbed her arms. The wind off the lake was cooler, and dark clouds bracketed the forested hills. She'd gotten what she wanted: a new start as the strong, independent woman she'd resolved to become.

Nick exhaled and the expression in his eyes was a lot like regret. "I'll walk you back to Charlie and Sean's."

"It's only five minutes. I'll be fine. Jay was headed to the airport anyway."

"I insist." His gaze locked with hers.

"Nick?"

"I don't want to lose you."

"You won't. We're friends." She tried to smile but instead buried her face in the front of his dress shirt and the warm, male smell of him.

"Friends," he murmured, his voice thick.

Mia blinked back tears. "If you come over to Charlie and Sean's with me, why don't you stay for dinner? The town has stocked them with freezer meals and desserts, so there's plenty of food."

"I can't." Nick stepped away and put his socks and shoes back on. "I have to work on a probate case, and I've booked time off to take Kylie to Burlington."

In that way, Nick was like Jay and her dad. Work always came first. Before her and before family.

"I see." Mia tightened the already tight clip that held her hair away from her face.

"Why don't we go out to dinner tomorrow night? We could take the girls and Mom with us. Celebrate your new job." His tone asked her to understand, give him a chance.

"Fine." The tightness in her chest didn't ease. She walked across the beach and Nick followed. "Do you plan on spending any time with Lexie?"

"Sure I do." The three words were too quick.

"You left early when Charlie and Sean brought Lexie home from the hospital."

The silence stretched between them as they went into

the woods and followed a faint green path. After a forest fire the summer before, young trees had already pushed up to seek the light. Nature's constant cycle of growth and renewal.

"I've been busy." Nick's voice was low. "There's the work at your house, Harbor House, and Kylie. I'm working on legal stuff at night because I take time off during the day."

"I appreciate everything you've done for me and everyone else, but when did you last take a vacation?" She wouldn't let him off the hook, not on this one.

"I...that's not fair. I had to get McGuire and Pelletier back on track and—"

"Allison's a partner in the firm, and she takes vacation but you don't. Allison also spends time with her nieces and nephews, and she volunteers at the county women's shelter twice a month."

"Mia, angel." There was a sad note in Nick's voice that caught her heart. "You're right. I should spend time with Lexie. Work can wait. I'll pull an all-nighter if I have to. I'll stay and eat with you."

"That's not what I meant. You shouldn't have to pull an all-nighter because you had dinner with your friends and spent time with your goddaughter." Mia put one foot ahead of the other on autopilot. While she hadn't paid attention, she'd fallen for Nick harder than she'd ever fallen for anyone.

Except, in falling for him, it turned out she wanted more than she'd ever expected. Maybe more than he could give.

"Do you want to stop and eat?" Nick glanced at Kylie slumped beside him in the passenger seat.

"No thanks." Kylie had stared out the window all the way to Burlington, and her baseball cap was pulled low over her eyes.

"If you don't want to stop at a restaurant, we could eat some of the food Mia packed. She made lots." Because Mia was a nurturer and one of the ways she showed her love for others was with food. Nick signaled to turn off the interstate onto an exit ramp as per the directions Kylie's social worker had emailed him.

"I'm not hungry." Kylie pulled at the zipper on her jacket in a monotonous rhythm.

Nick focused on the traffic as he merged onto a parkway. "Mia made those cowboy cookies for you. You can share them with your new foster family and take some to school in your lunch."

Kylie hugged the backpack he'd given her and rocked back and forth. "Mia said she'd call me tonight."

"Sure she will." That was also the kind of woman Mia was, one who kept her promises through thick and thin.

"Do you think you could maybe call me sometime?"

Nick took another exit onto a quieter street. "Of course. I'll miss you, kiddo."

He'd miss Kylie more than he'd admit to anyone, even Mia. He pulled into a parking lot next to a low-rise building surrounded by greenery. At least dropping Kylie off at her social worker's office meant he didn't have to see her with her new family.

"Here we are." He parked the Lexus beside a late-model red Toyota with a "Somebody in Vermont Loves You" decal on its dented bumper.

"Yeah." Kylie clutched the backpack so tight her fingers dug into the nylon.

"I'll get your suitcase and—"

"I've got it." Kylie scrambled out of the car and wrenched the suitcase from behind the seat, the new one he'd gotten her that held the clothes she'd picked out and presents from his mom and Mia and the girls.

"Wait." Nick caught up with her. "Don't forget the cookies from Mia and the other snacks." He grabbed the Firefly Lake market bag, but Kylie shook her head.

"You keep them."

"Kylie, wait." He pulled on the suitcase, but she held the handle in a viselike grip.

"I've got it, okay?" She pulled the case across the parking lot, and the wheels bumped against the asphalt. Her small body was bent almost double with the weight of the backpack.

"No, it's not okay." Nick reached the door of the building first and stood in front of it. "Let me help you."

She stopped and stared at him, and her chin was tucked into her chest. "If you really wanted to help me, you wouldn't make me go in here. You'd let me stay in Firefly Lake."

"You know that's not possible." Nick pulled the door open and stepped into the building. The reception desk was empty, and two spindly potted palms flanked several black plastic chairs.

"Why not?" Kylie stood with her feet apart and balanced the suitcase against one denim-clad knee.

"You need a family." Nick took the suitcase and rolled it toward a door marked FAMILY SERVICES.

"You could be my family." The pleading light in Kylie's eyes almost undid him.

"I'm a guy and you're a girl. I can't foster you."

Besides, he wasn't suited to foster any child, girl or boy.

"You and Mia could foster me and be my forever family." One of the laces on Kylie's sneakers was undone and her fingers shook as she bent to tie it.

"Mia and I aren't together. Not in that way."

In what way then? asked a little voice inside of him. He cared for Mia, maybe even loved her, but he couldn't let himself take the next step and risk losing more than he'd ever lost before.

"You don't want me." When Kylie straightened, the defiant look was back. The look that had been there the night he met her on the porch at Camp Rainbow. "Nobody wants me."

"That's not true. You're a great girl, and your social worker said your new family's excited about you moving in. They've got two daughters, and one's almost the same age as you. They've fostered several kids over the years who've stayed until they were eighteen. Kim thinks this family will be perfect for you. They can even take you to see your mom every two weeks."

Kylie laughed and cracked Nick's heart a bit more. "It'll be perfect, really perfect." She stuck out a hand. "Nice knowing you."

He took her sweaty palm in his. "I'll call you, and if you have something special at school, like a Christmas pageant, maybe I can come."

"Whatever." Her face was white under her tan.

"I'll come in with you and talk to Kim." He stopped at the office door. In there were people whose job it was to make everything okay for kids like Kylie.

"Don't bother. I know the drill." Her backpack bumped

against the door frame. "See you." She grabbed the suit-case, pushed the door open, and disappeared inside.

Nick raised his hand to catch the door as it closed, then let it swing shut. No. It was better this way. He fumbled his car keys out of his pocket. Quick, painless, and a clean break. He'd call Kim from the parking lot instead.

As he stood there, the door swung open again and Kylie barreled out, a package wrapped in purple paper in one hand. "Here, this is for you."

"Kylie…"

Then Nick's breath left his lungs as she wrapped her skinny arms around him and hugged him like she never wanted to let him go. "Thanks," she mumbled before she dashed back the way she'd come.

He grabbed the door and took a step forward only to be stopped by a gray-haired woman with a kind face. Kim, Kylie's social worker, spoke, but he didn't hear anything she said above the roar in his ears. Then Kim put her arm around Kylie and, as she led her away, Kylie looked back once, only those sharp green eyes giving away how much she hurt.

Nick took another step forward, but Kylie turned again. Her shoulders were stiff, and her hair stuck out the back of her ball cap in an untidy ponytail. To remind him, even as a chunk of his heart broke off and shattered, she was a girl who needed a family. A real family.

Back in the car, he drove forty-five minutes out of Burlington before he stopped at a rest area. Under a canopy of trees already tinged with autumn yellows and reds, he stopped the car. The package Kylie had given him was on the seat beside him.

He untied the lopsided purple ribbon bow, peeled back

the tape, and unfolded several layers of purple and white tissue. A twig frame decorated with purple feathers and glitter nestled in the paper and held a picture of him and Kylie. The two of them sat on the beach below Harbor House, and Kylie grinned at him with the teasing expression her face so rarely wore.

He traced the edge of the frame, where the wood was rough beneath his fingertips. Mia or his mom must have taken the picture when he wasn't looking, because they'd caught him in an unguarded moment. He and Kylie had their heads together, and his expression was open and relaxed.

He rewrapped the present in the paper and smoothed the ribbon.

Kylie would forget him. Or she'd make herself forget, like he'd made himself forget his dad and the times the two of them had spent on that same beach. Two guys shooting the breeze away from a houseful of women. Back when his dad was his hero and the man Nick had wanted to be.

He rested his hands on the steering wheel, and the interstate traffic was a distant hum. What if Kylie didn't forget and, no matter how hard he tried, he couldn't forget her either? What if he didn't want to forget her? What if he wanted to be more like the man in the photo? Someone who knew how to have fun and open his heart to a kid who needed him?

What was he thinking? The ridges on the wheel dug into his palms. The past few days had bewitched him. This temporary pull of who he might want to be went against everything he'd worked so hard to become.

A guy who was too busy fighting for justice to have

time for a kid in his life beyond occasional visits. A guy
who wasn't weighed down by memories and losses like a
Lake Champlain ferry in peak tourist season. And a guy
who didn't have roots that twisted and bound him tight
but that could still be torn loose in an instant to leave him
adrift and alone.

"Luc Simard came by while you were at school. He
rented Cat's old bedroom until next spring. He'll move in
next week after you and the girls are back in your house
and the painter's done." Gabrielle rested her weight on
a hoe and looked at Mia on her knees planting a yellow
potted rosebush. "Together with the money Nick's put toward the renovations instead of the bungalow, I can stay
in Harbor House."

"That's great." Mia's face was shaded by a floppy
white hat. "You got what you wanted."

Gabrielle stuck the hoe deeper into the soil. She had,
so why wasn't she happier about it? Maybe because she
didn't have everything she wanted. With Nick, with Nick
and Mia, and with Ward. "Luc's having a house built on
land he inherited from his grandparents by the lake near
the inn. Since his parents have downsized, he needs a
place to stay until his new house is ready."

"I knew everything would work out. Nick will be
thrilled." Mia's smile was forced. "You won't be alone,
and Luc's so big and strong. Remember how he towered
over Cat at the fashion show?"

"Yes." Gabrielle also remembered Cat's false cheerful-
ness that night and her daughter's awkwardness whenever
Luc's return to Firefly Lake was mentioned. "Luc's big,
all right. Pixie didn't leave my arms the whole time he

was here. I think she was scared he'd step on her by accident and crush her." Gabrielle left the hoe where it was and bent to Mia's level. "Let's sit on the patio and rest a while."

"Of course." Mia got to her feet and took Gabrielle's arm. "I'm sorry. I didn't think. You must be tired."

"Not that tired." Gabrielle left her hand on Mia's arm longer than she needed. "I'll miss you and the girls. I already miss Kylie. She's sure a bright spark."

Mia dropped her garden gloves on a bench. "She's with a nice family. Still, I miss Kylie more than I expected. Although the girls and I will miss you, unlike Kylie, we'll only be five minutes away. Whatever you need when Nick goes back to New York, you call me first, okay?"

"Okay." Except, all along she'd hoped Nick would stay and settle with Mia and the girls. Gabrielle moved toward the patio with Mia at her side.

"Have you heard from Ward?" Mia pulled out a patio chair for Gabrielle and adjusted the sun umbrella to shade the small space.

"I emailed him to say hi." Although she'd told him not to come back to Firefly Lake because she didn't want to get hurt again, she hurt anyway, and there was an ache in her heart not even Harbor House could ease.

Mia slid a chair beside hers. "Ward will get in touch. The way he looked at you, it was obvious he didn't want to leave."

"Once he left, he'd have soon come to his senses." Gabrielle sniffed and dug in her pocket for a tissue.

"That's ridiculous," Mia countered.

"Is it? I've seen how Nick looks at you, and he's still

set on going back to New York." Gabrielle's voice was quiet.

"That's different. I didn't tell him to leave." Mia blew out a breath.

"You haven't asked him to stay either, have you?"

"I can't." The two words were an anguished moan.

"You could, more than me." Gabrielle rested her hands on the table. Two of the knuckles were knotted with arthritis, and the backs were dotted with age spots. When had her hands grown older? "If I ask him to stay, I'd hold him back, whereas you—"

"I'd hold him back, too. I know all about men who work twenty-four/seven. I want to come first. I deserve to come first."

"You do, but Nick doesn't understand." She'd tried to do right by her children, but each of them was wounded. "I could talk to him."

"No, Nick's my friend. That's enough." Mia's eyes were dark with pain.

"Really?" Gabrielle crossed one leg over the other and her knees creaked. She hadn't noticed her knees getting older either.

"Of course." Mia twirled the pearl ring on the fourth finger of her right hand.

"That was your mother's ring, wasn't it?"

"My grandparents gave it to her for her sixteenth birthday."

"You always wear it, like I wear my mom's engagement ring." Gabrielle held out her right hand, where a trio of diamonds glinted in the light. "I didn't know your mom well. I only talked to her a few times in the market and such, but she sure loved you and Charlie. She wouldn't want you to spend the rest of your life alone because you're scared to risk your heart again."

Mia's expression was bleak. "She stayed with my dad all those years, even with his affairs. I knew she wasn't happy, and everybody here talked about how Dad ran around. Whenever we came into town, I saw how they looked at him and at us."

"What your dad did was wrong, and your mom got trapped. I expect she stayed with him because she thought she had to." Like she'd ignored the signs Brian wasn't who he'd seemed. Gabrielle swallowed hard. "Maybe in her family, like it was in mine, divorce was pretty much a mortal sin back then. But when you found yourself in the same situation, you had the courage to leave."

"I didn't leave the first time Jay cheated." Mia crossed her arms over her chest. "But when Tiffany got pregnant, I didn't have a choice."

"You always have a choice, honey." Gabrielle moved her chair closer and wrapped her arms around Mia's hunched shoulders. "I'm talking about me, too. Brian McGuire messed up my life, and he messed up my kids' lives. Even after all these years, he's still messing with us. Did Nick tell you he got in touch? All of a sudden Brian wants to see his kids and get to know Amy. He's never taken any interest in her before, but all of a sudden Amy's the grandchild he's longed for."

"Yes, but—"

"No buts." Gabrielle patted Mia's shoulder before she moved away. "Nick can do what he wants about his dad, and Cat and Georgia can too. What Brian did hasn't hurt me in a long time, but it's sure influenced how I live my life. It's held me back from what I want. From here on, that has to change, starting with me going into the house to call Ward. The worst he can say is thanks but no thanks."

She wouldn't think about the best thing he could say. She'd been raised by her traditional mother to wait for the man to make the first move and to please and accommodate. But it was a different world, one her mother couldn't have imagined.

"The girls will be home soon." Mia avoided Gabrielle's gaze. "Naomi and Ty took Emma bowling after school. Although she and Kylie had a rocky start, Emma was sad to see Kylie leave. I'll stay out here and wait for them to give you privacy for your call."

"Thank you." Gabrielle's heartbeat sped up like it always did when she thought of Ward. "You have a nice sit and think things over."

Mia was too much like the woman she'd once been, but Gabrielle was sixty-two, and the years had flown by until she'd been stopped short and made to stare death in the face. She'd won that battle, but if she didn't make some changes in her life soon, chances were she'd drift along, always planning to change but never actually doing so.

She took a deep breath and conjured Ward's face, the affection in his blue eyes when he looked at her and the safety and contentment she felt with him.

"It's only a phone call." Mia's mouth curved into a smile.

Except, it was a phone call that could change the rest of her life. Gabrielle pushed the doubts away. Sometimes a woman needed to take a risk. Unlike Brian, Ward was a man worth taking a risk for.

Chapter Seventeen

Jay hadn't wasted any time. Four days later, Mia ended yet another call with Allison and set her phone on the kitchen counter. The white worktop and maple cupboards and shelves Sean had installed gleamed in the light from the window. The same light bounced off the blue glass bottles she'd collected over the years at flea markets and thrift stores.

Those bottles represented one more thing Jay had found fault with. He'd wanted everything new and modern. Mia crumpled the email she'd printed out, the words already imprinted on her brain. It was from an attorney in Dallas to notify her Jay intended to sue her for sole custody of Naomi and Emma on the grounds that she was an unfit mother.

"He wants to scare you." Allison's voice had been strong and decisive. "He thinks if you're scared you'll come back to him. He doesn't have a shred of evidence you're an unfit parent, and unless there's drug addiction or abuse, sole custody arrangements are rare. Jay also travels three weeks out of four, and after how he treated you and the girls, no judge anywhere would give him sole custody."

Mia shoved the paper into a kitchen drawer and wished she could be so sure. She looked around the bright kitchen, small but functional, like the rest of the house. Her house, the home she'd made for her family and intended to keep.

Emma's laugh echoed from upstairs.

"No, you can't..." Naomi's voice was followed by a thump and more laughter.

Mia moved to the bottom of the stairs. "Girls?"

Two heads poked over the top of the banister, one dark and the other light. "Hey, Mom." Naomi grinned at her. "Our rooms look great. Uncle Sean and Nick and his friends did an amazing job."

"Great," Emma repeated as she waved a pink teddy. The bear she'd had since she was born, which still lived on her bed.

"Have you finished unpacking?" Mia pressed a hand to her chest as her heart filled with love for her daughters and this new life.

"Almost." Naomi's expression turned serious. "I still miss our old house, but now that it's all fixed up, this one's nice. It's a friendly house."

"It'll be a happy house, too." Although their house in Dallas had been big, with every convenience they could have wanted, it had been cold, unloved, and unhappy. The way Mia had felt for more years than she wanted to count. She jumped as the doorbell rang.

"That must be Nick," Emma said.

On her way to the door, Mia turned and looked upstairs again. "Is there something you want to tell me, Emma Rose?"

"I texted him on Naomi's phone. I may have said we needed help to move beds. Ouch." She squealed as Naomi elbowed her. "What? Mom said her bed was too heavy for us to lift."

"I also said I'd ask Uncle Sean to help us." Mia smoothed her hair as the doorbell rang again.

She wasn't sure what she wanted to say to Nick, or how to act around him. She'd avoided him for the past few days after they'd gone out for dinner, which had been easy because he'd been working on some urgent case. So Allison had said. It wasn't as if Mia had fished for information.

As Mia hesitated, Emma ran down the stairs and pulled open the front door. "Hey, Nick."

"Emma." He gave her a high five before she grabbed his hand and towed him into the hall.

"Nick." Mia put her hands behind her back and linked her fingers together. It would be easier if he weren't so hot, if he didn't remind her it how it felt to be a desirable woman.

"Emma said you need help moving furniture." He glanced into the living room. The taupe sofa had colorful pillows that echoed the colors in the abstract painting Gabrielle had given them as a housewarming present. A stalk of red hollyhocks from the garden at Harbor House was in a glass vase on the coffee table beside her mom's piano.

"I'm sorry we bothered you." Mia squeezed her hands tighter. "I planned to call Sean."

Nick wore a blue polo shirt, the same color as his eyes,

and a pair of worn Levi's that invited her to touch. The jeans hugged his legs. And his ass. Which were both very fine indeed.

"No bother." Nick grinned at Emma. "I planned to head over anyway in case you needed a hand."

She needed his hands all right, as well as his body. Upstairs in her bedroom in the new bed she'd picked out. A bed she'd never slept in with Jay. "It sounds like you've been busy at work."

"All done." Nick's smile widened to include Naomi, who'd followed her sister and stood behind Mia, quiet and watchful. "Since it's your first official night in your new house now it's all fixed up, we'll order in. Chinese, pizza or whatever you want, my treat." He pulled out his wallet.

"Mom?" Naomi's voice was uncertain.

"It's fine." Mia made herself smile. "Pizza or Chinese, you girls choose."

"Or we could get takeout from the diner." Nick's eyes twinkled. "Liz makes a great lemon meringue pie, and tonight's the fried chicken special."

"Mom loves lemon meringue pie and fried chicken," Emma said, "but Dad says if she eats stuff like that she'll get as fat as a pig."

"Emma...I...you...that's rude."

"Dad did say it." Her daughter's shrill treble was insistent.

"I'm sure he did, but you don't need to repeat it. Do you understand me?"

"Yeah, sorry." Emma bobbed her head.

Mia bit her lip. She didn't care what Jay said or thought, and so what if she indulged in pie and fried chicken on occasion? Nick knew her so well he knew exactly what was on her list of guilty pleasures, and he'd never complained about her body.

Above Emma's head, she caught his gaze again, but this time the teasing was gone. Without him saying a word, she knew Allison must have told him about the email from Jay's attorney.

"The diner it is," she said. "We can have a picnic outside. Your mom gave us a patio table and chairs she wasn't using."

"We have a plan." Nick gave Emma another high five. "Do you want to walk into town with me to get the food?"

"Can we get maple creemees for the walk back?" Emma slid her feet into her sneakers. "Ice cream is dairy and maple syrup is a fruit, sort of. It comes from a tree and has sugar in it. I learned that in school today."

"I like your logic, but your mom might have a different view." Nick laughed. "Mia, Naomi? Are you coming?"

"No." Naomi fiddled with a strand of hair. "I still need to do some stuff in my room and call Ty."

"Come on." Emma hopped on one foot. "You have to come. You can call Ty on the way."

"If you two don't come with us, we won't get any healthy food." Nick raised his eyebrows.

"We'll all come." Mia picked up her purse from the hall table.

"Mom." Naomi dropped her hair. "I'm sixteen. I've been babysitting for four years. I can stay by myself for half an hour."

She could, but Mia wouldn't give Jay any ammunition he could use to take the girls away. "We unpacked all weekend and today after school. We need some fresh air and exercise."

"Moving those boxes from the basement and the garage was exercise." Naomi grabbed her woven bag slung over the banister and stuck a pair of oversized sunglasses on her nose. "I should change and fix my hair."

"You look fine, sweetie." In navy capris and a white tank top, her baby looked more like a woman than a girl. "Beautiful sweet sixteen."

"Mom." Only a teenage girl could inject so much sarcasm into a single word, and even from behind the dark glasses, Mia didn't miss the eye roll.

"It's not like you'll bump into Ty," Emma said. "Before he kissed you good-bye yesterday, I heard him say it's his week with his mom and stepdad in Kincaid. Then he kissed you again, right on the lips, which was disgusting." Emma grimaced before she darted out the front door.

"You spied on us?" Naomi took her sneakers in one hand, before she ran after Emma barefoot.

"I guess that tells you everything you need to know about the friend thing Naomi and Ty have going on." Nick still stood in the hall, and his expression was amused.

It did, except who was Mia to judge her daughter? The "friend thing" was what she was supposed to have with Nick. Which didn't fool anybody, Naomi especially, so what kind of example was she setting?

Mia slipped her feet into her sandals and followed Nick out the door then locked it. Maybe Gabrielle was right. Maybe she should talk to Nick and tell him how she felt and what she wanted. Get what was between them out into the open, for her sake and her daughters'. Then, in addition to loving Naomi, she could better guide her and help her make good choices with Ty.

As Nick fell into step beside her, he talked about his day and asked about hers like he was interested and they were a couple. She glanced at the end of the street, where Naomi and Emma waited. Nick raised his hand and waved, and Emma waved back before she skipped toward them. Naomi followed at a saunter, too grown-up to skip.

Anybody who didn't know would think they were a family. A mom and dad and their two girls out for a walk on a small-town Monday night.

Mia wouldn't talk to Nick yet. She'd wait and enjoy what she had a bit longer. She was older and wiser than when she'd been with Jay. This time, she knew how to keep her heart safe.

"Are the girls asleep?" Nick turned as the patio door slid open and Mia came into the backyard. The moonlight etched the classic planes of her face above her plain white T-shirt, blue sweater, and jeans.

"Emma's out for the count, but Naomi's still on Facebook." Mia pulled out a patio chair and sat. Crickets chirped and, from a house two doors down, a dog barked.

Nick looked at the sky, where the first stars glimmered. When he was a kid, his dad had bought him a telescope, and he'd spent hours looking through it. Back then he'd wanted to be an astronaut or an air force pilot, a guy who wore his country's badge with pride. "Did you and Naomi talk?"

"Yes." Mia's voice was low and so sweet it made him ache deep in his gut. "She and Ty are serious about each other. No surprise there. But she's got a good head on her shoulders, and they're taking it slow. She knows she can talk to me."

"Despite what Jay said, there's no way you're an unfit mother."

"Allison told you?"

"Yes." Nick squeezed her hand and she squeezed back. "There's also no way Jay would win a sole custody suit, even though I doubt it'd ever go to court."

"You think?"

"I know." He fingered the inside of her wrist, and Mia trembled. "Even without Allison he wouldn't win, but with her, it's a no-brainer."

"She told me she wouldn't bill me until I get my first paycheck from the school, but even then I'm sure all this going back and forth between attorneys will cost a lot more than she said." Tension lined her beautiful mouth.

"The firm has a family and friends discount, remember?" Nick hadn't wanted to charge Mia anything, but knowing she wouldn't accept, he'd fixed the billing with Allison and sworn her to secrecy.

"It's very generous." The chair squeaked as Mia moved closer, and Nick looped one arm around her shoulders. Above the neckline of her sweater, her skin was warm with a hint of freesia scent, and his body hardened as she ran a hand along his bare arm.

"Have you talked to Kylie yet?" He seized on a distraction, since the girls were in the house.

"A few times." Mia leaned over and rested her head on his shoulder. "I also talked to her foster mom. It will take time for Kylie to settle in, but they're taking it one day at a time. Kylie misses you."

"Did she say so?" He hadn't called Kylie, afraid he'd upset her and make her think he was someone he wasn't.

"She didn't have to. It was more what she didn't say. She asked about everybody, even Pixie and Shadow, but not you."

"See, she's forgotten all about me." Nick's chest constricted.

"No, it means it would hurt her too much to talk about you. She put me off when I asked if she'd talked to her foster mom and social worker about spending a weekend here. Kylie hasn't had any adults she can count on in her life. My guess is she shuts herself off so she won't get hurt again." Mia studied him, her eyes soft.

Nick flinched. "I said I'd call, but I wanted to let her get settled first. If she needs anything, I told her she can call me. If she's in something at school, I said I'd come to it."

His throat tightened as he remembered the look on Kylie's face as she walked away and the expression in her green eyes. The moment he'd glimpsed himself, the kid he once was who'd been determined to not let anyone know how much he cared, or how much he hurt.

"I'm not talking about new clothes, school supplies, or showing up for a few hours at a school play or sports event. I'm talking about being a part of Kylie's life. Like a mentor or a role model, someone she can count on."

"Me?" Nick stared at Mia. "Maybe if she was a boy, but she's a girl and I'm not related to her."

"She's a child who needs stability. If I wasn't in this mess with Jay, I'd apply to foster her. She's rough around the edges, sure, but Kylie has a good heart and the potential to become a good woman." Mia hissed out a breath. "I don't mean you should foster her, but you have a chance to make an important difference in her life. The kind of difference I can't make. How many good men has she known?"

Nick opened his mouth but no words came out. He wasn't the kind of man a girl like Kylie needed.

"Whether you believe it or not, you are a good man. Trust yourself. You helped raise your sisters."

"Kylie's nothing like them."

"Kylie is Kylie." Mia's voice turned amused. "In a lot of ways, she reminds me of you."

"I...she..." Why was he surprised? Mia understood him in a way nobody else ever had, not even his mom.

"Sure she does. I remember you way back when." She gave him a small smile. "If there was ever a kid with attitude, you were it. Folks around here used to say trouble was your middle name."

And Nick had done his best to live up to it, causing trouble because it was the only way he could deal with his dad's abandonment, as well as the gossip that followed, which took years to subside.

"Kylie isn't trouble like I was."

"You weren't trouble, not really." Mia reached for the knife and slid the pie plate closer to cut herself another piece of lemon meringue. "You had trouble in your life, and Kylie has, too. You're the one who can help her the most because you get where she comes from."

Nick raised his glass of soda and drained it. He might get it, but that didn't mean he was the guy to fix it.

Mia dabbed at her mouth with a paper napkin.

"I..." He stared at her mouth, dotted in one corner with a blob of fluffy white meringue.

"What?" She patted her lips again before she set the napkin by her plate. "Talk to Kim and ask if you can spend a Saturday in Burlington to take Kylie to a movie, out for a meal, or to a sports event. Anything you do with her, she'd love."

Nick blinked. For a minute, he'd forgotten about Kylie. "Here." He retrieved Mia's napkin and blotted away the last smidgen of pie topping. "All gone."

"Thanks." She drew in a breath.

His finger grazed the outline of her cheekbone and traced a path to one ear.

Mia gave a needy moan, and the sweet sound lingered on the night air.

"I know we can't right now," he whispered, "not with Naomi and Emma in the house, but I want you." Wanted her so much it scared him and made him forget he'd be back to his real life in less than ten days.

"I want you, too." She rubbed her face against his, and her skin was soft against the stubble of his beard.

He rested his face against hers, content in a way he hadn't been in a long time, maybe ever. Although he wanted to take Mia up to her bedroom and be with her in the pretty, light-filled room with the white iron bed and the crisp green linens that made him think of a summer garden, he liked sitting here with her. And he could trick himself that this was his life and he and Mia lived here together with a few kids and a dog.

Mia tilted her head and her hair brushed his jaw. "Emma's going to a birthday party after school tomorrow, and Naomi's covering a shift at the diner for a friend. Why don't you come by?"

"Great." Nick's skin cooled as his stomach contracted. He was leaving Firefly Lake after Labor Day. And somehow he had to maintain the pretense that leaving this woman wouldn't tear him apart.

Chapter Eighteen

Gabrielle set the half-finished canvas back on the easel and stared out the dining room window. Harbor House groaned in the September wind, the patio was slick with rain, and the garden was cloaked in mist off the lake. She shivered and pulled on a sweater from the back of her chair.

She was too restless to paint and couldn't even settle enough to read the book for her book club. She walked to the front of the house and pulled back the living room curtain. The street outside was deserted, and leaves blew across the lawn to land in a puddle at the foot of the drive.

Dropping the curtain, she wandered into the kitchen. What was wrong with her? She'd never been lonely in Harbor House before. She'd wanted to stay here because it was her home and the place she was safe. Except she'd gotten used to it being filled with people again.

Luc had only left an hour ago to spend a few days in Montreal, but already the silence pressed in on her. She filled the kettle, plugged it in, and took a tea bag out of the canister.

She missed Mia and the girls and Kylie. And she missed Ward most of all. Her throat got a lump the size of a marble in it. He'd taken her at her word. No telephone calls or texts, and no reply to her email or the voice mail message she'd left him either. He'd disappeared from her life like he'd never existed.

"Hey, Pixie." Gabrielle leaned against the counter.

The dog stretched in her basket and whined. Her brown eyes were mournful, and her usually graceful tail drooped.

"You miss everybody, too, don't you?"

Pixie flipped onto her back and stuck her paws in the air so Gabrielle could rub her tummy. At least she still had Pixie. She'd already rebuilt her life once, twice. There was no reason she couldn't do it again.

Pixie cocked her ears then rolled onto her paws and looked toward the hall.

"It's only the wind." The kettle whistled, and Gabrielle switched it off and poured boiling water into her chintz teapot, as familiar and comforting as an old friend.

Pixie barked, ran to the front door, and scratched at it.

"Remember what Mia told you about jumping on that door? I let you get into bad habits."

Pixie jumped in circles and barked louder, almost drowning out the chime of the doorbell.

"Down, girl." Gabrielle unlocked the door and pulled it open. A gust of wind pushed her backward and sent rain swirling into the house.

"Gabby?"

Gabrielle blinked and brushed a hand across her face.

"May I come in?" Ward stood on the porch in a

battered black leather bomber jacket and jeans. His hair was slick with rain, and dark circles shadowed his eyes.

"Of course. Here, I'll take your coat. You must be cold. I've made a pot of tea and there are some of Mia's ginger cookies left and..." She was babbling like a teenager. Even Naomi wouldn't act in such a silly way.

"I didn't travel more than two days for tea and cookies." Ward shrugged out of his coat and draped it over the hall stand.

Pixie stopped barking and nosed his boots.

"That long?" Gabrielle's voice came out in a squeak.

"I was filming in a national park almost three hundred miles north of Chengdu." He pulled off his boots and patted Pixie. "China. Erica picked up the message you left at the house. You didn't call my cell."

Gabrielle backed toward the kitchen, trying to remember exactly what she'd said on the message and his daughter had heard. "I didn't want to bother you, but I sent an email."

"Which I didn't see until I landed in Shanghai." Ward followed her into the kitchen. His steps were purposeful, and even in his socks, he towered over her. "I was in a remote area, but after she listened to your message, Erica got hold of me."

"Oh." Gabrielle pulled out a kitchen chair and sat. "I didn't think—"

"I did." Ward pulled out another chair and sat in front of her, his knees almost touching hers. "Since I left here, you're pretty much all I've thought of. When Erica told me you wanted to talk, I came back as fast as I could. I wanted to talk, too, in person and not over the phone."

Gabrielle lifted Pixie and hugged her. "I'm sorry. I

made a mistake, but we haven't known each other long, and besides, I was sick and—"

"Gabby, honey." Ward leaned forward, scooped Pixie out of her arms, and put the dog in her basket. "I never told you how I lost my wife, but maybe it'll help you understand." He shook his head at Pixie, and the dog turned around twice and settled in the nest of blankets.

"You don't have to talk about Carol. It must be painful and..." Who was she to ask questions? She'd never told him about Brian.

"No, I have to do this for me and for us." He took both Gabrielle's hands in his and his voice roughened. "Carol was in her car. She'd dropped Erica off at a ballet lesson and a drunk driver in a stolen SUV came through a red light and hit her sideways. She never regained consciousness, and she died in the hospital two days later."

"Ward." Gabrielle's eyes watered, and she squeezed his hands tight. There were no words for that kind of loss.

"I still miss Carol, but I've lived a lot of years without her, and there's a place in my heart for you. If you want it." His blue eyes were misty. "Life can change in the blink of an eye. I'm ready to take a chance if you are."

Gabrielle's hands tingled, and heat radiated through her chest. After Brian, she'd never wanted to take chances, but life, and things she couldn't control, had snuck up on her anyway. She touched his check and the dear, rugged contours of his face. "I'm ready to take a chance, too."

He let out a breath. "I love you, Gabby." He lifted her onto his lap like she was a fragile piece of crystal. "Aw, heck. All the way back here, I thought about telling you how I feel. I wanted to make it romantic and look what I did? I went and blurted it out."

"I..." She traced the outline of his mouth. Although Gabrielle felt the love, she couldn't say it, at least not yet.

"It's okay." Ward smoothed her hair. "You don't have to say it just because I did."

"I care about you a lot." Gabrielle relaxed into his touch and the heat of his body.

"I know. I also know you and Brian didn't have the kind of relationship Carol and I did." Ward dropped a kiss on her forehead. "You don't have to say anything you aren't ready to say, and you don't have to tell me about Brian."

"I don't?" Gabrielle's heart pounded.

"Nope, not until you're ready, if you're ever ready. I heard all I need to from people in town. Everyone in Firefly Lake cares about you and looks out for you." His mouth quirked into a gentle smile. "I hope you believe me when I say I'd never do anything to hurt you or embarrass you."

"I do." Those words were a vow and a promise to bind the two of them together, no matter what the future held. Although she murmured them, she'd never meant any two words more than she meant those. And she'd cherish the expression on Ward's face for the rest of her life. The love and faith for her, and his belief in the two of them together.

He shifted her on his lap to pull her closer into his thighs.

Gabrielle wiggled and his arousal pushed into her.

"Gabby." His voice was strained. "I won't ask you to do anything you're not ready for. Besides, I need a shower and some sleep."

"I'll be right there beside you when you wake up." She was ready and had been for weeks. Even though she couldn't say the words of love to him yet, it was only a matter of time.

"Are you sure?" His warm breath caressed her ear.

"Yes." She twisted on his lap and looked into his face. "We have lots to work out, but I've never been more certain of anything."

Brian didn't matter, the cancer didn't matter, and even Harbor House, the place she'd fought so hard to keep, didn't matter. All that mattered was she was still alive and, with Ward by her side, she had a future to look forward to.

He lifted her into his arms, and she squealed.

Pixie bounded out of her basket with a chorus of barks.

"You think a guy in his sixties is too old for this?" Ward lifted her higher.

"No." Laughter started deep in Gabrielle's chest and spilled out.

"Watch your head."

She ducked as he carried her through the kitchen door. "You can't carry me all the way upstairs. I'm too heavy." She squirmed, but he held her tight.

"Most of the camera equipment I lug around is a lot heavier than you are. I want to give you something special to remember."

"You already have." She let her body go loose in his arms.

"It's only the beginning." He reached the top of the stairs and headed for her bedroom, then eased the door open with one foot.

"A new beginning," she added, before he bent his head, kissed her, and kicked the door closed.

"Spill." With one eye on Lexie, who gurgled on a play mat on Mia's living room floor, Charlie gave Mia a calculating look. "Tell me everything."

"About what?" Mia made her tone innocent.

"You and Nick."

"There's nothing to tell." Mia waved a soft red rattle shaped like a chicken, and the baby's eyes followed it. "You're a smart girl, aren't you, Lexie?"

"Smart like her mom, you mean?" Charlie moved to sit beside Mia on the sofa. "Lexie's precious, the most amazing baby ever, along with Naomi and Emma, but I won't let you use her to distract me." She grinned and made a grab for the rattle. "Sean won't be back with Naomi and Emma from that horse show for another hour, so we have lots of time to talk."

"Nick and I are friends." Which was a big, fat lie.

"So you say, but seriously, what's he like in bed?" Charlie's eyes twinkled. "All that buried intensity must be pretty hot."

"It is, but…I…we're not…" Mia clapped a hand over her mouth as shock reverberated through her.

"Got you." Charlie laughed and then hugged Mia to take away any sting in her words. "You forget I'm a professional."

"Busybody?" Mia sighed.

"No, journalist, investigative reporter. I'm paid to be nosy." Charlie tried and failed to look remorseful.

"Not with me you aren't." Mia reached for her glass of lemonade on the coffee table and took a sip. She loved and trusted her sister, and she had to talk to someone. "It's complicated. Jay wants full custody of the girls. He doesn't like Nick, and he said…" She bit her lip.

"Said what?"

"He guessed Nick and I are sleeping together, and he doesn't want him around Naomi and Emma. He blames Nick for Emma's accident, and he blames me for what's going on between Naomi and Ty and why Naomi's so determined to stay in Firefly Lake." A cycle of blame that, whichever way she cut it, all ended up with her.

"Jay always was big on blaming someone, usually you. Nobody else blames Nick for Emma jumping off the swim raft. As for Naomi and Ty, if he can't see they're both sensible kids, he's looking in the wrong direction." Charlie shook the rattle before she handed it to Lexie. "Jay never liked me or any of your friends, so, apart from the whole custody thing, he's still playing the same old games."

"We're divorced and he's moved on." Except, it still felt like Jay wanted to control her. The snide comments he made about her weight and her glasses, her house, her job, and Vermont and Firefly Lake. Nick was at the top of a long list of things Jay didn't like about her.

"Once Tiffany got wise to him, Jay realized how good he had it with you. That's why he's moved into threat mode."

"His attorney said Jay would get full custody of the girls if I kept seeing Nick." Which kept Mia awake at night worrying over questions for which she had no answers.

"He's bluffing. Do you think he could make something so ridiculous stick? Jay cheated on you with a woman almost half his age, fathered a child with her, and then she dumped him. Whereas Nick's a respectable guy, a pillar of the community these days, and he never did anything to Jay or the girls apart from saving Emma's life. Besides, Jay didn't object to you moving to Firefly Lake, did he?" Charlie was pissed on Mia's behalf, and Mia's heart warmed.

"Not in court." Which was all that mattered, despite what he'd said in private.

Mia tucked her feet under her. Already she loved this room with the simple touches that made it a home, as far removed from the sterile grandeur of the house in Dallas as possible. Her gaze landed on her mom's picture on top of the piano. Maybe her mom hadn't had a choice, but Mia did, and she wouldn't falter now.

"Jay travels all the time. Who'd look after the girls when he's away? A nanny? You can bet any judge would ask that question. Jay's the unfit parent, not you. Besides, you're so law-abiding you've never even had a speeding ticket." Charlie spat out the words before she cuddled Lexie and kissed the baby's tuft of dark hair. "There's no reason why you can't go after what you want with Nick."

Mia wanted to so much it scared her. "I don't know if Nick wants me like that." And she was afraid to be rejected and hurt again, afraid to destroy what they had by wanting something more.

"There's only one way to find out. Ask him. If you don't, won't you always wonder?" Charlie's voice was gentle.

"It's not so simple." At least it wasn't for her.

"Sure it is." Charlie inclined her head toward the picture of their mom. "Maybe it wasn't for Mom, though. She didn't have a job outside the house, and she was scared of Dad."

"With good reason." Mia's stomach tensed. "I was scared of Dad, too. Even though he never hit her, I always thought he could have."

"You mean he never hit her in front of us."

"You think?" Mia put a hand to her mouth.

"I don't know for sure." Charlie exhaled. "But Mom

never left him, and all of us tiptoed around Dad so as not to upset him. I got away from home as soon as I could for school and then work, and you married Jay."

"Because I wanted to get away, too. I wanted to make the family I didn't have." A choice that had landed Mia in a whole other kind of prison.

"You have your family." Charlie held her gaze. "As for Nick, he's nothing like Jay."

"True, but I have a job now and a whole new life." Mia had to make her sister understand. "I want to be independent like you've always been. I want to earn money and make decisions. I got married so young, I never had any of that."

"My independence came with a price. I was so focused on my career, I almost missed out on love, marriage, and a child." Charlie glanced at Lexie cuddled against her breast, and her look was so tender Mia's eyes misted. "Besides, I still earn my money and make a lot of independent decisions, and Sean does too, but it's nice to share my life with someone who's always in my corner, no matter what. Sean looks out for me, even when I don't think I need it."

"Whether you want him to or not?" Her sister was still the same forthright Charlie she'd always been, but a happy marriage and little Lexie had given her a glow that softened her features.

"Exactly." Charlie nodded. "I'm still independent, still me, but even more so because of Sean. Independence doesn't mean you and the girls have to be alone."

"I never thought about it like that." Mia stared at her sister in astonishment. "I've been so focused on standing on my own two feet as the kind of woman Jay said I couldn't be, I kind of forgot about the woman I want to be, all of her."

"Despite Jay, a big part of that woman is a wife and mother, a good one." Charlie reached for the last cookie on the plate Mia had set out earlier.

"Hey." Mia swatted Charlie's hand away. "Some of those were for you to take home to Sean and Ty. How many have you eaten?"

"I'm hungrier than usual since I'm feeding Lexie." Charlie grabbed the cookie and gave Mia a cheeky grin. "Will you call Nick?"

"Maybe." Mia grinned back. "No more information."

Charlie's cheeks bulged out with cookie like they had when she was a kid. "I'm your sister, the only one you've got."

"Which is why I've told you as much as I have." Mia reached over and hugged her. "No matter what happens between Nick and me, I'm thankful every day I moved here and you're nearby."

"Me too." Charlie returned her hug, replete with the smell of oatmeal cookies, milk, and Lexie. Good, honest smells. "Nick has to love you. How could he not?"

"I never said I love him." Even though Mia did, she wasn't sure he loved her or wanted her in the way she wanted him to.

"You didn't have to. It's written all over your face whenever you're with him. When you talk about him, even."

"It isn't." Mia's face got warm.

"You can fight it all you want, but love catches you when you least expect. I never expected I'd be Sean's wife, let alone a mom, but I found the courage to change and take a chance, and look what happened." Charlie's smile was smug.

"You found a happy-ever-after."

"No." Charlie transferred Lexie to her car seat as the baby's blue eyes closed and Lexie drifted into sleep. "You read too many romances. I found a happy day-by-day. Sean and I are both strong-willed and stubborn, but if we work on our relationship one day at a time, we'll make a happy-ever-after, too."

"There's nothing wrong with romances. Those books got me through some of the worst times with Jay." And they'd helped give her self-belief and the courage to start over.

"No arguments here." Charlie's laugh was rueful. "The books you lent me kept me distracted during that awful time Lexie was in New Hampshire. All I meant is a fictional hero's got nothing on a guy like Nick."

Mia stood and went to the window to look out at the tree-lined street. A small girl rode a bike along the sidewalk and wobbled from side to side on two wheels. She careened toward one of Mia's flower beds before her mom grabbed the bike's handlebars to head her off.

Until Nick, Mia had always played it safe. But she was a big girl, and big girls went after what they wanted. Even if they wobbled or took a detour along the way.

Chapter Nineteen

Nick sat on a flat rock by the lake behind Harbor House and stuck his hands in the pockets of his hooded jacket. Despite the sunlight that glittered on the white-capped waves, the wind was cool, and the lake was empty of boats. Another Labor Day was over, and by the end of the week he'd be back in New York. Back to the life he'd put on hold while his mom was sick.

He'd asked Mia to meet him here. To give her the final payment for the work she'd done for his mom and to say good-bye. This time in Firefly Lake had changed who he was, what he valued, and maybe even what he wanted. But it hadn't changed what he had to do today.

"Sorry I'm late." Mia's hair was windblown, and her cheeks were rosy. "I don't have long either. I have a lot of work to do for school." She sat on the rock next to his. "I was going to call you anyway. Naomi offered to stay with Emma tomorrow night. If you're free, we could have dinner at the Irish pub in Kincaid. The one with the live music."

Nick shoved his fists deeper into his pockets. "I can't. I'm sorry."

"Oh." The wind blew strands of Mia's hair against his sleeve, and he tensed. "Well, like I said, I have a lot to do for school. I still can't believe I have a music classroom of my very own. Even though the job's temporary, it's a dream come true."

Nick took the check he'd made out to her from his jacket pocket. "This is for the last of your work on Mom's house. You did a terrific job, far more than I paid you to do. I don't know what she'd have done without you."

"It was my pleasure." Mia smiled as she took the check, and her fingertips brushed his before she tucked the paper into the back pocket of her jeans. "I love your mom. To see her so happy with Ward and comfortable in her home, things couldn't have worked out better. Even Pixie adores him."

"Pixie adores anyone who feeds her."

"True." Mia gave that little chuckle that made Nick's heart beat faster.

"Ward's still going back to Asia."

"For a month because of his job." Mia's expression was earnest. "Ward and your mom want to be together, and somehow they'll work things out."

Nick took a deep breath. "Mia, look, I don't know how to say this but—"

"Wait." She touched a finger to his lips. "I want to say something to you first. I wanted to tell you the other day when Emma was at that party, but you distracted me."

Nick smothered a groan as guilt burned like acid in his stomach. He hadn't planned to make love to her one last time. He'd told himself he wouldn't, but one look in her eyes and he was lost. "We had a good time—"

"A good time? Is that all it meant to you? It was more than a good time, at least for me. That's what I want to talk to you about."

Nick took her cold hands in his. "I care about you and, like I said before, we can keep seeing each other when I'm back here. If you want, you can come to New York, too. Casual."

"Casual?" Her voice shook, and the look in her eyes was like a blade severing one of his arteries. "Casual as in we can see other people?"

His stomach lurched. "Neither of us wanted a relationship."

She gave a bitter laugh and yanked her hands away. "True. Except, it turns out I don't do casual. I made the mistake of falling in love with you."

"I'm flattered, honored, but I'm heading back to New York in two days."

"And you didn't think to mention that fact to me before?"

"You knew all along I was leaving after Labor Day. I don't want to upset you, but there's a big case the senior partner asked me to take the lead on. I said yes an hour ago." His heart got even heavier as he said the words aloud.

"Upset me?" Mia's eyes flashed. "Who will do your job at McGuire and Pelletier?"

"I'll still be involved, but I'll hire a guy who needs a clerkship to help out. It takes time to find a good attorney." He heard the panic in his voice and tried to will it away.

"I see." Mia's mouth was set in a flat line. "Who is this guy who needs a job? Law students aren't exactly thick on the ground around here."

"Travis is the brother of a friend from college. He wants to get licensed to practice law in Vermont, and he needs a break." Which was true, dammit, so why was Mia looking at him like he'd just drowned a litter of newborn kittens?

"How convenient."

Nick didn't miss the sarcasm in her voice.

"Travis is a good guy. You'll like him." And why did that thought make him feel worse instead of better?

"I'm sure I will, but this isn't about Travis. It's about us."

Her words hit him in the solar plexus. Nick hadn't been part of an "us" for a lot of years. He had to go back to New York before he got sucked in any deeper. Sucked in so far he couldn't get out, and then he'd be left alone like before.

"Mia, I like you. I love you for what you've done for my mom. You're great and you deserve a great guy." His thoughts whirled and he fought for breath. "Someone like Josh."

"Josh Tremblay?" Her voice wobbled. "He offered me a deal on a new furnace. I said no because I couldn't be indebted to him. Maybe he only wanted to help me out like he helps everyone around here, but I couldn't let him think I might ever like him in any way except as a friend."

Nick's throat was tight and raw. He'd told Josh that Mia wasn't his woman. There was no reason for him to want to punch the guy out. "Okay, maybe not Josh, but someone like him could give you a good life, a baby even."

"A baby?" Mia stumbled to her feet. "What makes you think I want another child?"

"I've seen you with Lexie." Seen how she cradled the baby in her arms with such love and tenderness. He'd also seen how she was with her girls. Mia was a born mother.

"Lexie's my niece and my goddaughter. I love her, but you've got the wrong idea. I don't want another baby." Her voice rose.

"You might." And he couldn't take that chance. If Nick thought he hurt now, he'd hurt even worse if he and Mia got together and she changed her mind about babies like Isobel had.

"This isn't about a baby, so what's really going on here?" Mia tugged on her sweatshirt, a white one she'd borrowed from him a few weeks back, which swamped her slender figure.

"I don't want a relationship. I never did." He got up from the rock, and pain shot through the knee he'd twisted playing baseball. Pain he welcomed because it displaced the pain in his heart.

"These last few weeks, I thought we were good together. Naomi and Emma like you, and I'm not going back to Jay, no matter how much he threatens me or criticizes my friends, the kind of mother I am, or anything else about me." On any other woman, her look would've been bitchy, but Mia never did bitchy.

They *were* good together, so good Nick couldn't let it go on because when it ended, he'd hurt a lot more than he already was. "This isn't about you, or the girls or Jay. It's about me. I don't deserve you."

"What?" Her eyebrows puckered in a frown.

"I can't have kids. That's why Isobel left me." He

curled his fingers into his palms to try to stop his hands from shaking. "When we met, Isobel didn't want kids. She was focused on her career. But that was before I knew...before we found out I couldn't. Then she sure wanted children, and she found somebody else to give them to her. A boy first, and there's another baby on the way."

"Whether you can have kids or not doesn't matter to me." Mia stared at him in disbelief.

"It matters to me." He pressed a hand to his chest as if he could physically keep the hurt in. "Besides, even if I could have kids, I'd be a lousy father. Look at the example I had. I couldn't be there for Naomi and Emma like you'd need a stepfather to be, whereas Josh is a great dad and—"

"Stop going on about Josh." Her voice was icy. "You would be a good stepfather. I've seen you with Kylie and my girls. And what about Amy? You love her, don't you?"

"She's my niece. That's different."

"Different how?" Her voice hitched. "Cat's a single mom."

"Cat doesn't need a father figure for Amy. Even if she did, she wouldn't expect it to be me." He shrugged to hide how much he cared that his sister had the child he never could.

Mia yanked his sweatshirt over her head and dropped it on the sand. "You've convinced yourself of things that aren't true to spend the rest of your life alone. I think you're making excuses. You're tired of me, like Jay was. Well, you know what?"

"What?" Nick bent to pick up his sweatshirt. Maybe it

was better she was mad because then she'd move on and forget him. His heart twisted tighter.

"I love you, but you're a fool, and maybe I am, too." She shivered in her thin red T-shirt. "You're right, I do deserve more than you. At least if I spend the rest of my life alone, it's by choice. Not because I was too scared of loss to open myself to love. I'm not Isobel. I'm not like your dad or your friends who got killed in the accident. We can't control the future. Your mom sure learned that lesson. I want to be part of your life forever, and if you can't believe me, that's your problem."

"Angel." The endearment slipped out before Nick could stop it.

"Don't you *angel* me." There were two red spots on Mia's cheeks, and her breath came in short pants. "In fact, don't ever call me or speak to me again unless it's something to do with your mom."

"I'm sorry," Nick murmured.

"You should be." Her eyes shimmered. "I'm sorry for you, too. That guy I remember? The one who rode around on the motorcycle? He may have been trouble, but he knew what he wanted, and he was fearless. What happened to him, Nick?"

A wave washed over his tennis shoes and cold water seeped through the thin canvas to chill his feet. "He almost drowned at the bottom of this lake inside the cab of a truck with his friends already dead in front of him. They died on impact. Even though he tried, he couldn't help them."

"You didn't die. You lived." The words came out of her like bullets.

"Only because I somehow managed to smash my way

out and the cops were right there." His breathing was uneven. Every detail of that night would always be etched in Nick's mind.

How he and two of his friends had been drinking on the beach behind the lifeguard station and then started a fight on the town green for the hell of it. How when the state troopers had arrived, the guys had panicked and piled into the truck to head out of town. How he'd argued with them and tried to take away the keys but instead had found himself in the backseat of the cab careening along Lake Road with the cops in pursuit.

"Because you lived, you had a chance to turn your life around, but somewhere along the way, you lost what made the guy I used to know so special." The pain in Mia's voice shredded what was left of Nick's heart. "Sure, he made mistakes, big ones, but he wasn't afraid to take a risk. He wasn't afraid to let himself care about people."

Nick bit his lower lip and tasted blood mixed with spray from the lake. He cared about Mia, more than he could say.

"I'll look out for your mom, and if she needs anything, I'll contact you, but otherwise, I won't." She stood at the water's edge for endless seconds, tall, beautiful, and strong, before she climbed the stone steps away from the beach and disappeared into the trees.

Mia stopped in Gabrielle's vegetable garden. Her chest heaved, and her vision blurred. Rain spattered the paving stones and big drops soaked through her T-shirt. She grabbed the umbrella Gabrielle kept in the toolshed and made her way to the patio. She could cut through the side gate and avoid Gabrielle, Ward, and the bubble of happiness that enveloped the two of them.

She eased the gate open and struggled with the umbrella as pine branches scratched her bare arms.

"Mia, honey?" Gabrielle came up the path in an orange slicker. At her side, Ward carried Pixie sheltered in a fold of his jacket. "What's wrong?"

"I got caught in the rain down by the lake. The storm sure blew in fast." She smiled until her mouth hurt with the effort.

"You...Nick..." Gabrielle looked at Mia, then at Ward, who shook his head. "You're half frozen. Come in for a cup of tea before we drive you home."

"I can walk." A gust of wind turned the umbrella inside out, and Mia made a frantic grab for the handle.

"You're soaked." Ward took the ruined umbrella.

He was right, but she couldn't handle their kindness. Besides, no matter how much she loved Gabrielle, she was still Nick's mom. "I'll borrow a rain jacket."

Gabrielle and Ward exchanged another glance.

"My blue coat with the hood is on the peg inside the kitchen door," she said.

"I'll get it." Ward patted Mia's shoulder. "Back in a minute."

"Thanks." Mia moved under the branch of a maple tree.

Beneath the hood of her slicker, Gabrielle's expression was worried. "What did my son do to you?"

"Nothing." Except throw her love back in her face and stomp her heart into little pieces.

"Or say?"

"He was honest." And Mia had learned her lesson.

"Stupid is more like it." Raindrops sparkled like silver teardrops on the edges of Gabrielle's hair.

"I never said—"

"You didn't have to. I'm Nick's mother, but I'm not blind to his faults." She rubbed Mia's cold hands between her warm ones. "Sometimes, the more you love somebody the more you hurt them."

"I don't..." What was the use of denying it? Gabrielle was savvy about people. "I'm sorry."

"Never be sorry for loving." Gabrielle smoothed Mia's wet hair away from her face, her touch motherly. "But I was talking about Nick."

"He doesn't love me." And she loved him too much.

"I'm not so sure of that."

"Nick thinks he can't be with me because he can't have children." Mia gulped in air. "Even if he could, he says he'd be a bad father."

Gabrielle's eyes widened. "What?"

Mia pulled a hand away and pressed it to her mouth. "You didn't know? Please don't tell him I told you."

"Of course not." Her expression was sad. "It explains such a lot, though. My poor boy. That must have been the root of the trouble with Isobel. And all this time he's had me and half the women in town pestering him about getting on with having kids."

"I forced him to spend time with Kylie." And Nick cared about the girl, Mia was certain of it.

"He won't let himself love her, either. He's hurt, Kylie's hurt, and you're hurt. Do you want another baby?" Gabrielle's blue gaze was tender.

"No." Mia hugged herself. "I almost died when I gave birth to Emma, and I was sick for the whole pregnancy. I

never want to go through that again. When I told Nick it
didn't matter to me if he could father a child, he wouldn't
listen. Then he said he couldn't be there for Naomi and
Emma like a stepfather would need to be."

"I think he's convinced himself he can't love or won't
let himself love, which pretty much amounts to the same
thing." Gabrielle's face got a faraway expression. "Nick's
had a lot of losses in his life, and he's wary. He doesn't
want to get hurt again."

"I can't change him." She'd already tried with Jay and
her dad and gotten nowhere.

"Maybe I—"

"No. If Nick ever changes, it has to come from inside
him." Another lesson Mia had learned.

"Here you go." Ward slung Gabrielle's blue coat
around Mia's shoulders. "Are you sure you won't let me
drive you home?"

"I'll be fine." Mia shrugged into the garment.

"Sure you will." Gabrielle tugged on the zipper and
pulled it up to Mia's chin.

"It's still raining hard," Ward said.

"I didn't mean the weather." Gabrielle patted Mia's
cheek. "I'll call you later."

"You promise you won't say anything?" The last thing
she needed was for Gabrielle, however well intentioned,
to talk to Nick. Whatever she'd imagined they shared was
over, and Mia had to pick herself up and move on.

"Not a word." Gabrielle's eyes were troubled. "I only
wish…"

Like Mia would've wished, if she hadn't stopped wish-
ing a long time ago, even before Jay left. She moved
away from Gabrielle with an effort. She'd gotten what she

wanted. Independence and a casual, no-strings relationship, which had put what she'd had with Jay firmly in the past.

Except, it had cost her a friend and showed her what she really wanted but had lost forever.

Chapter Twenty

I hope you know what you're doing." Gabrielle sat on the bottom porch step as Nick put the suitcase he'd borrowed from her into the trunk of his Lexus. The shrubs in the flower beds below the porch were wet with dew, and the sun nudged the eastern sky to envelop Harbor House in a rosy glow.

"Sure I do." Nick opened the driver's door, dragged off his suit jacket, and hung it on the hook behind the seat.

"I'm your mother." And it was time she started acting like it again. "Cancer took away my hair, my energy, and a lot of other things, but it didn't take away how I always know when you're lying to me."

Nick left the car door open and moved toward her. "When did I ever lie to you?" His smile was too quick.

Gabrielle patted the step beside her. "Maybe you're lying to yourself, then."

Nick rested an arm on the porch railing but didn't sit. "That's ridiculous."

"Really?" Gabrielle stood and moved up two steps so she faced him eye to eye and nose to nose. The wariness in his expression gave her hope she'd touched a nerve and he'd think about what she said. "I'm not senile either, even if you wanted to make me old before my time by stuffing me into a retirement bungalow."

"We got beyond all that." His smile slipped. "I'm going back to New York because it's after Labor Day and that was always the plan."

"Plans can change if you want them to." Gabrielle touched Nick's jaw with the small scar from the accident the years had made part of his face. "I love you and I want you to be happy."

"I love you too, Mom." His expression softened. "And I am happy. Now you've got a good guy like Ward in your life, I'm even happier."

"I want you to be happy for yourself, not on my account." Even though she didn't quite trust the happiness she'd found with Ward yet so they were taking things slow.

"You worry too much."

"I'm your mom, so it comes with the job." Gabrielle's throat tightened. "Mia left something for you. She asked me to give it to you before you headed out." She picked up the cardboard mailing tube from one of the porch chairs.

"What's this?" Nick's fingers closed around the roll, and a muscle in his jaw twitched.

"I don't know," she said, although she had a good idea. "Mia said was it was something she found in the closet in your old room and forgot to give to you."

"I better hit the road." Nick's eyes darkened from blue

to pewter as they'd done since childhood when he was upset about something. "I have a late afternoon meeting with the team. It's a big case. If I win, it'll make my career." The lines between his nose and mouth deepened, and in the early morning light, his eyes were purple shadowed.

"Drive safe." Gabrielle followed him to the car. "Call me when you get there."

"I always do." Nick hugged her. "Why don't you and Ward fly out and spend a weekend with me in New York?"

"I'd like that." She couldn't bring herself to say anything more.

He got into the car. "Call me if you need anything, and don't forget Cat and Amy will be here again soon."

"I won't." But it would be yet another brief visit, and her daughter had insisted on staying at a local bed and breakfast instead of Harbor House so they wouldn't be a bother. As if her child and grandchild could ever be anything but a blessing.

Nick waved, and the engine roared into life. The premium car told the world he was a success. Except, although the car was safer, Gabrielle sometimes preferred the old motorcycle.

"Bye," she whispered.

With another wave, Nick turned out onto the road and the engine sound died away to leave silence in its wake.

Gabrielle walked back to the house. She had her life to live. Her hand closed around her phone in her sweater pocket. Ward had promised he'd call later today when he got to Beijing. A world away, he'd think of her and dream of her.

"Did Nick just leave?" Luc jogged around the side of the house in black sweats and a Winnipeg Jets hockey T-shirt.

"Yes." She tried to smile.

"Give me twenty minutes to shower and change and I'll take you to breakfast at the diner. It's been too many years since I've had Liz Carmichael's buttermilk biscuits." He stopped at Gabrielle's side and patted her shoulder. "I'd enjoy your company."

"I don't mean to sound ungrateful, but a man like you would never be short of company."

He grinned. "Maybe, but you're the company I choose. Besides, Ward and Nick asked me to keep an eye on you, so you might say I'm only doing my job."

"They did, did they?" Gabrielle took one last look at the empty street before she pulled open the screen door and scooped Pixie into her arms. "We've got to have faith," she murmured to the dog, who wiggled in her grasp. "Nick has to come back. He and Mia were meant to be together."

Pixie licked her face.

Gabrielle laughed, and then the laugh turned into a sigh. Because things were meant to be didn't mean they would. She had to face facts and count her blessings. She'd done all she could. The changes she wanted Nick to make had to come from him, because he wanted them, too.

Almost four weeks later, Nick pushed his chair away from the desk and took a folder from the filing cabinet beside it. Lights gleamed out of the darkness, and New York traffic hummed from the street twenty floors below.

Beyond the pool of light from the desk lamp, the office was dark. Even the cleaners had gone home long ago. He turned back to the computer then glanced at the time on the screen and grabbed his phone. He'd intended to call Sean tonight but, as usual, he'd lost track of time. He scrolled to the number, and it rang in the house beside Firefly Lake. A house full of love, laughter, and everything that made a house a home.

"Nick?" Sean's voice was thick with sleep. "Why are you calling at this time of night? You aren't still at the office, are you?"

"I'm working on a case." Nick checked the time again. It was only ten thirty. "Are you keeping farmer's hours these days?"

"It's having a baby. Charlie and I have to sleep when we can." Sean murmured something. "Hang on a minute."

Nick moved a stack of files to find the picture included with the invitation to Lexie's baptism. Dressed head to toe in pink, the kid gave the camera a gummy smile. Charlie's smile. Mia's, too. His chest ached.

He turned back to the computer screen and, with an effort, clicked open the document with the police report and pictures of his socialite client with the black eye inflicted by her state senator husband. Soon to be her ex-husband and behind bars, if Nick got what he wanted.

"I'm back." Sean came on the phone again. "Are you okay?"

"Great, never better." Nick was doing what he wanted, and he'd win this case. Why wouldn't he be okay? "The firm's got a bunch of extra tickets for the hockey game on Saturday night. You want to come and stay with me? It's the Rangers against Vancouver."

"This weekend?" Sean hesitated. "Sorry, buddy. I can't. Lexie's still so little I don't want to leave Charlie alone overnight."

More like Sean didn't want to leave Charlie period. Or the baby. As if Lexie might do something he'd miss if he was away for more than a few hours.

"Can't Mia and the girls stay with her?" Nick stared at the stars and crescent moon that peeked out from behind the high-rise across the street.

"Mia's busy with school." Sean's voice cooled. "And stuff."

Nick had given up his right to know what that "stuff" was. "Mia's okay, isn't she?" He missed her friendship, apart from every other way.

"She's great. Everyone at the school loves her, and she's settled into Firefly Lake like she's a Vermonter born and bred."

"Wonderful." Nick's throat constricted. Why did Sean have to sound so smug? "Maybe we can catch a game some other time. I'm pretty busy." The client had paid the firm a shedload of money for him to stay busy.

"Really busy, or busy on purpose?"

Sean's words hit Nick in the pit of his stomach and ricocheted up his windpipe. "I've got a big case. It's high profile."

"After this big case, it'll be another one and then another." Sean sounded so reasonable Nick wanted to punch something. Or someone. "You ever get tired of it?"

So tired by the time he got to the end of the week he'd go to the gym, drag himself home, order takeout, and fall into bed. Alone and aching for Mia. "This client needs my help."

"They all need your help, but I think you might need help, too."

"What's with you? Has Charlie turned you into some sensitive new-age guy all of a sudden?"

Sean's laugh grated like sandpaper on Nick's ears. "Nope. I'm still the same guy I always was, only a happier one. Say, when you come for Lexie's baptism, you should stay a few days longer. You could have more time with your mom, and it'd give me a chance to kick your sorry ass at pool."

Nick pulled at his shirt collar. "Mom's fine. Having Luc as a housemate is great for her. Besides, Ward will be back by then."

"You're still coming to Lexie's baptism, aren't you?" Sean's voice roughened.

"Of course. I'm flying to Burlington on the Friday afternoon." Even though it meant he'd have to stand at the front of St. James Episcopal with Mia on the Sunday morning, the sight of her a fresh reminder of what he'd forced himself to let go.

"You're all set to pick up Kylie after school?"

"Kylie?" Nick dug under the stack of papers on his desk for the cream-colored invitation.

"Charlie emailed and texted you. Mia's got it all organized with Kylie's foster family and her social worker." There was more than a hint of frustration in Sean's voice. "If you get Kylie from her foster family's place after school on Friday, she can spend the weekend in Firefly Lake. Remember?"

Nick stopped looking for the invitation. "Of course. Sorry. I've had a lot going on." If he focused on work, he didn't have to think about the mess he'd made of the rest of his life.

"Kylie can't wait to see you. She's super excited about the weekend and Lexie's baptism. Hey, why don't you take Kylie and her foster family to the hockey game? You said the firm has a bunch of tickets and, with what you must bill, you could cover the tab for their flights and a hotel for the night. I bet Kylie would love to go."

Yeah, she would. And he'd like to take her. Buy her a team sweatshirt if she wanted one and eat hot dogs, drink soda, and hang out together. He glanced at Lexie's picture again and then, almost hidden behind his computer monitor, the second picture behind it. The one of him and Kylie on the beach framed by the twigs she'd glued together and all those purple feathers.

"It's short notice. Kylie's probably busy."

"Want to bet? Not for you she wouldn't be. Even if the whole family can't go, I'm sure her foster mom or dad would take her." Sean paused as a baby cried in the background. "I have to go. Lexie's fussing."

And Nick was left with the dial tone in his ear, the whir of the heating in his quiet office, and a court date in the morning that could make his career again and give him back his professional pride and the self-respect Isobel had taken away that night on the conference room table with the affair that, it turned out, everyone had known about but him.

He grabbed a Snickers bar from the drawer, tore off the wrapper, and inhaled the scent of chocolate and peanuts. A smell that took him back to when he sat with his dad in a boat on Firefly Lake with Snickers and soda stashed in a battered cooler. They'd spent hours out there with their fishing rods. A time when they'd talked about sports, the weirdness of girls, and motorcycles.

The motorcycle posters they'd collected together, which had papered the walls of Nick's bedroom. The posters he'd never been able to throw away but had forgotten about until Mia found them and asked his mom to give them to him. The posters he'd shoved in a closet in his apartment behind his skis and empty suitcases.

He could win this case. He would win this case, but maybe there were more important things in life than winning. He dropped the half-eaten candy bar and found his cell again to scroll to the number he'd memorized as soon as Kylie had given it to him.

She could always say no. Or she could say yes and take him a step closer to being the guy Mia talked about. The one he used to be.

Nick stopped. It was too late to call Kylie tonight. Even if she didn't think so, her foster mom sure would. He drummed his fingers on the desk.

What else had Mia said? The guy she remembered hadn't been afraid to take a risk. He continued scrolling through his contacts and found the number his mom had emailed him. The number he'd never called.

It was too late to call Kylie, but it was still early in Vegas.

He propped the picture of Kylie and him in front of his computer keyboard. Her smile warmed him and gave him unexpected courage. Unlike him, she'd never known her dad. He wasn't ready to forgive and forget, but if he wanted to move on, maybe he at least needed to listen to what Brian McGuire had to say.

"You must have known earlier it was your week to bring a snack for circle time." Mia stuffed the songbook for the third graders into her portfolio with one hand and an apple into Emma's lunch box with the other. "Why didn't you tell me?"

"I forgot." Emma leaned against the kitchen counter and lifted one leg in a graceful arc. "You can defrost cupcakes or something. Like you always do."

"Did." Mia handed Naomi her lunch and flute case. "I have a job outside the home. I don't have as much time to bake. I'll buy cupcakes at the bakery on the way to school."

"Mom." Emma's voice rose. "I don't want bakery cupcakes. I want your cupcakes. I already told my teacher and my whole class what an awesome cook you are."

Mia wiped toast crumbs off the counter and counted to five. She loved her girls, but she also loved her job, and there was no way she could produce twenty iced cupcakes in the ten minutes before she had to be in the car. "There's a loaf of banana bread in the freezer."

"Banana bread has fruit in it." Emma dropped her foot to the floor with a thud.

"Course it does," Naomi said. "Why else would it be called banana bread? Give Mom a break."

"You're mean." Emma opened the freezer and slid out the loaf Mia indicated.

"And you're a whiny baby," Naomi countered.

"Mommy." Emma's voice went up another octave.

"Girls, please." Mia found her car keys and checked to make sure she'd tucked the card for Naomi's after-school dentist appointment in her purse. "We have to leave or we'll be late and—"

"Nick's on TV." Emma slammed the freezer shut and pointed through the doorway at the television in the living room.

"What?" Mia whirled around, the appointment card forgotten. She'd trained herself to not think about Nick, at least not during the day. Who or what she thought about at night alone in bed was another matter.

"It's him all right," Naomi said. "Shush, listen."

Mia moved into the living room on autopilot. Nick stood outside a brick building with pillars, and he was flanked by reporters with microphones. His hair was windblown, and he wore a dark suit and tie. She sat on the nearest chair to listen.

"I'm confident the jury will reach the right decision." There was a steely glint in his eyes, along with warmth, passion, and a conviction justice would prevail.

Mia gripped her purse. In spite of everything, she still loved him. The camera panned the nearby crowd, some of whom waved placards.

"Violence isn't the solution, it's the problem." Emma sounded out the words. "There's no excuse for domestic abuse. What's that mean?"

"It means a bad man hurt his wife, and Nick's helping her." Naomi glanced at Mia.

"Nick helped me when I almost got drowned," Emma said.

"Yes, he did." Mia's throat clogged.

Nick helped people and causes he cared about. He'd tried to save his friends when the truck hit the water all those years ago. He looked out for his mom and his sisters, and he'd looked out for the girls and her.

"And he helped Kylie and her mom," Emma added.

Naomi flicked off the TV and touched Mia's shoulder. "We have to go or I'll miss the bus."

Her eyes burned as Mia moved into the hall, grabbed her

coat from the hook, and checked that the girls had lunches, school bags, and musical instruments as if by rote. "Put the banana bread in a plastic container," she told Emma. "The one with the blue lid in the cupboard over the sink."

"Mom?" Naomi took a sweater from the newel post as Emma darted to the kitchen. "Are you okay?"

"I'm fine." Her voice cracked. A stranger's voice.

Naomi slung her backpack over one shoulder. "Is it Nick?"

Her daughter was almost a woman, too old to be fobbed off with comforting lies or feeble excuses.

"I miss him." Mia missed him so much her heart ached with it and maybe always would.

"Even though you never said so, I knew things weren't great between you and Dad." Naomi's brown eyes were older than her years. "When I saw how he was with Tiffany in the summer, and then how he threatened to take Emma and me away from you, I guess I finally understood."

"Understood what?" Mia's tongue was thick.

"Dad's selfish. He doesn't think about other people like you do." Naomi's smile was wistful. "He doesn't want Emma and me to live with him, not really. He just wants to get the better of you, like all of us are one of his business deals."

"Honey, I'm sorry. Your dad loves you, even though he might not always show it in the right way." Mia hugged her daughter. "And I love you so much."

Naomi hugged her back, soft and with a familiar smell of strawberry shampoo. "I've asked Dad to back off over and over again, but last night I convinced Emma to talk to him with me. He listens to her more than me."

Mia studied Naomi's face for a long moment, seeing her daughter as a person in her own right.

"I think Dad's finally coming around. He's upset all of us, you most of all, so I told him if he forced Emma and me to live with him, I'd marry Ty the day I turned eighteen and wouldn't go to college."

"You don't mean that!" There'd been a teasing note in Naomi's voice, but Mia had to be sure.

"Chill, Mom. You know I'm not serious." Naomi gave her a knowing grin. "Dad doesn't, though, so he backed right off. He said he'd have his attorney call Allison, and he was sure we could work something out."

"What about Emma? How did you manage her?" Mia held her breath. Although Emma had come around, she'd always be her daddy's girl.

"Ty told me Uncle Sean sold a boat to this rich guy who has a horse farm south of town. The man's daughter's too big for her pony, but the pony's like a member of the family, so selling it would break the girl's heart." Naomi's grin broadened. "The family's looking for someone to ride the pony, and there's even a pony club that meets at the farm. Emma wants to learn how to ride a pony more than she wants to live with Dad."

Mia raised an eyebrow. "I thought your dad promised Emma a pony in California."

"He promised, sure, but you know what Dad's promises are worth." Naomi's smile disappeared. "He never even let us get a cat, so why would he all of a sudden spring for a horse? I didn't exactly tell Emma that, but I sort of led her to the right conclusion."

"Thank you." Mia's heart clenched.

Naomi moved closer. "About Nick, you should call him and tell him you miss him."

Like telling him how she felt had worked out so well for Mia before. "He's back in New York, and he's got a great career. You saw him on the news."

"Why won't you go out with anybody else?" Naomi's expression was demure. "Emma said the fire warden who came to talk to her class asked you to have lunch with him."

Emma saw and heard far too much for her age.

"I'm busy." Mia glanced toward the kitchen.

"Maybe Nick needs you as much as you need him. He just doesn't know it yet." Naomi opened the front door, and cool air rushed in with a scent of crisp October leaves.

Mia was getting relationship advice from a sixteen-year-old? "Hurry, Emma, we'll be late."

"You look after everyone else. You always have," Naomi said. "You tell Emma and me not to give up on our dreams and not to settle for anything or anybody that isn't right for us."

Because they were her girls and Mia wanted them to aim for the sky and be happy.

But she deserved to be happy. She had her house, her job, and her family. If Naomi was right, Jay would back off. Mia needed to stop thinking about Nick and find her future.

Without him.

Chapter Twenty-One

"How do I look?" Kylie twirled in front of the full-length mirror at the little boutique in Kincaid. Her hair had grown since the summer, and blond tendrils curled below her shoulders.

"Beautiful." Nick studied the dark purple dress the saleswoman had picked out. "After Lexie, you'll be the prettiest girl at the baptism."

Kylie bounced on her toes, and her cheeks flushed pink. "Naomi's gonna fix my hair, and Emma said she'd loan me a necklace she got for her last birthday." Kylie twirled again. The slim lines of the dress showed her figure, which was curvier than it had been when she was at Camp Rainbow.

"Does your daughter need shoes?" At Nick's elbow, the middle-aged saleswoman also watched Kylie.

"Uh, she's..." The woman's words slammed into Nick. The room spun, and the mirrors and windows blurred in the sunshine that streamed through the store window.

"I can wear my sneakers." Kylie stared at her feet. "Nobody will look at me anyway. I don't even need a dress."

"Of course you do. Remember what my mom said?" He forced himself to smile at the saleswoman—Marlene, according to the tag pinned to her black top. "And you can't wear sneakers with a fancy dress."

"I'll show you a few pairs to check for size." Marlene patted Kylie's shoulder and moved to the rear of the store.

"You don't have to buy me stuff." Kylie tugged at the sleeves of the dress. "Or take me places if you don't want to. Your mom made you bring me here."

He was busted. "Shopping's not my favorite thing, but we had fun at the hockey game, didn't we?" Nick searched her face and wished he could bring the light back into those wary green eyes.

"Yeah." She gave him a half smile. "That was different, though. My foster family was there."

"My mom would have taken you shopping if she could, but she was tired after her doctor's appointment yesterday." He marked the regular checkups to make sure the cancer hadn't come back on his calendar, and then breathed a sigh of relief each time she got through another one with the all-clear.

Kylie's smile broadened. "You brought me here because you didn't want your mom to kick your ass."

"True," Nick laughed, "but you shouldn't use that kind of language."

"You do. I've heard you."

Nick swallowed another laugh. "Yeah, but you might forget and use it when you shouldn't. Like around Mia." The woman who was never far from his thoughts, but

who he hadn't spoken to in four weeks. The longest
month of his life.

Kylie's smile disappeared, and she picked at a hangnail. "I'll try, but what I also meant is you don't have to
spend money on me. If you can't afford it."

"I can afford it." Nick's gut twisted. With what he was
earning in New York, he could afford anything he wanted,
except the one thing that mattered most. "And I like hanging out with you."

It had been easier than he'd expected to let Kylie into
his life. Maybe because after he'd called his dad, an awkward, stilted conversation with a guy he no longer knew,
he'd glimpsed the guy he could become. Old and alone,
consumed by bitterness and regrets.

"You like me, don't you?" Kylie's eyes were sharp. An
old soul in a girl's body.

"Of course I do. I'd never lie to you."

Reflected in the mirror beside him, Kylie's face was
serious. "You lied to Mia, though, didn't you?"

"What do you mean?" Nick looked for Marlene, but
the saleswoman was nowhere in sight.

"Mia calls me every Sunday night, but whenever I ask
about you, she either doesn't answer or she tries to distract me like I'm a little kid."

"Mia and I are friends, but she's busy with school, and
I've got work, and it's been—"

"See? You change the subject whenever I mention
Mia, and you stayed in the car when you dropped me off
at her place yesterday and picked me up this morning."
Kylie put her hands on her hips, a picture of pint-sized
feminine outrage. "Whatever you did, you fucked up big
time, and now you've gotta fix it."

"Kylie…"

"It's true. You did fuck up."

"I guess I did." He'd told the kid he wouldn't lie to her, but although he wanted to, he had no idea how to fix things with Mia. If he could fix things.

"You need to tell Mia you messed up." Kylie took an open shoebox from Marlene and stuck a pair of black shoes with lethal heels on her feet. "Apologize, give her flowers and jewelry. Women like shit like that."

"Kylie." Nick glanced at Marlene, whose lips twitched. "Remember what I said about your language."

"Every woman likes a bit of romance." Marlene gave Kylie a hand to help her balance in the heels.

Kylie teetered toward the mirror. "These shoes are way cool. They make me look fifteen, at least."

"Aren't the heels a bit high for a girl your age?" How could he talk to Mia? She never wanted to hear from him again. At least not about anything or anyone unless it involved his mom.

"Girls her age wear shoes like this for special occasions. Dads never want to see how their little girl is growing up." Marlene beamed at Kylie, who gave her a tentative smile in return.

"Please?" Kylie's eyes shone before she looked back at her feet and stuck each foot in front of her in turn. "They fit me real good."

Nick opened his mouth and closed it again. He couldn't destroy the excitement and pleasure in Kylie's eyes. "We'll take the shoes, the dress, and anything else she needs." He gestured to the stack of clothes Marlene had hung on the changing room door.

"I don't need nothing else." Kylie slipped out of the

shoes and tucked an arm through his. "But thank you," she added in a soft voice.

"For what?" Nick pulled his wallet out of his back pocket.

"For everything." Kylie squeezed his arm, and her touch was warm and confiding. "For picking me up in Burlington and bringing me to Firefly Lake. For getting me something to wear so I'll look okay at the baptism. And I know you're gonna talk to Mia."

"I didn't...I never said..." Nick stopped and handed his credit card to Marlene.

Kylie untangled herself from him and moved toward the changing room. "I trust you. You'll fix what you did, 'cause that's who you are." She disappeared behind the curtained door, and the rustle of clothing told him she was putting her jeans and sweater back on.

"You've got a girl with strong character there." Marlene put the shoes back in the box and tucked it into one of the boutique's pink paper bags. "Don't worry about her language. One of my daughters was the same way once she hit her teens. Liked to get a rise out of me, Lisa did, but she grew out of it. Your Kylie knows you love her and you'll be there for her. Nothing else matters."

Nick took the bag with the shoes. "You think?"

"Sure." Marlene handed him his credit card and receipt. "You'll make things right with that Mia Kylie talked about. Girls of Kylie's age need a woman's guidance, and it's not good for a man to be all alone."

Nick swallowed. "How did you guess?"

"Kylie talked you into those shoes real quick, didn't she?" Marlene's gray eyes crinkled at the corners. "If there was a woman in the picture, you'd have taken a lot more convincing and asked to see some other pairs."

He was a sucker for a blond-haired pixie with sparkling green eyes. A girl who'd brought fun, laughter, and love into his life, and who he'd been stupid enough to almost let go.

"Hey." Kylie burst through the changing room doorway and handed the dress to Marlene to fold into another pink bag.

"Hey, yourself." Nick passed Kylie the bag with the shoes. "Want to grab some lunch before we head back to Firefly Lake?"

"Sure, but no salad stuff. Mia's great, except she eats like a rabbit." Kylie took the dress bag from Marlene then looked at him, her gaze trusting as they went out of the store onto Kincaid's Main Street, where the fall foliage had just passed its peak. "While we eat, I can help you fix things with her."

"You're twelve."

"Thirteen next month, and I couldn't make stuff any worse than you already did, could I?" Kylie waved at Marlene through the store window.

"Okay." He dodged a group of late-season leaf peepers and steered Kylie toward the burger place across the street. "What do you think I need to do?"

Mia fixed her gaze on Reverend Arthur. Sunlight streamed through the stained glass window above his head, and Lexie gurgled in his arms as the baptismal robe worn by three generations of Carmichael babies billowed around her.

Sean's voice and then Charlie's said things. Nick said things.

Then her voice as she promised to be there for Lexie and guide her niece in life and faith. Reverend Arthur splashed water on Lexie's head, and she squealed, which earned muffled laughter from the congregation, who lined the pews behind. Sean's family, her girls and Kylie, Gabrielle and Ward with Cat and Amy, as well as most of the town.

"Mia." Charlie whispered and nudged her elbow.

"Sorry." She took Lexie from the minister as Sean and Charlie went to light a baptismal candle.

Mia stole a glance at Nick, who stood tall and serious to her left. She'd managed to avoid him all weekend, so she only had to get through the next few hours and he'd be gone again.

Then maybe the hurt in her heart would ease.

She rocked Lexie in her arms, and the baby rewarded her with a sunny smile. "All finished, sweetheart, and here's mommy back for you," she murmured as she and Nick followed Charlie and Sean to their place in the front pew.

Reverend Arthur opened his hymnbook for the final hymn. The organ music soared and echoed off the vaulted ceiling in the historic church.

"Mia." Nick's voice was a hiss under the cover of the music. "I need to talk to you."

She shook her head, opened her mouth, and pretended to sing. The hymn ended, and the minister gave the benediction before the organist launched into a recessional and the choir and baptismal party followed Reverend Arthur back down the center aisle.

"Wait." Nick stepped closer to Mia and took her arm in a firm grip. "I mean it. I need to talk to you."

But she didn't need to talk to him. "Not here." She smiled at Kylie on the end of a pew next to Gabrielle, then Liz Carmichael three rows back with Luc Simard and his folks.

"Then where?"

"I promised to help serve lunch in the parish hall. We're Lexie's godparents, and Charlie and Sean want to take pictures, so we can't—"

"I've already cleared it with Sean. They can manage without us for ten minutes, and I've drafted in Cat to serve lunch in your place. I have to speak to you."

His voice was urgent, and a little part of Mia melted. "We're still in church." Technically, although they'd reached the entryway, the front doors were wide open, and the bells in the tower pealed out to celebrate Lexie's special day.

"If a man can't say what's in his heart in church, where can he say it? Use my office, son." Reverend Arthur gestured to a door on the left of the foyer. A fringe of white hair encircled the minister's head like a halo, and he gave them a saint-like smile as he moved to open the door. "Take all the time you need."

"Thank you." Nick dropped Mia's arm and clasped her hand as the office door closed behind Reverend Arthur with a soft click.

Mia stared at Nick as if hypnotized. She couldn't make a run for it because, by now, not only her family but half the town would be milling about in the church entrance.

"Nick." He was the most private guy she knew. Didn't he realize how many people would have seen him pull her in here? The gossip would spread through Firefly Lake and beyond faster than a mountain wildfire.

He flashed her a devastating grin like he was way ahead of her. "I made a big mistake last month. I've made a lot of mistakes in my life because I didn't know any better." His smile turned tender and sweet. "Except, this mistake I knew better but I went ahead anyway."

"You did?" Mia's mouth got dry.

"Yes, and I'll always regret it. I hurt you, and I'm sorry. Sorrier than you'll ever know." His voice was low, raw. "You gave me your love, and I threw it aside like it was worthless."

Mia swallowed. "I—"

"No." Nick's gaze never left her face. "This whole mess is my fault. I was too stupid to recognize I love you back. Too stupid to realize I had to let go of the past and stuff that wasn't true anymore. Some of it wasn't ever true, but I thought it was, so I guess that amounts to the same thing."

Mia curled her fingers around Nick's and held on like he was a lifeline. "You love me?"

"I do, and I hope you still love me and can find it in your heart to forgive me." He moved closer, and his warm breath feathered Mia's cheek.

She breathed in his familiar aftershave, warm and comforting but sexy with a hint of danger. "If I forgive you, then what?" Even though a part of her wanted to forget about tomorrow, fall into his arms, and say yes to whatever he offered, she wasn't that woman anymore. She didn't want to be such a woman ever again.

"I want you to think about building a life with me. A forever life."

Mia took her hands away from Nick's. She'd had the promise of forever once. A proposal at sunset on a Florida beach with Jay on bended knee. A tiny box holding a massive diamond ring from a man who'd lied to her almost from the start of their life together.

"Those are nice words, but how can I be sure you mean them?" She might be throwing away the best thing to ever happen to her, but if she didn't ask, she'd always wonder if she'd given in too soon and started to lose herself again.

"That's a fair question." Nick gave her a half smile. "I love you even more for asking it. I can't promise the two of us together will be easy. I'm stubborn. I don't like to talk about my feelings, and I also work too much, but maybe you can help me with all that."

She gulped. "For us to be together, I'd have to come first, before your work."

"You would, I swear it."

Mia couldn't doubt the sincerity in his voice. Still ... she channeled the woman she was. All of her. "I need to know you love me for me." Jay never had, and Mia had spent almost half her life trying to be good enough. All for a man who'd never been good enough for her.

"Aw, angel." Nick's expression changed, uncertainty wiped away, and all the love he'd kept hidden showed in the blue-gray tenderness of his eyes. "I've never wanted you to be anyone but you. It may have taken me a lot of years to figure out, but you've always been one hell of a woman. You're the woman for me, and if you'll give me a chance, I want to be your man. I promise I'll always do my best for you and Naomi and Emma. I want us all to be a family, my family. It'll take time, but I'll figure out the stepdad thing. And if I start to go wrong, you'll steer me straight."

Hope bloomed in Mia's heart, as well as all the love for

Nick she'd buried but never lost. "You believe me when I say I don't want another baby?"

"Mom told me what happened at Emma's birth. I've also heard enough about babies from Sean. Lexie's great, but you and I don't have to have one. I like sleep too much. And other things." He gave her his bad-boy grin, and Mia knew exactly what those other things were.

"I love you, Nick, and I'll love you for as long as I live."

The office door banged open, and Kylie evaded Gabrielle's grasp. "Is this the part where you kiss her?"

"No, it's where I kiss him." Mia leaned in and wrapped her arms around the man who'd helped her figure out who she was.

And who she wanted to become, together.

Epilogue

December, seven weeks later

Nick stood in the front hall of Mia's house. Snowdrifts were already piled deep, but inside it was warm and cozy. A home, despite the scattered construction debris. Three backpacks were at the bottom of the stairs, together with a flute case, a Play-Doh horse, and a pair of purple swimming goggles.

"Girls?" he called. "If you don't get a move on, you'll miss the school bus."

"Not a chance." Kylie came out of the kitchen, with Pixie beside her, followed by Harley, Nick's rescue collie, and Chanel, Mia's kitten. "There's no way the driver will leave without Naomi."

"What are you talking about? Bert Stevens is sixty, at least." Nick handed her the swimming goggles, which she wedged into her backpack.

"His nephew isn't." Kylie grabbed her coat from the

hook beside the front door with her name on it. "Mr. Stevens has to have a hip replacement so Jordan's filling in. He's twenty-one and sex in a parka."

"Jordan Stevens is a grown man."

"Don't get all weird." Kylie heaved the heavy backpack onto her shoulders, and Nick winced. "The only guy Naomi notices is Ty."

Which he and Mia also worried about—the teens were too serious about each other too young.

"Girls?" he called again.

Emma slid down the banister and vaulted off.

"You're lucky my mom isn't here to see you do that." Nick ruffled her hair. "Whenever she caught me or my sisters sliding on the banister at Harbor House, we got a time-out."

"That's why you let me do it. You know how much fun it is." Emma gave Nick the sweet smile that got him every time. "When's Grandma Gabby coming home again?"

"On Saturday, so she has time to get ready for the holidays and the wedding. She's sure excited about your mom and me getting married on New Year's Eve and being a real grandma to you girls." When he'd spoken to her the previous night, his mom had sounded happier than ever, full of her trip to Arizona with Ward.

Mia and Naomi came down the stairs side by side, and Nick caught his breath. He still couldn't quite believe Mia would soon be his wife and this would be their life.

"You're here early this morning." Mia wore a pair of sexy red heels with slim black pants and a white shirt. Simple and elegant like always.

Nick gave her his hand for the last few steps. Not

because she needed it, but because he liked touching her. "The contractor wants to get an early start so the crew can finish Kylie's bedroom, my home office, and the family room by the end of next week." The addition to Mia's house, where he'd move after the wedding.

Mia bumped her hip against his, a fleeting gesture because of the girls. "Pixie, stop it."

Nick grabbed the Maltese while Mia took the kitten and nuzzled its face. "Pixie's a girl and she likes shoes." When his mom and Ward weren't around, Pixie was part of his life and the family he cherished every moment of every day.

"Since she all of a sudden likes shoes so much, why won't she chew on the ones I got her for that purpose?" Mia eyed him over the bundle of black and white fluff in her arms.

"Why chew on discount sneakers when designer's on offer?" He gave her a teasing grin.

"Pixie's gotten into bad habits. We should never have left her with Charlie and Sean when we went to the cabin to celebrate our engagement. Shadow influenced her." A smile hovered around Mia's full lips.

"Wasn't the weekend worth it?" Nick would've taken her anywhere, but Mia had chosen his mémère's cabin, where they'd spent an idyllic two days alone making love and planning the rest of their lives together.

Mia colored and stepped back. "Emma, don't forget your lunch." She waved the pink bag by its strap.

"You won't forget to come to my swimming showcase after school, will you? I can almost do the front crawl." Kylie paused on the doorstep, and her green eyes held only a hint of the wary expression of old.

"Of course I won't," Nick said. "I wouldn't miss seeing you swim for anything."

"All the other kids' dads are coming." Kylie gave him a shy smile. "I said mine was too."

"Kylie." Nick's heart almost stopped. He set Pixie on the floor and pulled the girl into a hug. "I'll always be there for you."

Kylie pulled Mia into the hug, then Naomi and Emma. "'Cause we're a family."

"We are." Mia's breath warmed his cheek.

"You're taking me to my first pony club meeting, aren't you?" Emma's voice came from the middle of the huddle. "My dad can't make it that weekend."

"I sure am." Above Emma's head, Nick's gaze met Mia's in wordless sympathy.

"And my band concert," Naomi added. "Dad can't make that either."

"Already in my calendar." Nick took a deep breath. "Don't forget that after the wedding you'll spend a few days in a hotel in Boston with your dad. He's a busy guy flying all over the world. I'm sure he'd be here if he could."

Even though Nick wasn't sure of any such thing, he could afford to be generous. He had what Jay didn't know he was missing, what his own dad had turned his back on and realized too late that he'd lost.

"Thank you," Mia whispered, and her beautiful eyes glistened.

"No problem," he mouthed back.

A horn sounded outside, and Pixie and Harley barked in unison as they skidded to the front door.

"Jordan stopped right in front of the house this

morning." Kylie poked Naomi's ribs. "A two-minute walk to the corner would be way too cold for a delicate Southern flower like you."

Naomi's face reddened. "I'm not a—"

"Kylie, you remember what I said about teasing...Pixie, no, Harley..." Mia hopped on one foot as both dogs went after her shoes.

"Sorry," Kylie shouted as the door slammed behind the three girls.

"Some mornings it's like air traffic control around here." Mia tucked her shoes under one arm and wiggled her toes as the kitten leaped toward the stairs.

Nick hung his coat on Kylie's empty hook. "You don't have any regrets, do you?"

He looked at the pictures they'd hung on the staircase wall. Framed school photos of Naomi and Emma and Kylie. One of him and Mia after Lexie's baptism, where the photographer had caught them leaning into each other, two people in love who weren't afraid to show it. There was also a picture of Kylie and her mom and brother because, although they'd worked out a long-term fostering arrangement, Kylie's birth family would always be part of her life.

"Not one." The sweetness of Mia's smile warmed him. "I'm a lucky woman."

"I'm sure a lucky man." He pulled her close and nudged Pixie and Harley aside. "I love you, Mia, with all my heart, and the day you become my wife will be the happiest one of my life."

"Not only because you won't have to live with your mom and Luc any longer? Between your mom's fussing over you, and those extra workout sessions Luc's roped you into, it must be tough." Her brown eyes teased him.

"I'm staying in Harbor House the weeks I don't work in New York because we both agreed we needed to set a good example for the girls."

"I know." Her voice went husky. "I love you, too. You're sure you're okay with all of us living here and not Harbor House? Your mom was so keen on you taking over the place."

"Harbor House is still her home, and we all need our space." He and Mia most of all. They'd figured out the love, now they needed to figure out the marriage. "Maybe someday we'll live there, if we both want to, but not now. Besides, I couldn't be the one to put Luc out on the street, could I?"

"No." Mia laughed then sobered. "You're a good dad."

"You heard what Kylie said?"

"I did. You don't have to father a child to be a dad." The love in her voice winded him and maybe always would. "And you don't need a good dad to be one yourself."

"You helped me see that." Like she'd helped him see a lot of things but, most of all, she'd helped him see himself. "Brian's trying." Like Nick had tried, and in time, the two of them might edge closer into an acquaintanceship, if not a father-son relationship. One-handed, he picked up the two motorcycle helmets from the hall table. "I forgot to put these away. No more biking for us until spring."

Mia looked at him from under her lashes. "Later."

"Oh?" He raised his eyebrows.

Mia took the helmets and set them back on the table. "Just how soon will the contractor be here? The fifth graders have a field trip without me, so I don't have to be at school for at least an hour. This house is empty of kids

for a change, and I've already finished my lesson prep."
She trailed a hand across his chest and lower, her touch
slow and deliberate.

He sucked in a breath. "I like the way you think, Mia
Gibbs."

"Soon to be Mia Gibbs-McGuire." She gave him a
saucy smile.

He pulled her toward him, and she slipped into his
arms, into his kiss, and even further into his heart.

Right where she was meant to be.

Former NHL star Luc Simard has experienced some hard knocks. After his wife's death and a career-ending injury, he's back home in Firefly Lake, coaching and rebuilding his life. But when Cat McGuire—and her daughter who lives and breathes hockey—moves to town, Luc can't deny he's intrigued.

But is this hometown hero ready to risk his heart again?

Turn the page to find out, in a free preview of *Back Home at Firefly Lake*!

Chapter One

"Next." The high-pitched, perky voice came from the woman behind the arena's reception desk.

Cat McGuire moved forward and wrinkled her nose. The pungent cocktail of stale beer, sweat, and hockey equipment invaded her senses. "Hi. I'm here to register my daughter for hockey." She glanced at twelve-year-old Amy beside her. Under the harsh, fluorescent light, Amy's dark-blond hair was limp and colorless, and above her Pittsburgh Penguins jersey her expression was sulky.

"Firefly Lake doesn't have any hockey teams for girls." The woman had long, highlighted brown hair and shiny pink lips and wore a too-tight white sweater.

"But when I called before Christmas the man I spoke to said we could register today in person." Cat dug her nails into her damp palms. "I told him Amy was a girl."

"That would've been the skate sharpening guy. He always gets mixed up. It doesn't matter, though, because girl or boy, this registration is only for kids five and under. The main hockey registration closed in September." She shuffled papers, brisk and officious. "No exceptions, not even for you." As the woman looked her up and down, faint recognition tugged at the edge of Cat's consciousness.

"Not even . . ." Cat stopped. "Stephanie?"

Stephanie Larocque, the girl Cat had envied and hated from kindergarten on, nodded and tossed her hair over her shoulders like she'd done in high school. "I heard you were back in town."

Cat didn't need to ask how. Although she'd been in Firefly Lake less than twenty-four hours, it was a small town and news traveled with the efficiency of a bush telegraph in the Australian outback.

"Then you also know I wasn't here in September." Cat tried to keep her voice even. She was an adult, Stephanie was too, and their school days were long behind them. "Are there any other options? Amy loves hockey."

"No." Stephanie gave her best cheerleader smile. "Rules are rules."

"Mom." Amy's voice was a whine mixed with an anguished wail. "It's bad enough you made me move to Vermont, but if I can't play hockey I'll die."

Cat's heart pounded. She had to fix this—and fast. "Sweetie, we'll work something out, I—"

"I can't have any kid dying on my watch." The voice was deep, male, and familiar. "Hey, Cat."

"Luc." Cat's head jerked up.

Next to her, Amy sucked in a breath.

The man who stood behind Stephanie smiled at them. The same easygoing smile Luc Simard had always given Cat, the one that had graced a thousand sports pages. He still had the same hair too, dark golden brown like maple syrup. "It's great news about the research grant. I never thought we'd see you back living in Firefly Lake."

Cat hadn't either, but desperate times called for desperate measures. If things worked out like she planned, she wouldn't have to live here permanently. Her stomach knotted. "Life can surprise you."

"It sure can." Luc's smile slipped and his blue eyes clouded.

Cat's face heated. More than anyone, Luc knew how life could throw you a curve.

"So what's the problem?" His voice was gruff.

"I..." Cat swallowed.

"The problem," Stephanie interjected, "is that Cat wants to register her daughter for hockey. I already told her we don't have hockey for girls, but even if we did, registration for any child older than five closed in September." Stephanie's voice had the same smug tone as in first grade when she'd told Cat the whole class had seen her underwear. She glanced at Luc and her expression warmed. "It's nothing for you to worry about, sugar."

Cat blinked. Stephanie had the same mix of Vermont and Quebec roots she did. As far as she could remember, nobody under the age of seventy had ever called anybody else sugar around here.

"Hockey spaces fill up fast." Luc rested one blue-jeaned leg against the desk. "I hear Amy's a good little player." His gaze shifted from Cat to her daughter. "Your grandma has told me lots about you."

"She has?" Amy's eyes widened.

"Absolutely, she's real proud of you." Luc reached over Stephanie's head of pageant hair and scooped several sheets of paper from the desk. "The girls here are into figure skating, not hockey, but there's nothing to say a girl who wants to play hockey can't. Since Amy's only turned twelve, if you give the go-ahead she can play on the boys' team. One more kid won't make a difference."

"But...but..." Stephanie stuttered. "It says right in here, no exceptions." She waved a blue binder. "You could get me fired. I need this job and—"

"You won't get fired." Luc's gaze swiveled from Stephanie to Cat and held. "No exceptions unless at the coach's discretion. Since Coach MacPherson fell off a ladder hanging up decorations for a New Year's Eve party and broke his leg in three places, I'm filling in. In this case, I'm making an exception." He quirked an eyebrow, and his smile was sweet and way too sexy for comfort.

"Mom?" The yearning in Amy's voice punched Cat's chest. "Please? You promised I could play no matter what, remember? It's not as if there's anything else here for me." Her face was white, her expression strained and etched with desperation.

Cat *had* promised, and she'd already taken Amy away from the only home she remembered, her team, and the hockey tournament. She drew in a breath. "There's family here and a good school for you." Cat had to get Amy back on track academically. And she had to give them both a better chance for stability and future financial security.

"School's a waste of time for me." Amy stared at her feet, but not before Cat caught the flicker of uncertainty in her light blue eyes, as well as the fear.

Her stomach clenched. Had she put that look in Amy's eyes? "I guess you can play with the boys, at least for now." She forced the words out and glanced up at Luc. "Thank you." The backs of her eyes burned. Luc was still kind, and although he hadn't been a real part of her life for years, he'd slipped right back in to looking out for her like he always had.

"Mom." This time, Amy's voice was an excited yelp. She jumped up and down, and her winter boots squeaked on the scuffed tile. "You're amazing. He's amazing. This is the most amazing thing that's ever happened to me. I promise you won't regret it."

Cat regretted it already, but she couldn't deny Amy something that would make her this happy and help her feel good about herself, too.

Luc pivoted away from Stephanie with surprising grace, and Cat's tongue got stuck to the roof of her mouth. She always forgot how big he was, and how he filled whatever space he was in and seemed to suck the air out of it—at least her air.

"Since there's a line of folks waiting to do whatever it is they need to do before we close, you go on and help them, and I'll handle Amy's registration." He smiled again, and Cat's heart skipped a beat.

"I...you..." Stephanie's face was a mottled red.

"Sometimes everyone needs a helping hand. No man or woman is an island." Luc's blue gaze drilled into Cat, the same blue as his crewneck Henley. The T-shirt molded to his broad chest and powerful forearms before it dipped below the waistband of his jeans to rest against...

Cat's hands tingled as warmth spread through her chest. She wouldn't go there. Not with anyone, but especially not with Luc. As toddlers, they'd gone to the same playgroup and attended the same birthday parties. He'd seen her with cake on her face and ice cream in her hair. He'd been her lab partner in chemistry senior year, and he'd rented her old bedroom in her mom's house for the past four months.

In all that time, he'd never looked at her except as a friend of the family. The kid with the thick glasses who'd skipped fifth grade, and who was so bad at sports she was the last one picked for any team except when he took pity on her.

In their small-town world, Luc had been a god. The kind of guy who'd dated the pretty, popular girls. Even if Cat had been the kind of woman for a man like him, having feelings for him would be wrong on so many levels. Her life had changed almost beyond recognition since high school, but it hadn't changed enough for that.

Luc opened the metal gate separating the reception desk from the arena foyer and waved Cat and Amy toward the cubbyhole that served as the coaching office. Even before Jim MacPherson's accident, the hockey program had been in chaos, so one more kid truly wouldn't make a difference. Even if it had, though, making that exception would have been worth it for the expression on Cat's face. Relief, gratitude, and something he didn't want to put a label on but that touched an emotion he'd forgotten he could feel.

As for Amy, he might not know much about kids, but her longing was palpable. She clearly needed to play hockey almost as much as she needed to breathe. "Take a seat." He gestured to the two chairs in front of the coach's desk, now his desk at least until the end of the season.

Cat nudged her daughter, who continued to stare at him like he'd sprouted an extra head.

"You...you'll be coaching me...like for real?" Amy's voice stuttered.

"Sure." Luc moved a stack of paperwork and several fishing magazines aside to make a clear space on the desk for the registration package. "You think you can handle that?"

"Yeah." Amy leaned forward. "You played in the NHL. You played for Tampa, and Chicago, and Vancouver, and Winnipeg. You were on the U.S. Olympic team and World Juniors and you..." She stopped as Cat gave her a silencing look.

And Luc had the scars to prove it, not only the physical ones but also those that couldn't be seen. "I retired after last season, so now I'm just a regular coach." He pulled a plastic portfolio from atop a pile. "Why don't you take a look at some of the player information while I talk to your mom? You can see the uniform, and there's a bunch of pictures from games."

Amy gave a quick nod and took the portfolio he held out.

Luc sat in the battered black vinyl chair and studied the woman across from him. Cat still had that serious look she'd had as a kid, and she wasn't much taller than when she'd joined his sixth-grade class, almost two years younger but a whole lot smarter than everyone else. But she'd been a sweet kid, and he'd looked out for her when he could. He'd never have expected her to produce a hockey player, though. It must have something to do with Amy's dad, a guy who'd never been in the picture and, unusually for Firefly Lake, nobody ever mentioned.

Cat glanced at her daughter, and her mouth tilted into a smile filled with so much love that Luc's heart caught.

He cleared his throat. "I feel bad you and Amy aren't staying at Harbor House with your mom. I already told her I can find another place to rent until my new house is ready."

"Of course not." Cat's face went pink, and she tucked a strand of blond hair behind one ear. Why had he never noticed she had pretty ears? "Even if you weren't staying there, Amy and I would still need our own space. Besides, I wouldn't think of inflicting my cats on Pixie." Her expression changed. Not defensive exactly, but watchful and tinged with apprehension.

"That little dog sure rules the roost at your mom's place." An unexpected prickle of sexual awareness whipped through him. Cat had a pretty face, too. Big blue eyes behind almost invisible glasses, delicate features, and a classic oval face. Why had he never noticed all that about her, either?

"I sublet my place in Boston and rented an apartment above the craft gallery on Main Street. I got a great deal on rent as part of helping the gallery owner. The winter months are quiet, but the gallery owner has a few buying trips coming up, so he needed to hire somebody to look after the store." She glanced at her daughter again and her face softened. "Like I tell Amy, everything works out somehow. You have to keep the faith."

Clearly, Cat was a glass half full person. The kind of person he used to be before he lost his wife and his hopes and dreams along with her.

Luc took a bulging folder from the bottom desk drawer and got his mind back on hockey, where it belonged. "The practice schedule is in here, along with the game dates and all the other information you need. The parent volunteer roster is already set, but if you want—"

"No." Cat's voice was laced with what might have

been panic. "I'm not really a hockey mom. I help out when I'm needed, but…" She took the folder from him and set it on her lap on top of a bulky black tote. "I want to help Amy get settled at her new school first. It's hard to change in the middle of the year."

"Of course." Luc's heart gave a painful thud. His mom had been a big hockey mom. Like his wife would have been if she'd had the chance.

"Thanks." Cat's smile was sweet and genuine. It shouldn't have been sexy but somehow was.

Luc tented his hands on the desk and tried to work moisture into his dry mouth. As far as women were concerned, he was off the market indefinitely and by choice. He shouldn't look at Cat's straight, blond hair and wonder how it would feel as it slipped through his fingers. And he definitely shouldn't wonder about her petite figure beneath her chunky gray sweater and tailored black coat. Despite all the women who'd made it clear they'd be interested in whatever he offered, Luc wasn't offering anything. Once the house he was having built was finished, coaching and working alongside his dad and uncles at Simard Creamery would be his life—his whole life.

"Your mom's real excited about your brother's wedding." He changed the subject with an effort. "She says it's so romantic that Nick and Mia are getting married on New Year's Eve."

"Yes." Cat smiled, and damn if the soft curve of her rosy lips didn't take Luc's thoughts right back to where they had no business going. "It's great to see Mom so happy, and Nick and Mia too. With Mia, it's like I'm getting another sister."

"Nick's been a good friend to me." And that was even

more reason why Luc shouldn't think about Cat like he'd been thinking about her. A guy didn't have those kinds of thoughts about a buddy's little sister.

Luc dragged his gaze away from Cat's mouth to stare at the frost-fringed office window. The tall pine trees outside were etched in white, and the open field behind the arena slept in a blanket of snow as it sloped in a gentle hill to the shore of the ice-covered lake. In the distance, wisps of wood smoke curled from chimneys in the small town of Firefly Lake cradled between the dark-green Vermont hills.

Home, family, and community. Everything Luc needed to get his life stable and back on track was right here. Apart from his wife and professional hockey, everything he'd ever wanted was here too.

"The uniform's great." Amy's excited voice brought him back to the present. "Does Mom need to fill out some forms and pay?"

"Yeah, she does." Luc's voice hitched.

"While I do that, why don't you go out to the rink?" Cat dug in her tote and pulled out a folded bill. "You can get yourself a hot chocolate and watch the figure skating practice."

"Mom." Amy made a disgusted face. "Figure skating's for girlie girls."

"Before she switched to hockey, my wife started out as a figure skater." Luc pushed the words out through lips that were all of a sudden numb. When it came to sports, Maggie had been as driven as him and as reckless. Between his failings and hers, he hadn't been with her when she needed him most. "My mom was a competitive figure skater, too. You have to be real fit to do those routines. Unlike in hockey, you aren't wearing gear to protect you from falls, either."

"Sure, but you'd never get me into one of those costumes." Amy gave him a dimpled grin. "I had to wear sequins for a school play once. I never itched so much in my whole entire life. Can you imagine skating in one of those outfits?"

"Nope." The force of Amy's smile kept the memories at bay and, despite himself, Luc managed a smile back. "Go on, we won't be long."

"Okay." With another grin, Amy took the bill from Cat and tucked it into the front pocket of her jeans.

When Amy had left, shutting the office door behind her, Luc turned back to Cat. There was no mistaking the sympathy in her eyes.

"It must be hard to talk about your wife. Amy's still a kid, so she doesn't think before she speaks."

"Life goes on." His voice caught again. Maybe it did for everyone else, but his life had stopped two years ago. Although he went through the motions and did what his family and everyone expected, the biggest part of him was numb. Until today, he'd been fine with that numbness. Then Cat had poked through it with her big blue eyes and a smile that was like a warm hug on a cold day. He cleared his throat. "What's up?"

"Nothing…I…" She fiddled with the strap of her bag. "Until my grant money comes through after New Year's, money's a bit tight. Amy needs new skates, and with my move, the holidays, and the wedding and all, I wondered…can I buy a secondhand pair anywhere?"

Luc's throat closed as guilt needled him. If money was that tight, Cat and Amy should be staying at Harbor

House, rent-free. Except they weren't, and he couldn't shake a sense it had something to do with him.

"Len's Hardware on Main sells used gear, but it goes fast." Although there was money in Firefly Lake, folks were thrifty New Englanders who could sniff out a bargain at twenty paces.

"Oh." She pulled out her checkbook. "Amy will have to make do—"

"Hang on." He stood and came around the desk to sit beside her in the chair Amy had vacated. "I can wait for the hockey registration fee. Put that money toward new skates instead. Len sells those too, and he gives a discount to local kids. Show him Amy's paperwork so she'll qualify." In the meantime, he'd square the registration fee with the arena manager. Cat would never have to know.

"Really?" Cat's cheeks reddened. "That would be great. I don't want to ask my mom or Nick. They'd both help me out, no question, but..." She gripped her bag and slid down in the chair.

Luc's heart squeezed. She was embarrassed to ask her family for help, like he'd have been embarrassed asking his. Except, that would never be an issue because he had more money than he could spend in one lifetime. Money to finance the creamery expansion his dad had talked about for years. And to send his folks on that cruise they'd hankered after but could never afford because of the cost of raising four kids and putting them through college. Money for everything except what mattered most— taking care of his wife and their child like he'd planned.

"Pay for the hockey registration when your grant comes through." He tried to smile. "I know you're good for it."

"Thanks." Cat's voice cracked and she took one hand away from her bag to rub it across her face. "Hockey means everything to Amy. I want her to be able to play, but she's growing so fast right now."

"Hockey's an expensive sport." He slid an arm around her shoulders and gave her a little squeeze. The same kind of friendly squeeze he'd given her all those times back in high school when she'd saved his butt in chemistry. Before today, however, his fingers had never tingled when he'd touched Cat. His body had never heated, either.

Cat started and pulled away at the same instant he did. "Hockey can be a dangerous sport too, and now Amy will be playing with boys. She hasn't played with boys since she was seven. She could get hurt."

Like he had, hurt so bad it had ended his career. "Amy's playing minor hockey. At her age, there is a rule about no body checking." He tried to make his tone reassuring. "I promise you I'll keep a close eye on her." It was his job as her coach, and he'd do the same for any kid. It had nothing to do with the strange and unexpected attraction he all of a sudden had for this woman he'd known his whole life, who he'd never really looked at until today.

A woman who wasn't Maggie. Luc's stomach clenched in a tangled lump of guilt and grief, tied tight with a slippery ribbon of disloyalty. Maggie was never coming back, but that didn't mean Luc could forget her. Or that he wanted to.

About the Author

Jen Gilroy grew up under the big sky of western Canada. After many years in England, she now lives in a small town in eastern Ontario where her Irish ancestors settled in the nineteenth century. She's worked in higher education and international marketing but, after spending too much time in airports and away from her family, traded the 9-5 to write contemporary romance to bring readers' hearts home.

A small-town girl at heart, Jen likes ice cream, diners, vintage style, and all things country. Her husband, Tech Guy, is her real-life romance hero, and her daughter, English Rose, teaches her to cherish the blessings in the everyday.

You can learn more at:
   www.jengilroy.com
   Twitter: @JenGilroy1
   http://facebook.com/JenGilroyAuthor

Fall in Love with Forever Romance

TOO SCOT TO HANDLE
By Grace Burrowes

From award-winning author Grace Burrowes comes the next installment in the *New York Times* bestselling Windham Brides series! As a newly titled gentleman, Colin MacHugh has no wish to entertain all the ladies suddenly clamoring for his attention. But when the intriguing Miss Anwen Windham asks for his help to save a London orphanage, he has no idea how much she'll change his life forever.

Fall in Love with Forever Romance

JEN GILROY

Summer on Firefly Lake

SUMMER ON FIREFLY LAKE
By Jen Gilroy

In the tradition of *New York Times* bestselling authors Susan Wiggs and RaeAnne Thayne comes an emotional new love story from Jen Gilroy. Single mom Mia Gibbs and divorcé Nick McGuire are content to live their lives alone—until they begin to fall for each other. Can the two find the courage to take a second chance on lasting love?

Fall in Love with Forever Romance

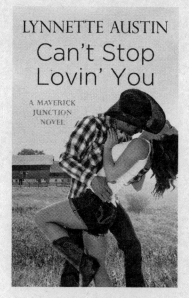

Can't Stop Lovin' You
By Lynnette Austin

Maggie Sullivan can't wait to get out of Texas. Luckily, she just got the break she needed to make her big-city dreams a reality. But then Brawley Odell swaggers back into Maverick Junction...Fed up with city life, Brawley jumps at the chance to return home—and get back to the smart, sassy woman he's never been able forget. But how will he convince Maggie that their one true home is with each other?